"HISTORICAL FICTION AT ITS BE~~ST~~
A DARKLY COMPE~~LLING~~

A gripping tale, and Busch's us~~e~~ ... y absorbing, rendering the characters a ... h a slow
grace that's gone from modern ... ishment
with a power all its own."

—*Albany Times Union*

"An act of massive imagination, rich with biblical nuance, precise historical recreation and psychological inquiry."

—*Time Out New York*

"In its dramatic visualizations of festering streets and battle-destroyed land-
scapes, its patiently wrought characterizations (both the stoical Melville and the
deeply conflicted Bartholomew are unforgettable figures), its deftly managed
period style, and especially its brooding, sorrowful empathy with all the scarred
and twisted souls who stalk its pages, this book seems to me the high-water mark,
as it were, of Busch's estimable career."

—*Raleigh News & Observer*

"A very good book because it does ring true, inspiring a fresh inspection about
the nature of our society now, and because it promises so much more meaning
on further reading."

—*Milwaukee Journal*

"With seamless effort, Busch moves us back and forth in time, from roiling New
York to the quiet and deadly southern landscape of Bartholomew's memory. . . .
[*The Night Inspector*] re-create[s] the post–Civil War world of New York City . . .
capture[s] the intensity of a Union marksman in the field and, most daunting of
all, bring[s] alive author Herman Melville in all his grandness and vulnerability. . . .
Filled with a strong cast of secondary characters and one resonant scene after
another, *The Night Inspector* carries a thematic and metaphoric richness missing
from so much contemporary fiction."

—*The Oregonian*

THE
NIGHT
INSPECTOR

A NOVEL

—⁂—

Frederick
Busch

Ballantine Books

NEW YORK

Grateful acknowledgment is given to the Library of Congress to reprint the following maps: on page 118, *Lloyd's Mammoth Map of the Business Portion of New York City*, by J. T. Lloyd, 1867; and on page 234, *General Map of the City of New York*, by Louis Aloys Risse, 1900.

Grateful acknowledgment is given to the Manhattan Borough President's Office to reprint the following map: on page viii, Untitled, by Daniel Ewen, 1827.

Grateful acknowledgment is given to the New-York Historical Society to reprint the following photographs: on page ii and iii, *Battery Park, c. 1885*; on page 76, *South Street, c. 1897*; on page 194, *New York Harbor, c.1860*; and on page 276, *Broadway at Spring Street, c. 1868*.

———— ✌ ————

A Ballantine Book
Published by The Ballantine Publishing Group

www.randomhouse.com/BB/

Library of Congress Card Number: 00-190145

ISBN 0-449-00615-8

This edition is published by arrangement with Harmony Books, a division of Random House, Inc.

Manufactured in the United States of America

Cover design and collage by Heather Kern
Cover photos © Corbis-Bettmann

First Trade Paperback Edition: May 2000

10 9 8 7 6 5 4 3 2

Dear Judy

I would, in sum, describe him as a man of size: Broad at the chest, long and thick of limb; and capable of flexuous motion, manifesting the dexterity and abandon, let us say, of the young New England brown bear in search of pike in icy rivers. He was known, once, to be fetching in his features: Saxon at the nose and jaw; clear of skin; evincing through all of his life, I am told, the trait I came to know so well—his manner of peering about through half-closed eyes, as if he searched the distance, or as if, like the bear, he knew himself to be, whatever ground he trod, not far from peril.

He kept his silence, and he pondered Creation. He seemed not fearful of the Universe, but distrusting of its benevolence. He took care not to display his tenderness, most especially in regard to himself. He was, I lament to conclude, the most wounded of men, a tattered spirit in need of much repair.

SAMUEL MORDECAI,
Inspector of the Night

THE
NIGHT
INSPECTOR

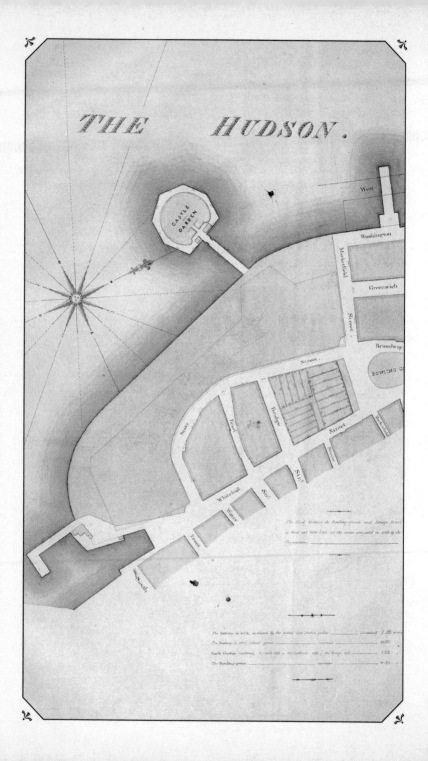

C H A P T E R   1

"No mouth," I told him.

"If I'm to craft a special order for you," he said.

"What is that, a special order?"

"Why, this." He held up the sketch. I looked away from it. "The mask, Mr. Bartholomew," he said. "I make arms. I make legs. I've never made a face, sir."

Through the smell of resin and shellac, through the balm of pine shavings, came the odor of his perspiration, and I thought of bivouac, and our stench on the wind. His thick, ragged, graying eyebrows were stippled with sawdust, as was his mustache. One of the knuckles of his broad hand was bloody, and the end of the other hand's long finger had been cut away many years before and had raggedly healed.

"Yes," I said. "Special. I thought at first you meant order of being. Race. A species of man, perhaps. A special order of nature. I cannot abide such speculation. We have collectively demonstrated, and not that many months before, the folly of such thinking."

He smiled at the drawing, but not at me, and he shook his head. "No, sir," he said. "You are enough like the rest of my custom. Only your face is maimed, Mr. Bartholomew. You have your limbs, God forgive us."

"I suggest that I am proof of His unreadiness to do so," I said.

We examined his sketch again, and he spoke to me of materials and money. It was to be of pasteboard, he decided, so that my head would not be weighed down. He would build many thin layers, each molded to the one beneath, and would protect them with paint, the better to keep away the deleterious effects of rain and snow. Withal, my head would not be burdened, on account of the lightness of construction. "Like a little craft on the sea," he suggested. I had to smile. He had, it was clear, to look away.

And in the end, he prevailed, and he shaped me a mouth.

I did hear of several who used a buffalo gun, and at first I thought it a lie. How could you haul such a heavy piece of metal and wood up a tree? Not to mention aim with accuracy, or reload with speed? From a hilltop redoubt: yes. With a tripod under the front of that immense, octagonal barrel. But never in a tree, I thought, and of course I was wrong. It was one of my lessons in this long education I received about and from my native country. Never consider a feat undone if the reward is of a size. We move what we must, whether barrels of meat or kegs of dead flesh, when at the farther end of the transaction there lies a crate of dollars. That is how we fare westward, in spite of reversals, anguish, and death.

That is why some very few of us served with the volunteers of New York as what we called marksmen. *Snipers,* the men of infantry or horse called us, and, behind our backs, *assassins.* An Englishman I met said *thugs.* In the woods around Paynes Corners, where I was born, the hamlet lying two hundred miles and more from Manhattan, a small crossroads and then a church and a fur-trading shop for victuals, I learned my forest craftiness. I could hide, and I could seek. I was a solitary child, and powerful of limb. And I was reckless, and born with great vision, though not, alas, of the interior, spiritual sort. But I saw in the dark if there was a hint of a sliver of moon in the sky. How natural, then, with my youth and young manhood passed in patrolling a trapline and hunting for my meals, that I would make a marksman when called to the War.

It was a Sharps that I carried into the trees. I wore a pannier of sixty rounds, and always a pistol in a holster at my back. The knife I wore at my left side, and I drew with my right. It was good for game, and bad for men, I once told the sergeant who saw me out and up and hunting Rebels.

"Kindly do not boast of the assassinations, Mr. Bartholomew. You fire your weapon, but in this chain of command, you *are* my weapon. And I think we owe it to the dead to never boast about our work."

"It is the brigadier's wish and your command that I take to the trees and shoot men down."

"Truly said, Mr. Bartholomew. I wonder if I rebuke myself while addressing you." He looked away as he spoke, though I was whole of face, and had smooth enough skin, and all of my nose and lips and jaw. I watched a fly hover at his ear. I thought to seize it, and I could have. He turned, and he read my expression, I suppose, and drew back a pace. "This triumph of ours," he said, "our killing them off, is no pleasure to me. Those are men like us."

"No, Sergeant," I said, "with all respect. They are dead, and we are not, and that's the nature of our transaction."

Smoke from the cooks' wagons blew in on us. He tried not to smile, I think. He said, "As you were, Mr. Bartholomew."

I drew myself taut.

He said, "I hope you return safe and well."

"Sergeant."

"And I wonder how you sleep, bless you."

"Fitfully," I said.

He nodded. He caressed his ginger beard, which did not give him the appearance of age I believe he sought. He covered his lips an instant with his fingers, and I saw his fatigue, and his fear, of course. He was from a village up on the Hudson and had been raised in wealth. He was a powerful leader in battle, and in sum a man of strength. Many months later, when the hunters took me down, I tried to ask him to kill me, but I could

3

not work my jaw. He only wrapped my head in what I later learned was his shirt, and he carried me across his saddle, propped against his breast, to a Southern farrier, who thought to cauterize some of the area of wound.

When I had stopped screaming, I heard the sergeant tell the farrier, "You enjoyed that." I heard him cock his piece, and I waited for him to fire. Someone, I remember thinking, should be shot. Then I remembered that I had already filled the bill.

But I did take precautions, and I lasted a good long while. I always fastened twigs and leaves to my cap and my shoulders and sleeves. I used cold coals from the cookfires and darkened my face, my wrists, and the backs of my hands. At three hundred yards and more, a hand in dense brush, if it is a white man's hand, will flare like the tail of a deer. I dulled the barrel of the Sharps with coal as well, to eliminate reflection, and I carried it by the barrel lest it shake the leaves above me. A Rebel sentry, on seeing the motion of the branches, might aim at them and fire, not having the skill to allow for the rolling of the earth and how a rifle ball, fired over long distance, falls. He'd miss the leaves and kill the man. I did not intend to die by accident, and I knew a good shooter had to believe that everything solid and still was an illusion, and that it all was always moving, up and down, around, away.

Into the tree, then, and up, then screened and with my back against the trunk if possible, I worked with telescope for surveillance and rifle scope for aiming. It then was a matter of resistance: wind against bullet; will to be still and invisible against the tickle of spider, ant, or fly; lungs against the seized breath; finger to trigger; cheek to stock; and, always, despair against an imitation of God Almighty in a tree to smite a boy perhaps not wearing shoes or a man who had removed his officer's insignia to hide his rank (the sign of value in a corpse) from someone like me. I always shook and wavered, and I always steadied up. I was, finally, a hunter, and I killed them.

At Yale College, where I was to study theology ancient and modern,

I read in the novels of Maria Edgeworth and the poetry of Keats. I ate sweets, in other words, and grew chubby of mind. When my uncle Sidney Cowper asked me to name the sage of our time, I told him Washington Irving. He threatened to remove his financial support, and my mother, who had given up life for a career in widowhood, naturally wept. I amended my deposition: William Ellery Channing, I testified. "Though," I added, for a taste of danger and as a sop to what I thought of as courage, "I do admire Mr. Charles Brockden Brown." Uncle had clearly read neither. He cleared his throat and urged the conversation toward finances and, in particular, the desperation of the chronically unemployed, among whose number he clearly foresaw me.

Although, I must say, Uncle Sidney Cowper did not dislike me. Indeed, he was as fond of me as any man I knew was fond of any man. He was a great, bulky fellow, as tall as my father and far more meaty. He was handsome in his way, my mother said, and he took his responsibilities—as surrogate for his brother, my father, dead of fever when I was but seven and my mother little more than a girl—with a responsibility I must call overzealous. He always braced me with his large, heavy hands: "Chin back, Billy. Head erect and unmoving. Don't *waver*, son! Keep your belly in"—he'd have done well to follow his own advice—"and puff out your chest like a soldier. *That's* a man." Throughout such advice, his hands worked my body as if it were clay, poking at the point of my chin and cupping the back of my head, patting my belly just above the balls and pulling at my tiny tits as if I were to be shaped for once and for all by him. I did not like his hands on me, and when I saw them on my mother—not her belly nor her breast, but over her shoulders and neck of a sufficiency—I decided that my regret over the loss of my father was redoubled: once for his death and my loneliness, and once because greedy Uncle Sidney was going to wear away the flesh of those my father had left behind.

At Yale College, I learned enough to learn enough, and I was therefore situated in Cheerie's Chop House on an evening in 1867 when I needed to be. It was undistinguished by its food or drink, but for me it was a kind of home. Cheerie had been a drover with us at Malvern Hill, and he had vowed to live as far from horses as he could, if he might live. He did, and so he lived on Eleventh Street and ran his chop house on Twenty-third, and he swore that he rarely roasted a horse to serve as venison to his patrons. He owned, I'd have thought, fifteen hairs, which he pasted with pomade to the top of his oval, pale head. He seated me without my asking it at a recessed table where the shadows fell. He left it to me to light the candle or not, depending upon whether I chose to read as I drank my wine, or eat in the gray-blue light that curtained me, permitting me to remove the mask in something like seclusion and wear only the dark silk veil.

M dined that night at eight. He had stopped on his way to the Customs in the morning, asking Cheerie to hold a small table for his supper. Cheerie was a good comrade. We had nearly died together in a canonade that killed a half a dozen horses and covered us in their blood and ropes of blue intestine. We gave each other courtesies. When he smiled his great white teeth, I thought of horses shrieking and exploding. Christ Himself may know what Cheerie thought of when he looked at me.

I had noticed M on Broadway as I walked the town at dawn and as he was going to his job. I knew his visage from a Boston paper. Then I had observed him; I had, during the War, been excellent at seeing how a man moved through his terrain. And, noting the place at which he worked, I had as well seen an acquaintanceship with him as something to possess. I stood. I was wearing the mask, not yet the veil. I walked slowly across the sawdust of the wooden floor among the peculiar rectangular tables that Cheerie had bought when a ladies' dresses manufactory had failed in one of the recent economic convulsions. I moved into the man's soft, myopic vision. Even his beard looked soft. He reminded me, though his hair was darker, of dead Sergeant Grafton.

"Sir," I said. He look up and squinted, as though I were dozens of yards away. I could study the pores of his strangely youthful skin. He did not, through his complexion, manifest his service on the sea or on the shore.

I said, "Sir. I beg your pardon for this intrusion. I have read your work. I have read *The Ambiguities* and its analysis of your profession. I have read *The Whale*. I think it a blinding brilliance, the epitaph of our economy."

His eyes dropped, then returned, squinting at the mask. "No," he said, "but with thanks. I wrote expressly *not* for money when I spake my piece about the whale. And I was given justice: I made no money. Though, to be sure, it remains the king of most kings." He could not keep his eyes from my mask, even as he knew I observed their fascinated study.

"Begging to differ," I said.

He gestured at the vacant chair, and I nodded, then sat.

"You were differing," he said.

"The whale does triumph over your captain's will, and that of the industry on whose behalf he fished. It's a type of the national economy that founders when nature, in the guise of a whale, decides to strike."

"But it was Ahab, a man, mighty or not, who struck through the . . ."

"Mask," I finished for him.

"My regrets. I could not say my thought without including your misfortune. My most profound regrets." He swallowed half his glass of claret wine, then waved his arm for a waiter, saying, "Please to dine with me, Mr.—"

"Bartholomew," I said. "William Bartholomew. I am honored."

"And I am flummoxed," he said, leaning back his large head, affecting to laugh, though uttering no sound, as his nose pointed toward the ceiling and his mouth gaped into the air.

My dinner was brought, and wine was poured. He sat silently when I replaced the mask with my veil, although he as well as I heard someone at a nearby table gasp. I watched him close his eyes as the mask came up and the veil dropped over my head. I was charmed by his willingness to shy away from what I thought he'd spent his life in trying to peruse. And then we spoke, as we ate pork and cabbage, of what he called his career. He reserved his anger not so much for those writers who had pronounced him mad, or simply gone dry on him, but for the Brothers Harper, who had printed his books. I noted my recollection of Putnam's, whose printing of his *Piazza Tales* I had read at with little interest. He asked me about something called *His Fifty Years of Exile* of which I had never heard, and I lied that I had read it.

"But it's the publishers you blame, sir."

He said, "They are mere manufacturers of black shapes on white pages. They post me invoices still, for books of theirs, often by me!, that I've been sent. But not a human word about the writing of language to be read by students of human ways."

"You see," I said, "that is what *The Whale* was, I maintain: a critique of the philosophy of numbers."

"You're a watchful man, Mr. Bartholomew."

"No—won't you call me Billy?"

"Call me Herman," he said.

"An honor."

"And likewise. But may I ask you, Billy, about your . . ."

"Face."

"Exactly that. Yes. Was it the War?"

"It was the War. The interests of money and the will of our Commander decreed it. Battle for the rights of the industrialists, battle for the rights of the agriculturists, battle on behalf of bullyrag Abe, who saw *himself*, I insist, as the issue: *my* will, *my* national entity, *my idea* of indivisibility. Crush the farmboys and the desperate Negroes into one another with a thunderclap. And see to it—be sure!—that one William Bartholomew receive the national hoofprint in his head. I'm a coin imprinted with Abe's earnestness."

He shook his head and permitted me to pour him more of Cheerie's sour wine. "I cannot reprove your bitterness," he said. "I know its taste. Though I believe the righteousness of the President's motives. You cannot start a nation and permit it to founder. The experiment is too holy, too vast. And the black slaves? What of them, Billy?"

"Engines of economy. It was money was the prize."

"Poor man," he said. Then: "I meant that of *all* men, not you, you understand."

"Poor man," I replied.

"You were struck with a minié ball? May I ask?"

"I saw my fellowman countless times, with a devastating insight. Twice, and once with devastation equal to that which I dispensed, he saw me in return."

He gazed and gazed, but I gave him nothing more. He dropped his red-rimmed eyes.

"Tell me," I said, "of that extraordinary moment when your Ishmael feels the hands of the other men as they squeeze the sperm of the killed whale on board their ship. It was an instant of brotherhood surpassing the interests of money, was it not? And would your man not feel a great sorrow, given his great gloom? Would he not sense, having felt the hand of brotherhood, that they were soon to lose hold of one another?"

"You have read the book," he answered, nodding slowly, permitting himself a smile. "You have *studied* it. Yet I must wonder: Have I written as much of economic matters as you seem to suggest? Did I not speak of the beef-and-ale of those actual men? And about the fishiness of the fishes? The brine of their sea? I did intend to. And, surely, I was intent, I can tell you, upon capturing—well, suggesting, at any rate, rendering as well as I could, the superb high will of Ahab. His shuddering desire to be dignified under heaven—under heaven's oppression." His hands moved with precision upon the surface of the table, though in service of exactly what I could not tell, at first. He arranged, as he spoke, the angles of cutlery to glass, of nappery to butter dish. His body seemed to seek the exactness of purpose about which he spoke. I realized then that he wanted—he was yearning—to write on paper with a pen. "I have some poems," he said.

"Would I dare to venture a request?"

"Perhaps we'd dine again," he said.

"And you might bring one?"

"Several," he said. "If you're willing, why flee from a reader?"

I wore the mask when I left, and, underneath its absurd slight smile, an arrangement of pasteboard and varnish and paint, what was left of my mouth stretched involuntarily to imitate his own uneasy smile.

On certain days in Manhattan, say in the Five Points, when I am passing the open drains that fester not that far from the communal pump, when the weather lays itself upon us, sealing the island beneath it as a cork in the top of a glass bottle, and nothing rises very far from the cobbles or mud—not steam from the manufactories, nor the stench of leather in tanneries, nor bowels of cattle slaughtered while they scream, nor the muggy dews of unsoaped flesh packed dozens in every room at the Old Brewery building—then I think of the smoke that choked Charleston. Stink was everywhere. I carry, behind the ruins of my face, inside my brain, the smell of excrement and pounded, flayed flesh stirred deep into the mud of the streets, the composted stench of decaying scrip and bank drafts and certificates of mortgage in the civil registry, and in the merchants' bank, and of course the bitter, corrosive wash against my bandages of shingle, lath, and floorboard as they burned. It was a time of odors. You could smell the putrefaction of wounds. You could smell the maggots in them, like the bitter, herbal smell of bats. The unbathed men, the starved, exhausted horses and mules, the shallow breathing of a vast despair—you could smell the staggered nation, now entire again as the President would have it, and the perfumed men of industry and capital and confidence, one of whom I vowed to become. Some of us with faces could be seen to smile. And on certain days in Manhattan, say in the Five Points, I, with my little carved mouth hole set below the excellent painting of a face—lashes drawn above the eyeholes, breathing holes under the handsome, Saxon nose, all of it on the pinkish-white face paint that shines with its protective lacquer—I smiled, too, because I so wished that I might mean to. I was always grateful for a falling barometer, and the fog from off the Battery, because I was not, I knew, a gladsome sight.

I had come, unseeing, through Charleston on my way back up to Washington. That was where they nursed me in spite of my cowardly begging, my tearing at the bandages with which they wound my head and covered my face. I ought to have bled to death, and I hoped to, and I failed.

"Have the goodness," I told the woman who volunteered to bathe the remains of my face in glycerine water, "have the cordial generosity, the sisterly affection, I beg you, Madame, to leave me be."

"Have the decency," she replied, with her memorable inability to say the letters *r* and *l* as anything other than *w*, "to reward my efforts and the surgeons' with your silence and your courage."

"It is my choice to live or die," I said. I should not say said. I whimpered, I believe. I hoped that someone might end me, although I could not say so outright. My head burned from within, like one of the ruined manorial houses, all roasted black shell and sullen embers, which I had seen before the hunters took me down.

"There is no more choice, sir," she said as if in tears. I could not see her. She had a husky voice and a cultured manner. "Choice is irrelevant. Henceforth, we may live with much, though with less than before. And not, I believe, with choice. If I may say."

I did not see her face for weeks. I thought, often, of strangling her, and, equally, of wedding her, the better to serve her unto death. I did not know her name. She refused to give it. I became tumescent, on her account, for the first time in months. I thought to see to myself, glowing like a stove inside my bandages and beneath the coarse hospital blanket.

"It's daylight," a man on a nearby cot said hoarsely. His voice was equal parts pity, contempt, and embarrassment.

"In here," I told him, "it's night."

"To the bald-headed hermit," he replied, "the time *is* always night.

But I thought you'd want to know it's late afternoon, and your blanket gives an appearance of being crowded and violent."

"My thanks for the tip."

"No, sir," he said. "The tip, the shaft, the bollocks and all are wholly your affair. My sole concern is to convince myself that no wrist aches beneath the arm they cut away. I thought it right to warn you for dignity's sake."

"Who among us has dignity?" I asked him.

"Neither you nor I, I'd say offhand," he said. "Did you hear that? Off-*hand?* I've a lot to learn."

"All of us, my friend."

"All of us," he said. "I'll tell you when it's gone dark."

Mrs. Hess was as usual reserved, perhaps this evening even distant. I wondered if she sensed an embarrassment in me. I always valued her decorum. Her house, in Yorkville, was frequented by a various clientele, among them the boy called Mal, on whom a few of the older women doted. He was muscular and loud and, they said, at the moment of disrobing, shy. He had enlisted in the Guard and was sorrowful, they said he claimed again and again, not to have served, by dint of his youth, in the War.

"Then serve in *this*," one of them repeated to a few of us, lounging in the parlor near dawn. "Do some active service *here*." The tired, drunken women nodded, and the men laughed aloud. The peacekeeper and factotum, Delgado, dark of mien and dark of complexion, a sure, fierce fighter, circulated in silence. It was a noteworthy moment in that tasteful room of gentian-colored, textured wallpaper, and colored prints of parrots and doves, and it did not pass me by.

If Mrs. Hess was withdrawn, she was impossible to overlook, on account of her bulk, the jeweled tiaras with which she held her yellow-white hair in place, and the pallor of her marble flesh, not unassisted in this wise, I thought, by the quantities of laudanum she took in. Jessie, too, listened more than she spoke. Her skin was the color of lumber, say pine or spruce, washed with a tincture of creosote and slightly aged out of doors: browner than white and lighter than, say, beans of coffee in their burlap sacks. She was slender, tall, powerfully made, a mix perhaps of a female South Sea islander and African, and a man, she thought, who had been some Seminole, some white, and some Negro slave. Her limbs were long, the muscles of her calves looked always clenched, and when she moved her arms, the long muscles writhed.

Watching them once, I told her, "You have a separate life inside you."

Beneath her breasts, such tender flesh, she was tattooed in small designs that she claimed were of significance to her and to her family. I could not decipher the figures, although I often pressed myself close enough to the place to trace the dark inscriptions on her darkness.

It is pathetically and laughably illogical that a man such as I would care, as I did, for such a woman. There were sufficient numbers of limbless, even faceless, men like me in Manhattan. Passersby regarded us with curiosity, with disquiet, with sorrow and pity and disgust. Men with pinned or flapping sleeves and men on crutches jerked and wobbled on Broadway. Men with specially fitted masks, with artificial jaws and gleaming ivory temple plates or metal cheekbones, swelled the crowds at Madison Square. I envied those who had visited the prosthetic specialists at Baltimore and had come away with more than a pasteboard mask. My wound, though it was closed, was always raw. The medicos claimed that the pain was mentally stimulated and the wound had healed. It was more than a wound, I'd replied. It was a topography, a climate and a landscape, a sculpture of furrows and hillocks, of gullies and caves and open field. I smelled it, some days—it made me think of pink roasted beef left for weeks in the cupboard and still, somehow, damp. When the air was cold, the mask bit. In humid weather, fluids dropped and collected, I thought, in a heavy, oil-like liquor. The doctors instructed me otherwise, and Jessie was emphatic in her own assessment contrary to

mine. But they had never been able, at Baltimore, to fit me with an artificial face. I howled at them about my pain, complained that it grated on
the bone. "He *desires* his anguish," one of them said in disgust. I made a
child's rebellious face at him. But, looking at me, how could he have
known?

In her fine room, on her broad bed, in the darkness I so appreciated,
she moved me with her powerful thighs and bony shoulders, and she
pinned me beneath her and held me still. She worked her lips and slow
tongue on me, and I envisioned at such times—I always did, each time—
her sad, light, greenish-brown Creole eyes. She climbed upon me, and
then she reached above my head to the oval deal table beside the bed. Her
breasts brushed my hair, and then she declined again, so that her chest
and arms and belly and legs matched mine.

That stretching motion was always to turn up the lamp. It preceded
by a moment the pulsing of her little pump against my loins, and then
her low, soft voice: "Now take off the mask."

I always did. And then we worked against each other, and then I
worked within her, though never for terribly long, and then I arrived and
so, I thought, or so she gave me to think, did Jessie. Each time, surprising
myself, I realized, as if it were the first time, I wept and wept, and she held
me as if I were her child.

Upon an evening soon again, I paid for the night, and I lay wrapped
in bed linen as if it were a winding sheet, listening to Jessie as she read.
The Methodists had taught her brilliantly; rather, I thought, she was brilliant, and she had been taught by someone literate. She wore a silk robe,
figured, in white on a blue background, to represent the wings of moths,
or mythical birds. Her radiantly black long hair she had put up in a kind
of knotted ring at the back, and tendrils hung down beside her face, so
that her head was naked and sheltered at once. A spike of tattooed figure
peeked from her bosom at the margin of the robe, and Jessie peered at
me, upon occasion, from within herself. And she read to me from a novel
named *St. Elmo,* which breathlessly announced Miss Augusta Jane

Evans's discovery of human qualities in the poor and inhuman depravities in the wealthy.

"Jessie," I said, "I beg your pardon for interrupting, for I love to hear you read. But am I wrong or is Miss Evans discovering that sunshine is hot and ice is cold?"

"Ice?" she said.

"I mean that this Evans discovers for us that those with wealth have got it through dint of effort, though it is perhaps cruelly applied, while the poor are . . . poor, Jessie."

"Yes, they are. Then I'll leave off, or read you something from the newspapers. I have procured *The New York Times* and *The Evening Post*. There's a good deal about money in the headlines. The Union Pacific Railroad has paused in the building of track for want of something or other."

"Funds," I said. "Everything is funds."

"And a credit something or other will be formed to do something else."

"Build the road in return for railroad stocks."

"And the losing of whichever is someone else's profit, I assume."

"You see, Jessie? I told you that anyone could understand the economy. You most of all, good heavens. You simply never cared."

"And isn't it peculiar," she said, "that I, who am a commodity, have chosen to remain ignorant of what you call the marketplace?"

"The invisible marketplace. Yes."

"Perhaps if I could see it," she said, stretching. The tattoo moved because her bosom did, and I could look nowhere else. She did not turn toward me, but sat at the low green wicker table in a matching wicker chair, the lamp beside her, the book on her lap, and the window before her, its curtains adjusted so that she could watch the streets as she wished. Yet, not seeing me, she said, "But you can see it, can't you, Bill?"

"You know that is not what I study at the moment."

"You study me?"

"You know."

She sat forward as if to look more closely at Eighty-sixth Street, hard by Third Avenue. And, as if in a bath, she slowly shrugged the robe from her shoulders. Gaslight fell upon her golden skin and she seemed to me the color of cherrywood boards, gleaming in the twilight of the room. She pulled at the belt of her robe, and with a motion of either arm arranged herself so that the robe was gathered at her rounded belly, and the hair of her sex just barely visible. She sat straight yet relaxed, as one who posed for a painter.

And then she brought up her right hand, which she'd leaned on the arm of her chair that was closer to me. She touched the side of her right breast, and my fingers moved in response. She let her fingers trail to the jutting dark nipple, and she touched it as if in discovery. Then she pulled up her robe, though she did not fasten it closed, but let it drape her nakedness so that a man on the bed, attending her every breath and gesture, might see much but hardly all of what he just had seen.

She leaned back. "Economics," she said. "Are they not the considerations by men who do not care for babies about the burdens imposed when women, large with children fathered by men, give birth in great pain?"

I knew so little of her, and I thought to learn more.

"What do you know about babies, Jessie?"

She shook her head. "I'll read to you."

"No," I said.

Then she turned in the chair to face me, the gown opening so that I might once more see her breasts, and so that she could fasten her dismaying light eyes upon me. I wondered who had passed down eyes of such coloration if her mother was African or Polynesian, and her father a slave. There was a white man in the woodpile, I thought. I thought, too, of the loveliness of her face, the strength of her long throat, the savagery in her tattoos. She was a letter I had read with my fingers, like a man long blind who at last has a message he was years before intended to receive.

She said, as tranquilly as if she offered to pour wine or turn up the lamp, "Then I'll swallow you down. Would you like that?"

She came toward the bed in slow, leonine paces.

"What, though, do you mean about babies?" I lay back, but on an arm, so that I might watch her face.

"There are children at the school still."

"In Florida?"

"Yes. In Florence. At . . . that place. They are, I suppose you would say, the last crop of slavery. They were intended as slaves, and now there is no legitimate market. There's your word again, Bill." She stood at the foot of the bed and reached back to unfasten her hair. All the while, she was expressionless; all the while, she regarded me unblinking. "They will be kept there and used."

"The trade goes on?"

"Everyplace. Dark skin is the color of money. It is everyplace still negotiated."

"Unless someone—the Freedman's Bureau?"

"They are saving adults in the Carolinas. We have enquired."

"We."

Suddenly she let her head hang. "I am—I am a member of a group. We are most of us colored. We are determined to rescue these children. These babies of slaves."

"Is one of them yours, Jessie?"

"Would it make a difference to you?"

"Jessie, are you a mother torn from her child? How can this be?"

"Can you help me, Bill?"

"Is there a profit in it?"

"Moral or commercial?" Her voice was low and even.

"Jessie, is there a commission in it for a man who trades?"

She said, "Their lives here will be difficult. But they will eat as they need to, and be free, as they come of age, to go as they please. There will be capital behind them, yes. So, yes. A commission for a trader? Yes, Bill.

And he—you—will be serving me. It is I who have begged you. It is I before you here."

So I said, "Yes."

Her head came up, her features curtained from me by her hair.

"Lie back," she said, moving toward me again. "Lie down, Billy."

"What do you know," M asked me after an evening of brandy I had bought us, "about what one might think of as 'high art'?"

I thought at once of the crotch of a tree, a butternut, perhaps, and of shivering in the cold of dawn because the tree wasn't thickly leafed. I came down from there and crawled back to the derision of my sergeant. But I was able to stand and piss a steaming arc onto the hardpan of our encampment, and I was alive to watch the steam and smell myself. The decision, made so promptly, to come safely down from the tree: high art, I thought.

I cannot say I trembled more vigorously when stalking my first than I did any number of men later. I was bade begin my special service, and I did. Several men waved me good-bye and even clapped me for luck on the shoulder. One called, "Greetings to Johnny Reb from the 109th Volunteers!" This practice was to greatly diminish, and at the last I was avoided, as if the men were frightened of a contagious disease of which I was the carrier. It was not I, myself, their manner intimated; it was the disease.

We were then in Culpeper, the weather warming smartly and the air a blur of flies drawn in by the horses and our own rank stench. In Paynes Corners, we had called them sweat bees, though the sergeant called them deer flies. They stayed with a man. They were not deterred. My head was wreathed with them as I crawled, then wriggled on my belly, through a long, stony meadow. Beyond it was a steep hill, and past the hill a depression of scree and weed and stunted firs. Beyond that lay an evergreen forest and, at its far edge, or so we'd been instructed, was a detachment of

Rebel horse. They were described as starved lean, and wonderfully trained, and stupidly brave. Of course, you could have described so many of them in that manner. And would I kindly, encased with sweat bees that circled and circled and stung and stung again, make my way over rabbit droppings and the skulls of mice or voles, owl pellets, anthills, and murder some Confederate raiders?

It took me all of the morning to approach the forest. Its floor was shaded and therefore a litter of needles and dead branches. Every step was a possible bone-crack alarm. In my soft deerhide moccasins, and as slowly as a dancer, feeling more prey than hunter, I took half of the afternoon, swollen with bites and running in sweat, to find the tree at the farther edge and begin my climb. The rifle weighed so heavily, the higher I rose, that I feared to drop it. The telescope and cartridges, fastened against me, had frayed my skin and bruised my ribs. My legs shook as I stood on the limb, facing back to the Union lines, and I took a final gulping breath before I stepped and shimmied and finally sat, halfway around on the side that faced the Confederates, hidden or partly disguised by branches, but surely a decent target if they sought one. They had hunted, most of them, in order not to starve. If they saw me, they would have me.

I was blackened and disguised with brush. But the blue of the uniform made a spectacular target. The sergeant had insisted I go uniformed lest, apprehending me, they hang me as a spy. The uniform would help them shoot me from the trees, I told him. But he served a lieutenant who served a colonel who served a brigadier, and I was therefore an extension of tactics, and therefore a target, faded and filthy and blue.

I could not hear them, for the wind came from behind me and carried sound in their direction. I heard only the flies, and the groaning of branch upon branch where one tree had fallen into another, and of course the wind as it blew around my ears. I slowly turned my head so that my right ear was straight-on to their camp. *Perhaps* I'd heard the noise of metal on metal, but it probably was my imagination, I thought—my bowel-deep fear. The scent of pitch mixed with gun oil was so powerful that I expected to see it, around me, as a cloud.

Finally, then, I dared the motion required to remove and extend the telescope. The pressure at my chest meant I'd been holding my breath, and I forced myself to shallowly, silently, breathe. A gray and white bird flew into me, quite nearly, and then veered away, scolding. The man I watched looked up at the sound, and he gazed at me, I thought. I held my breath. He looked away. There were several of them, ragged and bony and hard. Walking into a country tavern and spying them, a man of sage counsel would turn at once and depart.

One of them cleaned what I thought to be a muzzle-loader. I had heard of them using arrows and bows. The one who stood, who had stared at the woods, wore a blond beard and soft muslin clothing washed almost white, though not recently. They were exhausted, their horses were hollow-looking, and one had cocked his hind leg as if coming up lame. And this was what had defeated us again and again, I thought.

The officer removed spectacles from a pouch and put them on. I knew he was the officer because of his bearing, and because he studied documents. I stowed the telescope. I slowly extended the rifle. I sighted through the scope.

He moved his mouth as the wind shifted, and I heard the laughter of his men. I lost him then because of the shaking. The gray and white bird returned, shrieking, and, as my trembling eased, the officer's face came up. I squeezed away, and he went down, thank God, before I could see into his eyes. I heard my shot strike.

I reloaded, by the numbers, calmly, and I looked for my second target. The men had scattered, so I put two horses down. Horses were becoming more precious than men. The sound was of a board slapped hard against the side of a building, and then the animal collapsed. I killed the second one, and I was deafened by my own firing. You do not hunt when you cannot hear. I descended the tree. They fired a fusillade into the woods, but I was well on my way.

He had looked so studious in his spectacles, I thought. Though I remembered best of all, I realized, as I gave the day's parole and walked past the pickets into camp at nearly dusk, how, when his jaw dropped as the shot struck home, his face had looked so soft, and he had seemed about to speak his surprise. Instead of the sound of his voice, I heard in my deafness—I was alone in it for part of the night—the *smack,* once and then again, of the .52-caliber bullets as they tore the horses down.

After the War, I had become, you might say, a careful man. I was reckless as well, I think, but somehow in something of a careful manner. For example, I lived in the Points, although I could well have lived elsewhere. And the Five Points remained, for all the recent fits of municipal zeal, and the declarations by Trinity Church, a great landlord in the district, that moral improvement and the wrath of the Lord were on their way, nothing less than dangerous. I knew it. I had sought it, after all. But I never went unarmed, and I was prepared to do a fatal injury in defense of myself, and I held myself as one such, and they knew me there for a dangerous man. It is not impossible that my neighbors considered me as willing to die as to live, and it is not impossible they found the confusion overwhelming in such a man as myself, and with a face they could not read past the same almost-smiling first page.

As in the War, when I refused a transfer to Berdan's Sharpshooters because I did not wish to wear their green coat and look like a bottle fly and lie on hilltops with great long rifles on tripods to be picked off, surely, by one of the Rebels with a telescope of his own: I wished to run the risk by myself, I told the sergeant, who told the lieutenant, not lie in a file as they did in Berdan's. If I had to be shot for a shooter, I would suffer in private. And I did.

I had sought out M. I had met him. We had dined together and had spoken of philosophy, and he had become enchanted, I thought, by my mask. He would have to be. He had spent his squandered or cursed career as an author in writing men who struck through the mask or curtain or surface of things not to do harm by the striking *per se,* but to learn what lay on the other side. He was drawn by the desire to see it, to know it, as surely as the nation was drawn, on foot and on wheel and on the backs of starving, stumbling beasts, to see what lay beyond the Mississippi River, and the Rocky Mountains, the southwestern deserts, and the hills between the travelers and the sea.

Boarding one of the new, experimental Broadway streetcars—and of course it occurs as well upon entering a restaurant downtown, an office anteroom, the Steinway Hall—I struck those already there into silence. I imagine that I understand their reaction: the bright white mask, its profound deadness, the living eyes beneath—within—the holes, the sketched brows and gashed mouth, airholes embellished, a painting of a nose. Nevertheless. Yet I cannot blame them. But. Nevertheless. *I won this on your behalf,* I am tempted to cry, or pretend to. The specie of the nation, the coin of the realm, our dyspeptic economy, the glister and gauge of American gold: I was *hired* to wear it! For *you.* And *by* you.

On the Broadway car, breathing to the rhythm of the horses' hooves as we slowly rolled uptown, and in the lingering silence of the passengers, I remembered the pond in which I swam as a boy in Paynes Corners. You drifted out, your feet left the silt and lifted, and it was cold beneath while hot on your head. But when you paddled over the feeding spring, you gasped in surprise at the relentless cold. It was like that, entering a room, encountering their eyes. I had learned, however, not to gasp. I wasn't a boy.

No dragonflies followed me over the surface, no clouds of midge above or tickle of bass below, and in the chill of the car I thought of M again. He had eaten precisely, systematically, perhaps seeking in his own pursuit of food a relief from the vision of my forksful as they disappeared under my veil into what he wished to see and not to see. With capable workingman's broad and long-fingered hands, he cut wedges and rectangles of pale pork and then, like an Englishman, shoveled with his knife to maneuver red pickled cabbage and crumbs of boiled potato onto the morsel of meat, the whole then carried to the mouth like a loading boom to the hold of a ship. He studied his plate as he worked, but looked at my head a flickering instant as the food approached his face. I thought of him as eating in a trance.

The thin lips and tight mouth, the narrow head and curried beard, the exhausted, half-blind eyes to which his spectacles gave little apparent relief, were matched by a soft baritone voice that was given to hoarseness. He seemed to me within a very short distance of depletion.

When I spoke of his *The Ambiguities,* he seemed to nod agreement; it was as if I had alluded to a relative whose death had long been suspected. But when I spoke of his *Whale,* even the flesh of his face seemed more alert. This, I thought, was a matter to which I must return. I'd smite the sun if it insulted me, his Ahab raged.

Imagine, I thought, jolting over the street stones: Imagine the engine that ran a man liable, or so he thought, to being insulted by the very sun itself. I swung out of the car and onto Union Square, beneath the morning's very sun itself.

I killed men in a crowded tent they had erected against the side of a low hill in the lee of a pasture near no place I knew. By then we were a specialized unit, and my sergeant, LeMay Grafton, knew that his war would consist of feeding, protecting, and conveying me. As he scorned my necessary expertise, his superiors, he knew, would scorn but utilize his skill in utilizing mine. He and two privates became my pander and my maids. They escorted me; they kept me alive. They brought me to an area and they found me work, then left me to it. And they then avoided me in whatever place of safety to which they'd extracted me. And then we went on to the next.

The Brigadier's Capon, Sergeant Grafton said our lieutenant said of me. The brigadier, he feared, would not promote him to captain because he surely must revile the lieutenant's measure of cowardice in seeing to the shooting down of unprepared and unresisting men. I knew this. The lieutenant knew it. So did the colonel who passed along the commands. And so did Sergeant Grafton. We were one another's prisoner during our service together.

The tent, you might think, would protect a group of men from my vision and my fire. But what the Rebels had not considered was that I might eschew, this time, the safety of the trees and, in my camouflage, crawl—wriggle, really, never raising my arms from my sides—an inch and even less at a time through marshy grass and cow pies and wild thyme, pausing to breathe facedown, then crawl blindly ahead, dragging the Sharps and hoping I would not foul the mechanism with moist earth or excrement. When my head touched the pit mound of the great birch at which, hundreds of yards and many hours before, I had aimed myself, I stopped. A blackbird from the swamp whistled and screeched. He might as well have been a Rebel picket, I thought. I lay my head upon my arms and waited for the bird to become accustomed to me. I breathed in the scent of the grass I had crushed with my body, and the bitter, dark smell of birch roots, the bright saltiness of my own heated flesh.

When I heard him call from bushes some dozens of yards from me, and then from the marsh, I began to bring my piece along my body, inspecting the muzzle and sights and chamber as it traveled my length. Mud daubers had made a nest in the rotted tree; two of them stung me, and I held my breath, waiting to see if the colony would surge at my eyes and ears and mouth. One went after my hand, and I watched him and did not move. It was a cold kind of pain that spread along the surface of the skin. I then watched shadows grow longer. I could not catch their motion, no matter how open-eyed my stare: First they were short, then, magically, long, and then they were much longer.

It was time to remove my forage cap and look over the fallen birch tree. What they had not reckoned on, you see, was the orange-crimson glare of the setting sun that poured down and through the tent. Just before sundown as it was, the men inside were silhouetted, and I did not gamble on the sun's low glow along the barrel of the Sharps. I hastened, taking one, and then another, and they were clean kills, I think. They dropped like dead men. The third target howled, and he might have survived, though it was thousands of pounds of impact he endured if he did.

I was what my commanders used as distress, in other words; I was a disease. I was poison in their lean rations, alkali water in their horses' guts. A man must grow fearful, I thought, if he thought I might be nigh. And how could he know that I might not be? The Brigadier's Capon had balls and he had reach, I thought I might say to Sergeant Grafton and my lads. I never did. It would not do for them to even suspect the very possibility that I felt the briefest of exultations, like a voice stoppered in my chest and throat, when I aimed, just before I killed someone. I put on my forage cap and, like a swimmer in the ponds of my boyhood, lay on my back and pushed off from the birch, able to squint down my legs toward the enemy while writhing backward toward what would have to pass for home.

They would watch me come in. They would force me to use the day's parole despite having seen me through the glass. I could always have approached closer before allowing them to see me, but I did not wish to give them an excuse to shoot me down. Not one of them would tell the truth, and maybe one of them would sorrow. They would be reattached to the 109th, and with pleasure, and they would tell their comrades of the Brigadier's Capon, and how he died for want of a word, by misadventure, not far from the enemy's lines. I am pleased to report that I was mistaken, and that it is likely, I have come to think, that I disliked myself a good deal more bitterly than any of them.

It was, I repeat, our very own Trinity Parish that owned the four- and five-story tenements in the Points. Go to Canal, west of Mulberry, and look for Park and Worth and Baxter Streets. You'd have found half the Asians in America. You'd have found, nearby, on part of Thompson, in the place once known as Africa, the remainder of what was the equivalent of a Negro nation. And in the Points, west of Chatham Square, was one of the worst rookeries the city could boast or be shamed by. They lounged on the curbings and the stoops, they crowded to what few windows there were and on the iron fire escapes. It was air they were after, and a sight of something more than a dying opium eater or a whore who was bleeding from a customer's excess. The children wailed when they were young and were soundless as they grew older. They carried water up the steps from the pump. They lounged, as older boys, on the wagons outside the alley doors of the merchants. They were like sharks in a squalid sea, suddenly finning toward a stranger in the neighborhood, surrounding him, and stripping from him everything but flesh. And who—if it was night, and a boy unsettled because of a parent's agonies or angers—can say that they always left the flesh? I had my own room, and I had my own lock. A lock meant everything: It meant you were undisturbed coming in, greeted by no surprises; and it meant that you could leave behind a bit of your private life. And it was the right district for a man who had left his face in bloody fragments on the splintered stock of his murderer's gun. I had my room at the back, above an alley and over the porch of a saloon; I could jump to safety if a fire took the Old Brewery, which would burn as they said the armory burned in Columbia, South Carolina—with a vast roaring, like the interior of a furnace witnessed through its open iron door.

And, yes, it was the church itself that profited from the immigrants and thieves, and from the whores, some of whom worked up against shingled walls or prone atop the rubbish over the vaulted sewers; you could hear the giant rats in them come running, a feathery sort of stampede. The journalists (and, surely, the good men in black serge who, preying, prayed on behalf of their church for the fallen) laid the blame on Dutch landlords, or on Jews come from Liverpool. But it was the best of us, the cream at the top of the cream. The cream rose, the value of their investments rose, and the single stairwell, serving as a flue, in a six-story building hard by Canal, all but round the corner from us, made the fire rise. It went straight up as the dago, the hebe, the bohunk, the nigger came down and into it. An investigation was promised by the Parish and the police, but I can tell you now: It was money killed them, same as ever, same as it was money responsible for maiming us. In the Harper and Brothers *Weekly*, didn't I read that the Virginia legislature voted thirty thousand dollars for the purchase of limbs for disabled Rebel soldiers, while nothing was allotted for limbless men who had fought on the side that supposedly won? Because nobody won. It was money that won. As the credit notice in the advertisement says, *No Trust.*

I rarely slept, unless with Jessie. I walked in the city. I enjoyed the tingle that went over my arms and hands and fingers when, in a dangerous district, I approached a group of men who lounged and smoked cigars and passed a bottle around. They stiffened as they made me out. They attempted a nonchalance. But how do you not stare at a white-and-pink painted mask, a horrible clown who seems to stare unblinking as you try to seem to look someplace else? Some of them slipped away, some of them walked so quickly, they might as well have run. It was the genteel sorts who neither ambled nor ran. They affected not to see the little mouth hole, the painted nose, the deadness of the painted surface that rode toward them on my shoulders. The higher you rise, the less you permit yourself to flee. It was that way with the highest-ranking officer I took, a colonel of horse who insisted upon wearing his insignia despite my having killed two men in two weeks not six miles from his detachment of overworked horses. He wore the antique Rebel uniform, its dark blue so similar to that of the Union troops. He wore a planter's straw hat, broad-brimmed and circled by what seemed to be a lady's long silk kerchief, white with pink or purple figures. I was in a spruce, itching from the needles and from the resin that smeared my sweaty skin. I had him, and then he sensed me. He stood absolutely still. The captain whom he had just dismissed began at once to understand. But he did not freeze. At first he moved his mouth, and I could read the formulation of his words: *Good Lord, sir. The sniper?*

The colonel's mouth moved less, but I thought he said either *Yes* or, more dramatically, *Sure,* as if he knew that he'd run into his destiny as a man in the dark walks into a wall.

The captain stood where he was, for the time it takes a frightened heart to beat, say, half a dozen times. I thought him brave to have paused there so long. He dove, as if into water, and landed on his belly and balls. His legs were moving to scrabble at the ground they had stood upon, and they finally took purchase, and he lurched, flailing his arms, for the roped-in paddock they had fashioned on a sparse field where the horses grazed. He rolled under the rope and into their legs. They danced about, but were too used up to more than dart and paw, then steady down and drop their heads. I followed the captain's progress an instant, and then I swung back to the colonel, who surely could have escaped. I'd calculated he wouldn't, and I was right. He had stood to await me. He was a very brave man. I took him with a head shot, assuring that he would not feel his end, and I was gone from there like a ghost. They thought of me, I think, as ghostly. They thought me, maybe some of them, a ghost. Walking in Manhattan, inspecting the people of the nighttime streets while walking hard, a nearly military march, to tire myself, I laughed and didn't know why. I wish now that I knew. How I wish I could be gone like that, the ghost disappeared from the killing ground. How I wish I could be gone.

At Washington Street, where the Hudson is a harbor, and where funnels squat filthily on ships among the high wooden masts, carriages rumble and groan with God knows what inside them. Two vehicles resembling the lower Broadway horse cars, but with no roofs, rolled up toward Laight Street with a dozen or more Negro immigrants on board: The Freedman's Bureau had carried them from South Carolina or Georgia to what might have been considered safety, and even, they might have thought, opportunity, in Manhattan. I wondered if they would live in Africa, the Five Points, or the Tenderloin. Some of them grinned, perhaps in embarrassment. They wore dark seamen's clothing and fishermen's caps. Most of them seemed stilled by the weight of their fright. It is a hard city, and as full of cul-de-sacs as large opportunity. They had used to be a kind of currency. Now they sought the common coin in competition with the rest of us. With some of us. Perhaps, of course, as they jolted and wobbled past, they had smiled because they saw a clownish mask. I waved at the second wagon, and a small black child, with no expression, waved in return.

Two ships, arrived overnight or at dawn, were visible at the mouth of the Narrows, lying-to in quarantine before luggage was brought to the public store for appraisal and the cargo was evaluated at the sample offices. M had a hand in all that, he had told me with self-importance and denigration at once; he was complexity, this fellow who made so much and so little of himself. As our waiter had begun to stack the dishes and cutlery, my brand-new friend held dishes, glassware, and an empty bottle from wine in one broad hand. He watched me as I noted the muscularity of his hand and fingers, and I understood how proud he was to have been a powerful deckhand and how powerful he thought himself now. His pride would be useful to know, I thought.

The wind shifted, the masts of the smaller vessels rocked, and gulls, as if tilted by strings, adjusted their angle of descent and the pitch at which they skimmed the murky, broad water. The sun took on aqueous tones; water was everywhere in the air, and the small rowing boats of chandlers and lightermen grew hazed and hard to follow. Even his name, I thought, brought on a drizzle. He gave me a case of what my mother used to call the collywobbles—the usual, at once, seemed untoward, and you thought the village dogs were wolves, and were hungry, and were waiting for you.

I walked above the docks, but the collywobbles came along. I thought of my room, or Jessie's room at Mrs. Hess's house, or the several snug-

F R E D E R I C K   B U S C H

geries at Cheerie's with their oak and frosted glass partitions, or the carriage cars uptown from here. Once, I was at home in the open. I had even occasionally slept away from lodgings and in the woods around New Haven while at school, though speculators were building houses there, and timber merchants were clearing whole half-acres a day. I had been at home, that is, in the world. Now I lived within. The silences, the gasps, the shrill queries of puzzled children—my neighbors in the Old Brewery had little ones who peeped about *maschera*—that were hushed by hard hands; I found these preferable now to the vulnerability in open spaces.

The more I stalked them, of course, the more they'd stalked me. It hadn't occurred to me, probably until after the eighth or ninth, that they had given me a vulgar name and had come to think of me as a person instead of a series of events. Nor did I soon enough suspect that those men, woodsmen since birth, had started, in an uncoordinated but persistent way, to hunt for me. Naturally, once I had sensed it, I took to shadows, to edges, to the safe-seeming side of broad trees. I eschewed a horizon line. I slept restlessly, and I listened hard, sniffed deeply into a wind. My escort, I knew, would fret for their own safety and would not, in all likelihood, kill me out of fear or some holy distaste while I slept. But I had no other assurances, and I stood long watch on my life. For the duration of my war, I peered instead of regarded; my eyes were squinted, not open; and I slept, ate, stooled, and bathed with a weapon ready to hand.

I had asked him, "Do you see us all like your man Ishmael? In a perpetual November gloom? Peering out at the world from nooks and corners and . . . inner places?"

He sipped a Dutch gin and grimaced as he leaned back. I caught his arm, for we sat now in the saloon bar on benches across a narrow table.

"Shipmate," he said, "a provident lunge. I thank you. Now. November? Modern man, you suggest, a creature of perpetual gloom. Well." He sipped. "I used to deal, you see, in concrete realities, not assurances or declamations of the more general sort." He stroked the spade-cut bottom

30

of his beard. "*But.*" He held a finger in the air. "I did, for certain, stride along the back of the particular toward certain broad conclusions. What did you think—that is, did you find a moment for those poems of mine?"

"How I wish you were publishing your tales."

He nodded. "Yes. I cannot do that, though. I am by circumstance as well as volition in a kind of retreat from such efforts. You behold the nutmeg grater grated thin. But the poems . . ."

He waited.

I lied.

I looked out at him, and I lied.

But is there *not* something—especially in this engine of a city, this rattling, black heart that pumps the capital and laborers and stockyard animals out and about and in and under, through darkness, filth, and the forge-bright fire—is there not a sense of the new creatures of this time and place as peerers from secret places? Do we not live, somehow, within? Cleave to privacies, spy from transoms, and listen to the sounds through one another's wall?

Once I hunted. Now I lurk.

And he threatens now to write a poem about a man called Billy. He drinks too much. He writes too many poems.

I rambled in them all, in Squeeze Gut Alley and the Yankee Kitchen and Coenties Slip. Walnut Street was seven blocks of nastiness at night, where in the rain or mist the great mounds of coal and the mountainous granite dumps shone as if lighted from within. Vast, twisted shapes sat like immense dying animals as they rusted in the yard of the Allaire Iron Works, and still, not so far from the Hook that you might see a flesh-peddler discipline his girl—as I once saw—by slapping her with a flail of wet, rolled cloth; she would feel the pain and be frightened to obedience, but he would leave her without scars. It was business, I remember thinking. It was a conservation of inventory. The new world was business, with a frontier broader than the overall combined dimension of our every western state. It was how the national greatness, or its subtle, dark, most woeful appetites, would be expressed. As in the case of my friend M, the deputy inspector of Customs. He was a resource, and that I knew. As I surveyed the city by night and by the wet, gray dawn, so I surveyed the man who was capital to me.

Invest or go stagnant, I maintain. And here I was, the newest, fastest friend of a man once known as literary. He helped to guard the port. He went on board the ships, he told me, in a seeming sorrow and in a kind of pride, at once; he inspected the cargoes, and when he did, he pinned, on his thick serge suit coat, a small metal badge.

"Silver?" I asked him as we ordered German sausages and ale at Delmonico's. He set it on my palm and I said, "Tin, perhaps."

"And locks," he said, regarding the mask as if he were seeing me.

"And what do you lock, sir?"

"The hold. If the casks of spirit are of unlawful proof or seem of dubious quality. If we detect French letters."

"You are a postal inspector, then, as well as an assayer of rum?"

"The letters to which I refer," he said, "you might know as safes. American letters? Italian letters. Spanish ones, for heaven's sake!"

"You speak of eel skins," I ventured.

"And you, sir, tease me. Postal inspector!"

"Letters," I said. "What mail you must see."

"Male as in the *membrum virile*?"

"As in what's sent to you in envelopes."

He smiled gently, his small eyes not so much expressing humor as expecting it. "I believe you know an envelope's another word for letter."

"Of the worldly sort to which you have referred. I do. But back to business, sir. You've authority to lock a captain's hold?"

"And keep him anchored in the harbor until a full-fledged inspector arrives. Why, I can investigate a premises onshore, without a sworn warrant or other affidavit, if I've reason to believe there's contraband within."

"A lock is a powerful weapon," I said.

"A lock is everything," he replied. He shot the frayed cuffs of his loose white shirt, and he pulled at the lapels of his coat. Then, smoothing his beard, stroking it as if it were a cat, he said, "You may lock yourself in. You may lock others out. You may capture or safeguard a person or property. Much of life is given over to the operation of locks."

"And isn't a French letter something of a lock?" I asked him.

"As in a dead letter."

"Or a letter unopened, for that matter."

He sighed. His face lost its rosiness, and his eyes their little luster. He nodded. "A good deal of life, I find, can be spoken of in terms of such mail."

"Of the postal variety, I assume," I said.

He said, "What you will."

We made an arrangement for me to visit his district office—Number 4, it was called—at the foot of the Hudson, on West Street. His wife returning from Albany, he would be dining at home, he said. Unless, of course, it was his turn for night duty. Each inspector must serve, for a twelve-hour span after dark. Sometimes, as a deputy inspector, he served as substitute during a busy week.

"Do you lack for sleep? I, myself, am often up at night."

"I have stood watches, you remember, on heaving decks and in the yards." He took much air into his lungs and his chest swelled. I was to note his musculature, I realized, and I nodded, as if I understood what he had said. I probably had.

"I might visit you, if it is permitted by the Customs."

"We might drink tea and a sweetener of brandy, then. Come, by all means. I might tell you—well, I might not."

And I was to beg him for the information, I saw. "Please," I said.

"Nothing of great magnitude to a veteran such as yourself. Did I not mention the time I went down to Washington to see the War, in April of '64, as much as a gentleman of middle years who wore no weapon could see? And with these faltering eyes. We did ride, more than two hundred of us, in quest of Mosby and his irregulars. He stole into Washington itself, you know."

"He has stolen into business there. He is a fine Republican gentleman these days, I am told."

"We never found his headquarters. But it was a bold foray, and I was a boy again, riding with those boys. You've read my 'Scout Toward Aldie.' He could not read my face. He saw no face to read. I nodded, though, and he nodded in return, as though we'd told each other a truth. "Riding on the Little River," he said, "I knew I was alive."

"And now? Do you know it now?"

"Come visit," he said. "I will be the night inspector on next Thursday, I believe. Come whatever time you wish after dark, and listen to the river at night among the pilings. The dead float by, every now and again. Murdered or suicide, who knows?"

"Nobody cares," I said.

"No. And the chandlers' lads in their long, low craft, ferrying supplies by the light of their lantern, then drifting along the shore with the lantern dim, their voices cracking under the weight of their youth and their cheap cigars apuff—you can smell them on a still night. It gives the old river a sulfurous aspect, and you might think yourself anchored off an Oriental town. And then there's custom, and the lights flare, the gas roars in the pipeworks, and the pilot shouts from the vessel that he's hungry and he wants a proper warm meal and will *someone* not row out and look out the cargo?"

"And then you row out."

"I do, if I serve as the night inspector. It's what I'm there for. The anchor chain rumbling is a kind of deep music, still. Like an organ in chapel, the notes singing through the floor."

"Write us a story of the river at night," I suggested.

"I have," he said. "Think of Styx. I've written it again and again."

"But now," I said.

"But now I go to work there." He looked, this time, squarely into my eyes, and I felt as naked, an instant, as if I wore no mask. It wasn't all lies, my chattering praises, my dancing round him while throwing off respects. He was an alarming man. And he was deep. He said, as lightly as you might ask for the cellar of salt, "If I might have that little badge back, Billy."

During the Seven Days in Virginia, as I was making the reputation that would explode in my face, I separated from Sergeant Grafton and the men, and I posted watch on a house that was occupied, according to reports, by a civilian expert in the drawing of topographical maps. Nothing, not even food at this point, was in such short supply among the Confederates; they hadn't maps of their own Secessionist territories, and they fought, most of them, as blind as if they were in Russia. My target's name was Washburn; I have mislaid his given name, and I came to think of him as W, for it was somehow easier to do my work. And W he remains. I heard the pattering rattle of small arms, and the thunder of artillery. It seemed to never stop, and while I chewed on hardtack and sipped at a stream a half a mile from the house, I knew that flesh, reduced to a sort of gravy, was running on the grass not eight miles hence. I crawled for several hundred yards because the trees behind the house had been harvested for stove fires and the building of redoubts. I had to lie, for a half an hour, as the setting sun illuminated the grounds; a man, moving, could throw a shadow far enough and bold enough to bring a fusillade upon himself.

They sent their large, long-legged dog, maybe a bluetick, out to patrol the grounds, and what he did was take a few dozen steps, lifting his leg several times, and then whirl slowly in the weeds of the fallow garden and, panting, drop. I could hear from his thick, fast breaths how old he was, and he was deaf and stoppered at the nose as well, for I was upon him by the time he started a low-throated growl and winced his way to his feet. I threw myself upon him to knock the wind from his lungs and arrest his warning bark. As I lay on him and slashed and stabbed, poor fellow, and murdered him, he bucked in his panic and screamed in his throat. I held his muzzle to stifle him, and I slashed for my life. His jaws, in the grip of my left hand, were under my belly, and he heaved beneath me like someone at love. Up and down we jerked and rode and sawed, I like death itself come down on him from the evening, and the tired, ter-rified, dying dog like any one of us.

Then he stopped. A long sigh whispered out, and he was done. And who is to say that lovers who collapse away from one another in their gluey juices and whisper their sighs out and out, are so dissimilar from that sorry, frightened animal whose life I took as if I had a right to?

I took my position, in the garden, under a trellis hung with last year's bean vines, my fingers sticky with the old fellow's blood and the alluvial smell of his fur in my nose. I sat sideways to the house, my legs crossed at the ankle, and I leaned my left elbow on my left thigh, near the knee. It gave my back a crook, but moving to relieve it might render the crook permanent, for although the moon was a thin crescent, there was enough light for a man, sufficiently alert, to pick me out—to pick me off. Crawl-ing slowly, I had dragged the old fellow's corpse, a sack of bone and suet now, into the garden; I had thought to shoot with the Sharps braced on his bony flank, but I could not, and he lay behind me, redolent of dis-quiet and stink. Doves made low, wailing sounds, and something thrashed to the rear of the garden near the trees, then abruptly stopped, and I crouched in case the passage of men had silenced what I thought might have been an owl with a mouse. Nothing came, nobody approached, the dog's corpse cooled, and I watched the windows at the back of the house.

I might have slept. I would have sworn not. But I could remember thinking nothing more since the sound in the woods. And then the light came on upstairs, in the window where I'd seen someone, while it was day, setting what seemed to be glasses and a decanter on a surface just below my angle of vision. I wondered what sort of mind a cartographer possessed. Like me, he was in the occupation of seeing. We looked and looked; we somehow took hold of what we saw; and he drew lines while I fired along the lines I sensed but did not render; what we saw we owned. And there, at once, was W, wearing a shirt the color of nutmeg, and linen trousers in a rather ferocious tone of yellowish gold. His belly pushed at his shirt and his belt line. I could see, using my telescope, the dark, thick hair on the back of his hands and even his fingers. One hand was at the decanter I had seen earlier, and then, before it could grip, it was seized by the smaller, more slender hand of someone else. I had not shot a woman thus far.

She leaned forward to kiss the coarser hand, and then I did sit up from my shooter's crouch because it was a smaller man who kissed the hand, a fellow with muttonchops and thick mustache. He kissed the mapmaker's hand and he nibbled at his fingers. When they laughed, it was with the deep voices of manly fellows who appreciated a jest. The mapmaker leaned to kiss the smaller man at the bridge of his nose and then on the tip of the nose itself. He was going to kiss the mouth, and I closed the eye that peered through the telescope, but then I opened it. I had not seen quinces at play before, although I had known boys at Yale who were said, because of the way they carried themselves or with whom they were thought to sport, to be epicene. W and his bugger nibbled each other's lips and were framed in the window like a painting of perversity, although it is open to question just which party, at which end of the shooter's line of sight, was perverse. I aimed the rifle, and therefore I was the legislator of the night's morality. I killed the cartographer and had a linen cartridge in, and a cap in place, as the glass of the windowpane exploded outward, seemingly, an instant after his head erupted toward the ceiling of the room. There was neck and jaw, an ear, I think, and a geyser of blood, brilliant in the light of their lamp, and then I had the littler catamite inside my telescopic sight, and then I planted the shot inside his ear. He fell from sight while blood still pulsed upward from the earlier shot. Before I took him, his expression was studious: He seemed to examine, with as much curiosity as disbelief, the disintegration before him.

I petted the old dog a couple of times, to apologize, before I started to crawl through the rank garden and make my way back. I smelled the dog on my hands and clothing, and I made a note to find a laundress or a Negro soldier who would clean my clothes. Wander the perimeters in a cloud of odor such as this, and be taken off the first strong wind by a Confederate marksman with even a fair sense of smell. When I reported to Sergeant Grafton, he drank at his bitter coffee and poured some for me. We sat in the dark, near the horses, and I ate some cold rabbit they had saved for me.

"*Would* you have shot him if—that is, would you have shot the woman if she'd been one?"

"No."

"Then why the man? Perversions aside?"

"You think it perverse?" I asked.

"I plow a different row," the sergeant said. "We can leave it at that."

"All right."

"And you?"

"Women, thanks."

"Thank Christ," he said. "And you'd not have shot the woman."

"Obviously."

"Oh. I see. You're . . . scrupulous."

"I'm not a murderer."

"Yes, you are."

"No, Sergeant. In wartime, you shoot soldiers and, I don't know, mapmakers, and horse dealers and merchants, if need be. But you do not shoot women."

"I'll remember that," the sergeant said, "and with gratitude for the advice. But why, pray tell, did you shoot the rimadonna's boy?"

"Who was to say which end of the buggery our fellow was on? They directed us to his house. They told us that his wife was dead, or fled. You may guess which. They told me he had a lot of dark hair, that in the district farmers said he had more pelt than his dog. Neither man was bald. I couldn't tell. I—"

"You appeared in the whirlwind and you took them off."

"I did my work."

"So it's work, is it?"

"The production of death, Sergeant, is a type of work."

He poured some coffee onto the ground and stood slowly as if stiff in the back or legs. I tended to avoid his eyes because they were of a very light blue, an almost eerie, icy pallor, and he seemed to be staring hard at you even if, in fact, he was only being attentive.

"You have to pardon me," he said, "as I must pardon you. There's an awful odor about you. I have to believe it is physical, and not a moral decay, but you might see to it, Mr. Bartholomew."

"I'm grateful you pointed it out," I said. "I killed a dog lest he raise the alarm. I used a knife, and I hacked my way into his bowel, I fear."

"The place, that is, where you did your work. The bowel of a dog."

I know I would have riposted, but I remember nothing more, and I wakened hours later. I believe that I fell asleep sitting and uncovered by any blanket but the stench and blood I had carried home from the job.

And I am trying to say that you could feel the city coiling itself. In Manhattan, you could feel the national effort begin. Early in the day, when I might have been about for hours, when the ice wagons and scissors grinders and ragmen began to drive their rounds, then the sound came up of the iron of the horses' hooves, the thunder of the wooden and metal-rimmed wheels, the creak of springs and chime of harness bells and the cries of vendors and drovers, the sweet reek of the honey wagon rising with the industrial salts, the smoke of fires of wood and gas and coke, and the cries of children on roofs and stoops, the wails of women and small men (for it was a place in which to be strong, or championed, or fleet of foot). The din was what I daily heard over the streets and rivers and the canals of Brooklyn, which I had walked beside—shriek of whistle, scream of wounded creature, the ponderous friction of loading pallet on dock or rail, the immense, deep roar of limestone pouring, and the clatter of the shunting in the switchyards. And, over everything, the stink turned into smoke of a hundred kinds, and, past it, like a promise, visible upon occasion in the soot-streaked sky, especially near the Hudson or the East, a blue-white pallor, and the sun. This polluted energy, this vastness on a small island, was the national beginning of a new lunge toward—what? I did not know. The resources were in place, and the drive to use them was pulsing. Just so with my new friend.

CHAPTER 2

DID YOU KNOW THAT IN MY TIME THERE WERE minia-
ture broughams drawn through Central Park by teams of goats? Ragged
children in cobbled-together livery drew wealthy children in Eton suits
and pinafores among the polished balustrades and through the arbor
made of woven live branches. While rats ran under the sewers of the
lower neighborhoods, such as mine, the Harlem River steamboat took
the daytrippers over to Claremont, where the aqueducts from Croton
rested. You could walk the promenade and see, high above Manhattan,
the tall reservoir in which thousands of gallons of water were held for
those in the higher reaches of the city whose delivery pressure might
drop. In my district, of course, the water often ran dark. It was a broth of
invisible creatures, and when a Swamp Angel, hiding from the police
beneath the alleys, relieved himself, he was infecting the immigrant children who rested from their street games and drank at the pump.

But I had faith. I had fine vision, and I saw possibilities. Indeed, I
earned my livelihood from them, and of course from their overthrow. I
speculated—in currencies of all nations, which I willingly exchanged
(drachmas for rubles for pounds in sterling for German gold), in the
future demand for slaughtered hogs, for cattle on the hoof, for codfish
packed in salt, for, of course, the oil of sperm whales shipped in wooden
casks. I was an importer-exporter, a student of the markets, and therefore

41

a man who was watchful of human needs. I lamented the deaths at the minehead in Wales, but I celebrated the retrieval of every lump and boulder of coal. The port at which my friend was deputy inspector was a part of the heart of the great body I attended as Scheherazade attended her Shah. She was thrilled, I have always thought, not to receive his attention but to be allowed to lavish hers; it was the danger in which she won another night that rewarded her. So with me, from out of the Five Points and onto the Manhattan streets.

Before I attended my office, one morning after I had slept for several nighttime hours, I bathed in cold water and retrieved my shirts from Chun Ho, as she was called, the widow who supported her children and herself as a laundress. She steamed my suit and pressed it flat while I stood, indecent from the waist down and unbearable from the neck up, shifting and sighing as her household regarded me in the room's dim light. It smelled pleasantly of fish and sauces, and of harsh soap, and it was the temperature of my body; I could not feel my skin. Before I grew dizzy, the little tan woman with large, young eyes and bleached, shriveled hands held out my trousers. I leaned upon her as I stepped into them, and then she reached up to place my coat upon my back.

"We're like an old husband and wife, Chun Ho," I told her. Her daughter, who spoke a little English, giggled from behind a curtain that must serve them as a wall.

The woman bowed while her eyes appraised me. Her pretty mask was little different from mine, I thought. I reached a finger toward her. She stiffened, but she let me touch her cheek. The flesh was soft, and I felt a *frisson*, you must call it, almost as if someone stroked the bottoms of my feet. Her eyes regarded me from deep within. The sweet young face was still. I had taken liberties.

"I have taken liberties," I said.

She waited. I gave her twenty-five cents. She bowed and so, strangely, did I.

My office was a single room in the Equitable Building at 120 Broadway, above the small coffeehouse that would become the Café Savarin and then, with all the building, in a terrible winter inferno, burn up. I was around the corner from Pine Street, not far from Trinity Church and the Custom House, the Board of Brokers and the United States Treasury. I had a wooden chair that swiveled on an iron screw. I had a plain deal desk. I had cabinets of wood and gas lamps of brass and one window that looked out over Broad and Pine Streets, and one that might have looked upon Broadway in an earlier day that had been, for reasons I never learned, bricked up. So that I might better concentrate, I kept my desk before this window, and, staring out, looked in. The room was small, and stuffy in the warmer weather, and snug in winter, and, truly, unimportant in either regard; it was where I thought about my profit and my loss, unless I foolishly lay abed in my room in the Points and permitted my mind to race like a panicked horse on cobblestones, skittering hither and thither, scrabbling for a foothold, giving off sparks of iron against paving, and making no progress. Here, in the room in the neighborhood called Wall Street, with my name upon the half-wood, half-glass door—*Wlm. Bartholomew • General Transactions*—I planned my days and weeks; I offered, I withdrew; I bought and sold; I profited, or I had my investment for breakfast, meaning that I died overnight in some sharp fellow's ledger book.

And, yes, there were confidence bubbles, there were, indeed, declines. These are the natural inhalations and exhalations of the national economy. Your loss is the compost for what falters, then grows, then thrives. Great creatures were said to have walked upon the earth. They were banished by history. So, too, with nations—say, Atlantis or, less picturesquely, the Romans. They were here, then not. And in their place—who is to say not nourished by the fermentations of their ashes and bones—came others. They survived. So with companies of men, so with investments by the likes of me. Bubbles expand and burst, economies grow lame, and men wander the broken metal railings of the Battery, once grand with grand homes, now a gathering place for those who stare into the water and contemplate their ruin and—not infrequently—their drowning. Then they die. Others live. And what survives is stronger.

I had traveled, that morning, by the omnibus that ran to South Ferry. I tugged on the leather strap affixed to the driver's leg as we came to the Corn and Produce Exchange, and he sullenly slowed, but did not stop, so that I might clamber down. I did not blame the man, although he had a contract with the public; he took our money; he ought to have taken with something like grace the fact that he was tethered back to his passengers as the brace of horses that pulled us were tethered back to him. The wooden wheels creaked and clattered on, and I made my way across Whitehall Street to the Exchange, where I was owed money by Lapham Dumont, who paced the paving stones while doing business.

He watched me cross to him, and I studied him in return. He was a negligible man who was in debt to me and, because in debt, was dangerous, or anyway warranted watching. He was very tall, and he seemed to have no muscles, only bone beneath his brown wool suit. His red face, pointy and dominated by a fleshy nose, appeared to be damp. I cannot imagine—I lie: I can imagine—how my face, my mask, appeared to him. I was a living haunt. I was a fright. I was unreadable.

"William," he said in his basso. It was a voice suggesting strangulation, deep and weak at once.

"Lapham," I said. "In what currency shall we deal?"

"Verbal?"

"Ah. Excuses, you mean."

"Insufficiency."

"That isn't a meaning. That's a plea."

"I must plead, William."

"I must press you, then."

"It is said that you cannot press a stone," he said, wiping each hand with a sullied handkerchief.

"No, my friend. It is said that you cannot press *blood* from a *stone.*

You can always press blood from a man, and likewise, I like to think, money. It was *my* money, pressed at your request into service, that I invested on your behalf in the bear speculation, you'll remember.

"Bearskins," he sneered. "How could I have gone for such a dream? How could you have persuaded me? How could I have permitted you to?" He put the handkerchief into his pocket, drew it out as if he'd never seen it before, addressed it as if it were a book he would read, then blew his nose, wiped his face, dried his hands, and put it away again, looking at me all the while as if I had appeared before him that very second in a nimbus of purple flame. "It's summer," he said. "Why did I not, simply, tell you? It's *summer.* Who buys bearskins when the weather is fair?"

"Boers," I said, and "farmers in Australia and growers in New Zealand. We invest in the world, Lapham, we are not parochial. Nor are we whiners, pouters, nor gonnifs who pike out of debts. Are we?"

He shook his head.

"Are we, Lapham?"

He took out his handkerchief, which seemed to have gone grayer in the past few minutes, and stiffer with the fruits of his physiological functions. An emptying of his left nostril only, a scrub of the forehead and cheeks, then the drying of his hands and the restoration of the handkerchief to a pocket of his vest, seemed to restore him. "I am prepared to write a certificate of obligation," he said.

I said, "And I am prepared to come up, Lapham." I drew, with my toe, an imagined line between us. I placed my actual toe on the imaginary line. I lifted my fists, turning sideways toward him, and bounced a few times on the balls of my feet. "I am going to administer punishment. I am about to become a nation at war. My investments must be protected, and my word as unrelenting in collection must be known as sound. You will learn about international finance. For we are nations in conflict. Are you ready for me?"

He was not. He stepped back. Looking at the street—that is, looking down, a man already beaten—he said, "And, anyway, where would I hit you? In the papier-mâché?"

I struck. I was swift and practiced, and I slapped him hard with my open left hand.

"No," he said, stumbling. Several potbellied brokers came toward us.

I slapped him again, and he leaned against the wall of the Exchange. "Shall we meet in a week to conclude the matter, Lapham?"

He looked at the brokers who attended us. He knew them to be more concerned with debts unpaid than with the safety of a man whose face was beaten red as a sailor's. He nodded.

"Then I declare peace," I said, "and good day to you."

And that is how capital works, I thought, entering 120 Broadway and climbing the iron steps. There are the weak, there are the strong, and some survive. Some, without faces, survive. Some even grow stronger. I thought of poor M, a youthful man still in his middle age, a fellow justly proud, it seemed to me, of his powerful physique. He had invested his efforts, his constructions of language, upon the national markets of England and the United States. His initial offerings were seized upon, his latter efforts were ignored. It was that simple. Surely, what had failed might be, as he had said, his best work. I knew some of the early, a little of the late, and thought him right. He had not, to me, vouchsafed an anger or resentment, even—only a quiet, beaten aspect, as of a man who knew that he was through. It wasn't fair, perhaps, but it was true. Once famous, he was now unknown, a deputy inspector of Customs with his badge and government notebook and his locks. I wondered if he wrote his private stories in the federal book. I wondered how deep in his soul he accepted the verdict of the marketplace. The waters would roll over him, and he would be forgotten if, already, he wasn't yet; and someone else, who wrote what the public would have—stories of investments, I thought, and who can tell?—might be remembered.

It is all rise and fall, I thought; it is all the contest waged to see who stands at the end.

As when a North Carolina platoon had broken away from Hill's Third Corps and were moving in the direction of home. Sergeant Grafton rode up to us as we were eating squirrel in a stew, and looked at me with his abrasive blue eyes.

"So soon again?" I said.

"It is why they invented the likes of you, Mr. Bartholomew." He nodded to Private Burton and Private Mordecai, replacements latterly detached to us, and who remained with us until my service was done. They set about to roll their blankets up and gather the water bottles to fill before we left.

I counted cartridges and caps. I cleaned the mechanism again, and I saw to the lenses of my sight and telescope.

"You haven't asked me about our mission," Sergeant Grafton said.

Swarthy Private Samuel Mordecai, angelic of face in a halo of hair that looked like wire brush, said, "The man shoots people. Why ask who? They're alive, then their families are hanging blankets on the mirrors. Finished."

Private Burton said, "What about the mirrors, Sam?"

"Dead people's spirits don't delay their departure if they cannot see themselves," he said most earnestly. "Blankets. Or you could use a sheet. Anything that covers."

"I had not thought you people to be so primitive," Sergeant Grafton said.

"My family and I, Sergeant, have already enjoyed the advanced culture of some of *you* people. With the sergeant's permission."

Grafton laughed, and so did Burton, though Grafton seemed to sense who Mordecai was, while Burton knew mostly what he ate for supper or didn't, and how many miles were left that day to ride.

"Where?" I asked Grafton.

"Southwest of here. Rebs breaking ranks and going home. Maybe not quite a platoon in pursuit. The colonel believes that we can harvest their morale."

We rode hard, and it was night when I was close enough to smell their fire and their horses and the men themselves. Grafton and the lads were half a mile behind me, close enough to be endangered, and they waited warily, I knew, behind a breastwork of rotted tree limbs and earth the soldiers took turns in digging. And I, in my moccasins, with my face blackened by charcoal, took small, hesitant steps. Then I heard them, and not the pursuing party; these were the deserters. So I knew we had out-run the Rebel pursuit and were caught between the men ahead of me, disgruntled and homesick conscripts from North Carolina, according to the colonel's intelligence, and the twenty or thirty men who had been detailed to bring them home. They might grind us between them like grain. Or the pursuers might have turned off course, thus their late arrival; if they were slightly misdirected, we might still do the business of the night and survive.

I found myself grinning in the darkness. If the Rebel maps were inaccurate, for want of reliable cartographers, I knew a reason why. Then I thought of the dog and grew sorry. But then I had to grin again. I set my finger alongside the trigger, and then I dropped very slowly and began to crawl. In a sense, it was a return to my childhood in the upstate forests. I could have roamed them blind, and I was only slightly less accomplished here in Virginia. I wondered if I should return to Grafton and warn him that we'd overshot the enemy. Only, I thought, if our mission were to live; but it was to see that Southern soldiers didn't, and I happily crawled on through my fright, eminently containable, and through the clouds of insect, through the slimy trails of slugs.

They had tethered their horses across the little meadow from me, and they were huddled, in spite of the heat, at their cookfire. They were cold because they had crossed an unmapped boundary to which they would never return. They were cold because they wished to believe they were soon to be united with their parents or wives. They were cold because nothing now could ever come right.

I watched them in their tense dispersal in positions of apparent ease.

I stared at the bulge of the head above the back of the neck, at the muscles of jaws that moved as they chewed, at the winding and unwinding of harness strings, the random chopping with a knife into the earth between his legs of a soldier who could not face his food.

When I was standing behind a tree and breathing shallowly, for silence and control of my frame, and when I had stared at the sparse hairs of a young man's face, at the man who seemed to scratch at lice inside his pants, at the older man who lay on his side, supporting his weight on his arm—he stared past the fire and into the darkness, at nothing his companions could see—I held my breath and eased my finger around. I held him in my sight, his obvious regret and grim considerations, and I fired. I heard the *smack* as the shot went into his neck, but I was already reloading, and because I thought to kill them all, leaving a camp of corpses for the pursuers to find, I hurried my shot at the man who itched. I killed him, too, but it went in lower than I wished, between his shoulder blades, and I heard his lungs begin to bubble as the youngest one cried, "Oh, Jesus! Dear sweet Jesus Christ! Oh, Jesus Christ! Oh, Mother! They're killing us. Mother, they're—" And then he stopped because I took him in the face. I saw his teeth explode through his jaws—harbinger, if only I knew.

A couple of them had rolled by now behind their satchels and blanket rolls. I moved to a tree several dozen yards to my left, changing my angle of fire and confusing their angle of return. I reloaded. I put a rapid shot into their tack and two above it, in case the early shot had driven them up and back. I heard a sound like a whistle, though my right ear had stopped functioning, and it seemed to come a terribly long way; I knew it to be the lungs of the man I'd hit in the back. I thought I heard someone sobbing, perhaps a man I'd wounded with the last few shots, and then I scampered. I went back through the forest as if I'd walked these woods in daylight and dark all my life. I slammed into a tree and was floored for my confidence, gasping and seizing at my nose to feel whether I had burst it. I took two deep breaths, shifted my rifle to the hand not numb from my collision, and I jog-trotted from the edge of the woods toward our encampment. I did not hear myself thrashing in the forest or over the field because the shots reverberated in my right ear, while the left felt plugged with cotton wool.

I saw Sam Mordecai's narrow, wide-eyed face, and he saw mine. But he called for the parole; I assumed that his demand was what I could not hear. I slapped my deafened ear with my palm to show my difficulties and I whispered, or I thought I did, "Medusa."

"The lady with the snakes," he replied, shouting at my left ear.

"Look at me and turn to stone," I said. I was able to somewhat hear myself, but as though underwater. "Hurry, Sam. Their posse hasn't got here yet. They're on their way."

"In my faith," he shouted, "we could maybe look at you and turn to salt. A pillar, even, of salt. But that's my best offer."

And I said, "Done."

I said it again to her—"Done for good, I fear"—when Jessie could not rouse me past, let us say, a certain point. She was shameless with her mouth, venturing beyond scruples or their absence to an obvious pleasure she took, both in the pleasure she gave me and in sensations of which she did not speak but to which she obviously responded.

Now she lay beside me, completely unclothed, while I, still wearing the mask, lay in an unresponding nakedness. My hand, which dangled from the bed as droopily as my peter lay athwart my thigh, was, I realized, stroking the head of the bearskin rug with which I had presented her that night in celebration of my uncivilized behavior of the morning with Lapham Dumont.

She spoke in the carefully modulated tones of the superior student of the Florence, Florida, Methodist Academy where, the child of a slave, her mind was trained for a career of teaching by the Reverend Foster's wife, and her body groomed for her present position by the Reverend Foster himself. He dismissed her on account of her unsightly, unseemly, and un-Christian tattoos, never feeling the necessity to make clear to the student body or his faithful trustees how it was that he had come to see them in the first place, banding her lower breasts and torso as they did. Jessie said, sweetly, "Bumfodder, Billy. A couple of nights ago, you rose like the moon. You don't lose the ink in your pen that quickly."

"Are you sure?"

"Are you acquainted with anyone else who knows the subject better than I?"

"I don't like to think of it like that."

"Yes, you do."

"Well. Sometimes, perhaps."

"Do you think of me sucking away at some big Irishman? Slurping my mouth all over him? As if he were a piece of ice, and myself in heat, if you know."

"I know, Jessie." She put her hand on me and I flinched.

"Yes," she said, "but a little firmness there already, I'd say. Let's go one better. He's turned me over and pressed my face down into the pillow. We know what he wants, don't we? There goes his big, blunt finger, pressing in, and I say something about the cold cream, and so he must say something about his *hot* cream, and he presses his suit, let's say. Let's say he presses on. I'm facedown into the pillow, and he's immense in me. Christ! He—"

I turned over and I pressed the mask upon her. She tensed and went still.

"Sometimes," I said, "I would surrender an arm if I could kiss you."

"Take off the mask," she said.

"I'm—"

"Oh, no? What's this I'm feeling? Remove it, please. The mask, not your— That's right. Not your— No, you know what to do now, don't you?"

It was the night I asked her again to tell me what the tattoos represented.

"Well, I've just now told you," she said.

51

I left off asking, and I lay in my pride and in my childish resentment.

"You tell *me* something," she whispered.

I said, "Yes."

"What were you remembering? What were you thinking about? When you couldn't. When you thought you couldn't."

"Hue and cry," I said, "crimes, misdeeds, and misbehavior."

"You evade me." She turned and kissed the crushed, crimped bony flesh beneath the scars at the side of what was left of my face. She kissed my ear. She nipped it, and I felt it down through my spine. "Tell," she said.

"My work in the War."

"The rifle work."

"Assassinations, yes."

"The dead are burdening your body," she said.

"The dead bed me that I might not bed you?"

Jessie said, "Perhaps." Then: "This one," she said, taking my hand and moving my finger along her ribs to the swell of her breast, "this is my mother's time on Pukapuka. She was taken from there as a girl." She moved my hand along her to the other side; I cupped her breast lightly because the flesh was beautiful and perfectly smooth, and because she permitted and even wished me to. "This is the story of my father in the Indian encampments." I read the story with my hand, and with its fingers. My nerves read. I remained there, eyes closed, in the tale of the man escaped from captivity to whites, now captive again to redskinned people. I listened with the outer flesh of my body for the moment he met Jessie's mother, and how she came to be there in the Seminole place, and how they coupled, and how they parted. Then she moved my hand to her belly, my fingers lower and, as she moved her legs apart, in. I understood little but felt much, and I therefore was grateful and burdened at once.

I sighed and my breath went up the craters of my face.

Jessie said, in her dry, low, undramatic voice, "This is about Billy Bartholomew entering my life. Now you may take the mask off, Billy."

"But I have," I whispered.

"Not that one, dear," she said, as if I would understand.

I made my way, on the arranged evening, to the foot of the Hudson River, at West Street, where, on a barge moored fast to the pier, some dozen feet, down wooden steps, below the level of the street, the Customs man on duty sat his watch of night or of day. The wagon traffic was diminished and, although not silent, or even quiet, the shipping district murmured rather than roared. Individual teams of horses, pulling heavy loads, could be descried, and one could even tell from which direction came the barking of a dog or the shouts of drunken men, the wailing of a child. The wind was up that night, and with it fog, and the moonlight thus was in retreat. I could tell the slapping of waves kicked up by the wind against the hulls of anchored ships. I could hear the little dip-and-splash of a boat with several rowers; perhaps it was the river police, I speculated, or perhaps a smuggler of courage and enterprise who took advantage of the darkness and the fog (it looked yellowish in the light of lanterns hung on stanchions on the dock and on the sterns of ships). One could turn a powerful profit if the night inspector turned his head at the right moment. It was chancy, of course, but a businessman must never close his eyes to chance.

M was in a broad armchair the horsehair stuffing of which protruded through the rents in its cushions. Still, he looked comfortable. A lantern on a gimbal in the center of the room gave mellow light that swayed as the barge was moved by the water responding to gusts of air and wakes upon the river left by passing craft. An unopened book lay on his lap—something called *The Will as World and Idea,* he told me, by a fellow called Schopenhauer, whom I'd never read. ("The man's a scowling pessimist," he fondly said when I asked what his attractions were.) The room was hung with what seemed to be charts and schedules of duty. Closely printed forms lay in stacks on rows of shelves. Several sets of locks, their hasps unfastened, lay atop the forms perhaps as paper-weights. A small table with a box of pencils and a ruled notebook showed me where he worked. I thought of the sailor to Polynesia, the librarian of whales, inscribing poems no one might read in a government-issued notebook with the pencils given him for writing down the provenance of foodstuffs, the ownership of hides in stinking piles in the cargo holds of ships.

"Welcome, shipmate," he said, standing with a youthful flexuousness. I remarked to myself once more that he affected clothing—black suit, a collar none too clean, a shirt of equal smudginess—of unusual loose-ness. His boots seemed cracked and cheap. He squinted, as he usually did, and he rubbed at his shoulder.

"A bit of neuralgia from the dampness of the river," I suggested.

"Oh," he said, "you get the twinges near water. An old fracture from a wagon accident. In Pittsfield, I was known to let the horses have their head, and mine as well. I learned my lesson over all the months it took me to heal. I'm good as new, of course."

"Except for the twinges," I said. He indicated the easy chair, but I took the captain's chair at his desk, and then he sat, too.

"You know about them, then." He gestured at my mask.

"I can feel iron needles slide in, some nights, in the midst of one of my marathon walks. There—I have to confess it, I continue to resent the pain's continuation—there are days when my face bones ring like wagon wheels on paving stones. Sometimes I think I've just been wounded again, and I'm waking to find myself in the ambulance wagon way down South, or coming to in Washington and screaming for some-one to kill me."

"You did that," he said, with something of wonder, stroking his beard, narrowing his eyes. "Asked for death?"

"It seemed the only comfort I might find. I'm not proud of howling. But I howled."

"Yes," he said, "we do that. Did Job not howl?"

"And you?"

"Oh. No. I was proud, and I was among neighbors, for my household has always been too full. I wished them strangers so that I might have, I can promise you that. But no."

"No. And now?"

"And why now would I declaim upon the very narrow and not particularly gripping story of the self you've so generously come to see?"

"Well, sir, you're the one, instants ago, who mentioned Job. Unless you think his story pertains only to me."

"To the nation. To the martyred President. To you, Bill Bartholomew, for certain, and your comrades in battle."

"And to you?" I asked him. "Are you not one of us?"

He shook his head. He smiled without conviction. "My travails are not those of Job, but rather of a family man with too much family and too few funds to pay for family. And of a literary man without the literature. One mustn't complain, though."

"Not so's they can hear one," I said. He opened his mouth, like a cat yawning, to soundlessly laugh, or make the motions of laughter. It seemed to me, as I looked into the darkness of his mouth, that he dissembled, and that the man I saw and who saw me perhaps was not the man I thought to see. I wondered who, in fact, was seated before me, but I did not speculate aloud as we sat companionably, two strangers apparently at ease with one another and with the office that slowly rocked at the pier. Everything shifts, I thought. "No," I said, as if we had been reading one another's thoughts, "it is that you rose to such a pinnacle height."

"You have read my *Whale*. You have seen the masts go under, Tashtego's arm wielding the hammer to affix Ahab's flag as the masthead disappears beneath the sea. That is the natural course of events for pinnacles and heights, Bill. They plummet. I have plummeted. You know my *Confidence-Man*? It was published a decade ago, on April Fool's Day. At the end, a light not unlike this one"—he gestured at the ceiling fixture—"is extinguished. All the light by which I apprehended my subject was extinguished. April Fool. Something further may come of this masquerade."

"Pardon?" I did not know the book to which he referred, yet I did not wish to further insult his wounded pride.

"That was the final line of my book."

"Yes," I said, "of course."

"Something further. I'd no idea what. I stopped the book because my vitality or my kidney failed. It was about devilish business, and I had thought to navigate further in the matter. But I stopped. One fellow, an English journalist, called it an abortion. I had to ask a literary Dutchman of my acquaintance what the word meant. Are you familiar with it?"

"Certain ladies of my acquaintance are familiar with it."

He nodded. "The flesh makes clarion signals we cannot ignore."

"I have heard the word employed."

"In evaluating books?"

"No, sir. In describing a surgery."

"Exactly. It was used in connection with my *book*."

I said, "Such a sordid profession! To earn one's bread by commenting cruelly on a man's labors. Still, the judgment's a commodity."

"And life's a market, yes? I see the downtown stockyards, and the bellowing, dazed creatures, and the stench, the rising dust behind which the men, bloody from the abattoir, are hidden as the cattle prance in their panic. It's a gloomy, Satanic sight! I see the hammer descend, crushing their skulls, and I see the blood and brains leaking while, before they are dead, the cattle are flayed and filleted. They die as they are hung to bleed in choicest cuts. So with authors. For sale! For sale!" He was up, and lithe as a boy, marching toward a cupboard with a small keyhole. "For sale! Prime butchery! Beef on the hoof! Volumes fresh killed!" His soft voice rose, and then he pantomimed, turning to face me, his soundless laugh. He raised a ship's decanter, with its heavy base, and, a finger inside each one, lifted with his other hand a couple of etched blue glasses. "Let's drink to the market. To the meat yard. To the meat."

He poured brandy into each glass, a good deal more than a splash, and he delivered mine with a kind of hop, and skip, and jump.

"To your health," I ventured.

"Ah, Bill," he said, "to yours, and to that of the warriors you knew. To the souls of the generals who bade you ride into battle."

"To the souls of the dead," I said. "To the dead. To those we killed."

"And to Malcolm, dear fellow, who has insisted upon joining the National Guard. My son," he told me, "Malcolm, my son. He works at an infernal insurance firm, gambling, I think I can say, on early deaths. But he awaits military work, not to say martial. Poor fellow, and he hasn't even a gun. I must help him acquire one. They are expensive?"

I thought of the roisterer at Mrs. Hess's, the all-but-boy they called Mal, who drank himself stupid and who brayed in the parlor. Something further might come of *that* masquerade. "I know of one," I said.

"A reliable weapon? If he must go armed, he must be well-armed."

"The Navy Colt of 1860 is a fine sidearm for combat. Your boy has large hands—"

"He has? How do you know his hands?"

"No, sir. You misheard me. I *ask:* Has he sizable hands?"

"He's a well-proportioned fellow. Yes, I'd say."

"It's a well-balanced piece. The chambering device revolves, you see, and a cartridge is presented for the hammer to fall upon and fire every time the trigger is pulled. You must instruct him—they will, the Guard, of course—to *not* pull. You caress with increasing pressure. The weapon fires, and the next cartridge presents itself, ready to repeat. I carried it during the War. It's far too large for a man in a business suit. The barrel's intrusive on Broadway, though highly practical for defending yourself when there are a dozen yards and more between you and what endangers you. One. The shooter."

"You are a marksman, then?"

"I was."

"And you would part with this weapon?"

"As a service to my friend, I would. I keep Colt's caliber .31 within reach for practical matters."

"Practical matters. Well, what's more practical, I say, than matters of life and death?"

"Nothing but business," I said. "Malcolm, eh?"

"An industrious boy. Though he has been attracted by the demi-monde, I fear. There are signs."

"The smell of drink and strong tobacco? Women's perfume? A certain pastiness of the visage, a glazing of the eye?"

M sat back. He shook his head once, and then he contemplated his brandy. Looking up at last, he said, "Hardly."

"Well, then," I said, and I lifted the mask above the ruins of my mouth, and I drank, sighting along the inside lining to regard his inquisitive, acquisitive stare at the puckers into which I poured some drink. I pulled down the mask and said, "A cumbersome business, I fear."

"Ah! war thy theft," he said. I took it to be more poetry.

We sat a long while, he now frowning and shaking his head.

At last I asked him, "Do you not regard the purchase of the Alaskan Territory for two cents an acre something of a great steal? The Russians must be hugely in need of capital to sell a half a million acres so small."

He sighed. He roused himself enough to say, "Might I suggest that two cents for an acre of ice yields only an acre of ice? And you cannot bring it hither, you know. You must voyage forth for what will melt before you bring it home. I call that less than a bargain. I tend to never validate an estimation by anyone in the Department of State. I do not trust their judgment."

"Skins," I said. "Bear and otter. There are limitless skins."

"I have my own, thanks, thin as it is."

"And fishes of every sort, I understand."

"No," he said. "Surely not. I am through with fishes, little or large."

"Secretary Seward cannot earn your approval, then."

"I asked for his department's approval, and friends not distant from the founts of power also asked, and this is the largesse I received. Day inspector, night inspector, badge and notebook, locks and pens. The distance from this barge to the consulship in Hawaii, which I requested, and which I dared to think I deserved, is greater than that between Hawaii itself and West Street. With a son soon gone for a Guardsman, and a wife almost gone in pursuit of surcease, and often enough—too often—a houseful of mouths." Having refilled his glass, he said, "To feed. May I offer you more?"

"As I said, a cumbersome business."

"Stand to, then, and signify as required." He poured more brandy and drank it, clearly for the fire and not for the fiery taste.

"I will let you have that Colt at a lovely price," I said.

"I shall consult with Lizzie—she is my wife. We shall discuss it, for any sum of money is a sum with which to be reckoned. And because I hope that we shall enjoy each other's company soon again, I will predict the decision. I suspect it's yes."

"He'll not go undefended."

"I pray there's no defense necessary. Though if he travels west, it's the Indian wars, isn't it?"

"From what I hear, the wars are ours, the lives lost are, in the majority, the Indians."

"I would say, in the case of any other soldier," he said, "that the persecutors of Indians receive their due. But I fear for him."

"For anyone who soldiers, yes," I said.

"Were you a horse soldier?" he asked me.

"I was a marksman."

"Yes, of course." He held up the glass to lay blame. "I saw a print of a marksman, by Mr. Winslow Homer, the magazine artist," he said. "A fellow in a tree."

"That was me. I was pretty then, wasn't I?"

"That was you I saw!"

"Now, sir," I said. "You have imprinted far more paper, far more valuably, than I. Mr. Homer was struck, apparently, by the sharpshooting profession—something to do, I've little doubt, with the visual apprehension of others when they might not know, perhaps. Something along those lines. He sketched me as I sat in a tree, far from any target, I can tell you. We were camped. We were gathering to disperse: It is how armies function. But, yes, I fired the 1859 Sharps rifle when it was time to conduct my business. I extinguished men."

"Extinguished the light," he said.

"If you will."

I held my glass out, and he refilled it and then his own.

"You shot men from afar."

"Often. But sometimes I worked in close."

"And shot them down."

"Dead. Yes."

He shook his head.

"And then they wounded you."

"They did."

"A glory and a pity," he said. "I wish I might have written a man such as you when I wrote tales. I wish I could do you justice."

"Sir," I said, "I wish I could see justice done for *you*."

"I carry on. I write at an epic narrative in verse, Bill. About the Holy Land. About certain men whom I have known. It's something of a summing-up."

"The Holy Land's an epic subject," I said, although I'd no idea what it was I had said.

"A bitter place," he said.

And I said, "Sir? Are you truly not bitter?"

"I can tell you," he said, drinking his brandy off, "that I am not sweet."

And then he was climbing the stairs in his house on East Twenty-sixth Street. And then he was inside the shadows of the lamp he carried up—inside of the shadows: his description. Stroking his beard, laughing his soundless laugh and meaning no laughter, squinting because he could not see so very far with any strength, and telling me of his evenings and his Sabbath afternoons in the little room upstairs that looked out upon a waste ground, a little backyard in which not even grass grew, and over the hard-packed, barren earth of which an accumulation of newspaper sheets and bits of rag and blown grit became a substitute, in his failing sight and in his inner vision, for the earth itself. He thought it the Manhattan aspect of the Dead Sea. In the harsh vinegar smell of Lizzie's preserving of vegetables and fruit, and in the heavy, bland steam of her cookery, and in the sooty shadows of his lamp, and in the last silent room left to his claim, and to his lock, he wrote of the Holy Land, he corresponded intermittently with family and an occasional literary friend, though he knew that several had remarked to one another on the matter of his early death. A dead man needn't hurry his long poem. Nor need an abortion to concern himself with matters of life. And since, as Mr. Charles Eliot Norton had remarked, his *Battle-Pieces* on the War were anything but poetry, his obligations to verse in general, and the literary world in particular, had disappeared. He drank at times, he wrote, he wrote and drank a bit, and Lizzie brought his meal to his door of an afternoon or evening. And he strolled down through the city to the docks, or rode the new horse-drawn streetcars to Union Square, where he could ride down further on an omnibus, or walk at a healthy pace. And then he was the deputy inspector, of the night or of the day, and he saw to the legal unloading of cargoes, the legal entrance by travelers to the crowded parlor of the United States—as he saw Manhattan—and he bore the badge of national service on the left-hand collar of his greasy suit.

"I do lead a life," he said. "I *am* the man I was. I am my own secret now, however. I am my darkest, best-held secret. Do I wish to be? I would prefer not to. Do I choose? I do not. Shipmate: Like the nation, I was divided from myself; like the nation, I was wounded; riven, like the nation, I healed; like you now, Bill, I am healthy; we are whole."

We are untruthful, I thought. But for the first time in a day and night, I felt the profoundest attraction of sleep. I had been fatigued, of course. But now, in the gently rocking barge, under the hissing of the lamp and the clinking of his glass on his decanter, under the pouring stream of his throaty voice, its rise and fall, the deft articulation of his syllables like water over rock and log and streambed, and in the absoluteness of his despair, and the charm of his denying it, I felt—there is no other description—quite at home. I had him, or would have him soon. And his possession of me, or his attraction to me, his wish to know me because I mattered to his artist's demand for darkness, and his need to know what lay behind the apparent, and my sense of my advantage over him—the comfort of gain, which I felt with my sound flesh and through the deep ache inside my jaw and nose and neck—closed my eyes and set me, sprawling in my chair and loose-jointed, asleep.

"Ho!" he called, and I was up, blinking, my hand inside my coat and on the butt of the Colt. "A ship lies to," he said from the door that went up the short flight of stairs to the deck of the barge. "Are you in the mood for a bit of rowing, shipmate?"

I was too stupid with sleep, too weak with ease, to answer.

"Shake a leg," he called, seizing a heavy oilskin coat from a peg beside the door and holding it out for me. He was wearing another such coat, and a sailor's knit cap, and he looked, for the first time, like the man who had written of sailing on small, wooden craft to the other side of the world.

I put on the coat and tied a kerchief over my head so that it hung upon the mask—the less salt of the sea, the better for its paint and varnish. I set an oilskin cap he gave me over the kerchief, and thus I protected my face—from the elements, and from men's scrutiny—the more. Then we were out and up and down again, to a dinghy tied to the barge. M took the oars and at his direction I cast off. A lantern on a hook behind him swung in the wind and chop of the channel, and he peered above it out toward a looming, lit vessel, its outlines blurred by fog and mist, that rocked at her chains.

He worked at the oars like a boy, demonstrating great strength in his wrists and hands, and showing a fine eye as he subtly corrected his course. I did not enjoy feeling like a lump of supercargo, a leather pouch of mail, say, heaped into the back of the boat. When he did not look over his shoulder, he seemed to stare at me, leaning in and digging with the oars, then leaning back to propel us. Perhaps he looked over my shoulder to navigate according to a light onshore. I could not tell. But it seemed to me that he addressed my face, my mask upon my face, as he rowed backward into the mist.

A thumping combination of whistle and drum rolled in toward us and seemed to shatter against the mist and wind before it might strike. Several bursts of sound came tinnily in again, and he said, "Pilot's gone for the night. Cargo to be cursorily examined—we'll note there is one, and what its contents are. Inspection in the morning. I'll make for the larboard in hopes of a bit less motion when we tie to the ladderway."

I could not imagine a bit *more* motion, nor could I see myself, white signboard of a face lit beneath the ship's lights, coming up a ladder without terrorizing a man on watch, or falling into the black, oily waters of the harbor to drown. But we bumped rather more gently than I thought we might into the timbers at the side of the ship. And M made us fast quite expertly. Salt and mist and the reek of rotting vegetables, the stink of rat ordure and the corruption by the sea of wood itself, blew over us. Under it all, I could smell skin, and the vomitous musk of fear on my breath as it rose and was trapped beneath the mask. M set my hands and then feet aright, and as I climbed he followed close. No one greeted us, so he put his hands on my shoulders to steer me out of his way, and then led us to the gallery outside the captain's cabin.

The master, named Borofsky, shook our hands. I made him uneasy, and he backed toward his broad desk, which was covered with charts held down by books. He took a manifest from the drawer and showed it to M, who moved closer to the light and who accepted a glass of Polish spirits distilled from potatoes. Small and trim, careful in his motions, Borofsky poured a full one, and I knew that they had drunk together before. He lifted his own full glass before me, raising his eyebrows and averting his eyes, and I shook my head. He and M clinked glasses and drank the liquor down. Each smacked his lips and cleared his throat and made soft roaring sounds. M rubbed his full, bluntly trimmed beard, while Borofsky tugged at each end of his mustache and adjusted the buttons on his trim blue coat worn over dirty brown-red trousers.

"*Ça va?*" he said to M.

M answered, "*Je ne sait pas cet mot ci—ah: moment! Je comprends. Vous portez, donc, le cognac en barils, et quelque fromage de France. Hein?*"

"*Monsieur sait que c'est comme il faut.*"

"*Bien sur. Mais ma verre, elle est vide.*"

"*Je regrette, monsieur, et je reconnais mon erreur. Voilà.*"

The captain poured more of the clear liquor into the glass of the inspector, who toasted him and emptied his drink. They apparently agreed that the ship might receive its full inspection in the morning, and they shook hands. Borofsky bowed deeply, and M inclined his head.

"Thus," he said to me, "I stand on an unmoving deck. It is what I do in my life at home and in my office. The deck may slope or sway, but it goes no place in particular. Let's disembark, shipmate. Let's set out on the little voyage home."

I said to the captain, "Good night, sir."

"*Enchanté,*" he said, looking away.

In the dinghy, and moving through the chop toward the docks, I looked over M and saw the yellow and golden and sometimes green-looking lights as filtered by mist and a yellow fog and blown dark smoke.

"I shall leave you," he said.

"Pardon?"

"I must leave you at the office and return. We must not abandon the vessel, in fact, once we're aboard."

"You'll wait out the morning?" I thought of the potato spirits.

"Regulations established by the Surveyor of the Port of New York. I am a servant of the servants of the people, Bill. We'll have a night of it again, though."

"I look forward to it."

He said, "You've warmed my heart on a bleak night."

"I'll bring you the pistol, then."

"I'll find the money. How much, would you say?"

"Five dollars," I said. "No, four, let's say."

"A week's pay," he said.

"I'm in no hurry for the money."

"A debt's a debt. It's a creature I know by heart."

We sat in silence, but surrounded by noise—the small splash of his oars, wielded with power and efficiency, against the black waters; the roaring of a furnace on the shore; the seething of the wind against the surface and the perforations of my mask; the little grunt he made as he held an oar, like a rudder, in the water while digging in with the other to turn us. The man of oceans, of three-masted ships, of naked brown girls and sailors who stalked their boys with hard hands and filleting knives: He rowed me, I thought, in a little boat. How could he bear this disintegration?

"Land ho," I said, with what I hoped was jest in my voice. I regretted at once my having reminded him of real voyages, and of landings made after considerable danger.

"You sound like a sea dog" is all he said, letting us drift to the barge, lifting his face to silently laugh in the flare of the lantern, a smudge on the fog.

I had a furrow up my inner arm, tender and debilitating, because I fell from a tree like a boy in mid-climb who goes frightened, stiff, and incapable. In fact, they had begun to stalk me. I was not as frightened of dying, though I did not wish to, as I was unnerved by considering they thought of me as a creature one might shoot. I had been, for a while, invulnerable; I had been, for a while, an eye at the end of a telescopic sight, a finger on the trigger of the Sharps, but no one they might know. I was, when I hunted them, a force and not a man. And before my little detachment was sent to the western theater, while we still were hunting in Virginia, I was up a tree in a blind I had built—lashed boughs for a shooting platform, a breastworks of bushes and limbs for camouflage—and I was daily awaiting the passage below me of reinforcements for Spotsylvania. Hearing my fire, artillery hidden in a copse hard by would begin to bombard the road. I would make my escape because I was a creature of the woods, Sergeant Grafton had been informed by the lieutenant relaying orders.

"They think you virtually a ghost," the sergeant told me.

"From dying of fright," I said.

"Not you, Mr. Bartholomew. You're a cold one."

"That's *shivering*—from fright."

"That's trembling from eagerness to kill someone," he said, clapping me gently on the shoulder. "You aren't human, though you're decent enough for all that."

On the third day, kneeling to micturate over the edge of the blind, I heard the clatter of wheels; then a horse, perhaps because he caught my scent, whinnied. With my flies undone, I lay back to check my cap, and then I lay the blackened barrel over the breastworks and sighted on the road. The clatter, and now a creaking, approached the track below me, coming from the east, to my right, and moving toward the north and west. First I saw the two horses, nervously stepping because reined and harnessed to what frightened them, a platform on wagon wheels, swaying and making odd sounds because it was jerry-rigged and poorly balanced on the axle. In the platform, four men were kneeling, two at each side. Their rifles pointed south and north, one of each couple aiming at the tree line, one of each aiming at the thickets on the side of the road.

They were looking out for me, I thought. They didn't know my name or face, but they knew what I did. And you are, in this world, what you do. And they therefore *did* know me. They expected me. They wished to kill me, and I shook with the authority of my fright: They were after *me*.

I could take each man on my side of the cart, I thought, and surely one on the other side, and probably each and every one of the four. Someone behind them—for two ragged columns followed of lean, dark men, many of them with shaved heads because of the lice that infested them, all of them hard-looking, bitter, nourished only by rage or despair—one of them would harvest me.

Breathing was difficult, for I forced myself to breathe shallowly for silence's sake; yet I wished to gulp at the sky, to chew the air, to relieve my stoppered chest. I went over the side and dove off the limb like a squirrel. My foot caught, my rifle was nearly pulled from my grasp, and I hit, balls and belly and all, the limb beneath my blind. I held my weapon. I held the limb. They heard me and poured a dozen rounds, at least, into the tree. A ball went up the limb, possibly a ricochet from a complete miss, and it gathered bark and brought it through my shirt and up my arm, just above the armpit, and along the underside, leaving a furrow that ended at the forearm, loaded with sap and bark and bits of cloth.

I was away by then, running a line of retreat I had marked out days before. The barrage began and some of them were killed. We found the rolling platform from which they had cut the horses as they fled. I lay in the blood of the Rebels on the platform, tilted up on its two wheels, bracing myself at the bottom with my feet while Sergeant Grafton cut away my shirt and poured liniment into the wound.

I refused to cry out.

He swabbed with the fragments of my shirt to clean away the bits of cloth and tree, and then he poured more liniment on.

"Survive my tender attentions, Mr. Bartholomew, and you'll surely survive the wound."

"Agreed," I forced through my teeth.

"We'll get you a shirt from a corpse, if you like." He nodded at Sam, who stood reluctantly.

"No," I said to Sam, "don't bother with a shirt. Their skin will do me."

Sam looked at Sergeant Grafton, who said, "He's joking, Sam."

"You're sure?" Sam asked.

"No," Sergeant Grafton said.

I was still tender and sore when we made our way to harry the Army of Tennessee, which the Rebels wanted to bring from Tuscumbia toward Central Georgia to block Sherman's move out of Atlanta. We came down through North Charleston and were a long way from Milledgeville in Georgia, where couriers were to find us, when we stopped in a shabby hamlet the name of which none of us knew. I counted seven bullet-pocked houses, but Sergeant Grafton said there were only six, because one I had counted was only an estimable outhouse. Its seat was wide enough for two, and it was elevated with interior steps, a palace that reminded me of nothing so much as the privy at our place in Paynes Corners, home to my aging mother and, in a sense, to my unmourned uncle. All the structures were in need of paint, inside and out, as we found, moving warily from building to building by twosomes. We sheltered, once we had found ourselves alone, in a low house with a small porch and a back door; it was situated closest to the scrubby brush that ran toward the woods and farthest of them all from the long, uncultivated field that would be a killing ground if we were jumped.

We drew water from the well behind the house, and we cooked in the iron stove, plundering the fled householders' flour to make pan bread. We took four-hour turns walking watch around the house. The sergeant was willing to excuse me from patrolling, but I was too dependent on him and the lads for my life; I wanted their goodwill—it meant my safety—and I didn't mind losing sleep, and feeling the chafe of my wound against my side, in order to secure it. So it was true, as I later stated, that in spite of Mr. Homer having posed me in a tree for his picture of a marksman on picket duty, I was never compelled to patrol.

The houses were set fifty and more yards apart, and I left off circling our temporary house on my watch, walking into the warm night, in order to assure myself that we were alone and therefore safe. They had fled the fighting, of course, but I wondered why they hadn't returned. It is likely that no one else among us would have found the remains of the doll because they were not gifted with my eyesight; there was little even barely visible that I did not see. At the third house from ours, the farthest down the row, attached to the field, I found the face of a rag doll—only the small face, no bigger than my thumb, with inked dots for eyes and a vertical line for a nose, a curved line for its smiling mouth—abandoned at the ledge of the window at the front dooryard, hard by the porch. My lantern caught its white, coarse cloth. The wind shifted back against me, and it carried with it something of cellars, something like the small upstate caves outside which I had paused as a boy, smelling the cold, earthen odor of snakes. I regarded the staring fragment of doll, caught on the coarse wood of the sill, beneath the shattered glass.

But why would a child leave her doll? And why leave but a piece of it?

I assessed the glass, and the scars of bullets in the window's frame and above the sill. I slowly went to my knees and, seating the lantern on the porch beside the window, I lowered myself to the ground, fully prone, but propped on my hands, so that I could sniff the hard-packed soil of the dooryard. This was something I knew. Then, on my feet again, leaning my rifle against the porch, I walked the wall with the lantern high and close to it, from the doll face along to my right toward the sliding door of a small storage shed. The clapboard was well chewed by gunfire. Most of it seemed to have been concentrated at the same height.

Yes, I thought, slipping the doll's head into my belt and retrieving my rifle. I thought: No!

I knew to walk out behind the house and to hold my lantern low, to prod the earth with the toe of my boot, looking to pry loose clods. I found nothing for twenty yards in either direction right or left, and nothing fifteen or twenty yards back from the house.

"Well, of course," I instructed the overgrown field, the high, bright half of moon, the distant trees, the houseful of snoring men. Beyond the light my lantern threw, a creature moved off, and I wished I had gone with it. "Why," I asked, "would you dig when you hadn't to? When you were moving at a rapid march?" I should have known, I thought, expert as I was at hiding in sight.

I returned to the house and I pulled a loose finishing nail all the way out of the clapboard with my knife. Using the handle of the knife as a hammer, I affixed the nail above the door of the shed and hung my lantern there. I took up my rifle, though I knew that what I'd face could not be fought, and I slid the shed door open on its rough runner, crying out something in no words, employing the sound as something of a shield.

There was my memory of coiled, sleeping snakes. There was the blood I had smelled on the beaten clay of the dooryard. There was the hamlet, and there— Her arm was bent behind her; she was devoid of expression, although her gray-green blankness was punctuated by the movement of a rat across her mouth (for the flesh is tenderest there, and at the cheeks). I had pulled up and fired before I knew that I would, and of course I missed the rat and caved in the face of the six- or seven-year-old girl, bloated as it was with gases from the corrupted internal organs. Drawn by the sound of my shot, they came up in good time, armed and shouting.

Sam began to convulse in vomiting and tears, and it was contagious, and we all of us were ill. The smell was as nothing compared to what poured upon us from the heaped corpses in their clothing rent by bullet after bullet, and in their blood. Men and women were piled upon each other with no respect for the intimacy of their posture.

I could not help but be offended by this disregard for their modesty, I told Sergeant Grafton.

He looked at me as if he might speak, but then he returned, as did I, to pulling the corpses away from one another and laying them in rows.

Sam whimpered, and then cleared his throat, and made as if to adjust one of the lanterns one of them had hung from a post. "I wish we could know which family was which," he said. "It seems wrong to separate them like this."

"A small, a miniature wrong," the sergeant said.

"Yes. But they require rescuing," Sam said.

The sergeant only continued to drag the bodies and to line them up.

I was astonished at the number of children they had executed. I wondered if one of the men had shown resistance, or had even killed a Union soldier, to call down such a large and brutal vengeance. All that was ever required, of course, for such a massacre was for a soldier to shoot his piece at the wrong moment, when everyone was tense or fearful or fresh from a battle gone wrong. Of course, it also required an officer, I thought, to permit himself to be swept by the moment's emotional flood, and to organize the operation. So many men to herd the families, so many men to guard the perimeter as they were marched into place, and so many men to be willing to stand and pour the volley into the mothers huddled round their children or grasping their infants—we'd found three babies—while husbands raged or trembled or called to those they loved about courage or heaven, or threatened the soldiers, or begged. There were young boys and girls, and the babies, and probably the parents had been young, although they now looked very old—as old, I thought, as people get.

The shirts of some were burned at the entrance hole of the bullet. The women, I saw, were clothed, and perhaps they hadn't been raped. You could not tell, of course, for it's simple to lift the skirts of her dress up over her head and hold her thus for a comrade before he offers you a similar courtesy so that you may take your turn. I would not look beneath their clothing to see if any had been violated; there were young girls, and I could not bear to know.

Their flesh oozed liquids you would not know the body contained, and the skin was loose on them, as if a form of greenish clothing that might tear away when we moved them. The stench, now fully upon us, was like the fields after any battle, and it merely sickened us, and we were accustomed to such effluvia, so sweet and rich and full of bowel and the cuprousness of blood.

It was their faces I wished not to look upon. I had seen men killed, and I had killed them. I had smelled their corpses and the corpses other men had made. But I'd seen only the faces of men, condemned to die or dying gladly, though I think few do gladly die, and the expressions had, for the most part, been of little more than violence that had shaken the features, which, after days, in fact, begin to relax, go bland and loose and full. Here, however, I saw fury and despair, deep fright, and I sensed in them a diminution—that they had understood, ultimately, that to someone in the world with the power to enforce his conviction, they had not mattered at all.

"You are making something of this," Sergeant Grafton said. "You are constructing an insight."

I stood. I regarded him. I thought of striking him, and he knew it.

"Don't," he said. "There's no profit in it."

I thought of what he deemed an insight, my no doubt erroneous belief that these dead mattered more than any bodies I had produced as I descended upon them like Jehovah down upon the Egyptians. I thought, as well, of the profit and loss in striking the man who could see me summoned at a courts-martial, and who could see me abandoned on a hunt, and who could also, and probably with justification, shoot me down if I made to assault him.

"I haven't any idea what you mean," I said, and I commenced the search of dead hands for the fragments of missing, stuffed bits of chest, or arm, or leg, that had been clutched when the volleying had torn away the head and left it perched upon the house. I had vowed that I would investigate each hand of every child, but I could not. I pried open the small fists of one whose eyes were open, and could not force myself beyond the hands of one other, a girl, whose hair had caught fire from the heat of the shots as they entered her face and neck. I took the head of the doll from my belt and carried it to the end of a row and set it upon the straw: man with much of his arm and chest shot away; man with no apparent wound; man with all of one side of his rib cage showing;

woman with one shoe on; woman whose wound was in her shoulder, probably dead from the bleeding and shock; small girl; larger girl of seven or so; girl; a boy whose hands remained in fists I dared not open; boy without trousers; girl; the finger of cloth with its painted face.

We slept hard, afterward, each of us claiming not to have wakened to smell his hands or see them as they lay in the shed. I actually went, when I waked, to see if Sam had covered the mirror in the hallway of the house we used. He had.

We departed without burying them, although Sergeant Grafton drove a fence post into the earth outside the shed and hung upon it the tarnished silver crucifix that had encircled the neck of one of the women. We hurried along, agreeing that our orders called us away, agreeing without speech that what hurried us was what we left behind. After much of a day's hard riding, we entered swampy ground that sucked at the hooves of our horses and that worried the sergeant. He sent me up a tree to survey the landscape, and I saw solider ground to our west. We rode toward it, suffering much from insects not much larger than fleas that anguished our horses and flew in at our nose and mouth and eyes. As we climbed, they diminished, although the pitch grew steep and we led rather than rode the horses.

"What does this go to?" the sergeant asked me.

"Nothing pleasant," I said.

"In specific?"

"I haven't any idea," I said.

"Then please find out," he said, stopping us and sending me to a slender poplar that swayed as I went up. "Stop," the sergeant called, and I did. "Why burden yourself with the rifle?"

"It is what accompanies me up trees, Sergeant."

"See that it doesn't go off."

Despite the low crotch of the tree, because we had climbed a good distance, I was able to make out, instantly, motion in a copse a little more than three or four hundred yards from us. I used my telescope, and the sergeant hushed them, knowing that I used it only for a stalk. I enjoyed working with him; he was professional, and he offered me deference when the matter at hand concerned my work.

He looked up, waiting. I looked down to him and nodded. I presented the four fingers of my right hand, and he nodded. They led the horses back from the tree, and they readied their weapons. They would shelter behind a stone outcropping we had passed, calming the tethered horses and preparing to rescue or reinforce me.

I looked back, through the telescope, at the four men in their encampment. They seemed to have no horses, or to have left them somewhere. I could not find their mounts after sweeping the landscape, so I looked once more with the telescope and then replaced it in my kit. Now I looked upon them with my telescopic sight. I checked the arming of the Sharps. I selected the first of them, a man in an Indian squat some small distance from the others. I would take him and then quickly find a second target where the three of them waited.

Waited for what? was forming in my mind as I found the first one again and sighted him in. I looked down at a man in a blue shirt rimmed at the armpits by the salt of his sweat. His trousers were of buckskin, and his boots, I saw as I swept the glass down his body, were cracked and one was caked with dung. I wondered where their horses were.

Waited for what? I swept up to his head for the placement of my shot, and I looked into his telescopic sight.

Waited for him to take me.

They did not know I was me. But they knew me. You're your actions, and those they surely knew. They had been hunting me, perhaps in more than one party.

His companions waited for him to take me. He did. We fired at once. His ball must have struck the trigger guard or the metal at the breech. The rifle, at my shoulder and just below my right eye and right temple and right cheek, exploded into my face. I might have hit him, I realized much later, for they fled rather than come after me to see if they needed to finish. I did not fall from the tree, I realized later. I hung in the crotch, screaming. I heard myself. The metal of the mechanism, the splintered wood of the stock, were driven back into my face, as was, of course, the powder of the percussion pellet set upon the nipple. My face was the site of an explosion, yet my hearing was unaffected. I heard myself as I screamed and screamed, wiping at the teeth and gums and slices of face that fell upon my tongue as I made my undignified noises.

"Here we come," said Grafton, soothing even from a distance. "Here we come," he called, like a father to his frightened child. "We're coming," he called from the base of the tree. I went by wagon the rest of the way, rolling home inside a dream I dreamed was dreamt by someone else. After coming to consciousness, and begging for death, which I was not granted, I tried to imagine whose dream it had been.

I was wrapped in bandages and blind, because they did not know at first if my eyes were affected; but they had left an aperture at the mouth for breathing and speech. I used it when someone came into what I thought of as the dream to press my shoulder and ask how I fared.

"You could kill me," I said.

There was a pause, and then the hand was removed from my shoulder.

I said, "You could easily—"

"Yes," a stranger's voice replied.

CHAPTER 3

Off Elizabeth Street, at the Harlem Railroad embankment, where a kind of tunnel burrowed into a hill of earth and cobbles—the gandy dancers for the line stored sledgehammers and ties and spikes there, for use in making repairs—I was walking late, having trotted about early as well. I was tired of walking, but not, I thought, tired enough to sleep. So I had stopped at Uncle Ned's on the Bowery, at that time a notorious gathering place for gamblers, slaggards too filthy and used to be kept in a respectable house, and, of course, members of gangs like the Rabbits and the Ikes (who called themselves the House of Isaac—as nasty a bunch of Jews as the Rabbits were cannibal Irish). In front of a disused shop once specializing in trusses and like medical devices, and across from the embankment, I came, perhaps a little dizzy from dark rum, upon two white men beating a Negro. He dodged and wheeled, so I knew that he wished to resist; and, as he was burly and fit, broad of shoulder and lean of hip, with long, thick arms, I knew that while he chose to protect his head and face by shielding himself, he had deemed it wise not to give the account of himself of which I believed him capable.

"Hold still, Mose, and let me thrash your woolly head," the fatter of the two whites grunted. He slapped at the Negro with a thick black cane. He panted and sweated, and his face, in the gaslight at the corner stanchion, gleamed in oily unhealth. The other fellow, sturdy but short and quite narrow, swung what seemed to be a leather sap and, from its appearance of weight in his small hand, might have been filled with shot, or rock salt.

The fat one swung, this time with both hands, and he caught the Negro at the junction of neck and shoulder. The Negro went to his knees and seemed inclined to remain there. His breath was deep and uneven, whether from debility or fear I could not tell. I wanted to know. I wanted him to tell me.

"Gentlemen," I called, stopping just behind the smaller one. "Are you certain you have the numbers and the weapons you require? Or should I round up five or six armed men to pitch in and defend you from this fellow?"

The littler man, his sap up, turned to challenge me. I assessed his waxed mustache, his silk waistcoat and bright tan shoes. He said, "God almighty, what *are* you?"

"What you are not," I said.

"If you must involve yourself. This nigger was told to have a wagon-load of textiles here tonight, and he brings us himself but not the goods. We are out money, cloth, and reputation. A deal's gone dead, and he's to be punished. If, as I say, it's your affair."

"As a businessman," I said, "I hate to see a businessman lose face. But is this Negro not a businessman as well? You seem to be on the verge of robbing him, too, of a goodly portion of *his* face."

"As you seem to have lost most of yours. I wonder in what fashion," the fat one said, puffing and perspiring.

I smiled, but of course they could not tell.

To the black man, I said, "You held back because you thought them police, perhaps?"

He said, "I held back because I thought they were white men."

"Before the law, no whiter than you," I said.

"Look, why don't you, at the law a few more times." He searched my mask with red-rimmed eyes. "You don't have to shave that in the morning, I reckon."

I smiled again. Again, they could not tell.

"I apologize for that," the black man said.

"It was clever," I said, "and levelheaded. Do you understand me about the credentials of these men?"

"And do you understand me?"

"They are men of business. I don't know their commercial bona fides, but I can attest to them as men: They are, barely."

"Sir!" cried the fat one.

"Do you dare?" asked the littler man.

I seized his ear and twisted it. He whimpered, then wept. I kept hold of it with my left hand and gestured, far too dramatically, I fear, with my right. "If he raises his sap or, indeed, his body, I will have his ear for a watch fob. Would you, while we wait upon his course of action, see to— your name, sir? Hodboy? Fatcheek? Commander Bulk, perhaps? For you do throw about your weight with great panache."

The Negro climbed reluctantly, it seemed, to his feet, and he sidled toward the one with the cane, who leaned back from the Negro as that man shifted his balance and made a kind of crooning sound, a statement, I thought, of his reluctance to act. Then, grunting of a sudden, as if it were he, himself, who were struck, the Negro swung his punch. Because the fat man was moving, the blow missed his face and landed with a fearful, solid sound on the fat man's chest. He made a noise like a pig's bladder punctured, and he went a color that, in the gaslight, seemed quite green. I thought he was dead on the spot, but the assault, either to his lungs or his heart, was brief in effect—though it was a long moment in which he seemed suspended, and it must have seemed a good deal longer to the one on whose chest the blow had landed.

The little man whose ear I held made as if to rise, and I applied my thumb more firmly to the juncture of the ear and skull. It was a place, I remembered, where I'd once put a killing shot.

I said to the one whose ear I held, "Get him to his feet once he's able, and lead him away. It would be best to never burden this Negro again with your business arrangements. Make new ones."

I took the sap from his fingers as he stood. I gestured to the Negro—his hands were at his mouth, then eyes; he trembled as he moved his hands upon his face—and I said, "Let's walk, if you will, across the tracks. Down where the hill dips, on the other side."

He stayed where he was, and I saw he was weeping.

"Are you hurt?" I asked, watching the little man try to pry the fat one from the stones of the street. "Was it the blow to your neck?"

He cupped his face in his hands, at last, and he bathed himself in his own tears. Finally his bulkier assailant sat, and I took the Negro's elbow and moved him along with me.

"I never," he said, smearing his nose with the back of his hand.

We crossed the tracks of the Harlem line and went down the incline toward Rivington. There were fewer lights here, and the noises of the Jews in bakery shops and their crowded small rooms came as if from a forest warren one could smell—the sourness of yeast; the sweetness of fresh bread; the rich, dark smells of simmered inner organs of sheep and cow—but one could not descry them; those people were mysterious even in the homeliest of aspects.

Again, he said, as we drew near the coffee shop of Alsatian Jews with whom I had business dealings, "I never."

"What, then? You never what?"

"You were there," he said, though the "there" was almost—not quite—"dere."

"I was."

"You saw. How many of *that* have you seen?"

"Oh," I said. "Ah. Of course. I beg your pardon."

"You don't ever have to beg me for anything," he said. "Just ax one time."

"You were talking about the blow you struck."

"I never even did talk back to a white man. Then I up and hit one."

"You surely did. You squashed his breastbone and lit up his lights. You stopped his heart, I think."

"White man's heart."

"What passes for that particular white man's heart."

We stood at the shop, Alain Freres. I knew that he would not come in, so I tugged once more at the cloth of his shirt and we continued east.

"I hit me a white man," he said. "Do I thank you? Or do I curse you? Do I owe you, or do you owe me?"

"Will you tell me your name?"

"Tackabury's Adam is what they call me on the papers I was given. I *am* a freed man."

"You are all freed."

"Only some can walk around in any circles they choose, and others are freed to do what some white man says."

"Still," I said—as if what he told me was surprising. I did so for his dignity's sake.

He said, "Still, and forever and ever. Amen, if you like."

"Adam, then?"

"It's the name I use. Adam Tackabury."

"Adam. Where do you live?"

"Back that way and down. Centre Street."

"Near the Points. As do I."

"A gentleman in the Points?"

"Two of us gentlemen in the Points. I can find you by asking for Adam?"

He said, "You ax. I'll hear."

"I might, one day." I could smell jute on his shirt, and the wax from seals on cotton. He worked at the docks. I said, "I'm a tradesman, myself."

He nodded, waiting.

"You know a little, I think, about the edge of the river."

"It's how niggers live. On the edge of the water. If they will *get* to live. Railroad to dock or wagon to dock or brigantine to dock—we are the same as cargo, and we move how cargo moves. So I do know the edge of the river. And you can call on me. Can I know your name?"

"Bartholomew. William Bartholomew."

"Bartelmy."

"Close enough."

"Bartelmy. I'm in your debtedness, Mist Bartelmy."

"You're free, damn it."

"Did you earn that face in freeing me?"

"I do not need to shave it."

"Didn't mean an insult."

"None taken. What is under the mask, I every now and again must shave, however. Beards, you know, grow even on the flesh of the dead. And so with me."

"I did wonder. I do thank you."

"Adam, I won my wound in the pursuit of my own ends. Though I am heartily pleased to see no man enslaved."

"What was the end, Mist Bartelmy?"

"It is a question I haven't ever answered truly, even to myself. I do not know. I cannot learn it. It's an answer I await."

"Yes, sir," he said, as if I were lying.

"In truth," I said.

"Centre Street," he said, dismissing me. "You ax." He clasped his hands, for I think, in spite of his disappointment with me, he would have taken my arm or hand to say his thanks and his confusion. "Adam," he told me. "Ax."

He was the color of the night, and he went into it, and disappeared. For my part, I wandered back in the direction, on a whim, of the embankment where I'd found them beating him. I wondered if I would find a corpulent corpse, or a detective of police. I took from my pocket the sap I'd lifted from the littler assailant, and I threw it into the street. My face, it seemed to me, still stung from the impact of his question about my motives in the War. I was blushing, and I was pleased that neither I nor anyone else could see the furrows and puckers and craters of my face go crimson with what might be shame.

A sister of the streets, trawling in desperation before the dawn, opened her thin-lipped mouth as I stalked past. I stopped, for I wondered what she might say.

"Poor fellow," she whispered. She was scrawny and her naked arms were rough with exposure and not much care. I gave her twenty-five cents.

"For doing what?"

"For not being hungry."

"Do I look like a charity case?"

"You thought that I did."

"Then I beg your pardon if I insulted you. You are a veteran?"

She was already staring into the darkness down the street in hope of work. Cool air blew from the north and east, and she clasped her arms across her meager chest. She held my coin in her dark-knuckled hand; her fingernails, I had noticed, were far from clean.

"Sir?" she said. "What is your pleasure, then?"

"It lies, apparently, in assisting a man to give in to his blackest desire, and his greatest danger. I have probably led him to the edge of the world. And all he could think of, sad man, was the river's edge. Never mind."

She had stepped backward. "No," she said, "I never work with a male partner, though I could scare up a girl for the tribade if it suits your fancy. To tell you the truth, though, I would just as soon not, and it would cost you more than you've given me."

"Let's both not," I said.

"Then good night?"

"Then keep the two bits and good night."

"God bless you," she said.

I still doubted it. I made my way south and west, picking up Orange off Bayard. When I was that young man, in 1867, walking, despite the vapors, with some spring in my step, and with a Colt in my pocket, there were thousands, tens of thousands, of immigrant children, filthy and wild, dangerous as wolves, some of them, who came out with the sun each day in that district; they were there to collect what they could. Someone paid some money for everything. Little more than toddlers, some of them, squired by a brother not too much older, they collected coal that fell from the delivery wagon; there were rag pickers who sold to the Jews; why, there were little fellows who tore their fingers bloody while collecting bits of glass. Often, they were beaten badly by the adults in the trade with whom they competed. The hardiest and often most dangerous were the bone pickers. You found them, too, at dawn, as I found one now, carrying an oily-looking sack and armed with a stick that ended in a metal hook that he used for turning over mounds of ashes or dirt or other filth.

"Leonard," I said. "Up at the first hint of light, as usual."

"Morning, Mr. Bartholomew. Have you been to bed yet?"

"I'm on my way, Leonard."

"You've been carousing, I suppose."

He never looked at me or stopped his restless searching through as foul-smelling a two-foot heap of garbage as I had ever come across. He didn't seem to mind. He peered and stared and studied, like a myopic man reading a volume of fine print.

"Tonight, Leonard—last night by now—I took a man to his knees, made a new friend, cooperated in the slowing or stoppage of a fat man's heart, gave charity to a whore, drank dark rum, and ate the freshest bread. Would you call that carousing?"

"I would call this . . . *pewter*." He held the handle of an ale cup in his filthy hand. "Have a look, Mr. Bartholomew." He brought the stinking fragment toward me and, with it, the smell of his clothing and breath.

"That's not sweet," I said, "though no insult's intended, Leonard."

"None will be taken," he said, his dirty face, unshaven and pitted, arched—the brows, the broad mouth—in generosity.

"But it is," I said, "time to bathe your body and burn your clothes."

"Ah," he said, "it is the tendency of a man in my profession that he take on certain characteristics of the materials of his work."

"You're too wise for the work."

"No," he said, "I'm suited for it. I'm damnably good at it, begging your pardon."

"I do enjoy the company of happy men," I said, "and I thank you." I pressed coins upon his palm, then wiped my fingers on my coat.

"What are you buying, Mr. Bartholomew? Not that I ain't grateful."

"Or percipient," I said, moving on, past a band of feral boys who swaggered, at six or seven, in clothing so foul as to be collectible, by those who wore it, for a transaction at the ragmonger's. I put my hand upon the butt of my pistol and made certain that they saw me do so. One of them smiled, but it was not much warmer than the artificial mouth on my mask. Sunlight, cool but yellow, lay on the paving stones and on the warehouse walls, and on the horses who patiently stood in their traces while their drivers drank coffee or beer.

In the smell of refuse and ordure and the combined rank exhalations of the poor in their small rooms, I made my way to the Old Brewery. The taverns in the alleys were still noisy, but the sounds were somehow subdued, as if even the air itself that carried the exclamations and music and complaints were exhausted. I passed the door of Chun Ho and could smell the harsh, clean odor of hot water and powerful soap; she would let me bathe in a tin tub for the cost of laundering two shirts, and I thought with pleasure of the steam in which, maskless, I would wallow while she stared at me with her calm, appraising eyes. There was something about her very still face that compelled my attention. On the ground floor, entering the hive, I heard the snoring of Mr. Leone and the sobbing of one of his children. But children, here, were always in tears, and dogs were always howling. It was what gave vent to the general life of the Points—a voice, if you will, for what the populace could never say.

I unlocked my room and, entering, locked the door behind me. I poured a little water into the basin and washed my hands. Removing the mask, I washed the ruins and, gingerly, for I always ached there, dried myself with a towel that smelled of Chun Ho's brown soap. The bed was a military cot and, removing my clothes, I rolled into it as I had so many times when they'd assembled us at a major encampment. I closed my eyes. I had made promises to Jessie and, in a sense, to Adam as well. He could not be well served by me, I feared, for I had led him across a line—a boundary. I thought of him at the edges of rivers, his red-rimmed, yellowish eyes, his broad, dark nose, his mouth pressed tight with habit over so many years of biting his lip and holding his silence. And I had preached to him of freedom, and had led him to strike a white man down! I owed him some assistance, I thought.

And I was a tradesman, so I also remembered that he felt obliged to me. If owed, I thought, remembering my hand brushing back and forth on the head of the bearskin beside Jessie's bed, then I must collect. I spent the early morning and the forenoon in falling asleep, then waking myself with wild thoughts—drunken small girls who acted like whores dressed in rouge and furs, a boy with a pistol that he placed inside my mouth most painfully—and with memories: the faces of men I had killed at the instant of killing them. It was, you might say, the customary sleep.

I was invited, and I would go. In truth, I had seen to the invitation because I wished—I now needed—to go to East Twenty-sixth Street, off Madison Square. Business is business and so, of course, might friendship be, and I must confess that I had a bit of what the marksmen used to call buck fever. It had not been an affliction of mine in the War; I had stalked them, and had seen them square; I might have paused before firing, but not very long, and never with the shakes some of them suffered—to the point where their target fell out of their trembling sights. I did, though, sit on my cot, the mask beside my left leg, the Navy revolver beside my right, and wonder—like a raw recruit, like a city man on a bear hunt in the fastnesses of the north country—whether I was adequate to the task. I even considered the rights and the wrongs.

Finally, though, I rubbed my hands on the smoothly beautiful wooden butt; the oil from my fingers, over years, had permeated it, and I was rubbing upon myself, a peculiar kind of friction, yet something that gave me pleasure. It was a touching upon my own history. I had touched the pistol in difficult moments—when a detachment of Rebel horse came so close to our camp, so swiftly, that I was the only one armed, sitting with my buttocks hanging off a log of downed birch, caught in mid-stooling, my pistol in my hand, the defender of us all. Even while they paused, and while I prayed that my unfelicitous scent might not betray us, and while I squeezed the darkened walnut grip, I had my left hand to my mouth that I might smother my helpless giggling. It was a work of art, that revolver, and the falling to of the mechanism that brought the next chamber up was a smooth, heavy, inevitable motion. I would sell him my past for a song, then. Four dollars was a decent amount of money for a man who was slave to his wages; it was nothing to me for the Colt. Yet it could be much, and what men such as I were expert at was knowing when to invest, and with whom. Look at the Crédit Mobilier: I had every conviction that the railroad it protected would go bust; I had every confidence that the credit corporation itself would make fortunes for its investors. Men would go to prison, I thought, and men would go to the bank; I needed no compass to tell my own direction.

I put the pistol and some old brushes and a small bottle of gun oil wrapped in cloth inside a croker sack. In honor of our night on the harbor when the shipment of brandy came through, I carried a bottle of something older than I from the Continent, for I knew he liked his tot. I put on my good coat, and then my damned mask, and left, bearing gifts.

I found a cabriolet at Canal Street and had him carry me up Broadway. Even at that hour, verging on seven-thirty, Broadway was bright with light and noisy with prostitutes cackling about like geese. You cannot imagine how, in those days of accelerating growth of the city, the whores were everywhere, and particularly on Broadway. The men in city government who had a share in their care, feeding, and occasional policing were in a business as good as any I knew. I did not venture it myself because of Jessie; you may believe it as you will, but I had certain limits and a few proprieties, although I would not describe myself as being a man of much conscience. Thinking of my hands upon the pistol, and of my days in the War, I had thought that I survived the sniping as long as I did because of my age. I was no nimble boy when I did service. I had entered, in 1861, at twenty-six; I had been discovered as a marksman late in 1862, and I had survived into 1864. Almost thirty years old, then, when I was skipping in the tops of trees and killing men in numbers with a gun. You cannot discount experience, and the sense, which a man will have but not a boy, of what he can and cannot achieve, whether on the ground and peaceful, or in the trees and an Angel of Death. My host of the night was, I realized, nearly old enough to be my father if my father had gone a-pollinating at the age of sixteen. And here he was, with a boy of eighteen and three other children, and his various relations—according to a sodden night's complaint—moving in and out of the house as if Elizabeth, his wife, were a professional cook.

"Lumpy," he had confessed in a theatrical whisper, leaning across the tavern table and making a humorous face that, as usual, did not include any expression whatsoever of the eyes. He had laughed his silent, broad mouthful of shadows, and had repeated himself: "Lumpy. Lumps in the gravy, lumps hard as gristle in the very squash and beans, much less potatoes, and lumps in the rice pudding bigger than the currants themselves. She is a resolute and dangerous cook, my patient Lizzie."

No matter his joking, I thought, this was a man as given to the miseries as I was. You could look into my dead face and find my living eyes. In his case, the life and death were reversed, and the flesh of his face was living ground, while his eyes were little monuments to lifelessness buried therein.

He greeted me himself at the doors at the top of the outside stairs. "Shipmate," he said, holding his glass lantern aloft as if we were on a moving deck.

We shook hands, and then I presented the croker sack. "The aforementioned weapon," I said, "in case you did not wish it to be table talk. As for the payment: four dollars, as and when convenient."

He nodded, more acknowledgment than thanks, I thought, and then he surprised me. In his foyer, the shadows shifting as the lantern moved in his hand, he said nothing about my courtesies or his gratitude. Instead, hefting the sack, he asked, "Are there bullets?"

"Five in the chambers."

"It holds five?"

"Six, but I am, like many, overly careful with something so dangerous. The hammer is somehow caught, the trigger—it is delicate, you must tell your son—may be tripped, and then someone is maimed, or dead, or anyway frightened half to death. I recommend the five, though it is up to your boy."

"Mal."

"And this," I said, "is something for the end of the night, not that I wish to hurry its coming."

"Let's attend its beginning," he said, leading me past an interior staircase and along a narrow corridor toward what he described as the dining room. It was a very small and dark place that once might have been the bedroom of a servant, I thought. Standing at the foot of the table was Elizabeth, his wife, her face a little plain and pug, her figure stout, her hands red, her eyes as lively and expressive as his were not. She winced at the sight of my mask, and her eyes slid away; I watched her direct them back. Her dress, of dark blue, had an oval white apron atop it, and she had the appearance, thus, of a serving maid in uniform.

"Stanny has eaten," she said of their younger son, "and the girls are with relations for the week. So it is to be the four of us. This is Malcolm, sir"—the boy I had seen at Mrs. Hess's, broad of shoulder and spotty of skin, with angry eyes as mobile as his mother's and with his father's fine features—"and I understand that we are indebted to you for his equippage."

And so we sat down to dine. I turned from them to replace the mask with the dark silk veil, and they dealt as well with it as any. I set the mask on the broad planking of the dining room floor, at the edge of the braided rug, and when I looked down, it looked up at me. M gestured at it from his place at the head of the table, to my left, and he said, "Hawthorne wrote a tale about a skeleton and skull at the dinner table. Do you know it? It shook me, I recall."

"Do you liken me," I asked, "to the skeleton or skull?"

He held his spoon aloft and tilted his head to laugh the silent laugh.

"You do not hold it against your companions," Elizabeth said, "that they speak of your . . . misfortune."

"It makes the dining simpler, ma'am. Since the management of food beneath this veil, especially liquids, is no easy matter. People see what they see. They might as well say it."

"You're a hero," Malcolm said.

"Oh, no, sir. I was a military man and I suffered the consequences thereof."

"Not everyone did what you did. Father said you were a marksman!"

"Not everyone was," I allowed.

"I'm for the cavalry," Malcolm said. He seemed less thick and stupid than at Mrs. Hess's. It was his eagerness that worried me: Be a soldier reluctantly, I thought, and live awhile.

M brought the croker sack up and made a great sound with it against the dining table.

"Oh, no," Elizabeth said.

"Oh, a week's wages," her husband said, rather loudly.

Malcolm untied the sack and retrieved the pistol.

"It's loaded," I said.

He looked at me with something like fear tinged with merriment. I watched his father sip wine and I saw his wife attend the sipping.

"Perhaps," I said, "after dinner, if your mother agrees, I will show you how to be safe with it."

"Guns are for *not* being safe," the boy said loudly, reminding me now of the fellow whom he was in Mrs. Hess's house. I wondered that he did not recall me, and then I wondered that he drank himself so drunk that he *could* not recall me, yet had not given his father a hint, so it was said, of his fondness for the stuporous state.

"Sir, guns are for making *others* unsafe; for the fighting man, they are to be feared."

Elizabeth instructed him to place the weapon on the floor. His father nodded like a magistrate, and the young man, looking younger, removed the weapon from the table.

We discussed the muddy print on the wall behind me—a souvenir of Liverpool, I was told. We spoke of *Miss Ravenel's Conversion,* which he had not read, but of which, as a slight and popular thing, he disapproved. Elizabeth described for me her husband's family's land up the Hudson, where her daughters were, and then we chatted of her native Massachusetts. I had known men from New England in the War, especially some Vermont marksmen of Berdan's Greencoats, and a fellow from Maine whose life had been saved at Gettysburg, he claimed, by a collapsible tin cup that he kept in his breast pocket.

"He carried it as a talisman until the end of the War. But wars are nothing, in the end, but stories," I said. "Who knows which of them is true? Who knows which details, likewise, of the wars themselves?"

"There is the great historical cement that holds the stories together," M said. "It is the mucilage of the underground dead, do you not think? So many of them, Southern and Northern. The ghastly expense of life in a waste of— I was going to say 'shame.' Do you think it shameful, Bill?"

"Which 'it'?"

"The dying. The killing. Drummer boys and generals, President Lincoln, the bakers and the cooks and the quartermasters."

"I should like to hear from someone like yourself that the men still breathing, after Grant accepted the Confederate sword, were worthy of concern, much less such tears as you propose we shed."

"You feel ill-served by such remembrance?"

"No. I share its emotions with you. As to how I feel, with regard to public concern, I am unaware of any to be registered. We are absorbed, as best we can be, into our populace. There are many such as I to be resented for reminding our brothers and sisters at large that such a war took place and that such men had the misfortune to survive it."

"You are not resented!" the boy said, slapping the table. "You are reverenced."

"It seems to me," his father said, "that some of that populace has spoken."

"I thank you one and all."

"Such dry wit virtually squeaks," Elizabeth said. "Perhaps you will allow my husband to moisten it."

Her grave voice and darting, dark eyes, her ready wit, had me smiling. I gave the gruff male equivalent of a titter so that she might know my appreciation.

In fact, the fellow from Maine had been shot right through his folding tin cup, and he had died with lung blood bubbling on his lips and with the metal of the cup inside his chest.

M, I found, had been staring at my veil, as though to better see my thoughts. His small, weak, expressionless eyes could take on the appearance of prescience I associated with the Egyptian Sphinx, and I found him unsettling. He drank a good deal more of the bitter wine he had served, and we ate mutton that was bathed in something like horseradish and accompanied by very dry, hard greens. I was inspected as I ate by the man who had fallen from close to the sun. I was the object of speculations by the man who had made a book about a whaling voyage sound like the Holy Bible itself. And here he sat, a federal employee of small matter with a son determined to be killed in the Indian wars, and a wife who badgered him first, I felt, before he might badger her.

He nodded, as if he had been addressed, and he set down his forkful of meat with a violent gesture, as if the food offended him. Then he clapped his hands twice and smiled like a great cat at his son.

"Oh," his wife said, as if about to warn me.

Her husband clapped his mysterious applause once more and said, very loudly, "I *like* this good man!"

"Yes, Pa," Malcolm said. The boy sipped, as children are required to, from a goblet of water. His father drank down wine.

M said, "He brings into the rooms of our house, the mortgage of which is paid off, I might say, with my wife's largesse of resource and spirit, a kind of *memento mori.* And even though we break bread and chew and chew and chew at mutton, we are fortunate to be reminded of what I have called the charge through the hauntedness."

I saw that Elizabeth had hung her head and so had Malcolm. Evidently, they were accustomed to but not reconciled with such an apparent welling of emotion as this.

"We should be grateful," M said, "and we should be *drinking.* I propose a toast." He raised his glass, and so did they, then so did I. "To William Bartholomew, soldier, warrior, deliverer of bleak truths. To wit"—I tired of holding my glass aloft, particularly in my own name, and I brought it down; the others, in a strange obedience, held theirs in the air—"the churches are by and large occupied by scoundrels and cowards; the libraries are by and large occupied by frauds, villainies, and the language of spun sugar; the newspapers are filled, by and large, with canards, lies, and self-congratulation.

"But, by damn, I wrong you, Bill. For, as is obvious to a man of education, I have placed in your mouth, as it were, the words I wish to speak. I have, and I pray you forgive me, *written* you. You're a damned *character* of mine, and for that I must apologize. Though not overly. For I have given you harsh truths to convey. And truth, though with some it makes a wholesome breakfast, proves to all a supper too hearty. Hearty food, taken late, gives bad dreams. Do you say, Lizzie? Mal? Have I heaped upon this good, this finest, fellow a burden of truth too heavy to bear? *Miss Ravenel's Conversion,* by the undergarments of both Saints Peter and Paul! And Hawthorne in his grave and me in mine."

He shook his head slowly back and forth as it drooped toward the table. Elizabeth excused herself, gestured to Malcolm, and they began to clear.

"May I help, ma'am?" I asked her. But she affected not to have heard.

Her husband had. He said, "But you *have* helped, good fellow. We have spoken together of whales and cabbages and kings. Of Dutchmen and their papers, of poor Poe buried and remembered, and other scriveners buried and forgot." His voice had grown softer, and he spoke now as though he had a sore throat. "You know, Bill, I am not unaccustomed to the minstrations of Dr. Charles Eliot Norton himself. He has called me mad. Poor fellow! I am but weary. I might sleep."

Malcolm, returning to his place, said, "My father cannot always manage his wine."

The father's reddened eyes grew wide. His chin came up as if the end of his beard were a gunsight. He squinted down his face at Mal. "And you, sir," he told him, "seem to know too much about such management. Or, anyway, to profess too much acquaintance with it."

Mal held his stare, and I was astonished to watch his large, pale face seem to swell, as if it were a flower that opened before me. The boy's lips, of a sudden, seemed thicker, and his nostrils more flared. Even the bones beneath his white cheeks gave the impression of broadening. Lizzie stood before her place at the table, gripping her napkin as if it were fastened to the solidity to which she needed, for safety's sake, to hold. Her sad, sweet features seemed the face of a woman about to faint. The glow of perspiration I saw on Malcolm's upper lip I also saw on his mother's. His smile became a sneer, and I worried that father and son might fall upon one another.

I could imagine the boy as he strode through an Indian encampment, shooting the sick old men and terrified women. I could see him firing a rifle from the seat of a lurching wagon in some Western province, picking off an Indian rider not because they fought each other, but because the man was passing on a horse and made for a difficult shot placement and thus provided the boy with sport. And I saw him, of course, in Mrs. Hess's parlor, too drunk to remember the fellow with the store-bought face, all but poisoned with the excess of his pleasures.

M's red eyes narrowed, and he wiped at them as if the sight he had seen were too exhausting for the very tissue of his flesh. "I did not raise my son to be a lout. Nor to demonstrate my failures in fatherhood before a stranger at our board."

"Sir," Malcolm said, his face seeming to shrink.

"Whom do you address, boy?" his father whispered.

"Sir," Malcolm said to me, "I am heartily sorry. And sir"—he had turned to his father—"I regret my impulsive words. I respect no man as you, sir."

M's eyelids were fluttering, and he seemed not to hear.

"None," Malcolm said, as if he were dismissing a servant who proffered food.

And M lay his large head, as if it weighed fifty pounds and the muscles of his neck had given in, upon his cutlery, and he closed his eyes.

Again, Elizabeth said, "Oh."

"I have stayed too long and exhausted him," I said. I placed the mask beneath my arm and rose. "I brought brandy," I said. "It might remain in the pocket of his coat."

"He will doubtless find it," she said. "You were good to sell us the gun."

"It is a gift, ma'am. You will tell your husband the Colt is a gift of a former soldier and a grateful reader. Will you say that to him?"

"Exactly, I think you wish, as you have said it to me."

I affected a little bow. It was a botch because the veil began to slide forward and I had to mash my hand, already burdened with my hat, upon the top of my head to keep the veil in place.

She said, "I have watched him, grinning like a great, pale cat, pat the trees in Madison Square and thank them for growing. I have heard him, on the other hand, look as if into stormy winds and say nothing for a week at a time. He . . . ebbs and flows. With or without liquor, in the drinking of which he overindulges. His mother was a woman of appetites. His father was said to be a man of such swings of spirit, and I know for a fact it was an affliction of his brother. Sometimes I fear I see it in you, Mal. Oh, Mr. Bartholomew, it is as he said! We burden you. Forgive us."

Mal stood behind his chair, staring at her with dark eyes in a white face. He might have wished her dead, for all the affection I saw in his features.

"I would serve you, ma'am," I said, and I said it again at the door.

Someone, at any rate, would be served.

A little before dawn, when I finally slept, I dreamed a dream, and it wakened me. I dreamed, or I speculated upon, as I fell into sleep, or I was haunted by, the chambered drum of the Colt revolving. I could see it and, though it hung before me in this reverie, I could at the same time feel its weight in my hand. The weight was vast, but the drum turned smoothly, immensely, inevitably. It seemed to me that I felt the tremendous turning of the earth itself in the revolving of the drum.

She lived on the ground floor, and even her children helped, at dawn, to carry in the water she would use all day. They stored it in wooden barrels from pickled cucumbers and olives and whiskey I had seen her haul, as big around as she, from the alleys behind the merchants. From the steam above the tub, while Chun Ho poured more water in, as her stove roared and heated the room sufficiently to almost send me to sleep, I said, "The future of the nation is in railroads. I will, surely, invest more heavily. It would be useful to you and your children if I could invest some dollars on your behalf. And I would be pleased to extend you credit. May I do so?"

She had been looking at me. I could tell from the way she turned away as my gaze came up. Her clothing, which resembled a soldier's union suit, was soaked from steam and spilled water, and it clung to her child's limbs and womanly torso. Now it was she, with her immobile face, whose eyes interrupted mine and sent them skittering off.

"The Union Pacific to the West, of course. Mr. Vanderbilt's New York Central bringing trains across the Hudson. Any number of manufacturies of railroad cars, and steam boilers, and now our own American steel. Soon, Chun Ho, the island of Manhattan will boast an elevated railway from Battery Place up to Thirtieth Street on the western side—near Greenwich Street. Can you imagine? You can be drawn by steam, as I am here parboiled by it, virtually through the air above town. Would your children enjoy an aerial ride?"

She stood beside me, leaning away, looking away, to hand down a heavy bar of brown soap.

"Thank you," I said. "Where are your children?"

As if exasperated by my mannerliness, she turned toward me her smooth, expressionless face. Her eyes fell, and I felt the fall, as if of cold rain, upon my unmasked face, and then my throat and chest and then the water that covered my lap.

"Children—mother. Mother of Chun Ho."

"In this district? I mean: here? Near this house?"

She nodded once.

"Is your father here?"

She closed her eyes and I watched her control the composition of her face; it stayed as smooth as a painted picture. She shook her head.

"Your father is dead?"

She nodded once.

"How is it, do you think, that your husband and father did not survive this country, yet your mother and you, if she is like you, are tough as alleyway weeds?"

"Weeds?"

"Strong flowers."

"Woman is strong flower. Yes. You are some of woman, maybe?"

"Because I survived? Yes, maybe I am. Though I am, as I think you have seen, mostly man."

"Not see!"

"Oh, no?"

She giggled. She covered her mouth and recomposed herself. "Not see much."

"You mean there's not that much to see?"

She shook her head, then waved her palm at me, as if we were friends who played at teasing one another. "Plenty enough," she said, moving her hands to her mouth, then walking toward the stove.

I closed my eyes and reached up to soap my neck. I felt her fingers take hold of the soap, and I sank back toward her. She poured achingly hot water over my shoulders and I keened.

"Not so strong flower?" she said.

"Strong enough, I hope."

She scrubbed with a flannel cloth at my shoulders and, when I leaned forward, my back. I leaned against the tub again, waiting to see if she would come around and wash my chest. She did not.

"So may I invest a few dollars for you and the children? I predict no risk."

"Chun Ho give own some money Gongsi Fang."

"Who?"

"Oh! Take care of Chinese man, woman, baby. Many help us. Many is *fang*—many Chinese people, one bunch."

"Group?"

"Group."

"This *fang* helps people from China?"

"Sure. Rooms to live. Money. Funeral Chun Ho father. All the time. Group."

I lay back again and closed my eyes. From behind me, she reached to scrub at the underside of my left arm, and then along the elbow and fore-arm, and then the palm and knuckles; she reached for my right arm and did the same. The sound of the roaring stove drowned out the crashing of wheels, the shrieking of infants, the barking and howling of dogs— and I felt as a child while this child-sized woman with strong hands and powerful silences rubbed me clean.

"Sure," she said. I opened my eyes to find her large, dark eyes directed at the water that lay above my groin.

"I am bobbing to the surface," I said.

She fetched me a towel, then removed herself to the small table at which she and her children ate, and on which she folded laundry.

I stood to dry myself, and Chun Ho said, "Flower."

When Mrs. Hess had partaken of what her clients agreed was Lydia Pinkham's in ruby port wine, her dignified carriage grew famously erect; she looked, in fact, as though she might tip over from carrying herself all but on the balls of her feet in their patent leather slippers. Her mammoth bosom rose and fell rapidly at her prow as if a powdered creature transported into the parlor for applause. She blinked her eyes a good deal and spoke quite slowly, though I could not tell whether to herself she sounded quick and nimble of tongue. Malcolm seemed as spifflicated as she, though he did seem to recognize me, and to turn his face toward the woman to his right, who, at that instant, yawned.

"You've an admirer there, all right," a stocky man said as he lit his cigar. It was fairly apparent that he had set his sights on the slight, ruddy girl for whose company Malcolm had paid. I wondered what salary his insurance firm gave a boy who at best might be a clerk, that he might spend so much money on liquor and whores.

Because it was the end of the working night, Mrs. Hess's servant, whom we knew as Delgado, made his tour of the downstairs rooms, dimming the lights. He carried a short, thick truncheon in his coat and, although he was of stringy build and quiet demeanor, I had never seen a man stand up to him. Mrs. Hess sat beside Malcolm, on the other side from her girl, and soon she was snoring demurely; that would change, I knew, and we would all be treated to great, gasping noises unless Delgado removed her to her quarters in the back of the house.

Malcolm was pinching the girl's jaws with his hand, squeezing hard enough to bring tears to her eyes. I watched Delgado approach him from the rear of the sofa.

"If you must be a whore, you whore, then have some *manners* while you're at it," Malcolm said.

The stocky man said, "Do not address her in that wise. And drop your hand from her face."

"By jockies!" Malcolm said, trying to stand. The girl rubbed her face, and Malcolm gave up, sitting back, his fists raised, his eyes closed, stupid with drink.

"Sir," Delgado said.

"What is it?" the boy asked, his eyes still closed.

"It is time to retire, sir."

Malcolm opened his eyes. Delgado's suggestions were almost always accepted.

"A cabriolet, sir?"

Malcolm said, "Awoke."

Delgado turned to me. I said, "He means to say he'll walk, I think. But here." I held up some coins, and Delgado came around to accept them for Malcolm. "Send him home. He'll never make it on his own. He'll be lucky, any rate, if he's admitted at home."

"You know the gentleman, sir?"

"His father and I are, you might say, associates in trade, Mr. Delgado."

Delgado raised his sparse brows, took the coins, and lifted Malcolm from the divan as if he were a frail boy instead of a bulky cross between child and adult man.

"You might have a word with the father about the comportment of the son," the stocky fellow said.

I turned to him and stared. He dropped his eyes and attended to the girl whose face Malcolm had bruised. The stocky man addressed her with exaggerated concern, and she shrugged her shoulders and made to smile; it looked more like a leer.

I walked to the foyer, where I found Delgado about to descend the steps with his charge. "Allow me, Delgado," I said. "If you'll help me stuff him into the carriage, I'll escort him home. What I gave you for fare I hope you'll use for a drink."

"Mr. Bartholomew," he said. He inclined his head an inch. I had heard a rumor that on a Portuguese cod fisherman, somewhere off the English coast, he had cut a man very badly with a gaff and, while the fellow bled, Delgado had used the hook to keep the crew from coming to the man's assistance. According to the story, he had never said a word, from start of fight to death by exsanguination.

It was a mild enough night, but I took the blanket from the driver and laid it on Malcolm's shoulders and chest, more as a stay against his soiling his clothing if he took sick than as a protection from the night. We made our way south and west through the smells of coffee and bread and, once, the sour stink of a brewery.

"Mr. Face," Malcolm said.

"You'll be forgiven tonight," I said. "But Delgado will remember."

"Ooh," the boy said, and he affected to laugh. "Mr. Face," he said again.

I placed the thumb and forefinger of my left hand on his nostrils and pinched; the while, I clasped his lips between the thumb and forefinger of my right. He began to struggle, so I slapped with elbow and forearm upon his chest, and he went crimson. I squeezed and then let go with both my hands. "Don't call me that a third time," I said.

He began to go very pale, and I knew that he was about to heave his night's drink. "Driver!" I called. "To the curbing, if you please, at once!"

While Malcolm leaned out to the right, I climbed down from the left, gave the driver his instructions and his fare, and I made long strides to escape the sound of the boy's blubbering and spew.

I was at Seventy-second Street, and I would have a good night's walk in which to think. I had been fascinated by Jessie's tranquillity—not a word about the children until I referred to them, when I said only that I had an eye on an opportunity and that I must devote time to developing it, and hearing in return only her assurance that she knew me well enough to exercise patience. Of course, there was little about Jessie that did not fascinate me: her form, her face, the delicate tattoos and their location, and her ability to work for Mrs. Hess and keep herself fresh and somehow inviolate.

I said, "Ba!" A man carrying a heavy burlap sack came abreast and went faster as I spoke. I had addressed not him but myself. I was becoming foolish—inviolate, indeed!—and it occurred to me that I must see her less, or not at all, if I was to remain strong enough to survive in this city, and in my profession, and in, as a matter of fact, my own flesh. When I realized at once that I would not forsake seeing Jessie, and that I felt as if I *could* not, I also realized that something like my life was now at stake. I walked faster, as if to outrun my thoughts.

That pace, and the sound of my harsh, rapid breathing against the inside of the mask, reminded me of a story M had told me. I could not remember where it was set, or what the ship was called, but it concerned a man from the Isle of Man. I did recall how, as he said it to me, I reminded myself that I was hearing a tale from the man who had written perhaps the greatest story told by an American about American industry. His *Whale* was a hymn to the catching of enormous creatures and using them, blubber and ambergris, for the manufacture of oily light and the perfumed scent on golden breasts and dark brown nipples I had just recently left. How the owners failed to hire a captain who would serve their will was a lesson to every man of capital, and how they lost a ship laden with oil was the story's moral: If you have a plan, you must see it through, and if you have none, you have no business; hire slackly and lose your investment; do not risk your money with a man who covets none.

The fishing vessel had been caught by a freeze in a cove off Lyme

Regis, and the crew had actually watched the salt water thicken, first on the rigging and on the nets, and then on the bowsprit, and then in the sea that slapped, more and more slowly, against the hull itself. Within hours, as M told the story, the ship was halted, ringed with ice that lay tight against her, and the masts were like the limbs of trees in winter—bone-white, glinting. "It made the Ancient Mariner seem like a passenger on a pleasure craft," he told me, sitting forward to lean his elbows on his knees, rubbing his hands as if against the cold that came blowing into the room from out of his story.

"The captain pitched over dead," he said, "frozen on the spot. He fell out of his shoes, in fact, and they remained adhered to the deck by inches of ice that now lay over everything. This was—did I tell you?—the winter of 1832, famous for its killing chill. The frail were culled, and only the hearty survived the year, especially along the English coast.

"That left a first mate who was too drunk, whether with fear or gin I cannot say, and a second mate who was barely old enough to tell him*self* what to do, much less a crew of a dozen tars who had long before that, I daresay, considered catching and eating him."

"They were cannibals?" I remembered saying, gullible as a lamb in an abattoir.

"Shipmate, there's more than one way to devour a boy on a boat," he told me. "But to the inclemencies, then, shall we? Here they are: worse than becalmed because a ship with no wind can send a cutter out to tow her an inch at a time if needs must. And there's always the hope of a sudden gust of wind. But this was the dead of winter, mind. And the ship as fixed in the ice as a glass eye in a stuffed and mounted Muscovy duck. And the temperature falling, and night coming on, and the captain dead, the first mate incapacitated and soon enough to freeze to death.

"'What shall we do, sir?' calls the cabin boy to the second mate. The men fall about grunting—it would have been laughter in a fairer clime—at the sight of the little fellow thus questioning the fellow not much larger or older.

" 'We'll make a fire!' pipes the second mate, intent on doing his duty, and on seeing the crew through the fray.

" 'What shall we burn, then, lad,' groans an able-bodied, 'fish in blocks of ice?'

" 'Charts, the log, and every book on board,' cries the second mate.

"A fellow known as Button, Sterling Button, called by his shipmates either Silver or Bone, scholarly man with gold-rimmed spectacles tied round the back of his head to keep them on when he's up in the ropes, says, in his deep voice that matches his broad, manly shape, 'I'd rather perish, sir.'

" 'But you will,' the second mate is wise enough to note.

" 'Then I will, but I'll not burn my books.'

" 'What's in 'em, then?' asks one of the rugged net haulers, shivering in his boots and oilskins.

" 'Poetry,' Button tells them. 'Sweet music, hard truth, and wisdom. And a bit of sorrow, like spice in a Polynesian stew. Madness, even, though of the sane variety. And not for burning.'

"With that, he bolts, for he knows they're soon to act. He hies himself to his hammock and his seaman's trunk, a lovely structure of polished maple from his native New Hampshire and leather from a deer he shot when home. He opens the lid for an instant, looks in at the titles and the authors' names, and, bidding farewell to the likes of Ben Jonson and William Shakespeare and Laurence Sterne, he shuts the trunk and locks it, and he swallows the small metal key. 'They can cut it out of me when they've done their worst,' Button says. He opens his clasp knife and sits, awaiting them, perched atop his seaman's trunk in the middle of a frozen waste like an Anchorite in the sweltering sands of the Holy Land."

He had leaned, again, to refill our glasses, spilling a little after having drunk much.

"And there he sat."

"But what happened? I must beg you: finish," I said.

"No, shipmate. In the case of the tale of Button and his books, what happened matters less than Button's decision."

"To die for his books."

"Exactly. Perfectly spoken. Die for his books. *That,* shipmate, is a reader for whom a man might decide to write something and see it through the printers and reviewers. Die for his books."

"And that," I remember saying, disappointed and bemused, "is all?"

"It is everything," he said.

"You startle me with your unorthodoxy," I ventured to say, "but you do so surely tell a tale. I dare not complain."

"So they once said," he told me, and turned his attention to the blue, oily gin.

His son, I thought, stepping back from the wheels of a yellow-and-white ice wagon from which trailed some of the sawdust used to insulate the great, cloudy blocks, had none of the highly flavored language, none of the easy command of one's attention, nor any of the certainty—for all the uncertainty of M's latter days—that made him a present public official and, once, an author to be reckoned with. His son was, in fact, a bully and a lout. He would enjoy the murder of Indians, I wagered.

I knew men, I reminded myself, who had engaged in a war's worth of murder.

It was battle, I demurred. I was a soldier.

But the bully boy will also be a soldier, I told myself.

I could not have been more mistaken.

Outside the Five Points House of Industry that same night, I paused beside its smeared, unlighted window and its rugged wooden door. This was a refuge, I knew, for Chinese boys who wished to learn a trade other than their father's. Women, of course, did not attend, nor were they taught how to dress like Americans and speak the language of the United States. They were drowned at birth in China, I had heard men say at the coffeehouse beneath the Equitable Building. Surely, reading of gold miners in California and Oregon—it was where Chun Ho and her people had come from: "Oh-gin." "Where?" "*Oh*-gin!" "Oregon?" "Sure"—I had seen stories of the binding of women's feet at birth, of the uselessness, to their family, of girls, who would finally be of service as breeders for the groom's family. Chinese women rarely appeared on the streets, and I saw very few, and all of them were bulky in their silk pajamas and oval shoes, and none seemed to walk with the abrupt energy of Chun Ho or, for that matter, to sit with the profound contemplation I sensed in her. I had seen her lift filled laundry baskets, two of them, each balanced on the end of a stick, that were almost as tall as she. Somehow her mother had felt obliged to serve Chun Ho's wish for independence. Somehow Chun Ho had felt obliged to serve her own. I knew that she had a daughter and a son, and I knew that she would feel obliged to raise the daughter as an American person—a girl strong enough to live alone.

The Points, of course, were echoing as of wild creatures nailed inside barrels—calls, laughter, sexual cries, every variety of uneasiness and dismay, and the working sounds of the lower levels of industry composed of loom shuttles slapping, stable doors slamming, donkey carts rattling, honey wagons gurgling with the refuse of a tenement's month. But what I thought of, as I walked, immersed in the life I had chosen as if it were the sea and I a kind of misshapen fish, was obligation: Jessie's to her people, and Chun Ho to hers, and mine to gelt. To be sure, I felt loyalties of several sorts, emotional and otherwise; I was no monster, though I might be said to resemble one now and to have resembled one then. But I did not belong to a species or a people or a family or, say, *fang*, the group that gave general assistance, or, say, a *shantan*, which, as she explained it, was concerned with keeping a Chinese cemetery, and eventually transporting their dead back to China, as was, it seemed, their way. There was no group, from traders' organization to cemetery society, to which I cared to belong. So no one would bury me; I was for potter's field unless I gave instructions and left money in someplace safe for someone who cared to recover it and pay to cover me up.

Yet Sergeant Grafton had felt a loyalty to me. He had not wanted to, but I remembered, finally, his coming up the tree so swiftly, with such ferocity, and the gentleness of his voice: *Here we come. We're coming. Here we come.* The remembering him, and my thoughts of gentle Sam: Were those not loyalties?

I felt like someone with bonds and coin to deposit in a vault, and no bank in sight, and the need to save things powerful along my fingers and arms and in my head, and Irish Rabbits or Swamp Angels, those escaped convicts who lived in the sewers, coming toward me in the street. I smelled whatever it was they burned in a doss-house, and then I smelled stables, then the effluvium of a ditch engraved over time by the wastes that poured from a little hotel for whores and their customers who wished to rise from the streets in order to fall in rankness and disease.

I was thinking, of course—I must have been seeking *not* to think— of the warm, still evening in perhaps July, though it might have been August, when I walked on the toes of my moccasins to the edge of a Carolina wagon relay: raised wooden water tower, stable and farrier's, the little carpentry shop, and, radiating out from that cluster, a wooden fence in which horses might graze. There were to have been a hundred horses or more exchanged for looted Yankee silver, so the colonel had told the lieutenant who'd instructed Grafton and me. I counted nineteen horses, a few of them hale and well fed. The others were spindle-shanked and blown. But they were horses, and they could be hitched to cannon, ridden by men, and, if need be, served up for supper. I was sitting in my firing position on the top of the water tower, waiting for a good five seconds in the sights of either the chief drover who had brought the poor animals in, or his master, a man called Wickery or Hickory, or one of the Rebel officers who had come to take possession. I counted four horses with saddles on, their reins trailing on the yellowing grass.

I was to try to bring down the architect of the robbery—he'd robbed the Union, and now he would rob the Confederacy—and then to harvest whom I could in what time I had left. I assumed now that the fellow in the suit whose hands were not on the lantern as it was lit would be the man behind the deal. He had a thick, short beard of reddish-brown, and one of his nostrils seemed to be far wider than the other. I decided to place the shot up his nose. The lamp was set down, then adjusted; it flared, it subsided, an orange light slanted across the neck and then nose of the dealer as he bent to light his cigar at the chimney of the lamp. All right, I thought: I'll go down your nose instead of up. I should have apologized to him for taking him in an awkward stooping position while thinking derisively of his nose.

I did not apologize. I fired.

His forehead and nose blossomed, he leaned backward and I saw his devastated face, and then he went over. I loaded and aimed at the officer who crouched to the right of the table. I had him. But the charge failed. They began to fire wildly from the window, but upward; either they had sensed the origin of the original shot or they had been warned that I might be about. If so, what could have brought them to a lighted lamp in the frame of the window—a picture they posed for the transporter of their deaths?

I went down the ladder on the far side of the tower, and I propped the Sharps to recover when I was finished. I walked, as far as I can reconstruct it now, into their fire. A ball took off my hat, and something tugged my shirtsleeve. I drew the Navy Colt and, aiming it as best I could while I strode toward them, I fired deliberately, sighting this time with both eyes so that I could perceive their relationship toward my changing position.

When I was out of cartridges, I took them singly from the pouch I carried in my pocket (to distinguish them from the rifle ammunition in my leather pannier), and I reloaded three or four cylinders. I had no more time. I had been struck above the belt, on my left-hand side, though I could not tell then how deeply I had been explored by the shot. I held the Colt at arm's length and I fired and fired and fired as I walked to the window. I did not stop, I was surprised to learn. I stepped up and through the window, kicking aside the table and the lighted lamp. I stepped upon the first man I'd shot and went around the drover and the Rebel corporal who had come along to assist the officer, who stood propped against the far wall. He was slight and young, but unafraid. He was angry at me. He was raging, but he was also respectful. He stood and bled and shook.

"You murdered me," he said.

"I murdered *them* so far," I said, moving closer while he shot with his pistol and missed me. I said, "I haven't even aimed at you."

"You're the one put this in me," he said. His thigh was bloody, and the leg seemed ready to buckle.

"I didn't know it," I said. "I was just firing."

"For just firing, you mule-jism bastard, you did plenty of harm."

He brought his weapon up and fired and the hammer clattered down. "I'm out," he said. "I knew so. Oh, bastard, my *leg* hurts. I just wanted you to think, one time, you might die."

"That," I said, "I do think, every time out. If it's any consolation." I brought my Colt up and the hammer landed on an empty cylinder.

"Both of us," he said. "Maybe we should leave each other to go our ways, then?"

He wasn't begging. He preferred not to die, but he was brave enough. His leg collapsed, and after he'd hit the floor, he slid his sound leg out from under him and sat against the wall as if he'd chosen to.

I took the knife from my belt and I stooped as I stepped forward, thinking to do it quickly for him, and I stabbed him in the throat. The worst part was pulling it out as he gurgled and squealed with the pain of the blade coming back at a slightly different angle from its entrance. Blood geysered, for I had struck an artery, and I hated for him to have to watch it pulse out and up. He made a face of defiance, of disgust for me, and then he grew paler and more fatigued and closed his eyes. He would die in a minute or more.

I called down, as if he might take the words with him, "You were good. You were a stubborn soldier, do you hear? You were good."

He shook, as if with an ague, as if in the cold of an arctic night and not this moonless, windless summer dusk. His face was the dreamy, lost face of a boy deep asleep. The metallic smell of his blood was on my arms and hands and trouser legs. Then his bowel gave out the last that we leave in the world when we go: our embarrassment, our shame, the least of all of our aspects. He shook and his unwounded leg bounced upon the floor and then was still, and so was he.

"Plenty damned good," I said. I collected what papers I could find on the table and the floor. Outside, I grabbed for the horses' reins, but the stink of blood on me must have spooked them. They danced a dozen yards away and then, because they were trained and their reins were trailing, they stopped to wait. The only way I could keep them still so I might search the saddlebags for the silver I'd been told to retrieve was to reload my pistol and kill each one of the four. I searched with my hand for the cartridge pouch, and I found it; I had enough to load five cylinders with two more left.

But, you must think, I surely had to have been exhausted. I was. Might not I have been shaken by the battle? Absolutely. And, within it, the slaughter? Of course. And the death of the brave young man? And that without doubt. So that I rebelled at the killing of the mild, obedient horses?

I shot them down by holding the pistol in both hands and squeezing off as I saw those gentle, obedient eyes find me and look head-on; the sound was crunchy and slamming at once. I killed two with my first two shots; one ran off, then turned, as if in disbelief, and I shot him, too. The other I missed. He ran on, past the farrier's, and I found I hadn't the kidney any longer for a crippling shot and then the one with which to dispatch him. Only one seemed alive as I came up. He shuddered and looked to me as if—it was his training, after all—I brought reason and procedure and relief. I reloaded, standing above him while he watched, and I put the coup de grâce into the bony head of the sweet, betrayed creature. I went to the next one, and then to the farthest, and did all, at that moment, that I could: squeezed a shot away. The first one I'd taken had the bag I sought, a small canvas valise such as an artisan carries his tools in. I wondered what I would have done if the horse had pinned the bag beneath him. I thought of my knife. I thought of me in the geysering blood as I butchered the horse, hacked at him with axes from the woodworker's shop, sawed at his ribs, fell to above and within him with a mallet and chisel, until I had torn him apart and had fetched the bloody bag on which he'd lain. Instead, I cut the pigging string away from the handle of the valise, put away my revolver, stopped at a watering trough to rinse off the blade of my knife, and carried the valise toward the Sharps I'd left at the water tower.

Grafton was on watch as I came in. He didn't waste time with paroles. He came running clumsily through the high timothy weed and he got himself alongside, as if we both were ships on a rough channel, and he slipped his arm around me, grasping my belt, and tugged me along. He was soaked in blood, mine and the brave young soldier's, by the time we reached our bivouac. And I thought, near home in the Points, thinking still of the smell from the joss house, the odor of a people's obligation to an ancient ordering of life, I could feel obliged in my own way. I could feel a kind of loyalty to men like Grafton, and the men and horses and the single dog I had dispatched: my *fang*. And to the currency of the United States of America, to the growth of whose fortunes I had given straight lips, sound cheeks, most of a nose, much of a chin, and, no doubt, a goodly portion of my mind.

Sam Mordecai came to see me in Washington. He told the terse, wise, merciful woman at my bedside that we had served together in the fray. He said that: "Comrades in the fray."

"Poor fellow," she said.

"Oh, Samuel, you rabbi from consternation," I hissed up at him through the bandages, which seemed, on that particular moist, hot Washington afternoon, to be made of clay or rock and to have just come from the furnace in which they had baked all day. My words, I knew, were difficult to decipher, not nearly so clear, say, as Chun Ho's or Adam's to me.

"Billy," he said, "your eyes. Why are they covered?"

"He does not wish to see," she told him, "until he can be seen."

"Will that occur?"

She said, "I have told him probably not."

"It was their idea to bandage me, on the way here. Their thought was that my eyes were affected."

She said, "It was *yours* to keep them bandaged."

"She lies," I whispered, "this demimondaine of the casualty ward."

Young Sam said, "Surely, you do not wish to address her so. You always had the best of manners. Burton and I sought to emulate you."

"He wishes to drive me to fizz and sizzle," she said with, I thought, some pleasure. "But he cannot. This forenoon I assisted, in the absence of nurses, who were elsewhere at work, when the surgeons had off a poor fellow's leg. Knee and below," she said. "I was not driven away by that ghastly brutality, and I surely will not be offended by his attempts to woo my worst attentions."

"Sam, she's right. I am trying to get her into my narrow iron bed."

"You would not, if you could see my face," she said, "because I am the plainest of women. Let us cut holes in the bandage. Have a look."

"Billy," Sam said, "let's do it."

I said, "What brings you here, Sam?" I heard her release her breath, and then I heard the sound of her skirts against a neighboring bed as she moved away.

"You should let her, Billy. What a fine woman that is!"

"Sam. What?"

"Oh, Billy," he said, and I could hear him start to weep, then stop.

"Who?"

"Sergeant Grafton."

"How?"

"A cannonade. His poor horse went mad with the suddenness of it. His fright—"

"He threw him off?"

"He crushed his head. He danced on him in his fear. It was a jelly, his skull—white jelly and red jelly, bits of bone all through it. . . ."

I found no words. I breathed out against the hot, heavy bandages and then I breathed in. *We're coming,* I heard him say, as gently as if to a boy.

"Billy, I shot the horse."

"Sure," I said.

"You think I was right?"

"It's as good a deed as any other I can think of. Punishment for disobedience by an animal we've raised to serve us. Mercy, if horses are capable of pronouncing guilt upon themselves. Corrective, if another horse observed and could fathom it as retribution. Sam, my skin hurts, Jesus, it feels like they're boiling it and poor Grafton. He was a decent man. He should have been an officer. Though maybe he was decent because he was one of us. Oh, Sam: Take up your pistol, pretend I'm a horse."

He started in weeping again, and I put my hand up and he took it. He stopped, and so did I.

"You know what I intend to do, Billy? With this War? All of this?" I could feel the tension in his hand, the strength of his resistance to the strength in him of what he wanted to do—run mad, go screaming in the corridors and streets.

I lay back and let my hand drop. He kept it in his a few seconds more, then he released it.

"I am going to write something. For *Harper's Weekly* or one of the larger newspapers. Maybe even a book."

I heard the mockery in my voice. I fear that I did not wish to suppress it. "What will you call it? *Two Years in the Company of an Assassin? The Brains and Blood of a Superannuated Sergeant? A Jew's View of the War for Every Dollar?* I do beg your pardon, Sam. You know I think you a fine man and a fellow who protected me. Forgive me."

He was silent.

"I beg you, Sam. I beg your forgiveness. I am up to my former nostrils in self-pity. Apparently, I am not nearly so bold as I once thought."

"You're the bravest man I ever knew, Billy."

"You thought of me so?"

"I still do."

"But you forgive me."

He seized my arm and shook my hand.

"Bless you, Sam. The cruelty with which I turned on you!"

"Your wounds, Billy. It's your wounds."

"Tell me of what you would write. I swear I want to know."

"A kind of memoir, such as generals always write about their derring-do: And, oh, yes, the troops insisted upon dying every day, but here is how I sat in my saddle and sent them off to be burned alive and trampled to death and shot out of trees."

"The memoir of an ordinary soldier. It's a fine idea, Sam. I will be wealthy, I think, in spite of this face. I will somehow have money. If you do write the book, then come and see me, and perhaps I'll be able to help you pay your printing bills."

"Mr. Putnam or the Harper Brothers will do that. Or Mr. Fields, perhaps. Though I thank you."

"Well, remember me anyway, Sam. Keep me in mind."

"I will never forget you," he said.

"Don't you go writing me, mind. I have no wish to be a character in a book."

"I'm going to write about Sergeant Grafton," he said. "I'm going to keep him from disappearing away from us again."

"Can that be done?" I asked M. We sat over coffee at half past six o'clock in the morning at a round table of small diameter in the window of Charney's and Toller's Coffee House, hard by Rector Street, where we had met by appointment as he came on to duty at the river and I, up much of the night in roaming, had paused in my rounds of the rain-slicked nighttime streets.

He drank his coffee unsweetened and undiluted, as did I. It was pleasantly bitter there, where they imported their own beans and roasted them on the premises, and the smell was a kind of dark perfume. He leaned back and gave his silent laugh. "Can that be done," he finally said. "It is only the question that a man of letters asks himself each time he enters his room, shuts the door with a welcome kind of despair, and sits himself down before the awful, terrorizing whiteness of the white page. Can . . . that . . . be . . . done."

I placed a morsel of Irish soda bread, rich with currants yet the dough sternly unsweet, into my mouth beneath the veil. He drank at his coffee. I knew he would not stay away from the topic.

"Can— Bless you, shipmate. It is *the* question. And not only because it is so difficult. A man at his desk, poised above the awful blankness, must ask himself this: Do I seek a stay against oblivion on behalf of my little actors on the vast page? Or do I seek my own eternal life? In case of the latter, it's philosophy a man must drive for. If the former, a generous and a merciful and a slighter end, why then you can write down in their scratchy particularity the traits of a person and keep them fresh for as long as the paper lasts. If in some library in some city in some nation of the world that book exists, then your character's saved from oblivion— your remembered personage, I mean. Your own character, the outline and contents of your soul, that is neglected for the persiflage and rump-de-dumps, the lace collars and bone buttons, of romance. The choice is part of the danger. So's the oblivion, of course." He laughed, his mouth wide, his head tilted back, his little eyes staring at the smoke-browned ceiling of the coffeehouse, and no sound rising from his lips.

I had not listened with acute attention, for I was thinking of business—mine, and therefore his—while he had been explaining something about white paper. I could not help but wonder if, since blank, white pages were so fearful, one might not use another color of page and thereby cheat one's fears.

"And your comrade-in-arms, shipmate. Did he write his stay against the erasure by time?"

"I have not seen any notice of such a book."

"It seems a very good time to be issuing memoirs. If you have lived even but a little, but have knowledge of suffering of sorts, the same presses so hospitable to the ladies' books of household drama, thirty and forty years ago, now seem receptive to recollections of the utmost mundanity."

"Even, I understand, to works by Negro authors about their servitude," I said, for it was time to come to grips with our subject.

"Poor devils."

"From such works," I extemporized, "it has been learned—do you believe it?—that men of commerce continue to use slave labor? That slaves, indeed, are still kept? That the imprisonment of the darker brother, in certain Southern places, goes on?"

"Imprisonment is a condition, I fear, of humanity."

"But I am speaking, sir, not in the abstract, but of flesh-and-*blood* humanity."

"Yes," he said. He grew still, and I sensed that I would have to return to the topic on another day. I could wait. He said, "Forgive me. I am thinking of my children. Mal is out every night, and I worry. Stanny is silent and somehow removed. The girls argue with me as to how I wear my clothing and how many hours, of a weekend, I till the fields of language in my room." He shook his head, then drank the last of his coffee. "And I have lost the track, my friend. Forgive me. I cannot remember what we discussed."

"What could be more important than a man's repose among his children?"

"I surely did not speak of repose. *That* we do not entertain. What is repose?"

"Not, apparently, a family," I said. He laughed his imitation of laughter. We spoke of the ship he would inspect that morning, which had lain-to over the night, a Dutchman bearing molasses and rum.

"I'm off," he said suddenly, pushing back from the table and moving, as he often did, with the grace of someone younger. "I'm a man of action today. It's tonnage and seals. My *custom*ary chores." He clipped his little badge onto his lapel, patted my back, and walked off. I waved him good-bye and set my mask on under the veil before I removed it. I would broach the topic again, and at a suitable moment. I knew how to wait.

And in the end, by the by, I did permit them to unwind and to rewind the bandages, restoring to my sight the boy author of war, Samuel Mordecai, and the world he thought to write.

LLOYDS MAMMOTH MAP
OF THE
BUSINESS PORTION
OF
NEW YORK CITY
1867

J. T. LLOYD

Price in Sheets, 50 cts.
Sent by Mail to any part of the World.

NO MONEY TO BE PAID TO AGENTS IN ADVANCE.

CHAPTER 4

I NOTED, AS THOUGH OBSERVING SOMEONE ELSE—as though I were Sam Mordecai, or the man who once was M—that I brought shirts and handkerchiefs for cleaning although it was not the usual day. The boy, perhaps eight, was sulking as he struggled up the three stoop steps with his barrel of stained water. As I understood it, they made much of their boys and little of their girls, yet here was her son at the same labors—arms around the keg as if embracing it, yet with a face that said nothing of embrace—as were performed by his sister, who, younger than he, seemed stronger of arm and leg. He was chubby, while the girl was lean, like her mother, who bowed as she received the shirts and the red handkerchiefs I affected in those days (perhaps to demonstrate that once I had been a soldier in the field).

She looked at the rim of the collar. She brought the shirt to her face and sniffed, and I became embarrassed. The children stared at my mask. "Not so dirty," Chun Ho said.

"Really? Shall I take them back?"

"No back. I keep. Clean 'em."

"What are your children named, then?"

"Boy Kwang. Daughter Ng."

"How do you do?" I called. They stayed back by the stove and studied the apparition that had been greeted by their mother. Something

119

meaty and sweet was slowly cooking on the stove beside the great black kettle in which she heated water.

"No bath today," she said in a soft voice, as if it were an intimacy impossible to perform before children. Perhaps it was, I thought, regarding her stiff face, her lively eyes, the sweat stains at her arms, and the way her baggy clothes fell back against her flesh. I associated the cooking meat with appetite, the appetite with her, and I stepped away, then stopped.

"Boys work as girls do?"

"No. Always not."

"But your boy—but Kwang does." He looked up when I said his name.

"Now, Merica," she said. "Ogin. Fonia. New City. New *York* City. Merica States."

"The United States."

"Sure. United *States*. Wife of dead man, boy, girl: United *States*. Everybody work. You think?"

I said, in an eager way I am unaccustomed to hearing from my lips, "I *would* help you, you know. If you needed me to, I would help you."

She looked at me shrewdly; I felt weighed, evaluated as the steam and the scents of herbs and pork, perhaps, and of something corrosive— maybe a bleaching agent—rose at the low ceiling of the small, hot room. I thought of how she lifted my limbs to scrub them, of how she held each hand in turn to clean the knuckles, the palms.

I said to him, although I faced his mother, "Be good, Kwang. Be a small man."

"All men not so good," she finally said. "Some good."

We studied one another, I suppose you would have to call it.

"Shirts one day, two day. Yes?"

I shrugged.

Then she shrugged, as if in reply, and suddenly she smiled with a kind of abandon before she recomposed her face.

I thought, as I walked one step backward, then turned to leave, that I must remember what she had fleetingly looked like when she forgot to hide: *wife of dead man.*

At the office, I lit lamps, for the day was sullen and dark and very little light spilled down along the brick wall opposite my window, inches away. Mail came from the main post office on nearby Nassau Street, and I very much appreciated that, for the office had first been the Middle Dutch Church, which for me had the appearance of a bank in a nightmare. I had a notice of freight transfer from one of the wooden sidewheel steamers of the Collins Line, out of Liverpool, to the New York Central—bales of cloth for upstate merchant brokers. I had two letters concerning payment; one enclosed it in the form of a check drawn upon the Bank of New York, and the other begged for time in remunerating me for having purchased and sent by barge across the river to New Jersey a shipment of teak, brought over from the north of Siam through a brokerage in France, for the building of small boats. I wrote an angry note refusing to extend the debt; I would deliver it later to a small man in a large, empty office—he had a desk and two chairs in a room on Maiden Lane the size of a small restaurant—and he would write it gracefully and sign on my behalf and see it sent.

Having thought so recently of Sam Mordecai, I would not have been surprised to receive a letter from him, but nothing had arrived. I was not dismayed when events of which I had dreamed came to pass, nor had I changed in this wise since my boyhood. Once, when my uncle, staying (it felt like a decade) for several days, had lost his pocket notebook, and had become very much vexed and even more difficult than he usually was, I had dreamed of finding it behind the firewood I'd split and stacked, and which he had inspected like a grand vizier of the upstate forests. That is, I had seen the little leather book, had in my dreaming felt the textured surface of its cover, had shoved aside the fresh peach-colored surface of the quartered birch logs to seize it and hold it in the air before his quivering wattles and cloudy eyes. I had wakened and, still in my nightshirt, had walked barefoot into the autumn morning to move the wood about and hold it up. There had been no shaking it in the air before his face, however, because he was Uncle, after all, and he had kept us from falling further into debt and discomfort once my father was dead. But I would not have been surprised to see an envelope from Samuel Mordecai.

I found a strayed mare, on which we carried tarpaulins and blankets and food, rather early in my association with Sergeant Grafton when we were moving down through southern Pennsylvania. I sat back against a tree as he shouted at Burton and as Sam Mordecai went trotting off with a resoluteness I found charming, since he'd no idea where he should seek the horse.

The sergeant shouted, "Bartholomew, you lazy bugger assassin!" But I merely smiled and pulled my hat low upon my head and closed my eyes.

I opened them, only seconds later, and I called to him, "The fruits of my catnap, Sergeant. She's in a grove of plum trees."

He walked over and cut a chew of tobacco for himself and inserted it into his mouth. Then, around it, he said, "Specifically plum?"

"I do know a plum tree when I see one."

"And you saw one."

"Yes."

"Yes, Sergeant, goddamn it, Bartholomew. Stand up and give me a goddamned report!"

"Sergeant, the lazy bugger assassin"—and he began to smile—"reports that he dreamed of seeing the runaway mare in a grove of plums."

"I'm going to send Burton, on the strength of your dream, to look for plum trees. Is that what you suggest?"

"It is."

"And I'll never doubt you again, I suppose."

"I suppose you'll try, Sergeant. But you'll wonder."

He spat some tobacco juice between my feet. When he looked up, he was grinning. "Did you see me swallow any of this and choke to death?"

"I'm willing to be patient," I told him, and he began to sputter into a laugh.

Of course, we found the horse, and in a grove of trees that Burton thought, though he couldn't be sure, were plums.

It wasn't until we were pretty far south, halfway through the Carolinas, that I dreamed the dream about the woman and woke, shouting, to terrify Grafton and Burton and bring Mordecai running over from where he'd mounted watch. The night was cold and wet, heavy rain on everything for hours, and we were soaked and miserable to start with. We had rolled into our blankets and covered ourselves with tarpaulins because we hadn't the grit, nor had Grafton the heart to order us, to make shelters with rope and tent halves, using the low limbs of slender dogwoods, the only trees near where we had stopped.

"Are you drunk, Mr. Bartholomew?"

"No, Sergeant, and I wish I was."

"You were dreaming?"

"I'm afraid so."

"Because? Afraid because? Go back to your watching, Mr. Mordecai. Wake Mr. Burton in two hours and see if you can sleep. If not, find a way to make a fire in a rainstorm and I'll put you in for medals. Mr. Bartholomew? Why afraid?"

"Because of what I dreamed."

He slid down into his blanket and tarp and he rolled over. He murmured, "Which was?"

I slid down in my own blanket roll and pretended not to hear. I did hear his voice again, but I ignored it. He was snoring soon enough, as all soldiers learn to do, in rain or snow or landslide of mud or manure: Stop, do the necessaries, close your eyes, and sleep.

I tried to keep my eyes open in the cold and soak and darkness, for I did not want to live inside that dream again. I blinked myself awake a few times, but then I could not help but fall—as if down a cliff face or into a mining pit, for thousands of yards, and at great speed—into sleep. I was not invaded by the dream again, although I thought of it at once on waking, and left the camp, as if to relieve myself, because I did not wish to speak of it in any particulars. Fortunately, Sergeant Grafton was too uncomfortable and moody to demand an accounting of my nighttime vagaries.

I had dreamed of a tall woman in a dress the color of trilliums, that clean whiteness, who wore a gauzy cloth in her hair that matched the dress. Her arms were long, and I could see, as the light cloth was pressed against her by a wind, that her thighs were long as well. She had a long face, a long, straight nose, and a very wide mouth. Her throat was long, too, and it was arched, strained, as if she tried to hear. It was me, I thought in the dream. She was trying to listen for me, for she knew that I was on my way. She hadn't the face of anyone I knew, but it was a face to which I was powerfully attracted, and I coveted her body, thinking that I would spare her if she would lie down with me.

How wrong, I said in the dream, to kill her if she doesn't.

I was drenched, then, in someone's dark saliva. I smelled a stink, as of manure. But it was tobacco, of course, and Sergeant Grafton was passing along the lieutenant's instructions, handed down from the brigadier to the colonel to our lieutenant to Grafton, and then, in their vileness, to me. I choked at the smell. She turned, as if she'd heard me gasp.

I stared at her, stared into her dark, intense eyes. I ran my eyes like fingers along the frown marks at her mouth, etched beneath her tan. She nipped at my fingers, as if to promise pleasure. I closed my eyes, then opened them, and I stared at her lips. I felt charged, and full, and then I tingled with release, and I stared and I surged, and I cried aloud, and her face exploded as if I had caught it in my sight and fired.

So I waited for a week, and then for weeks, to learn that I'd been ordered to kill a woman.

What I wish to depose here is that I *never* had such a presentiment about Malcolm. Learning as I did, and learning what I did, I was as staggered as his parents must have been. But that cannot be, of course. But I was, indeed, staggered. And I did feel somehow responsible. And I did say "somehow" as a cowardly begging off. You see, my mind or nighttime soul or whatever aspect of us is involved in dreaming *is* a part of this recollection. That is what I mean to say. For, while the articles in the New York papers were either unsigned, or not by him, the editorial piece in the *Advertiser,* printed in Boston and left behind at my office by a Massachusetts traveler in French writing machines (for which he wanted much and promised little), was signed by one S. Mordecai. I read it two weeks after I had read the story in *The New York Times.*

But it had not happened yet on the afternoon of which I speak, and it had not happened that night. "He was the same boy," his father told me days afterward, as we sat in his office on the barge, he as inspector for the night and I as the comforting friend. The fire was high although it had been a sweltering September day, and he drank too much gin. He ran with sweat, and his tears ran with it; he was all a-glisten, and his broad workingman's hands trembled more than I had ever seen. "He was the same boy during the day before we found him. I have been assured. He skylarked with the other clerks at the Atlantic and Great Western. He was merry. Although I must report to you, shipmate, that he sported with the pistol. You told him it was a serious weapon. You repeatedly passed the warning along, and I somberly echoed it. But he listened to neither. He was careless with it, bringing it to work, apparently, although I didn't know, of course. I would otherwise have taken a hand."

He sighed. "I already did—had I told you? There had been too much coming home in the late watches of the night. We had given warning. I took his key away that opened the night latch, and I told him he must be in and quiet in his room by a decent hour, nine bells. We rise early, after all, and he had work as well. For two nights, he stayed in. His uniform, you see, had just arrived, and he must try it on in the evenings, and parade for his sisters. But, then, no: out into the night, and away until dawn, and we, rising and falling like a young man's feelings, staggering, then, through the long days' exhaustion. So it would not do."

"Of course not," I said, but he did not hear me.

"I came downstairs for my breakfast. Lizzie spoke of the night before. I had been asleep, having worked at something about the Holy Land after supper, but Lizzie, often a lighter sleeper, had gone downstairs at one or two of the morning, summoned by Malcolm's rapping at the door. She did remonstrate, she says, but in a motherly and gentle way. Can you not hear it? 'Dear fellow, this is simply *too* late. Can you not try harder for us?' So she says it was, and so it was. In and up goes Malcolm and up he remains in the morning, late for work. Lizzie sends one of the girls—I had left for work by now, and was at the river and plying what must forever be my trade. And she goes up and calls at his door, and he says, 'Yes.'

"That is his last word. And that it should be 'Yes,' in affirmation of his sister, or of home and domestic love, or of his own fault in jeopardizing his job, I find nearly intolerable in the weight of emotion with which it lands upon me, shipmate. 'Yes.'"

"Yes," I said.

"I told Lizzie to leave him be. His reception at work would be his own worst punishment, and he would learn, if from nothing else, then from that. A man must take the consequences, I told her, and off I went."

"Oh," I said. "I see. It was *then* that you went, and not earlier."

"Earlier? What was—earlier. Yes. Lizzie tried during the day, at odd hours, to rouse him. It was not unusual for him to sleep so hard, so deep, that he could not be wakened. He loved to sleep, that fellow, and so dearly he sleeps now at Woodlawn. Sleeps he and sleeps he, down at the bottom, where the oozy weeds about him twist.

"That was a day, you might recall, when we ate a chop and drank some ale and spoke of the War, and the need for compassion for those who surrendered. I did have difficulty in persuading you! But of course, you were there, and they tried to shoot you down, and you, in turn, them.

So much more simple for the unwounded man to be compassionate. I admired so your willingness to turn—ah, you see. . . ."

"The other cheek. Indeed. What's left of it. So I am given to understand that you were late returning."

"Returning?"

"Home. The night you found—"

"Tardy and tied to the masthead and lashed for it, I can promise you. She lit into me with the Cat that night. But paused to tell me of his long sleeping, his silence all the day, and the door locked from within. I had it down, I can tell you. I sent it off the hinges and down."

He poured gin and missed the glass with a good deal of it. I rose to take the bottle from his hands and pour again. He nodded his gratitude. He could not speak. His eyes looked painted on, not pained; his eyes looked dead in his gleaming face.

"In bed," he whispered. "In his nightclothes. Pistol on the pillow. Head at the far corner of the bedclothing. Eyes unclosed. A terrible wound in his temple. Bits of skull and skin, skeins of drying blood. Dead, dead, dead, dead, dead, dead, dead, my Malcolm dead. His eyes not shut, and looking at me"—his head came up, his own eyes rested upon me, giving little light forth—"and Lizzie atop him, pulling at his shoulders, demanding that her son wake up."

"Poor soul."

"He must have been playing with the pistol, for his hand was still around it, you see."

"Oh. Around it, then. I thought it was upon the pillow."

"As was the hand in which it lay. Of course."

"Of course. Please . . ."

"I took her from the room and then returned. I had to tell him good-bye."

According to a newspaper, the coroner's jury said this verdict: "That the said Child came to his death by Suicide by shooting himself in the head with a pistol at said place while laboring under temporary insanity of Mind." According to another: "The deceased was one of two sons in the family, their father well-known in literary circles." According to a third: "The youth, 18 years of age, son of a well-known literary gentleman, committed suicide yesterday by shooting himself with a pistol." And, weeks later, according to Mr. S. Mordecai, in the *Boston Weekly Advertiser:* "The boy was armed with a deadly pistol, suitable for military purposes. He was enlisted in the Guard of the Army of the United States. Soldiers die, with and without pistols, and perhaps there is solace in the boy's embrace of danger. By all accounts, his father knew dangerous days in his own youthful past, and perhaps he and his grieving wife can find comfort in what we might think of as the courage of their son." You sob sister, Sam, I thought as I read.

"In his coffin, he lay so sweetly, with the ease of a gentle nature. Ah, Mackie: You never gave me a disrespectful word, nor in any way ever failed in your filialness," he said, more to the gin in his glass than to me. If a ship came in, I thought, I would have to pretend to be the inspector. And I should like, I thought, to see the captain and the pilot who would hand the lading bill to a man in a little white mask.

Filialness, I thought.

"But just a boy," he said. "And his brother cannot *hear.* He wanders the house in his own interior silence, as if he has heard, already, far too much. The gunshot, I wonder." He looked up. "Do you think?"

"I have been deafened by shots."

"Just so."

"But they were shots that I fired. The detonation in the cartridge, you see, occurs at the level of the ear. It is natural, at times, for a loss of hearing to take place."

"But not, then, you think, if the shot occurs elsewhere? In a different room?"

"Perhaps your son—Stanwix?"

"Stanny, yes."

"It may be that he wishes not to have *heard.*"

He shook his head. "I must drink my drink," he said. "As to wishing and hearing: He has heard, and we all, one way and another, have heard. There is no retreat from knowledge. If there were— But you don't think him mad? My son?"

"Perhaps sad, then. Sad?"

"Sad," he said. "The universe is diminished and it closes in upon us when a child dies. Certainly, sad." He said, "We buried him in his military apparel, did I say? He has gone from us a soldier. But he fights no more."

It was half past five, and Mrs. Hess's place was still, it being too early for the nightbirds and too late for those who wandered through the city after midnight and into the dawn. Through the thick carpeting and past the flock of the wallpaper and under the heavy door with its brass handle and silent latch came sounds of women laughing or talking low while conducting the tasks one associates with kitchens in the latter afternoon. Jessie had not lit the lamps, and we lay in shadows and a kind of grainy light that strives for darkness. She smelled like the docks—of heat, and spices of the bitter sort, and heavy oils. She tasted like foods I had not eaten but had read about—mangoes, and the milk of coconuts. And, for all our long acquaintance and fondness, I despaired of knowing her.

She finally said, "Oh, my. Oh, well."

I reached for the floor beside the bed, then forced my hand from the mask. I returned the hand to my side and felt the chill of the heavy sheets. "It's the second time I've failed," I said.

"No, you mustn't regard it as failing." She rolled toward me and kissed my arm, while her long, naked leg lay hard against my own leg, hip to hip and knee to knee. "Could this, in fact, be the third?" she asked.

"Are you counting, you mercantile woman? And the word is *failed*. If I'm here to enter you and haven't and can't, then the transaction is a failure."

"No, dear. You aren't here to enter me. You have a tongue and fingers.

You have toes. There are candles on the stand, as long as you're careful. You could enter and set up housekeeping, for all that. Which, I would wager, is precisely why. You are not here to fuck like a stoat. You are here for me. There are emotions in the room."

It would have been an apt moment to inquire as to hers. Our relationship was predicated, no matter our intimacies, on asking little—asking less, asking least.

"Shall I tell you an exciting story, Billy?"

"Something splendid in its filth? To whip me along?"

"I have a whip, if that's what you'd like."

I turned and rubbed her buttocks and the dip in her spine. It reminded me of a topography I had known but could not recall. And it was smooth, golden and smooth, as exciting to touch as her breasts. I lay my forehead against her shoulder and said, "I could not wound such perfect skin. I could not do you harm."

"Do me good, then," she said. "I'll tell you again about the Irishman who loves to bugger."

"Please, no," I said. "Please do not. Tomorrow—"

"Ah," she said. "I am paid for a dinner party tomorrow. Three others and I. A gentleman wishes his gentleman friends entertained. We dine in private rooms at Broadway at half past eight and for all of the night we are together. He is said, the host and my dinner companion, to have been known by President Lincoln. He is a manufacturer of boilers for the steam trains."

She nipped my shoulder, then licked where she had bitten. Then she gently chewed at the place, as if I were to be her meal.

"What has he in mind?" I asked with what I hoped was a tone of idle curiosity.

"He wants, I would suppose, what most of these gentlemen want." She scraped her teeth against the flesh above the shoulder bone. "To tear our clothing away after they have made a decorous dinner of roasted beef and excellent Champagne. To rape us on the table among the gold and silver flatware and the platters from Limoges. To have us on the floor, or bent over chairs. To piss in our mouths. To spurt their mettle on our faces and our throats. The usual." She bit me harder, for she knew—did she not?—that I was growing hard and that what I hated to hear from her was also an incitement. I turned sideways now, and so did she. She lay her leg around me and pulled us with it closer together, she moving up and then down and upon me while seizing me with her left leg and arm. She was like the concubine of the Arabian prince, telling her stories, charming my flesh with her words, but hardly to save her life. She spoke for the sake of mine, I could not help but think. She charmed me into blinded action, away from my mind, and therefore safe for a while, and—so far as the sensations were concerned—entire again.

The woman I dreamed I must kill was not the woman I killed. She was a Rebel whore or, anyway, a whore who served the Rebel soldiers. Let me avoid all judgments and only say that she was a woman of business. It was a farm, and of course in a dip of the farmland that was flanked by low hills and then a long, gradual incline: Jessie's naked back. There were two large sheds or little houses instead of a single large building, and the men's horses were left in a rude corral made of rope affixed to saplings and some stakes impaled in the hard, dusty ground. No trees grew near the house, and I would have to crawl down from the hills. I would therefore have to wait for darkness, and thus rely upon lights at windows, unless I could take them as they departed the women. Since there were few windows, I chose the latter course.

It seemed to me that four women worked the two buildings, and I wondered how they would manage the traffic when seven men approached down the long, gentle incline in which a muddy stream hardly trickled. It made the line of Jessie's spine beneath my hands. Three of them waited outside after being greeted by two women, and the four men divided up and two went with each of those who had stood outside, one in what seemed to be a white slip—I wondered at the prediction by my dream—and the other, whose hair was boldly red, wore what seemed to be a very long man's shirt that covered her from shoulder to just above the knee, but which she wore unbuttoned. I could hear the deeper tones of the men and the laughter of the women, but discerned no words. I lay curled among large stones that someone, plowing, had dragged from the furrows at the end of what once was a crop field. I would be shooting slightly upward, so would have to correct by firing high to let the bullet drop. My hands would know the height.

I chewed a piece of jerky, as much to keep myself alert as to assuage any hunger. A vulture soared, and I worried lest he mistake me for a corpse and draw the eyes of the three Rebels to me. They sat and squatted near the corral, passing a bottle and smoking. I needed a little more time, I calculated, for the men inside to get busy—their careless-ness would assure me of more cooperative targets when they rushed outside.

The vulture dropped lower, and through the telescope I saw one of the men look up to watch its flight. It was necessary to rush, I decided, and, leaning against the roundness of a rock that must have weighed four hundred or five hundred pounds, I lay the rifle at the junction of left hand and boulder, and I took them, one and two and three. I caught the third as he was reaching the door of the rightmost shed.

They were quick. One came out, naked except for stockings, and I caught him in the chest. I had aimed for the neck or head, but he was moving jerkily, waving a pistol and calling to his companions. No one came from the shed to the left. Out of the right-hand building, on his knees, wearing no shirt and no shoes, his trousers unbuttoned, came a curiously tall and bony fellow aiming at this, at that, at nothing at all, and I fired up and along the barrel of his gun and saw his face explode. I heard another door and, reloading, moved to the left side of the boulder and sighted on the other structure, out of which walked the woman, now naked, who had worn the man's shirt—I could tell it was she from the frizzy red hair that waved up and out. Shots issued from the single small window behind her. They gave the percussion of handguns, and they were unaimed, simply fired off in fear or hope. Through my sight, I watched her shout. Her face was contorted, violent, and brave. She held a shotgun and would not have reached me. She fired it, and I watched it slam her naked shoulder back. Her breasts jumped.

She went to the men I had taken down, and she called to one, the fellow I had caught in the chest and who was bleeding to death, I was certain. She moved as though he had spoken in reply, and then she took up the rifle that lay near him. She knew to check its charge—it was an old flintlock, I thought—and from the ground near the wounded man she took up powder and balls.

The men in the house who hid behind her continued to fire randomly, while she knelt and, scowling ferociously, did a more than acceptable job of loading up.

She looked at me. I saw that in the sight. I had grown careless and had exposed myself to her while regarding her nakedness and her courage. She pointed at me with a short arm and a stubby finger. A rage danced across her unpretty face. Her nipples were extended, like tiny fingers. And she stood to point again, and then to start across the dusty field toward the rocks among which I waited.

I put a shot a yard or so before her. She stopped. The men behind her fired punily at nothing from the shelter of her shed. I checked its window and doorway and saw the other whore, wrapped in a coarse gray blanket, peering at my rocks. She held a telescope, and she called to the one with the rifle. I moved the sight to her again and watched her come toward me.

"Please," I said. She could not have heard me. "I beg you," I said.

She strode forward, and then she stopped to look down, as if for the first time aware that she was naked in the dust of her field.

She called to me—in the direction, at any rate, in which I lay from her—and I tried to read her lips. She called the same words again. *This is my house,* I thought she said, or *This is my home—get out.* I could not tell, but I knew that she was challenging me. And I did feel challenged.

She was a gallant, redheaded, absolutely naked whore who was armed with a heavy weapon that she hefted with authority.

I said, once more, "Oh, please."

I was watching as she called again, and watching still as she came closer, and because I had not fired again, the men at the house—I could tell from the sound of their shooting—had at last emerged. I put another shot into the earth near her and decided that it was time, at last, to go. I had stayed there far too long, enchanted by this wonderful woman I would have given much to greet, and to shake by the hand. I did not consider her as a partner in bed, I think, because she was more of a man than any of us men on her farm.

She walked closer and at last I could hear what she said: "All you can do is kill me, serpent. This is my *home.*"

She was not a silent soldier, I thought, but she was as gallant a foe as a man could have. I stood, in violation of my central tactic, as if we fought in a duel. She knew to react at once, lifting the rifle to her small shoulder and taking aim. I cut her down and loaded behind the rock, then stood to watch her through the sight. A number of shots from the house went no place near me. She was missing most of her throat and all of her chest: I had not wanted to damage her face. I kept the sight there, and I looked at her cheeks and nose and lips, but they were part now of a corpse; she was only meat now and her heroism would be kept, from here on, inside the man who had killed her.

I covered the house. One of them scuttled back, but the other paused, and I shot him on the spot. There were only a Rebel and a whore left to contend with, and I decided to risk open movement. I walked at a good marching pace up the low hill the way I had come. Every now and again, I stopped and turned to face the sheds and scrutinized the land with my telescope. If they were lucky, they'd be fucking each other, I thought, because there was nothing left to do in the face of so much slaughter except, of course, wail at the skies—where the vulture, I remembered, was poised.

"I love when you do that," Jessie said.

"You must tell no one."

"We are our secret," she said, wiping the tears at my eyes. "We are our good secret. No one knows about us except that you prefer me and will pay most dearly, and that I am pleased to be preferred." She lay against me now, her head on my chest. I could feel her breath against my breast as she spoke. "And within that secret," she said.

"Pardon?"

"The other one. About the poor children," she said.

"Of course. I have our man, and I am laying the ground."

"While *doing* a lay. A double lay, then, and one of them not for profit."

"But he has latterly had a death in the family, and I must be tentative. But I have not forgotten the children. And I wonder if the recent death will not be powerful motive for him to lend us a hand."

She moved her own hand and cradled me in it, cock and balls at rest. It was as if she held the whole of me.

Uncle Sidney Cowper, I came to realize, had admirably demonstrated the kind of discipline and restraint about which he had preached. This came to me of a wet, cold afternoon in my fourteenth year when I was out and at my chores—weather was no obstacle to the performance of duty, Uncle Sidney preached, and besides, we did need the wood to warm the house. I was splitting some limbs of birch to use as kindling in our kitchen stove and was concentrating on the blade of the axe in the greasy, chilly rain. I brought in an armful and was about to go out for another, pausing to filch a carrot from the simmering kettle of soup on the stove, when I heard a kind of snuffling from the pantry. It occurred to me that something large, say a raccoon, had got into our stores. At the door, just slightly ajar, I paused, for the snuffling had been joined by a lighter sound, as of panting, and it sounded more like a person, and less like a raccoon. I went to one knee at the door and listened, pressing my ear to the space between the door and the jamb.

The lighter sound became "He . . . will . . . hear," whispered in my mother's voice.

The deeper snuffling was, of course, the energetic gasping for breath as he grasped for my mother of Uncle Sidney Cowper.

I do not know what caused me to stand and kick the door shut, but I did, still dripping in my soaked canvas coat, before I went outside and set to splitting thick, heavy sections of birch. It was pleasing that no thoughts came into my head or, if they did, were instantly banished by my care with the heavy axe and my concentration on meeting the top of each section with the wet, sharp blade. When I heard the door from the mudroom off the kitchen slam to, I knew to stand and catch my breath. I held the axe across my body with both hands, and I was uncertain about my intentions with it.

This thought seemed to catch Uncle Sidney, for he stopped in his progress toward me and studied his nephew, but then, to his credit, he came up within inches of me and looked into my eyes. He wrapped the skirts of his long coat beneath his legs, and he sat on the chopping block. I stepped back a pace, whether for the easier placement of a blow or for safety's sake, I do not know.

Water poured off the shakes of the roof and into a couple of barrels, while the wind blew rain upon us and the spruces about the house nodded under the onslaught. My uncle said, "So what do you say, Billy? Was the slamming necessary? A gentleman doesn't slam doors. Nor does he invade the privacy of others. Don't pout, son."

"Uncle, would you not call me 'son'?"

"It's your dear father's prerogative, eh?"

I didn't know what *prerogative* was, but I nodded.

"Understood. Next?"

"Pardon, sir?"

"What's on your mind, Billy? Come along."

"Why . . . my *mother*, Uncle Sidney."

"Yes. We were conferring, she and I." He stared hard into my eyes, defying me to comment. "On matters of great moment."

"I don't think my father would approve, Uncle Sidney. I—may I speak frankly, sir?"

"As I've taught you, son—ah: lad. As you know to do. With courtesy."

"Sir, I don't think it's right, you making the beast with my mother."

I waited for the blow. None came. He smiled. He reached out his hand and cupped my thigh from behind. He kneaded gently and most intimately. He said, "I don't actually care very much which one of you it is," he said. "It could be you. It could be her. I'm pleased to let you choose which one." His hand came around to the front of my thigh and began to climb. I stepped back and raised the axe to my shoulder. "There are virtues to each," he said, smiling as if she had just set down his evening meal.

I said the only thought I had: "Do you mean, sir, that my mother is . . . with you because she's keeping you off *me?*"

His smile went wider, his eyes disappeared between the folds of skin beneath and around them, and then the smile faded and his eyes returned. He studied me, and I knew he knew me very well. He was certain, I thought, that I would permit her to sacrifice the wholeness of her intimate being to preserve the wholeness of mine.

I lifted the axe from my shoulder and my body tensed. So did his. He stood as I raised the axe above my head, and he moved backward, straddling the block, as I brought it down. He skipped backward, nimbly for such a large man, and I missed by him little. The blade was buried deep in the chopping block.

"You might have hurt me!" he said, his feelings apparently damaged though his body was sadly unscarred.

"I regret that I did not, Uncle Sidney."

"I suppose you do. I'm going back inside, Billy. Your mother and I must . . . talk. Why don't you stay out here and split more wood. Say for another half an hour? You won't get too wet, I pray."

He could dominate me physically, unless I killed him while he slept or while his back was turned. He would have me in a fashion I had heard about from boys in the district, but which I didn't entirely understand. I had to push and pry to get the axe out of the block, and I worked at that as I thought. Or he would have my mother—I again heard the snuffling of his breath, and the sound of my mother panting. I would have to kill him, I thought. I could not permit my mother to give herself to him, in violation of my father's memory and of herself.

Though she had not been weeping. I was certain of that. She had been concerned for their privacy, I thought, hearing again the way she said her concerns that someone might hear.

I would have to kill him, I thought again.

We sat in Madison Square and watched as a pointy-snouted street dog stalked doves. M was to imminently depart for his office, and I was coming off a night's wandering, intending to walk downtown with him in the direction of Mr. Lapham Dumont, whose services I had to enlist. He ate a small green apple that was sour-tasting, he said around small nibbles of the tight flesh of the fruit, as traffic pounded and whinnied and rattled on the stones where Broadway and Fifth Avenue crossed, the western street going east and the eastern going west. The island there was a cinched-in belt, a kind of waist of an X, a collection point for streams of commerce and conveyance and noise.

"Dr. Osgood read from 15th Corinthians," he said, as if to the apple. "Mal's company of volunteers was present, a good number of them, strapping and sorrowing lads. They carried his coffin from the house to the funeral cars—black vehicles, several black horses, though a few of them were chestnut; none were white. A white horse, I think, would have been frightening somehow. They first walked through the hall, single file, orderly, attentive, somber. They looked on Mal and then passed through. They returned again to take his coffin up. They, alive, in their uniforms, and he, so dead, in his. Elizabeth had dressed him. I know not how. The wound was so apparent, despite everyone's best efforts. Such wounds, you know, are taken up by those who live. Do you not think so? You have had experience—"

"In wounds? Oh, yes."

"No, Bill. In surviving the wounded dead and assuming their wounds. On the body of the soul, I say. Am I wrong?"

"No. I remember a man who was shot in the lungs. Whenever I cough, I think of his blood coming out between his lips."

"A fallen comrade," he said.

I made no reply.

"He was a boy. He was dressed as a man. Why not? He wished to be one. He even wore the ceremonial sword."

"They buried him with his sword?"

"Do you not think it fitting?"

"Of course. And his pistol? Was he buried wearing that?"

He turned to gaze on my mask and then at my eyes. Even as his vision was concentrated upon me, he seemed to me, as always, to be staring in more than out. "He wears only the sword. The coroner's jury have the pistol still." He waited for me to speak, but I did not. "You should have seen it. And you would have, leastwise, been invited to, on the strength of our deep acquaintanceship. It was only family there, you see. They carried him from the hearse to the cemetery ground. I must report myself composed. I think that Lizzie and I were both composed. Although when he was lowered in, tucked away for the last time in his boy's life, and the sound issued of earth as it fell upon the coffin, and Stanwix shuddered as if struck by lightning or some other force invisible, I wished to gnash and wail at the skies."

"Is that where you would look?"

"For what?"

"For God."

"I look nowhere for God. If he be manifested, I will see. If he be considered, it will be within my speculations." He nibbled at the core of the apple and tossed it to the dog, who ran from it, then ran back toward it, sniffed it cautiously, and chewed it down. "I regard my surviving son, a stripling boy, who cannot, often, hear. So perhaps I will learn to *listen* for God. Perhaps if I hear, Stanny will as well. Will we walk, then?" His eyes were wet, and he turned, so that I saw his back as we left the park; he was in hiding, behind himself.

I said, as we were closer to his striking off for the district office on the North River, and as I would turn toward the Exchange and, nearby, the office of Lapham Dumont, "We must protect the children, mustn't we?"

He stopped his long stride and lifted his head. "From what?"

"From the loss of their youth. From, in a case I know, actual slavery."

"To whom?"

"Agriculturists."

"Where?"

"South. Deep South."

"They are Negro youth?"

"Near infants, some of them."

"Whom we might rescue?"

I nodded.

"I would save a young life or two," he said.

"We might speak of it again. But it might serve the children were we to do so in confidence. *Entre-nous,* as they say."

"Confidence is my game," he said. As he heard his own words, his face brightened, and he smiled. "Confidence," he said.

"More on it later?" I said.

He clapped me across the shoulders with great power. "More," he said, as if someone were pouring him a drink.

I walked the length of the narrow second-story office that was shared by traders like Dumont who also shared clerical assistance and runners. He was in a room made of wooden half-walls with frosted glass from, say, the waist to just above the head of the average man. One might have the illusion of privacy if not the privacy itself. He sat in a wooden chair at his desk and opposite was a client's wooden chair. There were few books and no pictures. Light was from the gas fixtures suspended from the ceiling above each little office. He pushed his chair back as I stepped in and sat.

"No," I said, as if to the dog in the park, "you stay."

"It's useless," he whispered. "I'm in arrears. I haven't the money."

"Yet," I said.

"Of course." He had his gray handkerchief out, and he rubbed it on his face, then dried his hands in it. His red face shone, and his nose seemed lighted from within. "I *will* have your money. It's an obligation," he said. "Hate it though I might. The skins of bears. How *could* I?"

I permitted the mask to regard him. I compelled him, with its unreadable stare, I hammered him down until he was impaled in his seat. I waited seconds more. "The question," I said in a low, level voice, "is how *will* you?"

"Will what? That is: will I what? Do what?"

"Assist me."

"In what endeavor, sir?"

"In none about which you need to know or, indeed, *will* know. I require from you a manifest, an order for carting, and a receipt. Don't trouble yourself in dating the documents, since I will act, in this instance, as your clerk."

"Manifest of what? For what? Who to? Why?"

"The cargo will consist of whatever might come in tun or half-tun barrels."

He lifted his eyes to stare at the mask. "And what will you be placing in the barrels?"

"There might be nothing in them. There will, in all probability, *be* no barrels. That is not your concern. Yours is to produce the papers I require, signed by yourself."

"What protects me, Bartholomew?"

"I'll protect you, Dumont. Just as I have done."

"From who did you ever protect me?"

"William Bartholomew. He is an acid-etched man of measureless cruelty. A welsher needs protecting from a man like that. He would as soon tear your kidneys out and grill them with bacon for his dinner. I have it on authority he has forborne from devouring whatever's edible in you only because he wants you alive to pay your obligation to him. I believe this. Do you believe this?"

He nodded his long neck, his bony head. "A good deal of it I do. I do."

"Good. You sound married to my proposal," I said.

He nodded again, this time silently, as he rubbed at his face with his knuckly, long fingers.

"The paperwork," I said.

"Agreed. Do I need to shake your hand?"

I smiled. He could not see me. I stood and said, "Within the week, then?"

"Today," he said. "Tomorrow. As you wish."

"The money shortly thereafter?"

"That's as I can."

"It's as I say."

"The money thereafter. Rest assured."

"Yes, Lapham."

He wiped at his face with his handkerchief, and I left before he blew his nose.

Someone was hurting a child, though it might have been a woman I heard—perhaps a small woman, I thought. Over the noises of the city's dawn, as wagons slowly rolled on wheels that splintered upon the cobbles under the burden of hides, beef halves, dead poultry buried in ice, fresh flowers for the breakfast tables of the wealthy, or the furniture from households in arrears, I heard the steady cry of someone small, with a high voice, being hurt. It was remarkably regular, and soon enough it became one of the many sounds—you could even hear the doves coo,

and the scolding by dirty sparrows—that constituted the calling awake
of those who knew how to sleep.

Oh and *Oh* and *Oh.*

No, I thought: a child. I could not discern whether it was a response
to hard blows, or the prodding of some instrument—fire poker, knife,
the buckle of a belt—but it was regular and forceful, for the sounds were
clearly part of an expulsion of breath, a response to a shock.

An engine at the New York and Harlem freight depot on White Street
gave out a huffy demand, and I waited for the clash of metal that would
signal cars being joined or pulled separate. I kept my eyes closed and kept
my arms crossed as I lay on the cot. I thought of Malcolm lying in his
uniform, sword at his side and apparently not armed for his journey with
my revolver. It was an investment, but I would not mind its return. It had
traveled with me, after all, up and down several states along our
seaboard. It had saved my life and it had cost the lives of others. Seamen
and their scrimshaw and clasp knives and trunks: shooters and their
weapons.

The crying had grown ragged, the noises breaking into pieces as the
one who uttered them also must break. *Oh-uh, Oh-uh.* One of the manufactories shrieked its whistle to signal in the workers for the day. Now it
was *Uh* and then a silence, then *Uh.* Whoever administered the punishment was growing tired, I thought, and was pausing between blows. Of
course, it was also possible the child was dying. As the small noise among
a hundred loud ones became more and more noticeable for its absence,
I thought: unconscious or dead. I thought: That's a nice bit of luck for
someone.

Then I thought of Uncle Sidney Cowper, who would let me choose
which of us, my mother or I, would be snug harbor to his needs. It was
at this time in my life that I dreamed of his notebook and found it in the
woodpile and thought to incur his obligation by returning it. I learned
something about transactions, and it has stood me in good stead all my
life: Know the rules; do not trade with hope, but rather, if possible, with

advantage harvested and, like the fruits in glass my mother stored every summer, put by for a need. To wit: I should have read his entries and labored to decipher their use by me to keep him off us. Instead, I ambled and prattled and offered and smiled. He thanked me, but the violence with which he pulled the leather notebook from my outstretched hand instructed me that I had just let go of something useful. A resource is to be cherished: William Bartholomew on M. And watch it now come to fruit.

I went to college at fifteen, thanks to Uncle Sidney Cowper, and was glad to go at that age in order to escape him. I was alert and lonely and wretched, and I found difficulty in enjoying my few triumphs—the company of Melanie Levi, the daughter of a baker in New Haven who taught me French, both language and deed; my ability to tell my instructors what they wished to hear—because I thought, whether in the icy solitude of my small room or in the company of my pimpled, braying classmates, of Uncle Sidney Cowper atop my mother. And the more I learned from Melanie, the more my *cauchemars* grew detailed and more prurient, more fascinating and therefore more frightening. Soon, I frightened myself, for the vision of him tupping her was the least of my awful constructions. I did not know whom I blamed the more, my predatory uncle or myself, who chose to leave my mother in his hands.

It is the door, I told myself.

I had wakened to the sound of my panting, to the sound of my voice going *Oh* and *Oh*. It is someone at the door, I told myself, as if to calm a child.

I kept the discarded cracked haft of a street worker's shovel as a life preserver, which I leaned against the wall beside the door. Squinting against the day's light that filtered into my room, I seized the oak shaft and unlocked my door.

He made an inarticulated noise, a cry of fright and pity. I felt my hand go up to cover what I could of my face, for his sake and mine. I backed away, cursing like a wrangler of horses for my having gone to the door in such a daze of nightmare and fatigue that I forgot to don my mask. I kept the haft in my hand as I grasped for the mask.

"Wait," I warned him. "Wait at the door."

Then, covered, I turned to him again and found him in the doorway, his own hand at his face as if to imitate me of seconds before. "Billy," he said in a familiar voice. "Billy, I'm so sorry."

His hair was a wiry dark halo. I said, "Sam Mordecai. Now it's all right. You can look now."

He slowly dropped his arm, too long for the brown serge sleeve of his suit coat, and he slowly opened his eyes. "No," he said, closing them again, "no, it isn't all right." He took a breath and opened his eyes. "How it must have hurt beneath those bandages. How terrible, Billy."

"I dreamed about you," I said. "And here you are. I read your coverage of the suicide. In Boston?"

He nodded.

"And your memoir of the War?"

"I'm learning patience," he said.

I beckoned him in and pulled a chair to. He obediently sat. "You'll pardon the nightshirt," I said, "but I rise late and go late to my bed. You'll wait while I dress? And tell me, as I do, how you found me."

He had lost a good deal of weight and his face seemed longer, boyish still but also more muscled and more worked upon; as I knew, he had seen a great deal in the War. His dark, liquid eyes were not still.

"I found you by wandering about and saying your name and pointing to my face," he said, licking his lips and crossing and recrossing his arms. His energy was aboil. I thought him too uncontemplative, too keenly physical, to be a writer, and I thought it a piece of good luck because I wished him well. "I remembered your vow to become wealthy, so I asked questions of men in banks and at the gaming rooms on Broadway and at the Exchange. At each, you were known. No one knew where you lived, however." He took from his breast pocket a slender notebook in black leather, and he fanned through pages to find his notes. "Assuming, then, that you wished to be lost, I thought to discern what woods you would take to, in lying low. It was always your way. You always went for the thickets, the brambles at the bottom or the topmost parts of the leafiest trees. You were always, I realized, in hiding. Never did I think of you behind a mask, but even that makes sense."

"Sam, you needn't trouble yourself to make sense of me. I prefer, in fact, not to be made sense of." I was struck by a consideration: "Sam, you haven't hunted me down to put me in your book?"

"Of course not," he said. I thought that he lied. He was on the trail of something, and I was included in his hunt. His jaw muscles worked, and he compelled his arms to stillness, his legs to be crossed one over the other, further wrinkling his crumpled brown suit. "But I *am* composing the memoir of which I spoke to you. It has taken a different turning, although it makes use of my experience at war. I read a book of poetry, poems about the War by someone outside its immediate experience."

"*Battle-Pieces*," I said. "He writes so many poems. I have to confess to you that I find his meter too irregular for my crude taste."

"Yes, you with your New Haven degree."

"I have learned that having it pays nothing."

"What pays, then?"

"Profit."

"This fellow reaps no profit. I know little of poetry. But, at the end of his book, he writes a commentary, I suppose you might call it. Prose, Billy. He's a straight-talking man on the Negro question. And about not . . . hating."

"The South?"

"Yes."

"After years of laboring to kill them."

"And them to kill us. He is a complex man."

"Sam, he's a Republican, and that's their line, and that's their Administration giving him his badge and his paycheck and his pension." His face fell, and something about his dedication to the man I would employ brought my anger up. "So you found a whisper about the death of his son and you wrote a column lamenting it. You even wrote about his participation in that game played with a small ball—"

"Base ball, they call it. Yes. You read my column?" His face went boyish as he smiled his pleasure. "You see?"

"What's that, Sam?"

"How necessary it is for a writer to be read? You see how foolish and full of moonbeams I grow when you say you've seen my words?"

"And you're hunting him to see about a writer no one reads. The death provoked your interest in the life, in other words. Words again."

"All words, Billy. All of it's words."

"Words may convey dollars," I said.

"Ask the man without a son," he argued.

"He has another son left to him. Stanwix." Sam found a pencil and wrote down notes. "As I understand it, something about his older brother's death has made him go deaf."

"You see? And he cannot hear *words*, this son of a writer. It is, indeed, a story. It is a large story. How the United States will silence the voice of intellect, crush philosophical speculation, and stamp out the embers of our national literature. Have you read Charles Dickens on America?"

"I confess to not having read him on wherever it is he lives—the British Isles?" I was lacing my boots, but I looked up to smile for his enthusiasm. He could not tell. He looked distraught at my having not read Mr. Dickens. I made a note to read something by him, though my reading these days consisted of the newspapers and the news, in Mr. Morse's code, on the telegraph in the Savarin downstairs in the Equitable Building: the rise in corn, the fall in pork bellies. From under the mask, I said, "Take your ease, Sam. Take a breath. Take your time. We'll go to a coffeehouse and eat a breakfast and you'll tell me where you've been and what you've done. For how long will your editor permit you to remain in the city?"

"Jack Herman is a scrupulously intelligent man who knows what's news. He detests speculation, and he loves hard fact. He'll give me a few days at the Astor. If need be, I'll pay for more from my pocket. Or borrow it from you." He grinned, and the grin grew wider. "'The city,' you said." He was beaming now. "As if there were none other. You are a New Yorker, Billy."

"It's the capital of commerce, or soon will be."

"And you're a captain of commerce."

"Or soon will be."

"I love seeing you, Billy. I hate the damage done you by the Rebel marksman, but I am so pleased to be with my comrade again. You must permit me to be of service."

We shook hands. His was atremble, and damp. I said, "And you me."

"I fear," he said, "that I will burst into tears or burst into song, and neither is a pretty prospect. You know the poor fellow. Tell me how you know him. Tell me stories about his state of neglect, and I'll grow somber and professional."

"He is a badge-wearing deputy inspector for the Revenue Service of the Port of New York. He carries government locks, and he impounds things, I gather, if he thinks it important to keep them from coming ashore. He drinks a good deal—too much, I would say. His relations with his family strike me as tense, to say the best of it. Now, of course, with his son dead, who knows? Perhaps the boy was Isaac to his Abraham."

Sam looked up from writing his notes. "But the Lord delivered Isaac. He sent the angel to tell the father he might let the son live."

"I do not claim the boy was sacrificed to the father's God."

"I believe you implied it, Billy."

"You know, I believe that you're right, Sam."

He had been writing in his notebook as he stood. His face was clenched and his eyes were active, but it was not his face I was drawn to. Although his notebook was of black leather and Uncle Sidney Cowper's brown, I was reminded of my uncle and of how I had dreamed my way to his notebook, and how I had dreamed of Sam. It is said that a successful trader knows to predict events. He may as well dream them, I thought. But then I remembered how, in my dream, someone was cruelly hurt, over and again.

Sam said, "What, Billy? You stand so still."

"I was thinking, for some reason, of my uncle's sorry death."

"A recent loss?"

"No, you would have to call it a profit," I said.

I led him from my room, through the dark hallway, and down to the street. He stood back against the grimy brick wall of our tenement to observe: a child with a hoop; three stalking, sneering boys of nearly twelve, their teeth yellow in their gray faces; a tot of no more than three in diapers who stood as his mother, a whore from the next street over, tried to trade her favors for something from the fishmonger's wagon at the curbing. The sky was the color of soot, and flakes of it seemed to be drifting like coal-stained snow. The air smelled of heat and of metal, of the putrefaction of flesh. Sam's eyes were huge. Mine, perhaps from the dirty air, were smarting, and I was noticing the edges of the eyeholes in the mask, something I did only when very fatigued; I knew that I would spend the day in watching the edges of the holes as much as I would see what they were turned to.

In their dim flat on White Street, toward Broadway, I found the Pastrowycz family at their breakfast, and I asked Mrs. Pastrowycz to permit me to give her son, Benny, some money to run a note to my Negro friend, Adam. I did not know whether Adam could read, but I knew that he was intelligent and would find someone, if he could not, to read out my request. She went back to frying something fatty for their meal while the three daughters sat staring at their platters. I frightened them, but nothing frightened Benny, who knew the neighborhood and who knew how to keep himself safe. He was a sweet fellow, chubby at the cheek and sturdy of chest and shoulder, with hair the color of sand, and pale skin. He reminded me a little of Burton, the private in our detachment to whom fell the wrangling duties and who sometimes made a kind of fried bread dipped in egg, when we could forage eggs, on which he poured a little sorghum molasses for a treat.

"See it into his hands, Benny. Go now, for you'll have to trace him to the docks if you miss him. You'll do that? *And* take this other one to the North River. You understand the place?"

"Easy," Benny said.

To his mother: "May he take the message to the river?"

She looked at me and said, "No monkey fools?"

"Monkey *shines*, Ma," Benny said.

She smiled, and her gold tooth gleamed. She sewed at home while her husband was off digging sewers for the corporation of the City of New York. She minded the children in a hard place, yet she always smiled. I made the motion of blowing her a kiss as Benny left, and she did as ever: grinned her gold tooth and waved back.

"Lovely woman," Sam said as he stood in the street to make a note.

"Then why not omit her? Why condemn her to be captured behind your notations?"

"Billy, I propose to tell her *story*, not condemn her."

"You can take that up with your author. He receives the second message."

"What is it you're arranging?"

"A courtesy to you. A business arrangement for me. An expedition for us all to the Tenderloin. How do you feel on the question of steamed potatoes quartered and then fried with onions to flavor a small steak?"

CHAPTER 5

THE THREE OF US DINED AT CHEERIE'S, AND DURING the meal I saw Sam's hand stray often toward the breast pocket of his mud-colored suit. That was because he wished to make a note, I knew, and I felt a cruel pleasure that civility, if only for a time, prevented him from writing down what his idol so memorably said. Clearly, I had not, at the time, understood the need to write down life or state the having witnessed it.

As the veal was brought to us, Sam said, "Will you have some of this elixir of logwood?" He held up the bottle of red wine.

M looked at the bottle and looked at Sam. "You have read it, then?"

"The masquerade of the Confidence Man? Yes, sir, I have read it."

"A book," its author said to me, "in which I name such an elixir."

"Of course," I lied.

"A great book," Sam said. "A philosophical argumentation."

"As usual," its author said, "a matter of an argument between one man and nobody else. It takes two parties to argue, and whether the party of the second part—those who are *not* the author—be one or one thousand, that party must be a party to the contention. Otherwise, you have the lone author saying to the sky or the loamy earth beneath him, 'Given: That man is magnificent.' Or: 'That man is a dog.' " He sat back and leaned back his head and laughed, his dark mouth open and not emitting a sound. He then shook his head and leaned forward to address his viands. Sam looked at him, then reached for his notebook, then brought his hand back around to his wineglass.

I cut my meat into very small bits and brought them on my fork, one at a time, underneath the hem of the gray silk veil.

"May I ask," I said between bites, "how Elizabeth fares?"

"Lizzie," he sighed. He turned to Sam. "My son," he said, "is recently dead."

"I am so aggrieved on your account," Sam said. "I wrote of the matter. In the *Advertiser*?"

M set his implements down. He rubbed at his beard and then tugged it, then tugged it again. "You are the gentleman who wrote of my Malcolm's staying out late?"

Sam said, "It was known to many."

"Needed it be said? And how late? And how often? And why a matter of concern? To Lizzie? To me? To the both? To the readers in Boston who do not read me but do read *of* me?"

"It is history, recorded and observed, sir."

"And it needs to be said?"

"I do need generally to say it, sir. I believe it ought to be."

"Sharper than a serpent's tooth," he murmured, pulling down his whiskers. "And why do you ask in your paper how Malcolm came by the pistol? Should he not have had one, he a military man? Your article seems to suggest an impropriety. Should we have prevented him from arming himself? Is it now that soldiers of the National Guard ride into danger unprotected and unarmed? There had been rumors of their riding into danger in the West. Now I sit at my desk and, as I work, I look up at its bookcase, and on the shelves, behind the glass doors, I see recollections of the War. Each is by a military commander. Each makes no mention of casting aside weaponry but, rather, of gathering together all that money may buy or that may be impounded or borrowed.

"And is there some speculation that something was said that night, at the door, at the late hour, by my wife, who admitted him to the house? Or that something may have been said by me early in the day or in the week or month before his late arrival, or even afterward, through the locked door to his room?"

Sam looked miserable. "Sir," he said, "about the weapons: My editor thought it required saying, and so I said it. He is, if you know our paper, keen on the matter of civilians handing over their arms. I meant nothing subversive by it. I was pained by your pain, and still am. In no manner am I qualified to judge you as man or as parent to a son. I regard you too highly ever to trifle with your private feelings. I am grateful to receive their fruits, in your work, and I sorrow for you, and it is all."

"Sam is your name?"

"Yes, sir. Sam Mordecai."

"Yes," he said. He put his fingers to his eyes and rubbed gently at the closed lids. I have never been in the presence of someone whose eyes seemed so uncomfortable. When he had finished rubbing, they looked threaded through with bloody vessels, and almost unseeing. His face wore a bland expression from that moment through much of the night. "Mordecai, you say?"

"Yes," Sam said warily.

M placed his hand above Sam's dinner plate. "Shake, then. We may speak of it again. We may not. But we'll act as friends. It may be that we'll *be* friends. We'll be civil, though. A night is a long time to be together if we aren't."

I thought that Sam might weep for relief and for pleasure. "I'd always do my best for you, sir," he whispered.

M looked in my direction and raised his brows, then shook his head. "I look at *you*, shipmate, and I see the screen that is set over everything."

"Pleased to be of some use, then," I said, but more bitterly than I intended. He sat back as if I had gestured with menace. "I am being humorous," I said.

"You are not, I think, although I think you mean to be. It is my discourtesy. A man should not be employed by another as his emblem. Listen to us, then. We're all apologizing to one another for the wrongs in the world and the flaws in heaven. We'll have all the ills of the universe renounced by the time Mr. Cheerie brings us pies and puddings. And a tot or two more of this wine. We'll toast to right navigation, shall we? To the poor fellows who forgot how to put a bight in a hawser, or who forgot how to snug a hawser on a bollard. Their coal barge," he said, shaking his head, "drifted loose. It happens. It shouldn't. And the tide met the current in a grievous chop. And over went a small mountain of coal. And down went the barge, for having shipped too much river aboard. And now we've a tidy navigational hazard on the waterway. It's like making your way upriver in what we think of as actual life," he said.

I waited for him to explain, but he drank at his wine.

"Do you know the Tenderloin?" I asked him, pouring out the last of the bottle.

"I have been to places on the western side of the city," he said. "It is not where I would take Elizabeth and the girls for a stroll. Do you mean brothels and gambling dens, dance halls, saloons?"

"I do. And the remnants of Africa."

"But that was in the lower end of the city," he said. "Canal Street, Grand Street, am I right? Laurens? Thompson? It's all but disappeared."

"Because of the Loin."

"I have seen a number of dark faces there."

"White men pay to have black women," I said.

"Better than the old way," he said, "where they paid to *own* black women, who then gave birth to black women they might have."

The corner of Sam's notebook was in his hand.

"I am told that you are moderate on the Negro question."

"Oh? Moderate? I am not for any more war, if that's what you mean. Nor, though, am I—nor should I be!—moderate on the matter of the holding of slaves. It's the holding of grudges I would warn against, either side, either army, either color. Now is the time to get the black man what we may without requiring the South to carry it to him on bare feet. I said in a tale of mine once that the shadow of the Negro is a long one."

"Babo!" Sam said.

He reached to pat Sam's arm in acknowledgment. Sam's sallow face began to glow, though all the while his jaw muscles worked and his eyes, as if on mechanical swivels, moved from M to me and back.

"We are in for a difficult time," he said.

Sam said, "You mean tonight?"

"And tomorrow, shipmate. Many tomorrows from now." His focus disappeared, and his eyes seemed made of slate, absorbing light and giving little. He might, for all I knew, have been thinking of his son and then of his son, of his daughters, and his baffled, unhappy woman.

Sam had surrendered. His notebook was out, I had watched it move from his inside breast pocket to his hand and then to his lap, where, with a stub of pencil, he scribbled while saying, "Sorry. Very sorry—a moment, if I—"

M did not hear him. I, consulting my watch, declared against dessert and signaled for the bill.

As if waking of a sudden, M smiled his resigned, baffled smile. "So we'll voyage into darkest New York. We'll mingle with the darker brothers." He nodded his head. "I see them daily at the docks, of course. Once," he said, "I shipped with them. I slung a hammock beside theirs. I labored on the decks and in the rigging with them."

Sam, I saw, was racing across his little pages to get it all down. But Adam was waiting outside, I was certain, so I replaced the veil with the mask and I chivvied and prodded until Sam had tucked his notebook away and had hovered, assisting M from his chair, as if he were not more lithe and graceful than Sam himself. Cheerie threw a little salute, and I returned it, then we made our way among the tables and through the frightened or fascinated stares and out to the street where Adam—"You ax"—was waiting as I thought he would be.

He wore a clean, wrinkled shirt with long sleeves and without a collar. It was buttoned at the neck as though the night were cool, whereas it had grown sultry during the day, and occasional thunder scraped across the low clouds that had sealed the city in during the late afternoon. I could not see the clouds, but caught occasional flares of lightning on the edge of my vision against the eyeholes of the mask.

I introduced Adam to the company, and I insisted upon clasping him by the hand. His was as hard and scuffed as lumber. His broad nose and grim mouth, his red-rimmed eyes, which put me in mind of M, and his bulky shoulders and thick thighs made him formidable as, particularly when we entered the Loin, a companion and an escort and something of a guard. He was dressed in cast-off trousers too short for his long legs, and a pair of cracked high shoes that looked uncomfortable as he walked, and yet he commanded respect, I thought; he looked as though he owned the stones on which he trod.

"You have the money I sent."

He nodded. I regarded him, and he me, and finally he said, "Thank you."

"You'll earn it. You understand the errand?"

"Show these gentlemen the sights."

"No, sir. This is not a gentlemen's tour of darkest New York. I meant no humor. I want them to understand what it is to be poor and Negro and to struggle for a life in the city. I do not mean to entertain them."

I heard him expel a breath and then I saw him smile. "I can do that."

"And you will?"

"If that's what you want."

"No. You must want to as well—or at least be *willing* to."

"I am, Mist Bartelmy." M's head turned as Adam said this last. "I said it: You ax. That's what you did, and here I am. No money needed, tell you the truth."

"Thank you, Adam. It should be a transaction, however. One man pays, the other man receives. Done, then?"

He nodded.

I said, "We ought to begin, gentlemen. Westward, then, and down a few streets. I am armed."

Sam held up his notebook, as if it would defend us all.

M said, "I am beyond harming. I need no defense, thank you."

Adam opened his mouth, then closed it, and we wheeled to cross the avenue. "Go ahead," I told him. "Speak if you have words to tell us."

"Sir," he said, "isn't anyone past being harmed. And in the Loin, be thinking of the lion's den. People there, all kinds of colors, they would eat you up and swallow you down."

Sam stood to open his notebook and then catch up.

"You correct me truly, shipmate. It was wishfulness you heard, and sorrow for the self. May we all take care." Nevertheless, he trod on the toes of his boots and then lifted himself into the air to click his feet together and then, with equal grace, walk on.

"This gentleman's a minstrel," Adam said.

Sam made a sound of low pleasure, and he scribbled as he walked.

We entered the gaming house, set behind Seventh Avenue, through an alley off the street. It was narrow, and the bricks of the walls felt moist. Iron fire steps hung halfway down the wall to our left and then stopped: You would have to drop thirty feet, fleeing a fire, and then drive your broken anklebones up and into your shins. The light there was whatever fell from the dark sky or filtered through from the street. Adam opened a low door, perhaps five feet high, and we followed him in. Another door, of normal height, was opposite, in a gaslit vestibule. From outside came a sound as of grunting and then squealing and then a kind of high roar.

I heard M exclaim, and then I heard the squeal. Adam passed me as he returned to the alley, and soon enough he returned to say, "One of those pigs."

"It was a giant hog," M said. "Long and high and vicious."

I had seen them from time to time. Sam, evidently, had not. "Is this a farming district?" he asked Adam.

"No, sir. They eat the refuse behind the houses. They clean the streets."

"Then soil them, I take it," Sam said.

"Nobody thought of that when it started. Now they can't stop 'em, sir."

"Shipmate, you have just heard the story of how nature won't be tampered with or tamed. Great pigs roaming the streets like mako sharks in the sea."

"Like . . . whales," Sam ventured.

No one replied, and we entered the room. It was very long and brilliantly lighted and hot, from the massed bodies at the tables and the bar. Not all the girls were Negro, nor were all the customers white, but it was easy to see that a large measure of appeal was the color of the women's skin; some, like Adam, were dark and they gleamed, while some were almost the color of Jessie—without the lemony glow that colored her, it seemed to me, from within—and others were tan, and even white with a bridge of freckles, often, that shaded the cheeks and the nose. Every one of them was escorted, or embraced, or fondled intimately by a man whose skin and manner were obviously white: They made it clear that they owned, or had recently hired, the darker women whose pleasure it must be to give them pleasure. A very fat and sweating black woman played the piano; at that moment, she gave an expert rendition, I thought, of "When You and I Were Young, Maggie."

I smelled flesh and whiskey and cooked meats, the tallow of candles, hundreds of which bolstered the gas lamps above the huge circular bar. White men with large mustaches served at the bar, peering past its carved decorative lions and gryphons and bunches of grapes. The bar was of a very white marble, as was its rail, as were the decorations in the front of the bar. It was not possible to speak and be easily heard, so we stood in silence. We were not the only group of observers—each onlooker was white, I thought—beneath that vaulted, carved ceiling with its massed, glass-globed lights. Smoke hung between the lights and us, and it eddied and swayed as doors in the walls opened and closed.

Sometimes waiters—again, white men—entered, bearing circular trays of food, or bottles of wine or whiskey. Sometimes one of several black men in excellent suits entered or departed. I could tell that they were armed because their suits were fitted close to the body, and their pistols made a bulge. Once, a door across the room, past the gaming tables at which black men dealt to the gamblers white and black, opened out. One of the armed men came forward, followed by a child. He stopped for her to catch up with him once the door had closed. She took his arm with the gravity of an adult, and they made their way in our direction. She was perhaps eleven or twelve, I thought, with skin the color of new saddle leather. She wore kohl or some dark substance about her eyes, which were wide and striking. She wore rouge upon her lips. Her hair, very long and curly, was done up in a chignon held in place by ivory combs. What breasts she had were displayed in the gown cut square and low at the bosom and which went almost to the floor. Her escort wore a half smile, as if he enjoyed conveying such a striking attraction as this child.

When they passed near to us, in the fug of smoke and skin, in the loud chatter and the tinkle of piano keys, I made my way closer to M and said, "Watch this now."

He had been watching her, I saw. Who would not?

The escort halted behind a man at the farthest table, where only two men gambled, apparently against one another. No one dealt them hands; it was a matter of direct competition, the earnings of which would be shaved for a payment to the house. A broad-backed fellow in a dove-colored suit turned as his shoulder was tapped. His face was pale and rectangular, expressionless. He had no hair on his head and none I could see on his face. He gleamed in the smoke-cloaked lighting of the room.

The black escort handed over his charge. She curtsied. The bald man stroked her back and bottom. He moved his hand up to the back of her neck and bent her forward; she went where she was pushed—upon her knees, beside him. Instead of stiffening or remonstrating, she placed her little hand upon his thigh, then leaned to place her lips beside her fingers, then straightened on her knees again as her possessor for the evening returned to his cards. The Negro escort turned in our direction and, seeing us absorbed, smiled broadly, nodded his head, and walked toward and then past us.

"She is a night sister? That small child!" M turned away from the sight, but then he turned back.

Sam said, "I have seen it elsewhere. I have seen it in Baltimore."

Adam said, "People need to live. That's a way she can live."

M said, "It is the kind of moment life gives us when it laughs. It is the choosing without choice. A rich meagerness, that."

Sam was at his notebook again. I noticed M notice.

I said, "She is a kind of slave. She will earn some money and wear a shimmering gown. But she's enslaved. Imagine this in South Carolina, in Georgia, or in Florida."

"Down there," Adam said, "she works in the fields."

"As a slave?" M asked.

Adam snorted derisively, then remembered himself. He simply said, "Is she black?"

Outside, as we departed, Sam pointed out a great pile of turds.

"Wild street hog," M said.

"Or politician," I suggested.

Adam took us, then, farther along the alley instead of back to the avenue. It crossed another alley, which ran, at right angles, between the buildings for the length of the block. It was lighted by the lights within the flats that looked out, from right and left, upon each other. The smell of sewage was high and harsh and everywhere, for at our feet was the ditch into which the privies poured. Children keened here, and men shouted inarticulately, in either their pleasure or their rage.

A woman cried, "I can't. I can't. I can't. I can't." I heard no one reply. "I can't," she wailed. "Lord and Jesus O'mighty, I cannot." Then she was still, and I heard Sam hiss, as if struck, for she began again: "I can't. I can't. Oh, please to Jesus, no, I can't."

"You may hear her all over town," I whispered to M, "and she will be white as well as black. But here," I said, "she preponderates."

"It is the universal affliction of the Negro," he said. "I understand."

"The woman who cannot," I said, "may soon be setting fire to her infant and herself. Or drowning them both in the river. Or slitting the baby's throat and then her own. It is the despair. Could one envision one's child, the baby girl, in that room of carnivores? You are the father to girls."

"What are their names, sir?"

"I am not the subject of *reports*," M said.

"Of course not," Sam said, "and I beg your pardon."

"There are carnivores and then there are carnivores, young journalist."

"Oh, I can't," she cried.

Adam said to me, "We stay?"

"It's difficult for you," I said. "Of course. I regret it. No. Let's move on."

But Sam and M were halted at an opened window and were staring in. Adam and I walked back to them. In the grimy light of the alley, and even in the dim light that ran at us in waves of odor—spoiled food, dirty flesh—it was difficult to see. I leaned over Sam's shoulder while Adam remained behind us. A very small child, perhaps an infant, was screaming and screaming as its parents stood above it where it lay in a blanket in a box. The man of the household, naked except for his shoes, grimly held before him, as if he had struck something out of sight and was prepared to strike it again, a black iron skillet. The woman was lifting the child. When she touched the baby's face, she recoiled and held her hand up: bloody from a wound on the child.

"Rat bite," Adam said.

It had been this woman we had heard, for she cried it again: "I can't no more. I can't. I can't. I can't!"

Adam walked away as I turned to address him, and I followed. He was weeping. I said, "Go home."

He shook his head. "I made the arrangement, Mist Bartelmy. I gave you my word."

"Poor man. Can I break our compact for you?"

Adam shook his head. "But it is painful, sir," he said. I clasped his shoulder and he said, "It is painful to me."

I led him off, down the alley, and soon they followed us, and we came out near Eleventh Avenue, hard by a railroad depot. "We could dive back in," I said.

"I've enough," Sam told me. "I'm full of misery for the night."

M said, "Yet we have barely touched upon it. They must live there. I know what you have in mind, Billy, but I would remind you that the poor of the Europeans live in proximity to rats."

"It is the children whom I had in mind," I said. "I meant them, if I may be forgiven, as a lesson of sorts, you are right. The Europeans, for the most part, have chosen to come to New York."

"So have the blacks."

"But what if they cannot choose? What if they are enslaved?"

"What's that about lessons?" Adam said. Then he covered his mouth. "I beg you gentlemen's pardon," he said through his fingers.

"No," Sam said. "Why should you not speak your heart? These are your people."

M said, "They must be ghosts to a man who seeks to rise. They must pull him backwards by the tenderest emotions. To improve, you must flee. To be human, you must hear the voice behind you and turn and—"

I thought of Sam as picket, asking me for the parole, and telling me about the pillar of salt. I thought of men falling over and turning gray as they fell, their blood pulsing away. And I thought, of a sudden, about my uncle Sidney Cowper, who did not die as a pillar of salt, but who drowned in a privy in the cold, cruel countryside of upper New York State, turning even as he died into the substance that was at his core. He had grown heavy, as I could tell in those days when I returned, on a rare visit, from school; in the night, from my room in the little house, I heard my mother grunting as he had her. She sounded as though the strain upon her frame was great. And it was clear that her emotions were taxed. Her eyes were underscored with dark, lined flesh. Her mouth was bitter of expression, and she wept easily over small matters she would once not have noticed. When I asked after her health, she leaned upon me as if she would hide inside my chest.

I did chores during that Christmas season with a special fervor, and Uncle Sidney Cowper noticed my enthusiasm, rewarding it, as he said, with a little bit extra in an envelope that I might spend on food and drink at school. I worked about the house when he was gone, and passed enough time in the privy so that my mother inquired after the state of my digestion.

On the day of New Year's, when he was readying to ride to a little place called Poolville, over the hills from us, where he was determined to drink great quantities of a homemade corn whiskey prepared by two bachelor friends, one of whom was a schoolteacher, he visited the privy before departing.

We did not hear the crack of the dowels affixing the seat, already worn through with a wood rasp and touched up with creosote. We heard only a distant, muffled shout.

"Oh, dear," I said to my mother in the kitchen, where I was peeling apples for her. "I had better see what's happened." She was lost in the cooking preparations, or hiding herself within them, and she did not hear.

I put on my frayed mackinaw and went to the outhouse, where, as I expected—as I insisted I would find—Uncle Sidney Cowper had set his great bottom on the weakened seat and had plummeted through. It was a well-made privy, and the seat, built as it was on a platform that was sited on a raised floor, was a good five feet to the little lake of stool and piddle beneath. He was mewing his disgust and dread. From the dark corner, I retrieved a short birch bough and with it I kept my uncle Sidney Cowper where he belonged, drowning in shit. Each time he made a sound or tried to shape a word, I knew, he drew it in through his nostrils or mouth. I pressed, and I could hear him gag and struggle and strangle, and I smiled. I did not feel a regret. I could only hope that he might leave my mother a whopping sum for her agonies. Then, in not too long a while, I tossed in the bough.

I saw his little carpetbag on some stones near his horse, purchased from the Paynes Corner smithy, and I slipped the handles over the pommel of the saddle, slapped the horse's rump, and sent him on his way. He would amble in at the smithy's, I thought, and someone would reluctantly conclude that searching was a necessity. I did regret that decent men would have to suffer from the cold in such a futile hunt, and I was pleased that I could feel something like sorrow, even if only this distant cousin of the true emotion. I retrieved from our shed the new seat I had days before cut and darkened. Above him, where his body had turned, facedown, to float like the hugest of turds, I affixed the seat with new dowels.

I returned to the kitchen, hung up my coat, and sat again at the bowl of apples. I wiped my palms against my shirt, then set to.

"What was the matter, then, Billy?"

"I thought I heard a cry from far away in the woods."

"Nothing, eh?"

"Not a thing."

"And your uncle is off?"

"Seems long ago launched on his way."

She slumped against the edge of the table. She had lost weight, and had been slender to begin with. Now she looked old; now I felt older. She would spend the winter, once I left to return to New Haven, in covering his body with her stool. That would trouble her if he was found. On the other hand, I thought, he might do us a mighty favor and decompose with rapidity, and she might never need to know and I might never need to be hanged for murdering my uncle in a stew of corruption. I did not wish to die of choking, or a broken neck, but—and I was interested to learn it—I did not, finally, care.

"What's that," she said, "that makes you smile?"

I said, "Pardon?"

M said, "What have you and our dusky Virgil in mind for us now?"

"Adam, can you stand to lead us on one more descent?" I asked.

In the flare of the streetlight, he looked ill. He softly clapped his hands and rubbed them together, as if preparing to lift a great weight.

"Then, the crib?"

He nodded again, and turned and walked away. "Poor fellow," M said. "He is loyal and distraught and noble."

"Tashtego," Sam ventured, naming a character from the book about the whale.

"No, son, he was Indian, you'll recall."

It was not an alley we entered this time. It was a house, narrow and wooden, sandwiched between a piano manufactory and a dealer in scraps of metal and old machines. A dog as great as a small horse, with a blunt, smooth head, was tethered on a chain to the loading dock to guard the scraps of iron and pewter and steel inside the dull stone building. When we passed, many yards from him, and on the other side of a wrought iron fence, he stood absolutely still and fixed us with a glaring study. Sam made an affectionate, chucking sound to him, and he silently bared his fangs.

Adam spoke for us to someone at the door of the house, and we went in.

M asked of Adam, "What do they provide?"

Adam, looking sullen, said, "White girls. Brown boys. Blind men. Bleeding women. Egyptians. Bohunks. Niggers of every persuasion. Whatever you prefer."

Sam said, with more than a little apprehension, "I thought we were here to observe."

M tilted back his head, as if to swallow some of the darkness of the ocher-tinted vestibule with its single, small lamp, and he soundlessly laughed.

"So we are, Sam, I assure you," I said. I said to Adam, "You feel divided in this."

"I feel ashamed of myself," he said.

M gripped Adam's arm, then lay his own arm along the man's broad shoulders. "This is a brotherhood of shame," he said. "What pride can breathe in the airless coffin of this life? Except, perhaps, the pride in not dying when circumstances suggest that you must."

"I don't know about that," Adam said. "I just hate it."

A fat black woman in a maid's starched apron, her lips pursed in distaste, came to beckon us in and to our left, up an unlighted stairway and through a broad door and down a bright hall all covered in a dark blue textured cloth. We entered what seemed to be a small bedroom, and I gave her the money. She moved a painting of a waterfall, not a very alluring or realistic one, I would suggest, and then she dimmed the two gas lamps until we were in shadows. She gestured at the wall, as if to welcome us to what we might see, and then, turning the latch very quietly, she left.

It was awkward, fitting my mask to the small hole cushioned with velvet. I saw what they would see and gestured M to approach. He leaned to the aperture and stood very still. I heard his breath whistle. He stood there, and then he moved back. Sam went next, and he stared and stared, and then I returned to look once more. I turned to Adam, but he had gone to the far end of the room to sit at the head of the bed, his thick arms folded across his broad chest, his head drooped in a semblance of ease.

Inside the neighboring chamber, its bed lit by a single ceiling fixture, the scene reflected on a mirror at the opposite end of the room, a little colored girl, younger than the one we had seen at the gambling hall, absolutely naked except for a leather collar at her neck, and seemingly drunk or drugged, lay upon the body of a tall white man who was equally naked. The little child administered to him below the waist while a small white child, wearing a metal tiara and a collar that matched the black child's, sat upon his face as he sucked at her sex and spanked her black partner with a small black leather whip as she, her lips and cheeks straining, fellated the man.

The shadows at the end of their room moved and, coming first into the mirror and then into my view, I saw a black woman wearing what appeared to be leather underpants from which a long white object protruded, a carved kind of penis, I saw. As the black child ministered to the white man, the black woman seized her and spread her legs from behind. The child labored at the man, but drew her legs beneath her so that she might be mounted as she worked. The black woman seemed about to enter her, and I could look no further. M stepped to the aperture and watched for a few seconds, then stepped back in revulsion.

"I have been with dusky women in the Marquesas," he whispered. His sibilants hissed and coiled in the darkened room in that house of such darkness. "I have known, you could say, some dusky women. I have seen my share of sights, but never such a sight as that. It calls down fire from the heavens. No god could exist who would permit those children—"

Adam walked to the door and leaned his head against the jamb.

"We might leave," I said, "if you have seen enough."

And downstairs, on the dark and momentarily silent street, he said, "I must away. Lizzie will worry. And it was a long day of scampering through vessels even before this Dantean excursion was begun. Now, Mr. Mordecai."

"Sir." And Sam stood to attention as I had seen him do in the War.

"You and I have bones to pick. You have invaded my life, and my dear Mal's death, to write down your version of each."

"Sir."

"We may speak further on it. We may not. Mal would forgive you, for he was a fond and trusting child who never gave a fellow creature a difficult moment, and who bore no grudge. He'd have told you, 'God bless you, Mr. Mordecai.'"

Sam's head hung, and I could see no face, only the twisty, springy dark hair.

"So I tell you, on my dear boy's behalf, and for myself as well, in that spirit of forgiveness that transcends dying, 'God bless you, Mr. Mordecai.' We'll be friends."

He put out his broad hand and Sam reached for it with both of his as if he were drowning and he knew he'd be pulled up.

"Billy," M said. "I will speak with you further. I salute your gallant cause."

On the edge of the Loin of New York, then, and in the darkness pierced by the lanterns of cabriolets, and by the flicker of street lamps, M walked toward East Twenty-sixth Street while Adam lingered like a man at the scene of a railroad accident who has seen the bodies carted off but who is locked into place by emotions, not practical need, staring dully at the twisted metal and the bits of bloody cloth.

I put money in his hand and he let it fall. I retrieved it, and I placed it in his hand again.

"You have done me a service," I said.

"What did I sell you?"

"Energy. Expertise. Safety, perhaps. You were my courier—my guide."

"I showed you a look at bad behavior and sorrow. Like it was minstrels kicking and strumming just for you."

Sam slowly pulled his notebook out and opened it, then turned his back toward us and started to write.

Adam didn't notice. He said, "I beg your pardon." He held my hand and opened it out and deposited the money therein, then closed my fingers on it. "Excuse me," he said. It was like being touched with chilly wood. Then he said, "Mist Bartelmy, good night. If you are in trouble, you can ax for me. But I don't want to do this anymore."

"I will. And you won't. I thank you, Adam, and I wish you God-speed."

Sam had turned to watch us, and he was drawn so tall in observation, I thought he might throw a military salute, but he inclined his head and waved. Adam did not respond. He walked east, back into the Loin, and he disappeared into one of its alleys, and was gone.

"I would gargle with a bottle of something flame-y," Sam said.

"Flame-y? Indeed! You *are* inventive, Sam."

"I'll show you some of my notes. It's been a remarkable night."

"No need for the notes, though I thank you. After all, I was there. What can you have written down that I didn't witness with my own eyes?"

He smiled in his fondness, and then he shook his head. He put his notebook in his inside breast pocket. He said, "Then let's go someplace where all the whores are career officers and all the customers enlisted men. And where children are neither dead by suicide nor butt-shagged with scrimshaw."

"Was it *really* scrimshaw, Sam?"

He made a face of impish wisdom, and he tapped at his coat, over the place where the notebook lay. Then, as if he were the man of New York, and I the New England cousin, he led us out of the Loin, and east and south, and he bought us glasses of port in the saloon bar of the Astor, where, in the rosiness of its lamps and on the buttoned plush of our banquette, beneath a murky painting of a fox in flight from what I suppose were meant to be hounds but which looked to me like Shetland ponies gone carnivorous, Sam finished off a note and pushed the notebook over to me. Its cover was a heavy black leather binding, and the shiny pages sewn into it, five inches or so high, were ruled in black, with gold-tipped edges.

His handwriting ran across the page, leaning forward like a boy in flight, sprawling almost flat at times, as if the boy had fallen. I could sense the racing of his hand, as if it sought to keep pace with his scoutings-out and insights. How athletic, it seemed to me, of a sudden, must be the mind of such a willing and nimble observer.

I turned back a few sheets, as though searching for a single entry in particular, because I thought it would please him to see such concern. I already knew, from M, with what tender feelings an author might proffer his work. Sam had offered me his account of our night in the dark nation so alien, yet so much our own, but my fingers and my eyes, as if they were directed there, lighted upon the terrible dates when Malcolm, so late and so adrift, had returned to East Twenty-sixth Street as if in search of True North.

TUESDAY, SEPT 10: Boy returned at 3 of the morning—This could therefore count for Wednesday, the 11th—So soon do the actualities dwindle and the uncertainties predominate—A child as sweet as any I knew, who gave us joy and little worry, save for his welfare—Ghastly his welfare now, and ghastly to outlive your son!—So he returned at 3 of the morning, I asleep and Lizzie to the door, and she admitted him and of course did—must needs—reproach him for his inconsideration, for his breaking of his curfew and his vow—No scent nor display of the effects of liquor, swears his mother my wife who nearly departed the house in spite of *her* vow, but that's for another time or never—It cannot matter now—And so she did not scold, but chided him, and so he went to bed, having kissed her, she claims—Why should he not have? For he was the kindest of boys—And there's Fanny, in the morning, sent upstairs to waken him while I, at the table, smoked a pipe before work—Nothing but his voice, a single word, the child reports: He said, "Yes"—And in a life of everlasting No, I shall live, now, with his Yes—I can hear it in the inner ear—And so the father assembles the crew and gives the working orders for the day: the boy to sleep, then late into work at the Great

Western Marine, and surely to be scolded (if not fired!) by
Lathers, and where shall we find any other source of the $200
per annum?—Discipline's first, I tell them, and they make as
if to obey—From the girls, of course, this intelligence, that
Lizzie is up the stairs and down every 30 minutes and less,
knocking at his door—No answer—No answer—Is this not
the cry of man since Christ cried out to his father and received
No Answer, and the weight of his body at the nails on which
his cartilage and veins were hung?—No answer—and the
breaking down of the door at night—soreness in the shoulder
and hip from the collision with immovable wood and soreness in the soul from the sight with which it collided too—
The manchild like a baby, curled about his hand and the pistol
it held, curled about his wound as now I must curl in my
inmost self about the sight I forever carry—And the boy did
not drink liquor nor visit prostitutes nor engage in the vices
of other boys his age—He did twirl the pistol, we are told—
In the office and the street and at the luncheon place they frequented, he did twirl the pistol as if he were a desperado
crossing into Mexico—And she had decided, she said, that she
would do her duty as a wife and stay with me—She had done
her duty before, and she would do it now—It did him no
good, she insists, that I was gruff with him, or belittled his
engagement in the Guard—Men on ships are cruel with one
another—That is the world of men—That is the military
world, and he had better be accustomed, I said, after another
seizure of snuffling and sulking and her taking his side—
Fanny weeping and Lizzie and Stanny with his great, staring
eyes—I on the river, slowly spitting my spit into the foam of
the green, filthy water at the wharf, foam like slaver of mad
dog—Kneeling upon the lowest step of the wharf and dipping
into the water and tasting it and carrying all day the bitterness

of it—Bitter is it to be poor and bitter to be reviled, and Oh bitter are these waters of commerce and death, for the bodies of the drowned children do sprawl and swirl at the bottom—Dead animals cast up by the water, and sometimes a desperate woman in her suicide, but never are the children returned by the river and as for the ocean it is only in books that the tiny pip of humanity returns—

WEDNESDAY, SEPT 11: For a man to be accused in his own home of madness is madness redoubled and cruelty heaped upon cruelty—Is it not enough? Is it not enough, I said—I shrieked it, bellowed it, declaimed it in thunder—Is it not enough that a man be exiled from his profession, must he be exiled from his family too?—Lizzie, sitting upon her bed, weeping for an hour into the most absurdly small handkerchief—Live with your father, by all means, for it is with his money that we have lived and with yours we have purchased this house and with his smile of unmeant affection he may send you abroad as he has sent me—I have seen the Village of Lepers built upon a dung heap and I will be the leper, squatting on ordure, while you hasten to your father's house—You did not berate him, you say, and so he enters and you embrace in a sticky celebration of his abstemiousness and your benefaction, and up he goes, and off, and then to kill himself with a noisy gun while all the day long you hover near his door and yet do not hear the pistol's report.

TUESDAY, SEPT 10 & WEDNESDAY, SEPT 11: Must it, then, have been the gruffness of the father?—How else to account for a boy who stays out until dawn and is reported to have returned with no liquor upon his breath—The mother, unlatching the door for him, not having uttered any but wel-

coming words and, naturally, the mildest of reprovals—
"Down, dog, and kennel!" I'd have told him at the door—
Must it not have been the wicked father in his old, maritime
ways, who behaved toward his boy as if the boy had been a
boy—Who else but a boy, a man must wonder, could sleep so
many hours of the day—It was the staying up late, certainly,
and yet even of a weekend day, say Sunday, spent at home,
most of it was spent in bed—But might he not have spun the
pistol like someone in a Wild West magazine, instead of sleeping the days away?—Asleep or playing with his pistol, he
behaved like a boy and, like a boy, needed the discipline
administered by men—I had warned him too severely about
his character and habits, according to his mother, my devoted
wife—No sane man speaks such treason to himself without
he makes a mask from behind which to say his piece and beg
for peace—Sane madness—And here the man sits and writes
and says what he must or what he may, while his son sleeps
and wakes, sleeps and wakes, and then, waking finally, forever
sleeps—The night inspector at his occupation—Something
further might come of this—

TUESDAY, SEPT 10: Thought back to the day when she
claimed I lifted my hand to her—Aberration in the process of
observing and comprehending—It was on the *back* stairs,
Lizzie, not the front—Strong drink not involved—I, declaim-
ing with the righteousness that weakens my writing as well as
my speech—Lizzie prodding with her surprising, infrequently
manifested temper—A foul father, she cries, a fallow father, a
man of vast uselessness to his sons and daughters who
employs them as whipping posts for his temper—Not so, cries
the tyrannical husband and father, I have never laid hand
upon a one of them—Think you not that words, or mocking

laughter, or a blank and inattentive face may not cause wounds?—She cries out and out, I at the stairway top and she partway down on the narrow step with a hamper of laundry in hand—Disappeared, then, into the coppery nimbus, bright and dull at once, but she with no face, great spots in my vision and pain in the temple so vast that to have been shot there, as dear Malcolm was, would have been to sustain barely any pain—True, then, that my hand was upraised, as whose might not be in such a moment of despair—The body does know when to rescue the man from his mind—Hence blindness of the eye as a type of blindness in the brain—The spots before me like giant holes into which I might plunge to escape—Such a violence of feature to present, I think!—And so she, forgetting her place—Do I dare jest here?!—Lizzie stepping back upon the air and falling in place of her desperate, despairing husband, who would have fallen an instant later from the pain her mockery had given him—

WEDNESDAY, SEPT 11: Recalled with awful honesty the time I struck her as she stood before me at the landing of the front steps—I in from work and she with a kind of desperation rarely seen by me—Crying, wailing, as if a dervish in a fever-ish land—Anent the terrible pallor of Stanny and his silences and Mal's determination to use the Guard as a way to the West and then a way to find combat—Thinking, never saying, how the boy so lacking in discipline or energy would surely find a way, in warfare, to die—And why did I not speak to my daughters with more than a mocking smile nor do else but chastise my boys—Crying back to her, Not so!—The soles of my feet afire from the hot stones of the hellfire city where heat poured down from the sun and out from manufactories and up from furnaces and engines and the moisture hung in the air like a stench made visible—Clambering upon the cargo vessels, prying into packages and crates, thumping barrels and squinting with sore eyes the manifests of crooked owners and their crooked masters and their crooked bosuns and their mercantile accomplices lined, like great herring gulls, along the wharf—Scrawling in the government notebook with a government pencil—Pinning into the cloth of my lapel the inches of heavy, dull badge—Inspector U.S. Revenue, as if I am equally the government's property, along with my notebook and my federal locks—To lock in *what?* To lock *what* away?—And, true, I had gone by myself to Delmonico's, so close to home—The growling of garrulous men—Smoke of cigars and sweet, heavy shag I did smoke to contribute to the clouds of manhood in the dark, interior air—A chop as heavy as a chunk of ballast, and a wine from the Rioja spilling from its decanter into the table's candlelight a river of promise— Before me on the table, from August Brentano's newsstand, *The Reminiscences of Rufus Choate*—He knew the city as it once had been, to those of somewhat noble lineage, born to reign, but some only rained upon—And, no, Lizzie, I am not stupid with drink—Stupid, rather, with fatigue, and with regret at having spent such pleasant hours when she awaited me—As if I had forgot I had a wife and family and house and debts for the acquisition of each—The Choate, for example, purchased with an allowance for books made possible by Lizzie's decision that I'm a man of the book and thus must own books—To so chastise me for bookishness when it was she who once regarded that as no wound upon the family's opportunities, but a triumph of which to boast!—Did I, then, strike her in the face and send her backward, limbs flying gracelessly and dangerously against the banister and steps until she rested, still and still and still at the foot, in the foyer?

TUESDAY, SEPT 10: Malcolm home late—Lizzie at door—
Three A.M., and Lizzie still awake, thus at the door to admit
our boy—Pleasant of expression and filled, like a younger
child, with powerful regret—No odor of strong drink, nor
expressions from Lizzie of anything but her fatigue and disappointment—Slinging his arm around his mother's neck and
kissing her good night, his skin clear, his expression open to
inspection, and his words those of a boy en route to manhood—So to bed—For she never declaimed an anger or
resentment, eh?—And I was abed, not having warned him of
aught but duty, never a threat—So, twirling the pistol at the
edge of the bed, or even seated, lest, he might have thought, he
would be required by his duties as soldier to one day defend
himself while seated, say at a cookfire or in a mess tent—Silly
but understandable, and barely 18 years of age, a precious
boy—

WEDNESDAY, SEPT 11: Pain at the shoulder and rib and elbow
and thigh from flinging myself against the latched, heavy
door—Panting behind me of Lizzie and Bessie, while Fanny
wailed and Stanwix, alone among us as always, from where the
corridor curved, stood in his silence and the nighttime of his
solitude—In the door, then, and in myself with Lizzie and
Bess behind—The poor boy so pale, paler than the bedclothes, and his fine face stained with the startling boldness of
his blood, and so much of it—The weapon of his own
destruction in his square, strong hand—Then Fanny crowd-
ing in, and the cries as of seabirds in a frenzy on the water far
from home—The silence I felt, I *felt* it, from Stanwix Melville,
the only remaining male in our small family who might one
day sire a son—And no stern words behind us, like a pennant
on a scuttled vessel's mast—All had done their best—All had
done their all—Lord in whom I would believe and fear I may

not—How little he has done to deserve this dying—Why might you not have taken me?—I wished to say this to Lizzie—Could not—Lips sealed—Silences among us broader than the oceans of unspoken words in the past—My children blighted—Household boiling in silences of fever—Gall for dinner—Bile for tea—Great emptiness abounding in our rooms—

Tuesday, Sept 10: The boy returns—It is *Lizzie* who receives him—Their exchange—Dulcet tones, assuredly—And off to bed—

Wednesday, Sept 11: And nothing of the money needed and the money spent?—And no recriminations—Loving kiss from child to mother, and to bed—

Tuesday, Sept 10: The world revolving in the boy, perhaps—His feeling he is guilty of the sins against the house—Wastrel, roaring-boy, drunkard, pretender—The having done an awful deed for which there is no recompense—Yet we did not hear of such, we do not, will not—He was a boy on the verge of man—He died in purity, though surely he was tempted—I have been tempted—Flesh, drink, vanity, language—

Wednesday, Sept 11: Truly, I did belabor him for acquiring hurtful habits—Truly, I did threaten him with exile from the house—A boy alone in the grinding city—Only the Guard, sent on duty, would have given him a home—To be banished, nearly banished, from the rooms he had known—

Tuesday, Sept 10: Did she threaten him with *me?*—Was it the danger posed by his sometimes silent, sometimes cruel, sometimes angry father?—But why hast Thou forsaken me, so the Jewish stripling cried to his Father—People of The Law, they stood between a Father and His Son—Bitter truth, cruel salts of truth, ashes and gall, the unmoving lips of the Father, aloof—

WEDNESDAY, SEPT 11: Child, it is The Law compels and mangles *me*—Even Jehovah might lament—

TUESDAY, SEPT 10: His mother, awake and alone at three of the morning—Sitting in the darkness of her solitude—Taking refuge in another room—But what deep-diving men *are* easy in a life, a household, its empty, echoing rooms?

WEDNESDAY, SEPT 11: The batterer father, like wrath incarnate—Bursting through—And was it *then* the shot was fired?—Only then?—And Stanny, fearful at the pursuit, willing himself away from the world of such sounds?

TUESDAY, SEPT 10: I did not see him with my eyes—I did not sniff like a dog at his breath—Nor did I hear the timbre and tone of his mother's voice—What a sailor does not see he does not know—It is why some cruel god of the navigators invented heavy fog—The fear of the woman and her daughters through the ultimate day—

WEDNESDAY, SEPT 11: The shot—

TUESDAY, SEPT 10: It seems, now, such a small matter—Lizzie in the kitchen and the washing up undone because the girl was no longer retained—Money being once more an issue with us—With our creditors!—I upstairs in my little room, squinting against the glare of the spirit lamp—Gaslight too bright at night for my aching eyes—Mal in the small corridor swinging the pistol about, crying "Hey!" and "Ho!" and "Surrender your arms!"—The children shouting for fear, mock fear, I think—And I, emerging from the room to terrify them to silence with my visage and my thoughts, written upon my forehead, I suspect, like Cain's own brand, of such violence—Lizzie up from her chores to see—True mother, wary of the silence and not the former clattering and chattering—My roaring at them all to see to the dishes—Failure to respect their mother, etc.—Fanny weeping and Stanny struck dumb—Mal's scowl a mirror to my own, I think—Lizzie silent and suddenly pale—The moment of stillness like the failure of a heart to beat—Our little house suspended in the silence—The swing of my arm as if self-motivated, with not a consideration from my brain—Mal's pistol, which could have discharged at any or all, spilling from his fingers—His hand at his mouth, a fearful small boy, no man in the Guard with a sword at his belt and a pistol in hand—Fearful small boy—Are you such a poor shabby fellow? Are you a good, honorable one or good-for-nothing? Now you must announce it to me!—Monstrous man to hulk over them and bellow, glower, blink his weak, infernal eyes—

WEDNESDAY, SEPT 11: Lizzie tumbling slowly down the back staircase—Her white, loose thighs exposed—Not recently this naked to my eyes—Her thin cry of surprise, and then the fall—My sense that I had struck her—Probably not—It is not what I would seek to do—My arm upraised, perhaps, would startle her, as happens with horses and dogs—While true that I have spoken harshly to them all—My sense of despair mounting, my need to sleep and sleep not unlike Malcolm's, I think—The restlessness of the spirit in the Melvilles—My fury at small provocations, the sign of larger motivations to rage yet unannounced but present in the household and in my heart—Yet no harsh words to Mal upon his late arrival at home—No dire warnings beforehand, nor cruel greetings on the night—The door stove in, the bloody bedclothes and the bled, wounded boy—My girls and Lizzie in their sorrows, I in my own and separate sorrows, and my Stanwix, son, so silent and immense-eyed—The sword on the sash at Malcolm's side—

The waiter brought us more port. "It's very good," Sam said.

"Yes. It is, though—"

"I meant the fortified wine," Sam said. "However, I would admit to some confidence in what you have just read. What *do* you think?" His face demonstrated a carefully managed blankness, as if he feared to be accused of requiring me to express an approval. While I read, he had set down half a dozen brown stubs of pencil, of various lengths, and he had littered his side of the banquette table with cedar shavings. "If anything, of course," he said.

"Sam, did he tell you these thoughts?"

"Of course not, Billy. I wrote them. I created them."

"And you are certain of these insights, then? That he— Sam, how can you know this?"

He opened his mouth as if to speak, then seemed to think better of it, and he laid a finger upon his lips, and he smiled with a gentle, knowing humor. Finally he did speak, but to say only this: "Invention also speaks a certain truth, Billy. Have you not recounted your adventures in battle? And subtly altered what another might term *fact*?"

I did not reply. I found that I could not. And so I pressed on. "And why would he think—he so formerly famed for his abilities to recall and construct scenes of vividness and drama—why would he think so illogically? So repetitively? The dates repeated as if only they, of all the thirty in the month, had meaning. These thoughts are so contradictory and so unverifiable. So speculative, that is to say, Sam. Hysterical! You think of him as crazed?"

He no longer struck me as pleased. A frown had imposed itself upon his mouth, and I saw a kind of boy's pouting in his expression, as if I had failed him, and perhaps of a purpose. He worked at a pencil's sharp point as if to perfect it, and of course he pressed too far and was required to begin again. He scraped rather than whittled, and the sound of the pocket knife's blade against the pencil was a nervous scratching. I thought of damp dogs working with their claws against their ears.

"I am sorry," I said. "You know that I have only affection for you, and the best of hopes for your career. I do seek to comprehend. But, Sam, where is the truth of it, if one entry for September tenth is so different from that which follows soon after, but which is also labeled the tenth of September? Not, of course, that I know anything of authorship. Clearly, since you have thus done it, thus it is achieved. I apologize for my outburst. I am baffled and, when I am in that state, I become almost frightened—perhaps too aggressive, let us say, in my posing of questions, Sam."

His face was crimson, and I did not know whether with disappointment in my response, or anger at my myopia, or pleasure in my being all at sea.

"And—may I ask you another question without risking our friendship?"

"Never at risk," he said.

I turned a page and pointed, moving the notebook over to him.

He read aloud: "'He is careful not to display tenderness, most especially in regard to himself. Yet I view him as the most stung, the most wounded of men, a tattered spirit in need of much repair.'"

I asked, "Would that be your summary of him? A tattered spirit?"

"Of someone," he said, smiling, then restoring the notebook to its place in his coat.

"And those—forgive me—puzzling notations?"

"Entries in a log, as one might find in the belongings of a sailor."

"A log! So he records the events of his voyage, you say."

"On an inner ocean, Billy."

"Just so," I said.

He laughed a quick hiccup of an unhappy laugh, then shut himself into silence, smiling without pleasure at his port, and then drinking it off.

Yesterday morning, I dreamed them both and woke often, fearful each time that I would open my eyes to see M, face a blur behind the screening beard, and Sam, his face a banner of friendship, beside my bed, his notebook in hand, awaiting me. Each time I woke, I kept my eyes squeezed shut. Finally I slept through to the forenoon, although I was troubled with dreaming of the huge cylinder of the pistol, slowly and inevitably grinding around. The night had ended at Mrs. Hess's near dawn, with the clientele asleep upstairs or departed for home. Delgado, in the pantry at the back, had set down Vichy water and Madeira and a small, very heavy round Dutch cheese. While two of the girls lounged and lolled—Rachel in bloomers, undervest, and bright green shoes; Tillie in her gown with the straps down along her arms—Jessie sat beside me, wrapped in her figured blue-and-white robe, with her golden fingers clasped on the table beside her drink. Delgado stood beside the long refectory table and shook his arm in its black broadcloth jacket; a gravity knife slid into his hand, and he shook it once and the sharp, stubby blade emerged. He reached for the cheese, sealed in red wax, and began to peel it like a mango the size of a cannonball. Tillie, who was Rachel's lover, slowly ground her head with its thick, red hair up and back in the lap of Rachel, who sat, while Tillie sprawled, in a kind of deacon's bench against the wall.

Jessie said to Delgado, "Was it a busy night, then?"

He kept the wax coming in a single strip. "A bit less than crowded. How was the great man's dinner?"

She clasped and unclasped her hands, then she shrugged.

"Did he mind his manners?" Delgado asked.

"He never had any to mind," she said. "His idea of elegant dining is to hire a whore to chew his beefsteak and spit it into his mouth."

Tillie said, "Yum," and turned her head to nibble at Rachel, who slapped her, but did not push her face away.

"You're lucky," Delgado said, "if that's all he requires. So I hear."

"So you know. And it was not all that he required. Could I have whiskey, do you think, instead of this ladies' drink?"

"Locked it all away, Jessie. Madeira's not bad. This is a good one."

She nodded and drank.

The pantry grew silent. I listened to the gas hiss behind its pink, bright globe. I listened to the scrape of Delgado's knife between the rind of the cheese and the strip of red wax; it dropped, and I heard it strike the floor, though Delgado, for all his effort, seemed not to mind. He simply started another strip, and the cheese continued to appear. Tillie yawned and moved her head in Rachel's lap.

Jessie said, "I am not going to talk about the dinner, in case anyone is waiting."

No one spoke.

I watched her compress her lips, cause her brow to go flat, her eyes to open wider. When her smooth, glowing features were composed, she turned to me. "I would, if you wanted me to."

I said, "I'd just as soon not."

She nodded. "I would have, too. Are we any further along in—"

I put my finger to my ludicrous, artificial mouth and she closed her own. Delgado looked up. Rachel asked, "What are you two hatching?"

"Surely not eggs," Jessie said. Rachel giggled and Tillie affected to snore.

"Cheese," Delgado said. He placed it on the table and cut crescent-shaped pieces for the girls. "Sir?" he said to me, but I declined. One side of his face, near the nose, was shiny and pocked, and I would have bet that he'd been peppered with birdshot. I thought it remarkable that he'd survived. No doubt he thought me remarkable for similar reasons.

Jessie brought the chunk of hard orange cheese to her mouth and it rested against her lips, but she could not admit it between them. She lowered the cheese to the table and softly shook her head. Delgado raised his full, black eyebrows, then let them drop. Sam Mordecai, back at the Astor asleep, if he were present would have slowly drawn his notebook and opened it and set it upon his lap; then, with a child's self-pardoning smile, he would have set his stub of pencil scratching at the pages, setting down that silent exchange and all its implications.

William Bartholomew, trader and assassin, settled for gently touching the back of Jessie's golden hand and sitting within his mask while the night leaked out. William Bartholomew, stalking the streets as if he were in charge of them, peering through his eyeholes at cats leaping in a mound of very ripe garbage at the mouth of an alley at Seventy-ninth Street, made his way down to the Five Points and his bed. Whatever Delgado and Jessie had meant, I thought, by their exchange of glances, she had been through a ghastly night. I summoned grotesque pictures, and then I fought to banish them. In every one, Jessie's powerful haunches, the secrets of her thighs, were at the service—at the command—of paunchy men of business who were lollipopped, no doubt, while they chewed at their cigars. It was Jessie kneeling before them, was it not? But so small, as it were, a matter would not have driven her into such a sickened silence. I saw them using tableware and worse upon the girls. I heard the noises that they made.

A man with a filthy, unshaved face, half out of his clothing, obviously paralyzed by drink, lay across the street at Seventy-first. I stood above him, for I wanted to deliver a series of blows with my boot to his ribs. I did not know him, but I was atremble with the urge to wound someone.

He opened his eyes in mid-snore, and he looked up. I could not imagine what he thought, in the green glow of the gas lamp, he saw.

"Father Jesus!" he cried. "I'll stop. I'll never drink again. Don't take me off!"

"This is the last chance I'll give," I intoned.

"Never a drop by the Mother of God!"

"Go home," I told him.

He rolled onto his hands and his knees, then edged sideways to the stanchion of the lamp and pulled himself to his feet. I pointed east, and he went that way, tripping and sliding, although of course I had no idea where he might live. A fast cabriolet, its window blinds pulled down, almost struck him, and it seemed to me that two squat, bearded sailors, nearly as drunk as he, were altering their course to follow in his steps; he was hardly out of danger, I thought.

A family from India, it seemed—the father wore a dirty turban, his wife a sari of bright, stained yellow—were moving their household at dawn, along the railroad embankment at Hamilton Square at the corner of East Sixty-fifth. She carried a sleeping infant, swathed in blue, in her slender, hairy left arm; in her right, she steadied on her shoulder a long, thick wooden rod that rested, before her, on the shoulder of her man. To it were fastened deep baskets containing clothing, perhaps foodstuffs, implements, little wooden boxes round and square, and several sets of garments, some slippers and shoes. The father carried a sleeping child of two or so upon his other shoulder. They marched a peculiar dancing march to the rhythm established by the swinging weight of their household goods. They walked, in alternating darkness and light, communicating, so it seemed, through the distribution and redistribution of their burden. He, as he passed me, smiled; she, drawn and woeful, affected not to see me, although I watched her eyes widen as her view of me improved.

At the time of which I speak, you could enter Harry Hill's dance hall, on Houston Street, for twenty-five cents. Men and women alike were welcomed, but they had to pay, receive a little dish of oysters, and move upstairs toward the music. The wooden floorboards cracked and groaned beneath the dancers' weight, and everyone danced. Men in white-and-blue-striped sailor's jerseys circulated among the guests and they quickly compelled those not dancing, for more than one song's duration, to leave. It was all very respectable, and although I did not any longer dance, and of course I did not parade my visage in the hope of making female friends, it had never occurred to me that Hill's was anything but respectable. On behalf of workingmen and -women, I had always been appreciative. It took Jessie, of course, with her restrained and largely uninflected voice to tell me that on the floor above the music, a partial third floor—it did not run the breadth of the building—there were clean, inelegant private rooms where dancers might, for more than twenty-five cents, lock the door and make love—make, that is, whatever they were driven to.

"You have done this?" I remember asking her, one night in her room.

She said, into the flesh of my unmasked face, "I have done everything, Billy."

So, it seemed, had Lizzie and her girls, and possibly the silent, wracked Stanwix, waiting all the day, cajoling the silent son and brother, contemplating their wakefulness while Malcolm engaged in a sleep as alien to them, perhaps, as the winking sleep of dogs, the wintry sleep of bears. So, of course, had M. For so many of his young years, he had written what he could to make his way and make his wage; then, apparently, he had manufactured what he must, and he'd made neither. That is the way of the world, the ebb and flow of dollars, but knowing this could not have been of consolation; and in the pressure in the house—an atmosphere, like storm, as the barometric pressure dropped, and the very air pressed hard, in silence, at the inner doors of the rooms, the windows looking onto East Twenty-sixth Street—he drank his drinks and then escaped to walk to work, swallowing his own saliva as it welled like poison in his throat and mouth, and heard, from this remaining friend or that, how many of the other, former, friends were certain he had died.

So he had died. And yet he walked upon the cold or steamy streets. He smoked his pipe. Lizzie's life went on, and the children strove to live

in theirs, and he received his pay and bought his books and drank his drinks. He had imagined his way to, or had projected upon the page from within, a man so enormous in his woundedness and hate and malefi- cence—a man with tenderness, too, and a lover's eye for the shape, say, of the hunted whale's small ear—that he would risk a story about a man awaking in an inn with the leg of a stranger thrown, like a wife's, over his own. He would confess, that is to say, the hugeness of his own appetite in the body of a storytelling sailor. He would consider it a little moment in a momentousness: the story of a man who stabbed at all of the world, as if it were a mask, to reach through to—God, I suppose. Or the Satan we see as God. Or some absolutely other and dark indifference.

From tasking and tallying the whale, from daring the world with his story, he had gone to philosophical growls and speculations, and from there to saying less and less, and to counting the boxes and barrels on board merchant seamen lying-to in the Port of New York. From giving forth, he had declined to acting on behalf of those who received. If Lizzie had reported ball lightning on the chandeliers and banisters, a product of electric tension, I would not have been surprised. He had gone from life to a death-in-life, and was required—as husband, as father, as laborer for the Customs Collector of New York—to pretend that his failing stumble was a healthy trot. It was required that he not merely weep, or fall upon his sword, or, like his son, become his own assassin.

It was required—by my life, by Jessie's needs—that his unfortunate decline be as a resource to me; I must employ him, as the builder used lumber, as the chemist used salts, as the blacksmith used iron in his fire. As, it occurred to me, Sam Mordecai, his pencil in hand, his notebook open, used the sights I showed him and, it also occurred to me, might go so far as to use the driven man in his open-mouthed mask.

The heat in the city, and surely in the airless Points, had grown yeasty and wet. Folded papers expanded with moisture, cloth felt saturated, and the dirty walls and cobbles looked shiny, as if with the trails of slugs I used to see on the leaves of plants in my mother's garden and along the

fieldstone walls I had maintained. I carried my coat beneath my arm when I walked at night or went to the office at midday or later. Under the mask, I perspired uncomfortably, and was disgusted by what I thought was the odor of my own torn flesh. But I did go to the office, where I prepared papers to accompany those documents under preparation by Lapham Dumont and from which I issued orders to buy winter wheat upon speculation, or to invest in certain developments—railroads, absolutely, and the larger hotels in cities (now towns) destined for railheads—and I conducted intelligent business. I brought in crushed tomatoes in great vats for the growing appetite of the city (they were easier to ship if crushed, and in sauces and soups were not needed whole). I brought in citrus fruits from south and west (sustaining a loss in the shipment from California that came around by boat, breaking even on the southwestern shipments that were carted to the railroad at Chicago). I imported olives from Greece because the shipper sent them in stained terra-cotta amphorae, which—once the olives, transferred to barrels, were sold to wholesalers—I then sold, through professional consultants, as antiquarian relics to a surprising number of the rising upper-middle class in manufacturing and retail sales who required something noticeably new in their little palaces along Fifth Avenue.

It was at this time that Chun Ho's children, accustomed to me now, called me *Gui* when they thought I didn't hear, and then, soon enough, they said it aloud before me.

"What is *Gui*?" I asked her.

"They say it for this." She gently touched my painted cheek.

"They call me a name for my mask?"

She nodded. "Ghost, you say."

"I am a ghost to them?"

She solemnly shook her head. "*Look* like ghost. White face of spirit. You plenty alive. They know." She was folding laundry at most of her small table, although a few inches were reserved for Ng, who was required to practice English for school. She had made a list of words that,

in the evening, she and Kwang would chant at one another. Then Chun Ho looked up. She was wearing black wide-legged silk trousers under a kind of short black silk robe. Her light tan face, broad and impassive, under hair as black and silky as her clothes, was cocked in attention. She waited for my reaction to my name.

"You know I am more than this mask," I said.

"Sure. They young, small people."

"May I ask you, Chun Ho, why you look at me like that?"

"Want see," she said. "*I* ask: Why you come here? Sit here? Talk here? Listen here?"

"Why *do* you," Ng corrected her.

I said, "*I* want to see *you*, I suppose."

Often, she put her hand to her face and looked away if I embarrassed her with overmuch directness. This time, she stood straight and regarded me further. Then she nodded. She saw to the laundry but, I noticed, she smiled a little at the bedsheets and pillowcases and bath towels of strangers.

Kwang, too, was smiling, as if adults were amusing. Ng had her hand upon her mouth. These, I reminded myself, were the children of the dead man to whom Chun Ho was married. And, rather than watch laundry folded, I was embarked on an operation of considerable detail and difficulty. In my office, this time working with no sleep at all, I made my lists and wrote out my instructions to myself and having to do with M and Adam and Lapham Dumont and sundry carters and the acquisition, presumably well in hand, of barrels. Timing would be exquisite or ruinous. Endurance, of course, and courage, desperation, and the air supply—I noted *Reeds through staves*—would, obviously, prove crucial. The master of the vessel: I wrote this unknown quantity upon my list, although I could do nothing to affect it.

Sam had seen me thus, on nights before an engagement. Burton, of course, had seen me, too, but he had been curious about nothing but his horses and his meals, and, of course, his safety. But Grafton, interested enough, had left me alone; he had always been a great believer in men alone with their thoughts. Sam, on the other hand, had always intervened, just this side of rudeness, because his curiosity was so great and his taste for the lives of others a genuine appetite.

"How many times do you clean it, then?" he asked, moving away from the fire and out to where I sat with my gear.

"Are you counting, Mr. Mordecai?"

"I am, in fact, Mr. Bartholomew. Do I intrude?"

"Of course you do."

He sat. "I don't mean to."

I looked at him.

"Not a great deal," he said. "It's just— I just this minute realized you get nervous."

"Frightened."

"That's hard to believe. Normal soldiers, infantrymen, of course. You, though. You're William Bartholomew."

"The cold-blooded assassin."

"No. But you always look so . . . certain."

"Well, I am, Mr. Mordecai."

"Sam."

"But you can be certain and be scared. They shoot at me with *guns*, Sam. They want to *kill* me. And all because I shoot them down while they use the latrine or eat their grub or yawn. So I'm scared of what they'll do to me, with a little luck. And I'm certain that, if they don't, I can kill them."

"So you clean your weapon."

"So I think of where I might have to go to take them. I think of how I might approach my blind. A line of retreat when I'm finished with work."

"Work," he said. "It *is* work, isn't it?"

"War had better be work. If it got to be play, we'd be wrapped in wet sheets and gibbering, I think."

He nodded and sat while I replaced the cleaning rod and put the cap on the vial of oil. "War can also be righteous," he said.

"Is this a righteous war?"

He nodded. "I'm embarrassed to use a word like that for pissing down your pant leg with fear or watching someone drown in their blood. Yes, though. My people—not just the Mordecais, but the bunch of us, the *people* in America, Jews from Spain or Asia or Europe who ended up here. We're a step away from the Negroes, you know. Truly," he said, as I began to protest. "You've seen the signs: 'No Jews, Negroes, Dagos or Dogs.' All of that. They don't use us as slaves, but they revile us. We sell drink on Sundays. We don't do business on Saturdays. We lend money. We are a nation among and unto ourselves."

He stood, he walked in a series of very small circles and came back to where he had been sitting, and he sat. I was rubbing down the cartridges with a rag so that nothing might interfere with the accuracy of my shooting. Horses nickered and Sergeant Grafton spilled hot coffee on his hand and softly cursed, as amused by his own clumsiness as annoyed. Burton sat in thoughtless rest, like his horses, content to be still, uninterested in what wasn't.

"We would be next," Sam said. "Maybe not slaves, but only maybe. Surely reviled. Surely treated, often enough, with indecency. With insulting impatience or amusement. Revulsion. Hanged or whipped for punishment like Negroes? Who's to know. I don't *want* to know. I have the feeling that, if we win this—"

"It isn't about slavery, Sam." His face fell, as a child's does, when I told him the news he did not wish to hear. "It's about money. Economy. Agrarians need slave labor. Industrialists need *cheap* labor. The North will use your Jews in any way they can. If we make the slaves free of the Rebels, then the North will use your Negroes in any way they can. We're fighting for the oppportunity for men of business, manufacturers, to get their hands on black men, Jews, and broad-shouldered girls. It's money, Sam, they're waging the War about. The righteousness is only yours."

"No," he said.

I put my rifle cartridges away and began to sort through the pistol cartridges in my little pouch. Next I would hone my knife.

"It's a far keener cause than that."

"Noble," I said.

"You mock what you might die for?"

If we had sat closer, I would have reached for his shoulder and patted it or squeezed it. I looked at his thin face under its wiry hair beneath his forage cap. There was a poignance to his need. I said, "I do not mock what *you* might die for, and I intend to kill enough of them to prevent your dying."

"Why, then? Why work so hard at it? The killing. If you don't believe."

"Oh, Sam," I said, "I do believe."

"In *what?*"

"In me," I told him.

The next morning, as I hid behind a tree and men first on horseback and then on foot, pursuing me, went past, I heard myself pontificate again while, half a mile away, at a folding wooden writing desk, a colonel of horse cavalry lay covered in flies, unless someone had begun tending to his corpse. Flies were gathering at my face and hands, but I did not brush them away. I lay on wet moss among ferns in a forest of pines, and I blinked away the flies at my eyes, and I waited to be safe. I had taken the colonel while he wrote, and while a lieutenant in the tent behind him had—in truth—played in a minor key at a violin. The colonel was a girlish-looking young man in a creased but clean-looking uniform, and he had long, fine fingers with which he tapped on the air, as if working out the proper phrase, or, for all I knew, the rhyme scheme of a poem. I put a bullet into the side of his head, which appeared to disintegrate as he went over, hands and elbows loose in the air, a cloud of sprayed blood remaining behind an instant where he had been. The ink spilled, and the pen hung in the air although the writer was gone while the shot still echoed.

Then, of course, the playing stopped, and then the lieutenant came from the tent, violin in one hand and bow in the other. I shot him as he emerged, putting the bullet into his chest, completing my murder of the finer arts and accomplished Southern manhood. These were deaths, I thought, trying to shield my eyes from the horseflies, that I would not describe to Sam Mordecai. Although he seemed, when he was with me in New York, to know more of my peculiar history than I had ever thought he might.

CHAPTER 6

"Yes," he said, "but a shipment of precisely what?"

"A secret, Sam."

"A shipment of secrets. Who but you, Billy, pitching into the trader's game, would import a shipload of secrets? It is a path you would feel impelled to take. And who will buy these secrets once you have them carted and in stock?"

I said, "For once in a long time, this is not a matter of sale. Or of resale. This is a favor to a friend." Homage to a friend, I thought. Obeisance to a friend. The gesture of a kneeling man who has no face. Has he the friend? Has she him?

"Trade between friends is said to be dangerous," Sam said knowingly, and I turned to examine him as we walked west to Gansevoort Street and, from there, farther west to the river. Wagons and carters on foot crowded the street as the masts in the air above the street crowded the riverside sky over the warehouses and the seamen's taverns. The masts and empty yardarms wobbled slowly in the warm, thick breeze, giving hints of the vessels beneath them, invisible to us, but exerting their massive weight on what we did see—ponderousness hinting the imponderable.

"How do you mean, Sam? That is: What do you know?"

His was the innocent face of a child, despite his being in his twenties, and despite his having been seasoned in our cruel engagements in the War. "Only what I say, Billy. That friends, it is said—it was said, in fact, by my father, who was a small tradesman all his life. He had a partnership at one time with a man from Georgia, by which I mean the country near Russia, not the state in which we—the bodies in the shed."

"Yes," I said, "the doll. En route to Milledgeville. The head of the little doll."

He cleared his throat and spat upon the street, a common enough undertaking—our cobbles and paths were moist from the mouths of our citizens—but nothing I had seen him do. He was a fastidious fellow, bathing more than the rest of us, and wandering farthest from camp to attend to his stool. "My father," he said hoarsely, "invested money with a man who was a neighbor in Boston and a friend. The man sold out their assets, cheap, because his wife became ill and he was in need of cash, and quickly, for surgeons and special foods. It was a disorder of the stomach. And my father lost a great deal of money, though his partner maintained his wife a few months more. He could not complain to the fellow, though he'd never asked my father or spoken in any way so as to suggest regret. Matters of trade and the amity of friends, he said, were not to be confused. That is all I know. Have I upset you? You sound perturbed."

"It's the mask," I said. "It muffles me."

"You sound clear as a bell," he said. "Might I know any particulars of the dockland adventure you seem to have in store for us?"

"Let me tell you a story," I said.

"But not in reply to my question, I take it."

"I know a widow in the Points. She lives not far from me, with her two children." I described the months at work in the Oregon gold fields, and the being transported by wagon to California. I told him that she had not spoken of the violence, but that her description of her husband's death implied a suddenness the effects of which still gripped her, and that I sensed her withholding of matters of violence to her own person and to her mother. "I find her remarkably brave," I told him, and I spoke of the boy and girl, and the large room and little room in which they lived with her and where she worked. I enumerated what I thought was the schedule of their days, suggesting the small steps of the children with their arms around the barrels of water from the pump, and the dragging, strong steps of Chun Ho as she transported twin baskets of clothing on the bamboo rod. I talked of her support from the *fang,* and how her mother lived with friends instead of with her because she would not raise her children in traditional ways. "She wishes, you see, to be an American. I find that . . . moving."

Sam studied me as I spoke, as if he might read my expression, or, that failing, and it would, then find a suggestion of my feelings in the rise and fall of my voice.

"And is it for this person that we are engaged upon the secret matters?"

"No."

"Perhaps it should be," Sam said.

"Her children call me *Gui.*"

"Gooey's a lump of mucus, Billy, among the soldiering men. These children must hold you in some strange regard."

"*Gui,* apparently, means devil. Or ghost. It's the mask, of course."

"The Secessionists called you a ghost, I remember, or think to remember. It is how we used to say they thought of you. But now it's a pet name, I take it. Something to do with endearment? Something like, oh, Daddy? Uncle, at the least?"

"Thank you, Sam. No."

"Perhaps it should be," he said.

As we clambered down the wooden steps from the shipping office to the cargo dock, I was thinking of Jessie's voice, and how I had tried to read it—hence, the familiarity of Sam's expression as he attempted reading mine. She sat at her little writing desk with its several compartments and its folded-down front, and I stood to its side. It was as if she were my employer, and I had come to report. Her fine, golden features were composed and without much evidence of her thinking. I found her eyes impenetrable, light and flecked and as focused within as M's small, dark eyes were inward in their attentiveness. She was always fond with me, and I never feared for the loss of her feelings, although I could not have summarized their nature. But she was removed that afternoon, and I felt a bit like the man who sees a vessel unmoored and speculates. At what rate did the dock grow smaller to a man on board the ship? At what rate did the ship grow smaller to a dockside observer? Something was happening, and I could not name it. I thought of describing it for Sam, who seemed able to reduce any event to a set of employable words. It was M, of course, who might sum it up philosophically. But I found that I did not wish to know. I simply thought of her writing desk, and of her distance from me, and how I strolled the room, attempting not to yammer and stumble in my speech. We discussed the contents of the telegraph message she had, and we agreed on further messages to send and to expect to receive.

Jessie looked down at her desk and then, raising her low voice to transcend the noises from the Yorkville streets, and pulling at the balloon sleeves of her dark red dress, she said, "You have a great need to touch me, haven't you, Billy?"

"Now, do you mean? Or all of the time?"

"This minute."

"Yes. I didn't think so, but yes."

"You find me distant?"

"A little, I think."

"Men need to penetrate what will not otherwise stay to hand? You fuck me to keep me?"

"I do not know what men need, Jessie. I do not always know what *I* need. And I wonder how *anyone* might keep you, if you mean against time or the attentions of others."

She smiled with what I thought was a true affection of some sort. It was early afternoon, and the strong light fell across her face and bosom and the deep cherry tones of her desk. Her eyes grew lighter, I thought, and I felt, as often I did, that she knew a great deal more than most of us.

"You find me beautiful?"

"I find you beautiful."

"And I, Billy, find you deep and dark and very frightening. And I smell soaps on your skin, or oils. And a kind of—fish? Do you eat something made from fish? Where do you spend your hours away from me? Do I know you, still?"

"I do not intend to be a different man. Nor do I mean to be—what was it? Deep? Frightening?"

"No. You were made so. You were tempered and constructed and made hard."

"Not so hard as I may seem."

She smiled. "I know that. I know you when you're soft, and when terribly hard. *No* one knows you as I do. Will you come close now and forgive me for thinking of our transactions in Florida instead of here? While I forgive you for simply leading a life away from mine? I am imprisoned here as much as I take refuge, you know."

"No," I said, although I was tumescent and all but trembling for her. "I would rather serve you in these matters to *your* satisfaction than wag my tail and beg for mine. You have transmitted to them the name of the dock and the hour it is best to arrive?"

"You know precisely what I have transmitted," she said, standing and moving toward her bed. "We have just discussed what I have transmitted. Would you, Billy, please come here?"

It is called a whipsaw, and we used them in the forest near Paynes Corners. Two men are required for efficiency, and each tugs, then pushes, on a vertical wooden handle at either end of the four- or five-foot saw. You push and then pull, push and then pull, to saw through downed trees or, working sideways, to cut down standing timber. It is called a whipsaw, as well, when you are cut at or torn in two directions, back and forth, so that, no matter your efforts, you are pulled and then pushed until you are cut apart. She said, undoing the tiny garnet-colored buttons that went from her neck to her waist—I had estimated twenty of them, talking to her over the little writing desk—"Will you come to me?"

"Sometime in the small hours," I told him, "when he is the night inspector. He can give the orders to off-load, and I will have a carter operating that cargo boom." Its ropes smacked the long shaft of the boom as the warm but welcome winds came up. "Not that there isn't risk, Sam. Never mind the river police or someone from Customs deciding to pop in. He may give them his permission to unload. But he is required to have a certificate from the Collector of Customs. If it is sought by someone, then hell is come to the Port of New York."

"Don't worry about me," Sam said, grinning like a boy. He waved his notebook in the air. "I am but a concerned journalist protecting the public weal. I was there, Honored Magistrate, in the interest of the body politic and, I admit it, a good story for the *Boston Weekly Advertiser*. But you, Billy? And our distinguished friend?"

I said nothing.

"Emulating dear old Abe, tell them. Tell them you're freeing the slaves. Now, why would you keep that a secret from me, Billy?"

"I should not have. I am engaged in the matter because of a friend. She—"

"Ha! A she! The one with the children who think you a ghost?"

"They merely *call* me Ghost. And no, it is not she."

"Another one, Billy! You *have* kept your powder dry. And now you spend it all. Her identity is the secret, then?"

"It is all a secret, Sam. I must have your hand on the matter of your silence."

He offered it, saying, "Until it is done. And then I may write it?"

"Until it is done."

She left the last two buttons, at the waist, for me, requiring that I undo each one by myself, and help her to pull the dress down over her hips, and then remove her camisole, and then the rest. She smelled like lemons at first, and then like fresh-baked bread.

"Billy," Sam was saying, "and then I may *write* it. Yes? You would have to shoot me down to keep me from telling this story, you know."

Telling, telling, telling: It was Sam's madness, perhaps because of the War, and perhaps what carried him—my accuracy notwithstanding—through the perils of the War. Now we stood, Sam and M and I, at the curbing of the cobbled street early in the morning. We had gathered for coffee, Sam late as was common with him, for he walked to us from the Astor, and was always halted by some sight, a New York sight, he would call it, which he wrote to retell to his editor in the hope of earning his expenses back. He had a small story about M, and a large city to describe, which pulsed like a wound, and the need to tell what he had seen or, I suppose, imagined on the basis of whatever he had seen.

We were gathered, with the sun slanting through the cross streets, at the corner of Murray and West Broadway, crumbs still clustered at the base of M's beard from the sweet French rolls he had eaten, and Sam was of course engaged in capturing a scene for his notebook. Seven or eight urchins, all dressed in filthy clothing, some of which was little more than rags—short pants or canvas overalls, few shoes in evidence, little sign of hygiene except for the heads of a few that had been shaved against lice—were seated at the curbing, where the stones abutted a cement ditch, into which some of them hung their feet, inches above the effluvium of the streets, which included the manure and urine of horses, one of which lay three feet from the children. Its body was bloated, its eyes and ears were covered with flies, and its front hooves touched the curbing as if it tried to brace itself against the continual falling away that was its death.

The children had gathered because of the horse, I thought, but now were accustomed to it, and sat, some with their back to it, chattering with serious, old faces and ignoring us. Men at carriages and outside warehouse doors spoke idly and passed one another and went to their work. The boys spoke, and one laughed. The one who neither spoke nor laughed, a tall fellow of seven or so, carried what seemed to me to be a bow for a cello or bass fiddle. He held it with some delicacy, and I thought, of course, of the lieutenant I had killed as he'd stopped playing and emerged from his tent in time to see the colonel go over and then to receive a bullet of his own.

Sam had a look of terrible concentration, and I wondered whether it was the smell of the horse as its rotting began, or the sad adult sense of limitations accepted which we could see in the children's faces; and then I understood: He was thinking of Sergeant Grafton, killed by his terrified horse, and then, of course, he was thinking of the horse, which, after all, he had destroyed.

So I waited for Sam, the teller, to begin his tale. However, in the sound of the chatter of the boys, and in the general din and motion, it was M who spoke up first. He said to no one in particular, while he gazed at the boys and at the horse, "I, for myself, have made up my mind to be annihilated." He wore his little badge, for he was on his way to his job, and he carried in his hand a book, the title of which I could not see and about which I was little concerned.

I said, because politeness required it, "Annihilated? You mean killed?"

"Something will kill me, shipmate," he said. "But no. I mean the moments after the agent of my destruction sees to my death. I mean the afterlife we hope for and in which some believe. I mean that when I am finished, I am *finished*."

Sam looked studious. He fished in his pocket for another pencil, the one, I presume, having dulled with overmuch use. I thought M looked deranged.

One of the wagons down the block began to move toward us. The carter pulled the horse by his bridle, talking to the big, chestnut dray which did not seem to want to approach his fellow on the cobbles.

"And," he continued, "I have come to regard this matter of fame as the most transparent of all vanities. Though, mind you, I will not diminish or disregard that most secret of all passions, ambition. I will confess to having been fertile ground for its seeds and its shoots. As potatoes turn to stone in the ground, as corn crops wither—and I have seen them dry into husks and curl and lie so low—so do other plantings. And, often, tender ambition may wither, and may never attain to the sweet, nourishing fullness of fame. And so be it."

Sam kept writing as M fell into silence and as the wagon was turned in a circle, and the dray forced backward with it. Then the driver looped his rope around the long, heavy-looking head of the dead horse. He mounted his wagon and called up his horse, who responded. Off they went, at a slow walk, the dead fellow slapping and flopping and, finally, giving forth a belch from the muzzle, or a passage of wind from the flanks, which buzzed along the street and sent the urchins flying in a celebration of body noises, the final manifestation of life in the great corpse.

Waiting for Sam to finish, and to at last return his notebook to his inside pocket, we began our progress down West Broadway and then to West Street. We were silent for a time, but then Sam blurted—as if the thought had been compressed inside his head, pushing at his eyeballs and his forehead—"Sir! May I— Am I correct in inferring from what you told us that the absence of fame is the *cause* of this 'annihilation'?"

M turned to me and gripped my arm with his powerful hand. He nodded as if in agreement with something that I had not said. "He's a wonderful one, is he not? He studies the visual, clamps on to the audial, and he jots and jots and jots. I was not unlike you, Sam Mordecai. Although I must confess that I wrote only what paid until I saw that what paid I could no longer write. It was *then*, already having strayed some— *Mardi*? Do you ken it? And of course my great fish broiled in hellfire: *There's* a meal to test your stomach! But then, Sam, I wrote what I would, not what *they* would have me write. And I served my ambition, though I killed off my fame. I inspected the slimy floor of the sea and the serpents under the floorboards in the cellar of the citizenry. Now, for that citizenry, I inspect the vessels that wallow behind the wind at the mouth of the North River." He mildly belched, then stopped and pointed—we must needs stop and thus regard.

"Annihilation," he said, "commencing before the condition of the posthumous sets in, and recompensing an old sailor at twelve hundred dollars per annum. Night duty paying no extra, for it is part of the job." He looked at me as he said this last, and I smiled for his emphasis, which was meant, I thought, to reassure me about our arrangement. Of course, he did not see me smile in return.

We walked again, about to separate, for M must be at his job. I was prepared to leave assured, for we had talked of our schedule and of our concerns.

He combed his beard with his fingers and said, "One matter, Billy. It really is *the* matter. I will say it in the charging of this pipe." He lifted a coarse, oily shag from a small leather pouch and, returning it to his pocket, began to tamp it by the single pinch at a time, into the charred, high bowl of his pipe, which, from the charring at its top and the oil of his fingers on the rest, was nearly black. "A man knows what is right," he said, packing the tobacco down, "and he knows what is required. It seems to be my topmost thought, since I have spoken on it often to you, and moments ago most latterly, in fact. I must do for you what I must not do, on pain of punishment at law. I must do it for *them*, and in the name of humankind. I do believe this. You have convinced me, and I will act." He had the pipe stuffed and tamped now, and he struck a match against the buckle of his belt and pulled it, trailing smoke and flame, up almost through his beard as he shielded the bowl from the wind with his other hand and sucked and sucked at the stem, so that the flame of the bowl dropped deep inside and then flared up past his fingers. "I must be unde-ceived in this. Tell me," he said, "that I serve only the right."

"I do believe it to be the case," I said, "and I swear myself confounded not a little by the fact that I, too, engage in this transaction. For there's no profit in it."

"Except the moral," Sam said, staring at me, perhaps remembering the woman to whom I had referred, perhaps posing me a question in his statement.

But M nodded his approval, and I did not reply to Sam.

M, around his pipe stem, said, "What do you say, Billy?"

"Why, I think I have said what I know and what I think. Does it not suffice?"

"It does," he said, and Sam smiled tentatively. Then he looked behind us, and then looked grim.

M, walking west and away from us, paused. He asked, "What?"

Sam shook his head. "No, you must depart, sir."

"But, Sam, *what?*" he asked.

"I was remembering a day in the hospital at Washington, when I visited Billy. He was in much discomfort. He was very brave. And I told him—I had to tell him of a horse I was forced to kill. I was not forced by any orders to do it."

"I was hardly brave," I said. "I killed like other men. And killed off other men. And of course you were not required by an officer to kill the horse," I said. "You felt you had to as a kind of revenge." To M I said, "The horse had killed a beloved sergeant of ours. Trampled him to death, in a panic induced by an artillery barrage."

"A horse conjures forth from memory a horse," M said. "The streets of New York bring forth the War. We live in several moments, several places, at once."

Sam made a noise not unlike a gasp. He wrenched his notebook out.

"You have told him something crucial," I said.

M, leaving us now, said, "Shipmates, it would be rewarding to think so."

What I saw, as he went, was the face of the woman who had cared for me, and who, while Sam had nervously chattered like a squirrel, unwrapped and then rewrapped my face, this time with spaces for my eyes. Hers was the first face I saw. Her nose was broad and her mouth was small and tight. Her hair, curly with humidity and the color of tree bark, clung to her square head.

Her eyes had slid away from mine when she smiled an angry smile and said, "You see? I told you I was plain."

"If you would come into this bed with me, I would worship you," I said.

She flushed to her neck, but on her unfortunate, oily skin, it seemed a kind of rash. She said, "You're regaining your health, I see, and growing rude as you do."

"I would kiss every inch of your flesh with these scabrous lips," I said.

Sam, I remembered noticing, had also flushed.

And her thick, square body had gone quite still, and then she had peered at me, her face still angry. "Liar," she said, as if I had betrayed her.

Sam's head had risen, and he was motionless in his concentration.

"Not so," I said.

"No," she mocked.

"But no," I said.

And she had stared and stared, taking the measure of me, whose body she knew and which she had served so generously.

I looked back into her eyes.

Then she noisily took in a breath, and she turned her face from mine and carried away the soiled bandages.

And M, embarked now for the intersection of Laight and Washington Streets, and the thump of steam whistles, the clash of metal gears and the grinding of sea-soaked wood, called back as he strode his long paces away, "You ride your horse, Sam."

While Sam visited the telegraph office to demonstrate to his editors in Boston that his story—of a great national treasure gone into neglect— would repay the cost of his sleeping and eating and drinking very well, I made for my office. I had no check from Lapham Dumont, but I did have a set of papers that would have made a national treasure, or even a journeyman, proud if his profession was the composition of fiction. For, according to these papers, a shipper in Corpus Christi had received a cargo of rum from Haiti; he had sent it from his warehouse on a

schooner bound for the Port of New York, which had paused for replacement of its gaff sail boom at Savannah. It was due in tomorrow, three
dozen tun and half-tun barrels of bonded spirits. A carter, led by Adam,
would receive the shipment in the high light of noon—according to
the papers—although Adam knew, and M knew, and Jessie knew, and
Dumont did not, I prayed, that the wagons would be loaded and would
roll—up Washington or Greenwich Street, some perhaps up Broadway—ponderous and piled, and alive with small black children who had
hours before been scampering on the decks of Captain Corbeil's ship.
These papers did not represent the sums forwarded, and received, for the
captain's fee, and for two adult Negro women to supervise the conduct,
and see to the comfort, of the children on their voyage from slavery to
freedom. The amounts expended for food and drink and bribes for the
skeleton crew were not listed. Nor were there details of how they had
been freed; it was a shadow freedman's bureau, Jessie implied, not trusting even me with names or locations, for the South was still a dangerous
place. There was a bill of lading and a receipt of shipment. There were
carter's fees, marked as paid in full. And there were the warehouse
receipts.

Missing was the Special License required for landing goods from on
board a cargo vessel, as required in the statutes governing the tax Surveyor of the Port of New York; that license had to be provided to the
night inspector by the Collector's Office. I had written one out for M,
and he was going to sign it. There was also missing a certificate of duties
paid, a Customs House form, and M would also sign that. He would
become, instead of the teller of truths, a liar on federal forms: a felon and
a forger. This, I thought, is how fiction is constructed—of felonies and
forgeries, of lies about hogsheads swung ashore, against the laws, at
night.

What I did not yet know was whether M would sustain his enthusiasm. For he had said to me at last, "If we can save these children, we
must." He had faltered and gone silent, and I'd looked away. I heard the

gurgle of spirits and then his voice again: "Law must be required to kneel before the right. *That* is what happened at times in the War."

"This I do know," I had told him.

"And it did not occur in my home."

I knew that he was thinking of Malcolm, and that something to do with his household laws had been obliquely touched upon. I could not see it. I could feel it, though.

"We must see to what is right. There is risk—an income, a pension, the frayed remnants of a reputation."

"Life," I had told him, "and limb."

His breath met the level of the liquor in his glass. I heard his breathing fill up the glass. "They are as nothing, or at any rate little. A man falls from the yardarm and crushes his skull and dies. He is sewn into a shroud of sailcloth loaded with scraps of ballast or balls of shot, and he is slid from under a flag off the deck to lie on the floor of the sea forever and ever. That he broke, and how, are of small moment. They are life and limb. But was he, at a moment of his life, in the *right*? I will sign the forms, Billy. We will off-load in darkness. The children shall be free. And *then* may heaven protect them."

It was all too much of principle for me, and overmuch protestation. I must see him sign before I might speculate on right, wrong, sailcloth shrouds, or freedom. What I engaged in were transactions. The rest of it, I thought, were words—some of them, I had to allow, said by Jessie.

There were other documents to read and sign, and a check to write, and one to bank, and a proposal from a speculator in real estate sold or leased for theatrical purposes; he had become one of the underwriters, and he urged me to purchase a share of his share, of appearances in New York by Mr. Charles Dickens, who, in January, would give what the notice said were readings. That is to say, the English writer would appear in the Steinway Hall, which was built to hold an audience of over two thousand, and he would dramatize scenes, as I understood it, from his many popular books. Sam had spoken of Dickens, and he was the sort of fellow who might buy several tickets. There might be many such, according to the esteem in which Dickens seemed to be held. It seemed to me an endeavor in which I might participate, and I knew that Sam would be charmed; perhaps he would return to New York for the readings, although, according to the proposal, Dickens would also appear in Boston. But it might be a jolly occasion, I heard myself saying to Sam, and it was, after all, the season that men alone, in large cities and, I speculated, on frozen prairies and ships at sea, might find most trying. Sam, I heard myself suggest, come down to New York for a holiday! I wrote a counterproposal and pinned to it a check, the transmission of which, with other innocent documents, I would see to later in the day.

I read in the *Times* of streets torn up for replacement of the surface with stone blocks instead of cobbles. Crack a cobble, I thought, and it's one small, broken stone; crack a large stone block, and you've holes, soon enough, that you might lose a wagon in. And they called this progress. I thought of the laborers who would do the work, the Bohemians and Scandinavians, the sturdy Irishmen, the slender, powerful Chinese—if the Europeans permitted them to join the crews. And of course I thought of the woman who was married to a dead man. I thought of Jessie, tracing my fingers on the tattooed figures on her stomach and her breasts. I thought, in turn, of the dead horse in the road, and of the unnamed, squarish woman, so generous and weary, who had nursed me through considerable pain and shame and my wish to surrender, and who had goaded me to want to see again, and to dare being seen. The papers would be signed by the night inspector, and the unseen children would be taken uptown to an address that Jessie would provide. At the end of it, I would have served her, and Adam would have served his people and me, and M would have served Malcolm or, anyway, his memory of him, and Sam would not have served; he would have *ob*served, which seemed to constitute his passion.

And where, then, I wondered, would each of us go? For this would have been a small event of such large moment in our lives, that a change or shift or long pause for reflection would feel necessary, I thought. And I wished I knew what I hoped for from Jessie. My work toward the end she sought was, after all, a transaction. Would one between us then begin? Or would it have concluded? I had been in the company of Sam, with his speculations and his formulations, for too long, I thought. It had not occurred to me, during our time in the War, that he might exert such an influence upon my life.

Had I seen this madness of the notebook during our fighting days? I wondered. And I could not recall. In fact, I thought, I had hardly noticed him, except as an extension of Sergeant Grafton and Private Burton and their mission as a group in detachment: to care for me. Burton had curried my horse and seen to his hooves and his tack. Sam had fed me when they cooked and while Burton fed the horses; the sergeant had seen to my few wounds and occasional sprains of the knee or shoulder, had waited out with me my sometime deafness after shooting, had gone over with me maps and escape routes, had established paroles and set out Sam and Burton as pickets while I was off on the hunt. I recalled Sam's curious, wide eyes, his wiry hair, his sallowness and attentiveness and, in general, his seriousness, often leavened with humor; I suspected that some of the seriousness could be laid to fear, and it was a condition general to the four of us. We were alone, in Rebel country, and always about to come under their fire.

No notebook, though, and no frantic, frowning scrawl of notes. It had come after, I thought. After Sergeant Grafton's brains had spilled upon Sam's trouser legs and boots. After the blood of his horse had sprayed Sam's face.

I recalled how I had teased him, when I had wished only to fall on the ground near his feet and groan, when I returned, winded, from a mission. I had been in a vulnerable position, which is to say that although I was camouflaged with branches and leaf and grass I had tied upon myself and over even my forage cap, I was without cover, spraddle-legged on the rise above their camp. I could kill some, but then, if they had some nerve and could remember what good marksmen most of them were, they would have a clean shot into me as I rolled—it was my plan—away and down until the hill protected me from their fire.

I could not still the racing of my heart, nor the sighing of my breaths, which I drank rather than inhaled. I was certain they would hear me, had perhaps already heard me and were lying in wait while a few—I counted seven—pretended to build the fire up for the heating of lead to pour into the shot molds I saw through my telescope. At one instant, I closed my eyes and braced my body on the ground, head sideways on the scrubby grass, all of me shivering as if a terrible fever were passing through my body. No shot came, of course, for they were unaware of me, and I forced myself to count to ten. On the final count, I required that I raise my head. I did. And then I ordered my eyes to open. They obeyed.

Before me, on the ground, inches from my slowly moving head, was a bright blue bird with a duller blue breast that was brighter, still, than any blue I had seen, including those of the bluebird in my own upstate countryside, and the blues of Union soldiers and the first Confederate uniforms, and the blues of poor countrywomen like my mother, dressed in dull and inexpensive hues. I did not know its name, nor do I know it now. But I can see him. For he stood before me, a slowly writhing dark red worm in his mouth, and he stared along his blunt beak as if to challenge me to contend for the meal. My life, in the War, had so many times been held, like a worm, and like the worms to which I consigned my targets, at the mercies of a small creature of large appetite. I must find the lesson in this, I instructed myself.

I extended my rifle, and I lined up the first shot, having, with the telescope, now stowed in my jacket, selected the second and the third. I sighted, first, on the small black kettle that was on, really in, the fire. A sergeant with leather gloves and a stained leather cloth held in one gauntleted hand was preparing to pour the lead. The bright blue bird flew up, and one of the ranks—a country boy like me, I supposed—stuck out a hand, no doubt out of reflex in response to the color and motion.

Another looked up, and I froze. But I was too convinced they had spotted me to do what was wisest: remain in position and let their eyes accept me as an aspect of the countryside. I breathed out, and I fired. I fired again. The kettle took the first shot, and the second struck the fire—wasted powder. The sergeant was caught in the face and chest as he kneeled above the lead, and he began to scream. I saw his flesh give off a dirty smoke that rose around him.

Several of them came to his assistance, while the veterans moved away, toward their picketed horses and the trees. I caught one of them first, for he would be a cleverer soldier than those who had gone toward the wounded target. I then swung back, and I took the first one to reach the screaming sergeant, and then the second, who had halted while I shot. Some of them were firing, and one of them was good. He was excellent. He burned the back of my neck where I lay, and I howled. Then I remembered to roll, and I went flailing down the hill, bruising myself on the ammunition case and on my pistol every time I went around. I held on to the rifle so that my elbows and upper arms might take the brunt of my striking the ground, for I would need the rifle far more than I would hate the soreness of my arms. Nevertheless, I struck my face twice with my own firing mechanism, and I could feel the blood from the back of my neck.

I was moving through the evergreen forest below the little rise and well into its shadows before they could mount a pursuit. I panted and groaned my way, stilling myself twice to listen for them, then running on, whimpering by now like a child. I stopped close to the farther edge of the woods, and I caught my breath; it seemed to take me half an hour, although it was moments only, and then I forced my head back, although it stung, and more than that, and then I walked with a feigned ease back toward our encampment.

"Jupiter," Sam called out.

I replied with "Your anus."

"It's *Ur*-anus, Mr. Bartholomew."

But I was already there, closer to him than he had thought, and I was enjoying a bit, I confess, his exclamations over the blood at my neck and the bruises and cuts upon my face and hands.

He said, "I'll fetch the sergeant to see to your wounds. I heard the firing."

I was about to nod to his wide eyes, and to affect a veteran's silence, when my intestines crawled about and began to thrash within me as if some animal, the size, say, of a raccoon or mink, had burrowed into my belly to dig its home. I leaned my rifle at him, and he caught it with a kind of surprise. "Trench," I confessed, and I ran to it, crossing our camp and frightening one of the horses. If he brought our pursuers with his nickering, I would probably be killed as I sat on the log at our trench, but I would be fortunate to get there, and not to be caught with my trousers on the ground or filled with my wastes.

It was the burning, watery discharge of pure fear, and I was grateful to Burton for having left behind a few sheets of an Athens newspaper he had found. I did not think about smearing myself, as the flies gathered and my own odor choked me as it rose, with the facts or lies the Rebels told themselves about the War. I was happy to have lived, and happy to be through some of my terror in a private moment, and happy enough to consider that I would soon have to do it, or something very like it, again.

Later, as we led our horses with their hooves wrapped in pieces of flannel that Burton carried in a sack for the purpose, Sam, beside me, whispered, "I have never known you to leave your weapon, Mr. Bartholomew."

"Nature is the breaker of habits," I replied.

"It was an honor to be trusted."

"I was, shall we say, relieved, Sam."

Sergeant Grafton hushed us angrily, and he was right. I patted Sam on his bony shoulder, and he turned his head in surprise, no doubt at the intimacy of my gesture. I saw him lay his wide, intelligent eyes upon me, and I knew that he was—as I considered wind and drop and angle when I laid a shot—puzzling out a way in which to think about me.

While I, in the remainder of that morning's march, as the sun came fully up and we stripped the horses' hooves and rode, was remembering how, when spring came to Paynes Corners, I came home to build a new outhouse at my mother's place. I made the seat narrow, but sturdy, and I built the inside platform a little lower to the ground. Although I did salvage some of the wood from the old one, I set most of it afire where it stood and, guarding against leaping sparks with a ready bucket of water, I watched the flames, and then the sinking wood, and then the dropping of the platform, the crashing of the walls, and the burning of what lay beneath the wood and in the soil. I expected to smell something, at some point, like the roasting of beef. But it all finally smelled the same—a kind of acrid, intimate odor rode on the darker smell of burning wood. We were all, finally, the same, waste and lumber and Uncle Sidney. That evening, I noticed that my mother was gaining weight, and we roasted early lamb and gnawed the small rib bones.

I did not, however, see him making notes that day or in the camp that night. Sergeant Grafton insisted on disinfecting my neck with horse liniment; while Burton saw to the horses, the sergeant saw to me. And Sam, at his chores, did keep his eyes upon me, until I became nervy and snapped at him once when he asked a question about the charge of powder in the cartridges I employed.

"What difference can it make, Sam, for Christ's sake?"

"In how they die and how you live, Mr. Bartholomew."

"Well said," the sergeant said from his blankets, where he lounged and smoked, his men having been seen to and Burton set upon patrolling the perimeter.

"Truly," I relented. "I might be a little . . . eccentric tonight."

"It was close this morning," the sergeant said.

"Always, I suppose. But this morning, I felt as though, from the start, they had me."

"And?"

"They weren't that close," I said.

"A half an inch away," the sergeant said.

"How frightened were you?" Sam was young enough to ask it.

I was either veteran enough, or very young, and silence, in either case, would seem the only reply. I told him nothing.

Sam looked at me with his wide eyes, and I felt the pressure of his speculations. And I feel them now.

And here we poised, on the eve of the day of the eve. It was the middle of September, and hot in New York, but on the evening winds off the river there had come a hint of more than soiled water, and more than the dusty cliffs of New Jersey, and more than the smoke, dust, and corruption of the manufacturing process that was as dark upon the air as it was clamorous around our heads. It was a touch, barely a dilution in the general heat and stench and turmoil, of something cool, something like the seasons hinging toward fall. So we might change again, I thought.

I had been walking through the night. A vast hog had confronted me at St. John Street, once verging upon Africa, and we had stood there across from St. John's Park, perhaps his bower and patrol, as if we were fighters in a duel, he sniffing my odor and backing up a pace, then coming forward a pace, as if he could not decide which part of me to snap and then suck down into his very large belly. His face seemed mild, almost comical, for he had a wound or growth near the bottom of his great lips on the rightmost side, and it made him look as if I struck him humorously.

"I will not be imprisoned on this street for you," I told the hog. I had drawn my pistol, and I knew that I would fire.

Two women, quite pale and old and drawn inside the vast, dark skirts of their costumes, looking, really, like seamed, gray children in the clothing of adults, were about to pass me and cross toward the park when they saw what I stood before.

"Gretchen," one of them said, "that man has a gun."

"He has a wild pig, Eleanor."

"Is he going to kill it?"

"Shall we ask him? Sir," she called.

"Madam." I turned to respond and, finally seeing me through their myopia, they each took several steps back.

"Gretchen, that man has a mask. Is he an outlaw?"

I wondered if it had been my grotesque appearance that gave the pig pause. "I advise that you effect a detour, ladies. Return, perhaps, to the corner of the street behind us and cross over there to the park."

They fled me, and when I turned to the pig, he as well decided that I was a formidable presence and made his way along Canal. If he continued, I thought, he would arrive at the wharf of the Collins Liverpool Steamship line; embarking, he might become some of the famous Liverpool sausages.

I continued toward my home district, quite nearby to the east, and I was caught at the corner of Broadway and Leonard by a feeling I had known in the War. I wondered, in fact, if I roamed the city in an effort to capture these vagaries of mine; when I was unawares, and afoot, and adrift—for all my conspicuousness somehow still in hiding within the mask and the wound behind it—I walked into emotions that drifted upon the atmosphere of the streets as if they were smoke, or odors; in midstep, I was transported into a place I had been that was not New York and was not now. I thought, of a sudden, on the night before the day of our rescue of the Negro children, of a time when Sergeant Grafton found me outside our encampment in the week or thereabouts before they hunted me down.

"Mr. Bartholomew," he said, coming up behind me and pausing. I had read the sounds of his approach and, from the size of the stride and sound of his breathing, I had known who approached.

"Sergeant," I said.

"I have a sense that you are troubled," he said, "and I wondered if I might be of some assistance."

I turned to face him under a moonless sky and, in the darkness of those dense woods, I watched him swat at nighttime insects, a shape more than a particular man. "If you could see my face," I said, "you would see me smile. I am grateful, but you cannot protect me from ghosts as if I were a child from whose dream I required rescuing. The ghosts, of course, are actual. Does that make any sense to you?"

"But you enjoy your work, Mr. Bartholomew. Or am I mistaken?"

"I cannot know what you mean by 'enjoy,' Sergeant. But I likewise cannot imagine that whatever pleasures a marksman might take in the execution of his duties have any effect upon the spirits of the dead."

"You are haunted," he said.

"Why are you not?"

"I do not kill them in that manner."

"You believe," I said, "that the manner of killing is a matter of any moment to the dead? Or, for that matter, to those who effect the death?"

"It is why there are rules."

"There no longer are. Wars are fought between nations? Not the present one. Wars are a contest in the moral theater? Not this economic contest. Wars are for our right? Has Abe not abridged what once was promised by our Constitution? I do not know your rules, Sergeant. I am killing these people as best I can, and I am enduring the consequences. Cause and effect. If that is my lot, or being shot out of a tree by a Secessionist marksman intended to be my target, then cause will have been served by effect."

I heard myself panting, and I required of my breathing that it grow quiet.

"You are attempting, then, to come to terms with your own conclusion," Sergeant Grafton said. "You are an old man in some ways, are you not?"

"It is likely that I may not become one in the matter of years spent in breathing upon the earth. It's therefore just as well that I age while I can, Sergeant."

"Come in as soon as you can, then. Sam Mordecai is worried that you are unescorted in the forest."

"Strange fellow," I said. I ratcheted back the hammer of the Sharps. "I am never unarmed. You might tell him that."

The sergeant paused, turned, then paused again and said, "When we have done with all this, when it is through, Mr. Bartholomew, and we are demobilized, as I pray will occur to you and me and our fellows back in the camp, I would like you to come as a guest to my home, my father's home, in Saugerties. Do you know it?"

"On the Hudson," I said, "far north of New York City. It is below where I live."

"Which is?"

"Paynes Corners. A small settlement in the center of the state of New York. A hundred and more miles, I believe, north of you. Little is there, although the Payne after whom it is named is said to be a relative of the patriot who changed the spelling of his name because he was a loyalist during the War of Revolution. There weren't rules in that one either, by the by. Which is how the Americans won."

"You study war, then."

"For the time being, Sergeant, war is what I am."

The dampness of the dark forest, the distant smell of horse manure and horses, unwashed men, the smell of roasted rabbit which Burton had trapped, and something almost rotten, perhaps my own terrified sweat that rose about me as I moved in the forest, seeking someplace solitary where I might huddle with my arms about my own knees and thus take hold of myself for what comfort I might provide while I shook—that was all of what seized me at Leonard Street. I was near a notorious alleyway in the Points, running as it did behind a terrible crib above a vicious saloon, and situated as it was above a tunnel that came from the central sewers. It was here that we had seen enormous rats, and where more than one infant, left alone in its blankets and sucking on a flavored bit of ice, had been attacked while the mother was seeing to her business within.

The minders they hired were cripples and drunks who were of little use but who, for a penny or two, claimed to keep an eye upon the babes, and to comfort them if they required attention. The flavored ice was offered in place of food, and they soon enough dropped it because of the cold or because their little fingers could not manage the grip.

I wondered if the worst element I smelled was something dead. The alley was lighted only from the windows above, and few of them were illuminated at that moment. I saw motion in the alley's mouth, not far from where I had paused, and I took hold of my pistol and cocked it. I wanted any observer to hear that I was armed. And no one in those streets at night could mistake the cocking of a gun. It is a cold and very clear and ultimate sort of sound, tending to carry much farther than you might imagine, even in the clamor of those streets. And then, because I was alert to menace, as was often the case, I found myself drawn to it— sooner the ugly stench and almost liquid darkness of the alley, I chided myself, than a street I must share with a pig of the streets.

I walked slowly into the alley, and light from the thoroughfare disappeared as if the lamps had been blown out. I waited then in the dark, for my eyes to grow accustomed to it. And soon enough, I could see motion farther in, and then see figures. A piece of the street seemed to rise, and I understood that someone had opened a cellarway or a cover for one of the new drains meant to accommodate the rising tides of sewage and the floods of fresh water from storms. I closed my eyes, and I smelled what I had smelled during the War, when I went off into the woods to shake and weep. Some of that was the concentration of cooking odors and the general stink of stained bedclothes and unhealthy whores. Some was cheap or debased spirits. Some was the corruption of household and commercial garbage in mounds that had been heaped against the bricks and clapboard of the structures that formed the alley. There was probably a dead dog or cat or even horse that rotted under one of the mounds—it might have been a person; so many went missing in these places and never were found—but I could, for all my efforts, not identify the deep and rank and familiar olfactory note that probably, of all the smells, had brought me into this other world abutting the more familiar one.

As I walked farther in, toward the part of the walkway that had risen, I listened, through the mechanical piano playing and the shrieks of false gaiety, the grumbling deep noises of men at rut or next door to stupor, for a sound betokening threat. I heard it—a mechanical grating at once thin and loud: the cocking of a weapon—as I recollected the nature of the smell. It was fear, which had driven me before it into the forest during the War. I sniffed at my own odor and wondered whether it was derived from my being here, or whether my fear of the morrow, and our rescue, and its consequences, had sent me down the alleyway.

I stood in my place, the pistol in my hand, which hung at my side. "Good evening," I said into the darkness.

"You're here for a reason?"

"The reason is that I didn't go somewhere else."

Someone laughed. Light came up then from the stones of the street itself, and I saw that they—I made out two of them in the light—had been in the sewers and were emerging, or were about to descend.

From up the alley a woman's voice called, "They opened hell again, girls!"

"I will *not* do a swallow-cock on Satan," another woman replied. "My throat's off duty for the night."

The first one replied, "Yes, dearie, but the mouth in your ass does double duty, doesn't it?"

"Is your business with me?" the man called softly.

"What's your business, then?"

"You would know, if you were supposed to be here."

"You're one of the Swamp Angels," I said. "Did you escape from the Tombs? Or are you some other municipality's prisoners? Former prisoners," I amended.

"You're police?"

I went closer. I cannot say why I was thus drawn. Perhaps I was driven by my fear to prove—to me, perhaps somehow to *it*—that I would not be controlled; surely, I seemed to need to assert it to the man with the weapon. In the light that came up, a poor and wavering light, so perhaps from a lantern or candles, I saw that he wore a dark, dirty kerchief around his mouth and nose below his eyes. The smell of raw sewage rose with the light, and it was possible that he wore the mask against the stench, although, seeing my veil, he seemed actually to become less apprehensive and to make something of a show of uncocking his pistol, a large, nickel-plated weapon with a snubbed barrel. I uncocked the .31 and replaced it in my belt, at the back, beneath my coat. His clothes looked shabby and long unwashed. His shoes were surprisingly delicate in appearance and workmanship, and I suspected that he wore them beneath fisherman's boots that he had discarded on his way up.

"You aren't police," he said. "We don't invite visitors. We turn them away. Some of us were about to come up for, well, recreation."

"One of them said her jaws were tired."

"All of them have more than jaws."

A stovepipe head slowly rose in the light and the terrible smell, and then a small man wearing a white muslin mask about his mouth and nose came up beneath it. He had one eye and a puckered hole where the other had come out. He was missing most of his ear on that same side, and his stovepipe listed in the same direction. He noted my veil, I saw, and was assured.

"Evening," I said. "Or is it morning now?"

"Soon," the little fellow said.

I noted the approach of the second man I had initially observed. He wore a long coat that nearly touched the stones of the alley, and a sailor's wool cap. I had thought, at first, that I saw M in his oilskins, but this was a man with no beard I could see who also wore a mask he had fashioned from a large, figured red bandana. He stood beside the first man and then walked around him to stand closer to me. Even his eyes, little and

fatigued, slightly closer together than in most faces, reminded me of M. We had stood at the wharfs one late afternoon, when after my own day's work I had come to meet him at the conclusion of his. We were to take a meal, and drink some strong ale, and tell stories. He had, always, to tell stories—they were his only form of intimacy, Sam had said, upon meeting him. It was a point with which I could neither agree nor disagree, for I did not wholly understand its meaning.

But there we stood, he in his long oilskin coat and watch cap, I unprotected from the rain except by my hat. I had stowed the mask beneath my coat, to protect it, and was holding the veil in place as the winds came in with some force. M had scrupulously observed me as I held the mask and sited it beneath the jacket of my suit, which I fastened with some care. He looked at my face as I covered it and replaced my hat.

"You have penetrating eyes, Billy," he had commented, looking away, at the roiled and pockmarked surface of the river. "You see things, don't you? Short, quick probings at the axis of reality, and then back undercover, if you don't mind my saying it. Back beneath the mask."

"I am flattered to have been so studied, and to have been so considered."

"It's the mask that reinforces the study, I think. And it's the mask that lets you say the wise, brooding words I enjoy in our exchanges. You have read Shakespeare, I know."

"I was a boy, at Yale."

"An oceangoing vessel underneath a cloud of canvas was my Yale. But I have read the dark characters of Hamlet, Timon, Lear, and Iago, through whose mouths he so craftily says, or sometimes insinuates the things, which we feel to be so terrifically true." He leaned closer and, although we were of a similar height, he reached around me as if to loom at my ear from a height. He succeeded in dripping water from his sleeve down the back of my coat. I shivered with the cold of it as he said, almost into my ear, "Those things he says, shipmate. Those true, terrible things, he tells through the mouths of his *characters*. Do you see? For it would

be all but madness for any good man—Shakespeare or Bartholomew—in his own, proper character, to utter or even hint of the truth. Remember Lear! I feel so close to him, Billy! That frantic king tears off *his* mask and speaks the sane madness of vital truth. But, Billy, it is Shakespeare behind him. It is Shakespeare who wears his face, his soul. Lear is, you understand me, *Shakespeare's* mask! How else might we tell the world our terrible thoughts except through these masks?"

I had nothing noteworthy to reply on the subject, although it had crossed my mind that I might mention how little choice I had in the matter of my own mask. Yet, I thought, it had been my idea to commission one. I tried to ponder his words as the rain was whipped at us by rising winds.

"I came to think in this manner after encountering Nathaniel Hawthorne the man while simultaneously encountering his work. I was shocked, as if coming upon myself unawares in a mirror. He never, to my knowledge, paid the same, thrilled courtesy to my own fishy efforts. And he is dead, poor man. Too soon taken. On your guard, Billy. Take care. This business of mortality is, I think, contagious, for men are dying, willy-nilly, every day. You need only see an evening paper or two."

"We have business," the one in the red bandana said.

"You and I?" I asked him.

He shook his head. "Us. You don't belong here."

"No," I said. "Although I am a businessman."

"Good for you," he said. "We moved in the other day. We don't want to make friends with our neighbors. It's bad enough, living down there."

"You're awaiting a boat," I suggested.

"Who told you?" He put his hand into his coat, and I did the same, reaching behind me for the .31.

"I said I'm a businessman. I have access to a schooner that won't be full as of tomorrow night. Perhaps I should name a figure."

"Don't name anything," he said. "Don't say anything. To anybody. We don't want your boat. Go away."

"That's the extent of our business, then. I'll go away."

"I'll watch you leave," he said. The two others had descended again, although I could not imagine how. The smell seemed to grow worse the longer it hovered there. Drawn in by the smell and the menace, I was sent away by them, and I was happy to be leaving. When I emerged from the alley and its convention of wary men in masks, I smiled beneath my own to consider how pleased he would have been, with his Hamlet, his Timon, his Lear, to have witnessed us. M would no doubt have spotted them—he lived in a kind of crow's nest and was always on the lookout—but I wondered, our fear and curiosity aside, what great truths we could possibly have touched upon as, covered up and armed and circling like gaunt, wild dogs, each man had addressed the other through his mask.

As we did again, in hours, I reckoned, although I hadn't the opportunity to consult my watch. They hammered at the door, and I was up, having barely gone to bed.

"Fire," the man seemed to say, and I ducked my head and slid, crouching, to the floor, as I expected a volley of shots. I realized soon enough, of course, that the voice was not commanding someone to shoot me, but had cried a warning.

"Fire!" the voice called once more. And then I heard the hammering of fists upon neighboring doors, and, of a sudden, the Old Brewery, huge and dark and leaning, stinking of yeast and the intimacies of too many bodies, and made of old, alcohol-soaked wood, and ready as a wick to be lit, began to shudder. "*Fire!*" the fellow cried louder. There was a set of stairs nearby that ran to the roof from the ground, passing my door, and I could hear the terrified inhabitants of the upper floors as they poured from their tinderbox rooms and fled downstairs. I heard people cry out as they were trampled, and of course the small children began to shriek their terror.

I did not retrieve my pistol from the heap of my clothing at the side of the cot, nor did I bother to fetch anything with me except the keys to my Broadway office.

"Fire!" the man in the hallway called again, his voice mingling with the roars of the panicking mob.

I took up my cudgel, thinking that I might be required to pry my way into those who sought escape or blocked the way.

I sniffed at the edges of the door, and surely I did smell something powerful yet familiar, and with a tinge to it of flame or hot wax. Without thinking further—and that's always the end of your luck, isn't it?—I undid the lock, barely stepping back in time to avoid being struck as the door swung violently in. They were, of course, the threesome from the alley, Angels, as they were called by some, devils, as they were named by the whores upstairs, but men, at any rate, who were desperate to stay out of prison, and who knew how to see to themselves. The fleeing tenants poured through them, but they held their place until the one with the red bandana pushed me backward, and I stumbled but kept to my feet, backing up as they entered, waiting as they closed my door against rescue. I hefted the persuader. He showed me his stubby-barreled pistol. The other two seemed not to be armed, although the little one-eyed fellow in the stovepipe hat kept patting his suit coat at his heart, as if to remind me that he was but an arm's thrust away from a gun. He carried a squat miner's candle, which was set, on his open left palm, in a pool of its own drippings. The flickering light was sufficient for us to see one another and, I suspected, for me, as was usual in such events, to see best. To them the room was a shifting of light and dark shadows, while for me it was merely a darker version of a dark or foggy day.

The dirtiest of them, whom I had encountered first, said, "What'd you do to your face?"

"He took his veil off," the armed one said.

"No," the first one said. "It ain't a face. He put a mask on."

"Why do you not take off yours?" I suggested. "We can all be naked-faced and ugly together."

"Why do you not find us your pocketbook and your gemstones?" asked the one with the pistol.

"In this place? Gemstones? What makes you think I can procure money?"

The gunman said, "A man who has a ship has money."

"I said I knew a ship. I do not own one."

"In my life, mister, you're as good as an owner. But we don't want your ship. We have one coming in. We want for cash. We need meanwhile-money. While the boat comes up the coast. Food, weapons, clothes."

"Your clothing smells like a house afire. That is how you duped me."

"A fire can still be arranged," the other tall one said.

The little one, an animated candle stand with one ear and one eye, slapped his pocket and arched his small brows at me. His face, in the light of his candle, was seamed deeply, figured in cross-hatchings that his difficult life had etched upon him.

I swung the shovel haft with all my strength at the man with the snub-nosed pistol. I had intended to hit him at the junction of the elbow and forearm, for I knew that to be struck there sharply was to go so numb as to become unable to aim or fire a gun. I missed the elbow and hit him on the upper arm, but with great force, and I could have sworn I heard the bone crack. He howled, and I struck the arm again. He dropped the pistol, and I reached for it. But the little fellow, by then, had come forward, dropping the candle, which lay guttering while he stabbed with the folding knife he had drawn, no doubt from the pocket above his heart.

Since the blade was stuck through my nightshirt and into my arm, I removed both arm and blade from the little man's reach, and I swung the haft again, dislodging the knife and spraying my blood across the man who had dropped his pistol as well as the little man whom I struck in the side of the head and rendered unconscious. I retrieved the pistol and I stuck it into its charging owner, for I wanted, even in the heart of the Points, amid the hysterical cries and chatter of the crowd outside, to muffle the shot with his body. The flare of the discharge was obscured and he went down to his knees at once. I scrambled backward, until I reached the edge of my cot, and aimed the pistol, with unsteady hand and arm, but with the authority of a man who had lived with firearms, at the other tall Swamp Angel, who had been stalled in his place by, I assumed, the suddenness of my violence.

"Come here," I said to him. He walked toward me as if he were, at once, drunk. "Now halt," I instructed. He was but a few feet from me, and I did not wish him to become sufficiently emboldened by our proximity to fall upon me. Giving no warning, I swung the shovel haft with my left hand and caught him across the bridge of the nose, which cracked, pouring blood from his nostrils and flooding the flesh around his eyes with interior blood. He, too, went to his knees, cupping his face.

"Excellent," I said. "Now, the first man who may stand erect will not be shot. Who's for it?" The fellow with the broken nose moved to make the attempt. So, though he was weakened by the shock of the bullet and by his pain, did the other tall one. I said to the man whose nose I had split, "Take your friends by hand or belt or hair and bring them to their feet."

He did so, moaning the while, as did the other tall one, who helped him bring the smaller fellow erect, though hardly conscious.

"Now attend. You are businessmen, and you have plied your trade. You take money. I make it, and I keep it; that is *my* trade. So our transaction is over. I would like to hear you agree." They made liquid, nasal sounds, which I took for assent. "I have no desire to affect your further conduct of business. Is that clear? There's no profit for me in sending you off to the Tombs. But there's no profit in your further association with me. Wait in hell for your boat, and then travel on it. Agreed?" They made more sounds.

I said, "Then, good night."

But I did not lock the door behind them. I felt as though the room was violated, polluted, and that locking it at once was somehow more of a gesture than a deed. So I picked up a broken lamp globe and papers that had been scattered, and I straightened the furniture that had been tossed about. I poured water into a basin and made an effort to wash my hands and neck and forehead. The cleft near my brow was irritated, as if it had been wounded once more, and I took care to use soap and to lave it well, then gently pat it dry. I was unused to invasion. I was dismayed by feeling vulnerable. I found myself walking in small, tight circles, and they reminded me of the stiff-legged way those men and I, in the alley, earlier, had edged about near one another. I found the mask, on the floor beneath the head of the bed, and I put it on. I sat on the edge of the bed and listened to the rasp of my breathing, the diminishing sounds of the terrified tenants as, little by little, it became a fact that our tenement was not ablaze. With a kerchief, I bound the gash on my arm, the bleeding from which had decreased. I moved then and found clean clothing and, as I stripped myself to put on fresh linen, I held a shirt to my face and breathed in its harsh odor of strong soap, a kind of rough perfume of cleanliness.

It was dawn, and her children slept. She drew aside the curtain to display them in the weak light of the candle she held, yellow-white tallow dripping—I watched it—upon her small, tea-colored hands. The heat from the stove was oppressive in the large room, but the sleeping place seemed slightly cooler, and both Kwang and Ng were under the same white comforter in the narrow bed. Ng's eyes opened, of a sudden, and I feared for her as she observed us in our study of her.

She narrowed her eyes, and then she closed them. "*Gui,*" she said. Her brother stirred, and they both slept.

Chun Ho stepped back and so did I, and she drew the curtain to. The heat was from the stove, of course, on which she heated water.

"Have you been to sleep?" I asked her.

She shook her head. She wore light-colored trousers and a kind of shirt that clung to her and was darkened with sweat, creating such an intimate appearance that I was both embarrassed and impelled to look more closely at the outlines of her form, and its simultaneous proximity and distance. She smelled of soap and of her own perspiration.

"You must work all night?" I asked.

"Too hot for sleeping. Not sleep, then work."

"If you didn't keep the fire going, perhaps you could sleep."

"But you want bath."

"That isn't why the stove is fired, is it?"

She covered her mouth and laughed. "Should be, perhaps. Is not. Not sleeping, so work. Want bath?"

I did not reply. I took off my boots, and then my trousers and my jacket and shirt. I lay my hat upside down on the floor beside my clothing, and in it I placed the Colt .31. She poured the water into the tub, and I took off my mask. I stood where I was, attempting to formulate adequate words for what had possessed my body.

She said, with no expression, and this time looking into my face, "Strong flower."

I stepped into the tub. She placed the candle on a small gold-and-red lacquered dish upon her table and dipped water from the stove into a heavy, short-handled iron pot, which she carried over. The water she poured upon me was scalding hot in a humid, hot night in the close, steamy room, but it was renewing. I thought my body might glow. Without speaking, she unwrapped the handkerchief about my left forearm, and she pressed it beneath the surface of the bathwater. Then, pulling it back with both of her small, strong hands, she touched the puckered surface of the wound. I made no sound, nor did she. From a shelf near the stove, she secured a small, dark bottle.

"Hurt," she said, as she poured the violet liquid upon me.

"Yes, it surely does! Perhaps somewhat more than the injury."

"Help you to not be sick."

"Infected," I speculated.

"So many words."

She soaped a flannel cloth and then sat upon the rim of the tub, behind me, pouring more water and scrubbing my back and my neck, as if I were her child. I closed my eyes and let my head droop toward my chest. My breathing was deep, almost a sort of snoring, and I listened to it, and to the slight rasp of the flannel cloth upon my skin. Chun Ho reached around me to scrub at my throat and then my chest, and I felt the cloth of her shirt and then the solidity of her nipples, the muscle at the junction of her breast and her arm. I knew that when I looked at her next, I would see her clothing soaked in upon her bosom.

I let my head sag further and, from behind, I felt her own head lie upon my neck and shoulder blades as her arm, around me and pressing at my own chest, lay still. She held me thus, and thus she held herself, as we sat in the diminishing steam of the bathwater. We did not have to see each other seeing the other one and so, in a sense, we were safe from ourselves and each other, we were suspended in the restless sounds of the working stove, in the slight stirring of the bathwater, and in the breathing rhythms we slowly composed in simultaneity; were you there, unseeing but attendant to the noises in the room, you might have concluded that only one person drew breath.

Abruptly, she shifted her weight, and I felt her leave. I slumped down under the water as far as I could to lie upon my back. Perhaps she would come and pour more upon me, I thought. But, instead, she came to the tub and it was herself she poured. As I felt her enter the tub, I felt her lie against me and along me. I drew my knees up, and she lay between them, her head near my jaw. I dared to open my eyes in the flickering light of the low-burnt candle, and I saw that her own eyes in her raised head were shut. Then she opened them and looked along my wounds and up my face.

She wept, and I did not know, nor do I now, whether her sorrow was for herself or for my face. I watched lines appear on her visage that never before had appeared to me, for her face had always been a kind of mask in itself, occasionally cracked by a smile or a tender appraisal at the eyes. Now, however, her emotions played and disappeared like shadows thrown against a lantern light. She looked wicked and full of appetite, and then playful, with hungers less dark, and then she was blank and unreadable, and then moist at the eyes with a kind of pity, and then she seemed wise, as I had seen her when one of her children had given her a humorous sort of pleasure. Her nostrils reflected her hunger again, and the weeping went away, banished by what drove her—"*Strong* flower," she whispered—to stuff me into her as she moved up and down upon me in the soapy, warm water, and then clasped me to her with both her powerful arms around my waist as she moved us both, back and forth, up and down, water coursing over the edge of the tin tub and onto the tin plating at the floor.

I feared that we would wake her children. I feared that we would stop. We did neither. And then she permitted me to towel her delicate collarbones and sturdy, small chest and her breasts. Then I kneeled upon the slick, sudsy tin at the foot of the tub to rub her stomach and loins, to run the towel the length of her thigh and down to her ankles. She stood facing me then as I pulled her against me and dried her back and buttocks, cupping each and pulling it from her body to explore with the towel and my fingers her crack and cleft and what was cupped within. I stood and rubbed at her hair, tossing down the towel to feel her hair's silkiness, and then I rubbed with my fingertips at her back again, and buttocks. She leaned against me, her arms at her sides, in a signal to me, I thought.

She took a blanket from a hook and wore it over her shoulders as she made a pot of tea.

"You look much," she said.

"You, too, watch more than you speak."

"You think I a whore kind of woman?"

"Did you come to the tub as a whore?"

Her face went absolutely impassive.

"No," I said, "let me say it this way, please. Will you hear me? I did not think you came to me that way."

"Whore," she said.

"I did not think it. I thought—it was a gift. I'm sorry. It was an expression—"

"Confused man."

"Man whose words are failing him, Chun Ho. It was a beautiful bath. You were beautiful water in the bath."

Her sudden smile was pleased, and it more than flickered in her face.

"Flower and water. I water flower."

"Yes, you did."

"Not whore. Never whore. Only if children die for no food."

"Never. I will purchase them food if they are hungry."

"Chun Ho work."

"Yes. Good. But only at laundry."

"Sure." And then she said, "Tell me American?"

"Tell you— Do you mean that you would like me to *teach* you? Instruct you? Chun Ho: *Show* you something?"

"Tell me. Ah, teach me. In-ruct me. Sure. 'This is teapot.' You say, 'Ah! Teapot! American say'"—and here she mouthed broadly, as if to mimick a teacher of elocution—"'teeee-pote.' Tell me. Teach me. In-ah-ruct me."

"Bless your soul. You want to speak English."

She shook her head. "American."

"Yes. English *is* American. It is *termed* American. Chun Ho, I understand. I understand. Yes. I will teach you Eng— I will teach you American. Words for things in America, that is to say. Am I correct?"

She said, "Cor-rect," with great difficulty and great dignity, and then she poured us our tea. It was very smoky in odor, and its taste and effect were powerful; I felt it in the back of my head almost as if it were a brandy.

"Green tea," she said, pushing the *r* into being with her tongue and her palate and reminding me, of course, of the square-faced, angry, compassionate woman who had nursed me in Washington, contending with my anger and my sorrow and my overmuch attention to my own pain. I looked about for the mask, intending of a sudden to don it again, when Chun Ho, who had seemed to be gazing elsewhere, but of course was looking inside me, said, "You will tell me about American? Teach. In-ah-ruct. In-*struct*."

I said, "Yes."

"And you."

"Me?"

"Tell me."

"I will tell you, yes. I will teach you. I promise it."

"No," she said, placing the porcelain cup beside the white candle and creating new shades of white and amber with the gold of wavering candlelight, the white of the candle itself, the white of the cups, and the white and amber, combined, of her skin. She pointed, and then with her small finger, which she lay upon my paler arm, she punctuated her wish. "Tell me—teach me—*you*."

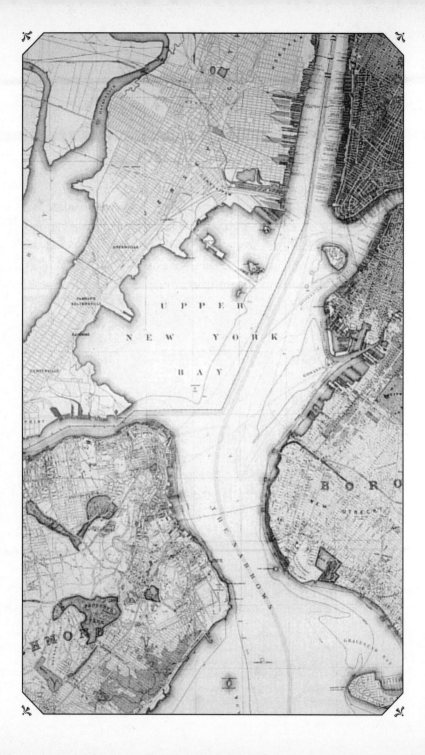

C H A P T E R 7

AND SO WE DREW TOGETHER, AT LAST, UPON THE DOCK between Hubert and Laight Streets, in the darkness of a late autumn night in New York. Lanterns at the Cunard Liverpool Steamship wharf in New Jersey ought to have been visible, but they were not. Nor were the lights of the inspector's office, nor those, downriver, of the water police. The weather was shutting us in, and so we wished it to. The low, gray ceiling of the sky showed neither cloud nor star, only an absence of what the eye might fasten to, although I thought, as I tried to survey our preparations, that I had discerned, for only an instant, a brilliant golden light, above the darkness, that was the storm; now invisible, it seemed to construct itself by sucking upward the very air at which we gulped.

Sam, at the cargo boom, was to supervise the unloading of the ship upon which the children had been transported in tuns, some, I had been told, the size of a large man and some about half of that. When I tried to imagine the children asleep in the barrels, like cod in salt, I could not—or, rather, did not wish to. It must be attributable to me in some wise, I thought, if the children were injured. Did I not contribute to their misery as I sought to offer—I could think of no other word for it—tribute to Jessie's desire to free them? Yet what might freedom be worth if a less than terrible price were affixed to it? I sounded to myself like Abe in the worst of his pufferies, and I left such thoughts behind as I sought the three wagons for which I had arranged. The children would be set upon them and covered with tarpaulins before Jessie directed the drivers to the places of refuge for which she had arranged. M would offer the documents I had acquired, and Sam—whom I could not deter from accompanying me—would record for private, not journalistic purposes, the evening's events. Although I was puzzled at how he might write with his pencil stubs upon paper certain to be soaked by the gathering moisture that, at any instant, would become a storm's sheeting rain.

The apprehension in the atmosphere was as powerful and prominent as the expectation we could feel, I might have said, from one another. M, despite the heat and the sweating oils that shimmered upon his face, wore his oilskins and his woolen cap. He was very pale, as if ill with a miscreant's conscience, yet his little eyes were active, even restless, and he squinted into the dark flannel of the night, and he spoke and spoke. And Sam, to M's apparent pleasure, seemed to note his every word.

"It's a sizable storm. Mark, for example, the polite nodding of the vessels at their chains. They'll soon grow vociferous with their silent brows, and will bob like bachelors at a long night's do." The masts of the anchored ships did, indeed, pitch busily upon the active water. There was much foam visible, and M said, "More than harbor water will be broken tonight, I wager." Sam smiled with pleasure as he labored in his notebook. "We might wish to encourage our brothers in this endeavor to offload with something like alacrity, Billy. I'm pleased to see you here at last."

It is true that I was the final one of our group to appear. I knew that Sam had engaged to meet with M at his office on the barge, so tantalized had he become by my account of where the man sat to drink his drink and read at his philosophy, and where he paced, and how he kept his papers in their federal bins. He had brought to M a bottle of something—"grog" was what he had boyishly said to me—and I had been pleased to remain alone in my little lair in the Points. Adam, too, had wished to come by himself, and I had watched him drift toward the docks, walking as I did a mere block behind him, with what I would have called reluctance. He was going to demonstrate the last of his loyalty to me, for my friendship, or employment—what you will—had clearly demanded a difficult price; he felt, I believe, that he betrayed his own people while serving me, and in despite of his knowing, I thought, that I did labor on behalf of those very same people. Never mind my ultimate motive, my fealty to a golden woman in a Yorkville house, who had charmed, hypnotized, or otherwise compelled me to the service we were gathered to perform. It was a labor for the right, I thought, although so very much wrong was required to perform it. I thought of the tattooed signs on Jessie's torso, and on the soft skin of the bottom halves of her breasts. I thought of her fingers moving my fingers on the intimacies of her flesh as I read her story while she recited it.

And then Adam stood at Sam's elbow as M described the mechanics of the gathering of a storm, and then I stood behind Adam. "I think he is right," I said low. "I think it is going to pour upon us. Shall we secure you a coat?"

Adam turned to me and said, "My black skin has been wet black and dry black and always in the morning it was just the same shade of black, and I don't see any coat make some change in that, Mist Bartelmy."

I touched his shoulder as I had touched Sam's or Burton's or Sergeant Grafton's, precedent to my crawling off or climbing off or loping off on one of my hunts in the War. Adam's reddened eyes and strong face showed only sorrow in response. He looked at me a little longer and then he looked away. Below us, the little schooner, her sails hanging on the yards but not furled, for she was going to make her way away in despite of any weather, was snugged at the bollards of the dock, and a narrow planking ran from her rail to the wood of the wharf. Adam walked away and down the steps and soon—I watched the whiteness of his shirt as it mingled with the darker clothing of the dockhands he commanded—large men, working without benefit of brazier, torch, or lantern, were wrestling tuns in the forward hold. A mist of rain appeared but did not cool us. The air seemed to diminish further, and each movement slicked me with my own liquids underneath the airless moisture of the night.

Sam said, "Adam is not at peace with this."

"He feels he owes it. He also feels that he is misused."

"And?"

"I suspect that he is, and that possibly—but I am far from certain—he also does."

"Owe it to you?"

I shrugged. "Perhaps to the fate that made him black, and that placed him in the United States, and that gave him a complexity of conscience."

"And to whom or what do *you* owe this venture?" Sam asked.

I pointed to the group beside the loading boom, at the winding handles of which Adam had begun to labor. Slowly, the long boom swung over to the cargo hold of the schooner, the name of which had been obscured by canvas hung over the side. Behind Adam, and looking alternately into the ship and up at us, was Delgado, in a long coat of thick leather and wearing a cap such as a captain at sea might employ. He stood alongside Jessie, who was in a black cloak with a hood that protected her from the gathering rain and the eyes of strangers. Two other men were with her and Delgado; they were strangers to me, one black and one white, and each carried a broad umbrella that threatened to fly away in the rising winds. I wondered if I ought to be there among them. I knew the speculation well; it was a desire to claim her in some fashion, and I remained where I was. She would come to me, as the evening progressed, or she would not. I no longer understood the nature of her claim on me. Let the evening roll on, I thought, and we'll know. We'll know.

Delgado, as if he had intercepted my thoughts, or at least felt their intensity, turned at that instant and looked up toward us—toward me, I was certain. I nodded. He nodded in turn. I waited for Jessie to turn, but she did not. To guard my mask against the effects of the increasing rain, I removed from the pocket of the black rubber coat I wore against the weather a scarf I used in winter at my neck. I tied it across the mask, over the mouth hole and my lovely painted nose, and I secured it at the back with a knot. I pressed my hat low over my head, and was as secure against damage as I could make myself. Of course, the .31 was in the right-hand pocket of the rubber coat. I wondered where Delgado's gravity knife might be, but did not wish, really, to have to learn. Jessie pointed, and I represented to myself more than saw the tawny flesh of her arm as her hand came up.

One of the larger tuns was in the netting of the boom, and Adam and another carter wound the heavy line back up. It went slowly, and I feared for an interruption by the river police before we had completed the task. The weather might keep them occupied, I thought, but the unloading was taking far longer than I wished. Now the tun was in the air, and now, as Adam and the other fellow labored, it had barely cleared the lip of the hold. They walked the boom around, and the great barrel, swathed in its rope netting, hovered above the dock.

I said, to M or to Sam or to no one, "But where are the wagons?"

The scene had nagged at me, and, of course, thinking of Jessie's thighs and Jessie's mouth and Jessie's breasts, I had not considered that something aside from her tantalizing proximity and disappointing distance might be the cause. In the forests, on the hunt, I had not permitted myself to be so blind. That is what the city had done to me. And it was Jessie, of course, as well.

Sam said, "I see none."

M was muttering. His hands gripped the wooden rail before us where we three were lined up, like dark herring gulls awaiting our share of the leavings. The sky pressed lower and the wind brought the rain now, and any visibility was all but closed down. M raised a hand and spoke to himself behind his beard and in his secrecies.

"Sir!" I called to him. "What is it?"

He pointed. Lower in the water than the schooner, and either hidden before and just hove to, or shielded from our sight because we expected nothing to present itself, was a small vessel, say the size of a brig, but with no sail mounted on the masts that were aft and forward of the thick, squat metal chimney, you might call it; the vessel was a steam-powered lighter large enough to take the cargo on and powerful enough to drive through a storm.

I said, "No such vessel was part of the arrangement."

"No word of it was mentioned?"

"None," I said, and M shook his head.

"That," he said, "is the matter with plans. They are important only if lives or reputations hang upon them. And plans do so rarely eventuate as conceived. If that vessel is not of the tissue of our planning, and it isn't, then I begin to have fears."

"Perhaps there's an innocent explanation."

"Perhaps the only innocence within a hundred yards is that of Adam and the children laid like anchovies inside those tuns. Billy, we have broken the laws of the Port, the Surveyor, and the Customs Department. Must I bid my pension farewell?"

"I'll see to this," I said. "Perhaps they decided to take them upriver, or around to Brooklyn."

"And did not wish to bother you with their amendments to the plan which originated with you?" I thought that he might lean his shadowy face back and laugh the silent laugh. If he did, I might have bellowed something terrible at him. But he shook his head and offered me a glance so full of disgust and disappointment that I understood, for an instant, how his son might have felt under the weight of such a dismal evaluation.

"We'll see," I said.

"He is dangerous," Sam told M, "when he employs that tone."

I said, "We'll see." I set my hand in my right-hand pocket, and I pulled my hat down hard, then set off. By now, I could see, Delgado was behind Adam and was directing the working of the boom. Small tuns came up two at a time in the netting now, and Sam and the other fellow labored without cease in spite of the weight of the load. That, I was certain, could be laid to Delgado's powerful persuasion.

I went down the wooden steps, which were slick now with the hot rain, holding on to the rail for my life. Out on the river, an incoming ship had hove to and was making for the Jersey shore before the wind; with luck, she might make the Atlantic Street harbor, at the intersection of North Twelfth, a kind of jagged pocket on the coast in which vessels had, in other hard storms, found shelter. A barely discernible light at the ship's pole, above the royal mast, dipped dangerously low and then swung laboriously to. Little else that far out was visible and, even close by, in the stairwell I descended, or upon the docks beyond the boom, I could not see much.

Adam's shirt had collapsed into darkness upon his dark skin. He worked, I saw, with his eyes closed. And I could not blame him, for how to understand what he saw: a majestic slender woman, even under a cloak and hood, her face animated as if she watched a sport of brave dimensions; a matched set of broad, tall men, one white, one black, whose heads and eyes in response to her commentary swiveled and roamed; a clearly dangerous man in a leather coat that glistened like a serpent's skin who tapped Adam's shoulder with the handle—threat enough—of his knife; the gallery, above and behind, of M and, behind him, Sam, solemn, pale-faced observers; the heavy, wet tuns that were swung and set, swung and set, from the hold of a pitching schooner to the deck of a steam-driven lighter.

He saw me as Delgado did. I said, "Adam, I do not know of this. Why not stop your labors while I learn what I can?"

Delgado, in his calm and uninflected voice, said, "Good evening, Mr. Bartholomew."

"Mist Bartelmy," Adam said. "We did all that walking in the Loin, saw all that misery, to help somebody make up their mind to come here and get fooled? Is that what I hear in your voice?"

"Yes. I think it is possibly so."

"Do you feel foolish, Mist Bartelmy?" He did not cease to work, nor did the other man, also Negro, far more slender than Adam, but apparently quite powerful. They wheeled, they swung the boom, they let their cargo down, and then, the net emptied, they swung the boom back and let down its rope for the next load.

I said, "I may be heartily sorry to have involved you in this."

"What *is* this, Mist Bartelmy?"

"I cannot tell you, Adam, for I do not know. I think now that I must find out. Delgado?"

"Ask her." He indicated Jessie.

"Will you let these men rest while I inquire?"

"I cannot, Mr. Bartholomew. Our schedule is a difficult one."

"Shall I try to force you to cease, Delgado?"

"I fear for their safety if you do," he said politely, tapping the handle of his knife upon Adam's straining back. Water had gathered upon the shiny, pocked patch of skin beside Delgado's nose, and it looked as if it were constructed of something artificial, a kind of pale gutta-percha. His eyes were unreadable, as ever, and he looked more confident than a minister taking the pulpit.

I backed away, then walked around Delgado, and away from the boom, toward Jessie and her escort. The tuns brought the lighter lower in the water, and I found it fascinating to watch the cargo press the ship upon the river, and to see it drop in comparison to the level of the dock. It seemed that at any moment it might sink away from us. But, knowing Jessie as I did, I was certain that she had calculated the load.

"Billy," she said, smiling from within the hood with her sad eyes and with a kindness at her mouth. "Hello, Billy. We are more than halfway done."

"With what?"

"Oh," she said. Then: "Billy, these gentlemen are among the principals in this . . . affair. Mr. Henry Porter, who is, in a managerial capacity, a purveyor of the services of laborers." The burly white man nodded, almost in a kind of bow, and demonstrated no surprise at the mask with which he was confronted. "Mr. Porter is well known for having sustained at Gettysburg a savage wound from which it was thought, at first, he might not recover. He wears the mangled bullet, which spun and bounced inside him, upon a chain at the throat." I knew, of course, how Jessie knew about the chain and about the nature of his wounds, and I knew, too, how she had comforted him.

"And this is Mr. North. He has assisted me in matters of administration and finances."

"I would have—"

"I know, Billy. But you were the overall organizer. And you secured the assistance of our friend who has signed the documents. Each man has his part."

"Of you?"

She said, "I must ask you to leave your emotions to the side in this, Billy. It is the children, after all, whom we serve."

"And you are donating to them a river voyage on a coal-fired boat as part of the service? I cannot recall our discussing this. I remember wagons. I engaged wagons, Jessie."

"Mr. North, at my request, informed the carters that we had reconsidered. It is always useful, I've been told, to have a number of plans and to see that no one knows all of them. Mr. North, for example, was unaware of the services of our . . . friend."

"Our friend. Just so," Mr. North said, in a handsome, well-spoken baritone.

"Just so," I said.

"We have two-thirds, I would say, on board," Jessie announced. The rain now was almost horizontal, and her face was running with it, although she barely blinked and she never wiped at her eyes or mouth. The wind pulled Mr. Porter's umbrella backward over its frame and peeled it away. Mr. Porter merely held his hat brim and leaned into the wind. I looked into his eyes and then into Jessie's. The boom swung over, and another tun was on the deck of the brig. I might shoot them all, I thought. Kill the two men, turn and fire twice to hit Delgado, and then deal with Jessie at my leisure.

I wondered about the children, and where they must be taken, and in whose care.

Jessie said, "I am reading you, Billy."

I saw her light, cold eyes, and I knew that I feared as much as desired her. She was of the madness I had always thought was in, or about to envelop, me. But her astonishing beauty, her willingness, and not for the money, to go anywhere in the darkness in any kind of sudden savagery and pain—and not for the money, I'd insisted, sleeping with a whore for whose company I paid by the block of hours to a laudanum addict.

She said, "I know your thoughts."

I thought, I know what it says on your body.

She said, "I told you the stories, Billy. Stories aren't always the truth. Not all of it."

I had to smile. She could not see it. "No," I said aloud. "I enjoyed them, however."

"And I did, too, dear Billy."

"What did you mean?"

"How much of it did I mean? Or what was my meaning?"

"Either," I said. "Both."

But she was looking past me, and I turned. M, carrying a small storm lantern, had walked down the dangerous steps—he had probably sprung, like a ship's boy on his voyage out—and had walked past Delgado. I would have enjoyed watching that—and he had come now to the laden lighter, onto which he stepped. A man forward on the brig called to him, and M waved his hand but continued on his way. He stood, and he shouted into the wind, which prevented us from hearing him.

"Billy, what does he say?" Jessie asked.

M was pinning his little badge upon the cloaking flap on the front of his oilskins.

"I imagine that he says," I replied, "'I am an inspector. Thus, I inspect.'"

"Truly," she said, with some wonder in her voice.

"It is what I would expect," I said.

M produced a bone-handled folding knife, and he cut away at the net about the tun.

"The cost of the net diminishes the profits," Mr. North said, almost singing. He had the practiced ability to make any statement into song—the less musical the statement, the more, apparently, he sang it: Life is a tale full of sound and fury, sung by an idiot. I thought of M and his Hamlet, his Iago, his Timon, his Lear.

M now labored at the tun, standing on his toes and working to gain access to what might have been two hundred gallons and more, but which in its place should have been children, born into slavery and freed by Jessie and Porter and North, by M and by me.

M beckoned, and Jessie said, "Do not go, sweet Billy."

"Kiss me good-bye, Jessie."

"Farewell, you mean?"

"Please."

She stepped forward, removing her hood, inclining her wonderful sad face, and put her arms on mine. She turned her head and kissed the scarf at the mouth of the mask. Then she leaned in beneath the mask and nipped at the flesh of my neck. She sucked upon it, and she bit it hard, and then she licked it, as if she were a child. Then she looked up and into my eyes and pulled the hood back over her. She patted my arms and stepped back.

"Thank you," I whispered.

Jessie nodded, and smiled her smile of regret. She said, "It was Lydia Pinkham's mixed in with the juices of fruits."

I recited those words as I turned and went along the dock of the wharf to the brig, sitting low in the water which sometimes lapped over onto her deck. I could not understand her meaning: the juices of fruits, the Lydia Pinkham's. I stepped on, slipping as the rhythm of the rocking of the ship betrayed me, but M was there to catch me by each shoulder with his broad hands and to steady me.

"We're in horror, shipmate," he said. "This is a cargo out of the imagination of someone more stirring and capable than I." He held up the lantern and directed me to peer down and in.

I smelled the vomit first, and then the stench of the leavings of locked-in bodies. The contents were, I saw, three children, or four, heaped in upon each other. It struck me as likely that they had been in there for days; I could not imagine their surviving the entire journey in this fashion, although I had of course no assurance now that Florida had been their home port. They might have come up from Philadelphia, for all I knew, and they might have made the entire journey in the tun. What Jessie had meant about juices of fruits and Lydia Pinkham's was now, naturally, clear. They had been offered refreshment, and it had struck them unconscious; drugged, they were packed in their barrels and carried only heaven knew how far, for how long.

What had not been clear to her, or to her operatives, was how much of the opium dissolved in alcohol could be tolerated by a child who was deprived of fresh air and exercise, perhaps on account of the cost, and perhaps because the traders did not know. Now they might know. Terrified and helpless, without adequate air to breathe, and in the absolute dark, they had been accidentally poisoned and purposely shipped. You are born, and the world bends down to feed you, and its teat is icy, its pap is poisoned, and you are dead because a child, and black.

"All dead?" I asked him. "Not a breath from them?"

"The child on top, the little portion of person, is dead, I perceive. I do not harbor hope for the others."

"We must open the tuns and have them out," I said.

"Get off my boat," the fellow behind us said.

I watched M tug at his oilskins and turn. "I am a deputy inspector of Customs in the Port of New York," he said. "I carry, with this badge, the authority of the federal government."

"*I* carry," the other said, "with this peacekeeper, the authority of point five six calibers of half a dozen cartridges, and more where they came from. And I seen your hand in your pocket, you, and I am told you always goes armed. Hands out, nothing in 'em, all easy and slow, thank you, gentlemen. I am the captain, and my word, as you know, is law. This"—he motioned with his pistol—"is its authority, you could say."

"Jessie spoke of us—of me—to you?"

"Don't know no Jessie. Mr. North told me."

"He must have sung it."

The captain, bald, short, soaked through in his long-sleeved seaman's shirt, smiled his dirty gray-yellow fangs. He held a cavalry pistol upon us by crossing his left hand in front of his face and, with his right, resting his weapon upon his left forearm. He knew what he was about, and I did not wish to see M wounded. So I brought my hands out, but insisted on leaving them at my sides and not up.

"He does croon whatever in hell he says, doesn't he, our Mr. North?"

"Jessie must have arranged this with Mr. North," I said to M.

"I don't work with any Jessie, I told you."

"Neither, I think, do I," I said.

"You *are* full of mystifications, ain't you? Off the vessel, please, gents." We stood then on the dock as the other tuns came over.

M said to the man with the gun, "There are children in the cargo."

"It's a cargo *of* children, as I understand it. Some large ones, one or two as what you might call an adult. But it's little slavies for the most part."

"Slaves," I said.

"Remember them?" the gunman said, smiling. "We recently had some disputations on the subject. Slaves? The niggers we bred?"

"Great and brave and small men died for this," M said. "That we might come, in so short a period, to *this*. And at her behest."

"Yes."

"A black woman and, beside her, a black man, engaged in the selling—"

"White men, too, are involved," I said.

"Yes, shipmate. But that is not the astonishment. Is it?"

I shook my head. M saw a pale, painted mask bound up in a sodden gray cloth that moved in nervous gestures. Sam, I realized, and I turned to find his face, was seeing it all. I saw his face beneath his narrow-brimmed, round derby hat as he leaned at the rail—beyond the conspirators, above them and Adam and the schooner and the brig, and over us, of course, looking down to study us, memorize us, make of us something larger and more of some whole about which, I had no doubt, he was thinking so hard that his sad eyes bulged and his sallow cheeks were round as if with held breath.

I was going to kill the one on board the brig who held the gun. I turned to face him, and I moved away from M so that any return of fire at me might miss him. I slowly inserted my hand into my right-hand pocket, and I forced myself to breathe out and then in as I grasped the butt of the .31.

"I beg that you do not," Mr. North sang behind me. "I beg that you consider our captain and his armament. It is about profit and loss, Mr. Bartholomew. It is not—it need not be—about a loss of actual life."

"Unless it's the life of a black-skinned child in a barrel on a boat," I said.

"There are contingencies in every aspect of existence," he crooned. "Life is fraught with peril."

M said, "You are, sir, to a man who endeavors to do good, as a boxful of newspaper critics to a man who endeavors to write what might be thought of as poetic. You are the adder in the garden. You are the fleshy manifestation of everything wrong. Do I make myself clear?"

"Meaning no disrespect, sir, which I might *not* say likewise about you, you would do well to stay away from any endeavors involving the poetic. Stick to the solidity of numbers, and the logic of the profit and the loss." This was in the form, virtually, of an aria to canniness. I looked at M, and his features seemed to virtually melt in his rage or beneath the onslaught of the rain.

If anything, the heat had mounted. The tuns were on the deck, a[...] Jessie and Mr. Porter, followed by Delgado at his leisurely pace, we[...] stepping on board. I moved toward the lighter, and Mr. North accom[...] nied me.

Jessie, seeing me, came closer. "Billy," she said.

"What will you do with them? Those who are alive?"

"Forgive me," she said.

"The sorrowful girlhood, the depravities of the Methodists, the d[...] and nights in sweltering Florida? All right. I understand that people[...] But lies are the least of it, I suspect."

"The tattoos I showed to you—"

"Read to me."

"Yes."

"Permitted me to read."

"Yes."

"They, too, were a lie?"

The rain drove at us, and then merely fell, and then only drop[...] pattering. She responded by opening her hood and pulling it back, [...] mitting her head and face and hair, which she shook, to profit from [...] air. Her golden skin, I thought, nearly glowed in the darkness. Her [...] were enormous, as if to gather, from M's lantern and from the glow[...] gold behind the mackerel pattern in the serried dark clouds, what l[...] light was available.

M, behind me, said, "I will not remain among these people, s[...] mate."

"Please," I said.

"No. Any man—woman, madam—who wishes to do me corp[...] harm is hereby warned that I will not permit myself to be fur[...] detained."

"He'll bring the authorities, Billy!"

"I cannot protect you, Jessie."

"Oh," she said, smiling in sorrow, "oh, my dear, I always thoug[...] was me protecting you."

Delgado, returned now from the boom, told her, "We're leaving." He had passed M on the greasy dock and had not bothered to capture him. We were not of use, nor were we a threat. We did not, in terms of their transactions, exist, and I knew that Jessie would agree with me.

A dreadful noise, the firing furnace in the belly of the lighter, overwhelmed her words. M, by now, was back at the boom, a hand on each of Adam's shoulders, addressing him. I thought I saw Adam nod. I returned to watching the ship and saw sparks burst from the smokestack, and then dark clouds come up upon the darkness of the sodden night.

M called, "Billy!"

I continued, because I was a fool, to wait for Jessie to call to me again, but she was back at the cargo, holding to a tun, as Mr. Porter and Mr. North turned one of the great barrels onto its side and leaned in, presumably to begin the pulling forth of the children. Her back was to me now, and I turned mine as I started what seemed a very long, arduous walk, to M and Adam at the boom, and Sam, above us at the rail. Now that the rain had diminished, he was holding his notebook again, and setting down whatever it was that he deemed important about this little demonstration of the profit and the loss.

As I drew near him, M regarded me sternly. "Empiricism, shipmate. It may be the death of us all. Can you do it, Adam?"

Poor Adam nodded his head. A man freed from whoever Tackabury was, a freedman in the great, expanding city, and he had the dire fortune to be rescued—so it might once have been construed to seem—by the man inside of the mask who had danced, before men, gods, former slaves, former authors, Boston journalists, the chanting North and the wounded Porter, in graceless indignity. Before Jessie, and the book of her body I had thought to learn to read.

"We are on the fly, Billy. To the wharf, adjacent, whence you and I made our way to the incoming vessel. Do you recall?"

"I do recall," I said. I did not care.

"You have your pistol?"

I nodded.

"Eh?"

I unwrapped the soaking scarf and thrust it into a pocket of the rubber coat.

"I remain armed. How little good it did us!"

From inside his oilskins, he drew a sack, heavy and familiar in appearance, and I knew it was the Navy Colt.

"From the lip of the grave," M said, dropping it. My hand, as if possessed by his will, sought and caught it.

"I will bring them, some of them, to theirs," I said.

"Then we pursue them," M said.

"From your—you mean in the dinghy?"

"The little catboat against which she's moored. It gives us a mast, a sail, ten-foot oars, and a shallow, broad cabin where some of the children might shelter."

"A small catboat," I speculated.

"Yes," he said, "but adequate to our purposes and less of a load to propel."

"In pursuit of a coal-fired ship. Against the current."

M said, "Mark the waters, will you?" I looked at them and saw only darkness and chop. "The tide makes *in*," he said. "Did you not understand the river to be tidal? We'll labor upriver against the current but with the power of the tide behind us. We'll raise a sail when the wind's right. Now we're off. You *are* with us, shipmate?"

Sam had made his way to us, and he looked into the face of each, the mask of one. "Who will tell me now what that was all about?"

M turned, and Adam followed him. I, in turn, set out, tugging at the sleeve of Sam's coat. "We'll tell you on the way."

"Way where, Billy?"

"Upriver."

"After that boat?"

"After that boat."

"Who was the woman who kissed you? The way she . . . But—Billy!"

"Yes, Sam."

"She was the one! The reason all this—"

"She was the one, Sam."

"And it was a double cross?"

I hurried him along, for M was setting a terrible pace, bouncing on his toes like a boy, while Adam was close behind him. "Everything's a double cross," I said, sounding sulky even to myself.

The river grows vast as you are closer to its middle, and as you go farther upsteam, especially, its marshes and the reaches at the shore through which canals are cut breed speculation upon who might live there, and how, and in what strange relationship to the river and its traffic and its distance from the City of New York. But even at some proximity to the shore, and so far downtown, passing the ships at anchor, and the pleasure craft upon which the wealthy pass their nights in pleasures to which the likes of us might not have pretended, we all, I think, experienced the power of the deep, swift river, and the fear that cannot help but reside, awaiting travelers, in that dark water.

The waxing and waning of the storm made it impossible for me to read the shoreline and know where we were. At times, gasping, I thought to guess, from the shapes of new brick buildings, or the sprawl of old ones made of wood, the street we might have passed. I ventured to note our passage of Desbrosses Street, but then I stopped, for we fought the power of the salty surge that propelled us, and were oppressed by the lightlessness of the giant river that seemed, in this storm and in the night's emergency and—it is not too large a word for these events—despair, to be as broad and as merciless as the sea from which the tide ran up the river.

The darkness of the Hudson was the equivalent, below, of the night under which Adam and I, side by side, toiled to sweep the oars to move the boat. Spray from the current battered the craft and soaked us deeper, if that was possible. The spume poured in upon our legs and feet; soon enough, despite the heat of this night, my limbs were nearly numb, for the water of the river was cruelly cold. Sam was in the prow, behind us, holding the lantern and warning us of no specific dangers, but only that we must be careful. At one point, he went so far as to call, "Land, ho!" We took care to avoid the boom when M drew the small sail taut. And, standing before us, one foot near the gunwale, the tiller in one hand while the other seized the gaff hook on its long pole, planted, for balance, against the ribbed flooring of the boat, his oilskins open and glinting in what light we passed or was thrown by the lantern, M, in his closed and bearded face, stared forward, over us and over Sam, toward the distant, retreating chimney that spouted gouts of fire and threw up sparks and made the sound of a railroad locomotive roaring away with a considerable portion of our dignity and hope.

"Land, ho!" Sam called again.

M, between his teeth, said, "We are in a river. Laterally speaking, land is *always* ho."

"Shut up, Sam," I said, and really could not spare the breath.

M saw the outline of a sloop anchored too far out, and he commanded that we swing to the west to avoid it. No traffic confronted or observed us, and the docks of Manhattan passed by, as did the sloop, which seemed, when we rowed next to its hull, as large as a tenement house in the Tenderloin.

Rowing toward the receding ship with the thick, heavy oars, looking ahead of me to M in the stern, I felt as though I were trying to propel us toward him. I strained, and Adam strained, and the little sail crackled, and yet he remained proximate but mysterious, detached. I wondered how much he thought I had preyed upon him, and how much of our companionship he now considered a ploy. He thought, always, of causalities, and it was not impossible that he thought me—hence his little disquisition on empiricism—a blackguard and betrayer. I rowed as if toward him, and he stayed away. He was right.

"Adam," I panted.

"Mist Barthelmy."

"I am truly sorry."

"Yes, sir."

"You believe me?"

"Yes, sir."

"But the belief," I tried to say clearly, "brings no comfort."

"No, sir."

"I *am,* Adam."

"Yes, sir," he said.

"I will row now," Sam called.

M said, "We need a powerful stroke, shipmate. I will row, as well."

"No, sir," Adam said, "with due respect. They told me you're a literary gentleman. That's a soft-hand business. My hands are *hard.*"

"Like wood," I said.

"Like wood," Sam whispered, maybe memorizing it, I thought.

"I am a workingman," M said as we passed an empty wharf. "I possess a workingman's paws."

"A literary gentleman *with* paws," Adam said, pulling hard to compensate for my having lost half of the stroke. "But that's still a literary," he said.

"And so I am," M muttered.

"So are we all," Sam said. "Ship them," he called, and we kept them out of the water long enough to permit me to scramble forward and Sam to take my place. I lay on the deck forward of the flat cabin. "Ready," he said, and they began. "I sculled in the Charles," Sam said.

"I don't know him," Adam said.

I extended my legs to rest my knees, and I tried not to pant as hard as I wished to. I could smell myself above the smell of the river water, and the stab wound in my forearm throbbed. I thought of Chun Ho bathing me, and of Jessie, who had bathed me with her mouth. I drew the .31 from my pocket to rest beside the Navy Colt and, thinking to clean it with my wet scarf, I drew that from the opposite pocket. "Wait," I said, but no one heard me. Under the scarf, I found folded, wet papers. "The documents," I called louder, and M shifted at his post in response. "I never turned them over. They were fictitious, remember, and there was no real inquiry from any real policeman or Customs officer. We were so fortunate—they were so fortunate—that no inquiries were posed. Sir," I called to him, "I can destroy these papers, and at least the forms bearing your signature will be forever lost. They can flutter back into fiction, and you may leave them behind."

He waved his hand in the air. "Lose them forever, then, if you will, shipmate. Then I must merely contend with my anger and my shame."

I set the pistol on the deck and tore at any proof of malfeasance—any, that is, except the dark children in the imprisoning tuns. The fragments, like a tiny snow, blew past Sam and fell upon the Hudson River and soon would sink, and M, at least, was now free to be only an official who had happened upon a crime and had done his utmost to bring some villains to brook.

I withdrew the pouch of cartridges from the croker sack and felt only four. I saw that the chambers were empty, and I prayed that I might recover my former skills, for the .31 would serve us only at proximity; our long gun, and the salvation of the children, must be what sent M's Malcolm into the earth.

As if I soon might have a shot, I lay my gun hand on the deck and, supporting it with my left, I sighted on the smokestack and its sparks, and I thought to squeeze off. But the ship was so far ahead of us that I could not imagine our capturing her. Which her: the question I posed for myself. And why? Because she had gulled me—there is no embarrassment greater, for a New York man such as I, than to be fooled, like the country cousin, by a striking woman of Manhattan—or because she had committed a crime? The nature of the crime was very terrible, for a woman who was (probably) the product of slaves was now, herself, a slaver; like the Africans who sold the slaves to Dutchmen or the Portuguese, she was enslaving her own for the profit. She was no better, I thought, than a white. Yet it was she, naked beside me or upon me, who had whispered my name on my flesh; somehow, I became more authentically myself when she had done that. Just so with her farewell kiss, when she had intimately planted her lips upon the scarf that masked the mask beneath which I sheltered. It was as if she reminded me that I was a man in hiding—as, indeed, I had been throughout the War—and then, with her chewing and sucking at my throat, as if she reminded me that the twice-masked man was this flesh, and this blood, and he was actual.

I came forward, saying, "Adam, I insist now."

"Your hands, Mist Bartelmy, aren't even literary like *this* man's," he said.

But he and Sam shipped their oars, and I exchanged places with Adam, and I was pleased, in spite of the burning of my palms and fingers, to be rowing again.

Sam said, "Will we catch them? I can feel the wind rising at us, can I not?"

"Ask the captain," I said.

"'Ask the captain,' eh?" M roared, of a sudden, as if I had inspired him. He swung the little jib, then gave up as the wind blew hard from New Jersey, and he let the sail slacken, then tied it loosely to the jib.

He took up the spearlike gaff and shifted it upon the flooring. He adjusted his legs in their stance. Lifting his chin, he said, "Were I the wind, I'd blow no more on such a wicked, miserable world. Babies unsafe, men unsound, danger everywhere to the frailest. Billy," he called.

I had the breath to utter, "Sir," but little more.

"Did you fight your War for the world to come to this?"

"I did not think," I gasped in a kind of hoarse whisper, "that it might come to too much more."

"We should have known each other years ago," he said.

It occurred to me that no one knew him. And I wondered if that was also true of me. It seemed to me, in that dark and soaking night of so many disappointments, that I wished for anyone to say that I was not unknown to them.

The wind beat at us in such a way as to drive us landward, and M required that Sam ship his oar while I row so as to bring us away. The rowing was even more difficult, and the water came over the prow upon us with considerable weight. The power of the tide propelled us, but endangered us as well, for, always, we seemed in danger of losing control. Still, Sam and I pressed on against the waves.

"Drive!" M called. "*Bend,* men!"

Adam, squatting in the stern beside him, said, "Is that the literary part or the workingman part?"

"Great heavens," Sam said. "I could tell him."

"Tell what? Tell who?" I asked. "What *are,*" I panted, "all these words you are slinging about?"

"Their fire has gone out," M said. "Or, anyway, it has diminished. They cannot progress unless they make sail. To do so—well, let us hope that they do not do so. It is the price of empiricism, shipmates. The motors in the world, each and every one, are subject to the laws of motors: They must be started, and they *will,* willy-nilly, come to rest. Each and every one. As here, tonight. Now *bend,* lads! With a will! Will you break your backs, my fellows? Will you crack your spines?"

And instead of repudiating his hyperbole, Sam and I did bend to the oars and press and pull and then press again, stroking with our shoulders and arms, pushing with our knees down into our legs, leaning forward, pulling back, and driving us on, even faster, despite the higher waves and harder wind, than we had previously gone.

"Will you *bend,*" he begged us, as if more, even than the lives of the children, even more than our outrage and pride, were at stake. And we bent. And, scrutinizing us, he leaned back his large, shaggy head, and his eyes rolled up as he bent at the knees and laughed his soundless laughter, mouth open to the nighttime skies.

And then, of a sudden, he ceased to be that person who all but lashed us to row, and he appeared to be more like the night inspector who used to write books. He peered beyond us, and Sam and I rowed, and Adam, clambering past us to the prow, said, "I see 'em better. We're closer now."

"With a will," M growled at us, and I waited for him to shift his being once again, and to become whomever he was when he drove a boat's crew onward. But he said nothing more, and I rowed as if my life were at stake.

It was M, then, the sailor, and the officer upon the Hudson, who said, "Did you hear about the coal barge?"

"It is like a blessing, Sam," I whispered. "I swear it. Like a sign."

"Broke her moorings," M said, "and filled and sank. Well, partly sank. Where they were dredging, do you know?"

Sam gasped, "Good thing, Billy?"

"Yes. The best. Shallow." And then I had to stop because I couldn't breathe.

M said, "Drafts in the thirties of feet there, when dredging's complete. But the barge sank because it *wasn't* complete. The vessel turned over on top of the dredger's barge, and they're both down there, like a reef. It's not the engine that defeats them so much as the life of the river itself. They're fast on the topmost barge, and they've driven themselves snug!"

Adam called back, "They are working, all of them. Everybody's dancing. No! But everybody's moving around."

"I must get up front," I told M. "I have a marksman's eyes, and excellent night vision."

"How much you have missed with them," he said sadly, but then he suggested that we ship our oars, that Adam return to rowing, and that I, in the prow, report on what approached.

He asked of Adam, "Are you sound? Hands and arms are fit? Your back, poor fellow?"

"That's free," Adam said, to none of us in particular. "When they ax."

He and Sam began the stroke, and I lay on my belly, legs splayed under the thwart that shifted beneath their weight as they rowed. I could feel the power of the river beneath my legs as I put my sore, puffy hands above my eyes, as if the visor of a cap, and attempted to concentrate my vision upon the thick, dark ship. Adam had been correct, I thought, for there did appear to be a kind of orchestrated movement about the cargo and back and forth; I thought I saw Jessie, her exposed head floating above the darkness of her cloak. It was she who led the dance. We drew closer. Every shape but hers that was the size of an adult was now my target, and I sighted on the silhouettes.

I heard a large-bore pistol shot. M was encouraging Sam and Adam to press a little harder at the oars, for we did make progress. When I looked over my shoulder at him, I saw that his expression was sorrowful. I returned my study to the boat we pursued, and foaming splashes became evident, I surmised, from the far side of their ship. Jessie was no longer visible in her dance, and Porter and North seemed not to be in sight, although the splashes came more quickly.

One of them lost his stroke, and we began to spin in the tide. I looked back. M said nothing. He pointed at Sam, plunging his hands down, and Sam understood, placing his oar unmoving in the river so that the other side of our craft came around again, and then Adam and he knew to take up their rhythm of rowing once more, and we began again to progress toward the lighter, ferrying our own cargo—the dull, fat cartridges we carried in the chambers of my gun. I saw no sparks at the stack, and I grew optimistic. That was just before I sighted the first.

I called to M, and he soon enough made it out as well. They had, it eventuated, not unsealed all of the great casks, for one came down to us—or, rather, we came to it while it whirled very slowly in a stately manner, dipping in the drive of the current that pitched it against the drive of the tide. It made its progress sideways more than down the river, and as golden light broke through the serried ranks of cloud, I could see the heat, trailing vapors, drift up. In the ribbons and then curtains of what seemed to be steam, as dawn came upon us, I saw the tun.

I said, "Not so."

M, in the stern, used his gaff and leaned to bring it closer. Adam ceased his rowing and took hold of M's waist lest he be pulled over. I scrambled past Sam, who sat, his mouth open, his chest heaving, slowly shaking his head. The great cask was open, and in it was Jessie, with a foolish expression at her mouth because of the blood that had filled it and then leaked out along her ruined lips. She glared at us from her death. I saw at last where the bullet had entered, in the back of her neck, where the hair was damp and heated, as if she were a sweaty child at play outside the school in Florence, Florida, free for a time of the minister and his instruction—if all or any of that was true. The bullet had emerged from her mouth, shattering teeth and lips. I thought: Cruel joke upon us, Jessie, for you, had you lived, would also have needed a mask. I held her head while M held the tun fast to us, and I at last patted her cheek once and let her go. Below her were dead children, their limbs jammed into place, the stench of their vomitus and excrement a kind of terrible sweet sourness: Lydia Pinkham's in the juices of fruit. They probably had never wakened, and now Jessie, whose waking I had more than once watched— a taut peacefulness going watchful and engaged—also would not waken. Neither would Delgado, who had sought at the end to protect her, I wagered; for we could see his black hair and pale forehead underneath a small, dark child.

Adam said, "Isn't that justice, Lord?"

"Is that what it is, Adam?"

He looked at me and said no more.

M said, "The children beneath her."

I nodded.

"They never wakened," he said.

"Sir, I was thinking that. She had thought to see to them, and she had protested their lightening the load. Surely that is what they're about now. Throwing overboard their investment."

"They're bad businessmen, then," he said, "for they invested a great deal of money in these lives."

"They're entangled in the business of avoiding imprisonment. They're scrabbling for *their* lives now. At the end, Adam, I think she must have thought of the children."

He looked away. He did not reply.

M said to me, "Were you thinking of Mal? He went to sleep and they went to sleep, and none of them did wake." He said then, with only a small pause, "Will you, Adam, first of men, take hold of the mouth of this great barrel? It will be for only a moment, I promise."

Adam moved around him to the gunwale, and he seized the lip of the tun with both hands.

"That is right. You understand. For only a moment, now." Adam pulled against the current and M, standing back and then lunging, dashed the pole of the gaff against the side of the tun. He reared back and did it again, then again. Staves parted, and one split. He struck hard, he was breathing hard, and the color was up in his pale face. Soon enough, the staves parted wide, and we could see her drawn-up thighs between them. I would have pulled her skirts down to cover them if M had let me, but, seeing me about to move, he ceased his battering and held his hand aloft. "We are engaged now, Billy, in a burial."

Sam said, low, "She must be hid, then?"

M replied, "They all must be hid. Hence, to the awful floor, cinnamon-colored child."

I said, "She is no child."

"She was somebody's child," M said.

Adam, staring at the tun he held against the current, said, "Maybe she's my child."

I said, "Truly, Adam?"

"Truly enough," Sam said, as if he knew.

Adam said, "Truly enough."

"Enough," M said. He said, "Adam, let them go. And may there be a Lord, and may He await them."

Adam stepped back and sat, and the tun fell away, then began to bob and revolve and then speed up, dipping, catching the river as it poured upon them within, dipping lower now, bobbing less, spinning and then, of a sudden, out of sight beneath the river's surface as if they never had been born. Some others now drifted near us, bobbing, sealed, lives put by as if canned for use a season hence.

M said, "And what meaning lurks in this? What cause? How dare we witness this and *live?* And yet we do, and then we do."

"Can we rescue them?" Sam asked.

"You must row, Sam," I said.

"He is right," M said. "Row, good fellows, will you? Can we not catch them up?"

"They might be alive inside," Sam said. "One of them might breathe."

"Contraband," Adam said. "Slaves. They didn't know you need to keep them alive."

M said, "I suspect they will roll them all overboard. Some will drift to an embankment, or over to New Jersey, where they will snag on the reeds and marsh grass, or come to rest, poor children, in gravel or mud. Or they may sail, when the tide goes out, all the way from the North River and out past the Battery, past Dimond Reef, into the East River's mouth. They'll grow waterlogged, no matter how earnestly the cooper worked to seal the tuns. They'll sink at sea, or they'll sink in harbor, or they'll sink before they drift past Christopher Street."

"We must hook them and bring them aside and open them up and give the living children asylum. One might live. Two! One, maybe."

As I spoke, a second tun went under.

"They are drowning before us," I said to M, as if he were the captain and I were his crew. "How *dare* we not rescue them?"

"There is no rescue," he said. "The one that came to us was opened. These are shut. We cannot wrestle them on board, for each is greater than any one of us, and loaded with—yes, and waterlogged, I think. And if we open them in the water, surely they will ship a hundred gallons of river in and drown them in place or sink them under. There is no asylum," M said. "And all of them, you know it, are dead of asphyxiation or from swallowing their own liquids or some other cause. It does not matter, to them, what the cause might have been. You know it."

We sat in the silence that his words made among us.

Then I pointed ahead of us. "They," I said, "are cutting their losses, as it is called. So that when they have discarded these small lives in great barrels, they may reverse their engines and back away from the wreck—the reef, as you call it—and may live to invest another day."

"The black folks are the losses," Adam said. "I don't see but one white corpse come down on us. Plenty of black ones, though, in the water, under it, everyplace—dead black babies in the water. Why'd they bother and be born?"

"There is Mr. North still left, Adam," I said.

"No," Adam said, "he's pretty much white, sir."

"Get us closer, can you? I beg you. Get me a little closer to them?" I said it to the men behind me, but I stared ahead, at a third spinning cask, and at the investors on board their boat.

"*Will* you?" M cried. There were tears in his eyes and on his seamed cheeks. "*Will* you haul us to them? Will you *bend*?"

We made more speed as the light brightened further, and I lay at the prow once more, my legs behind me in a marksman's delta, my scarf, so sodden as to retain the shape of whatever pressed upon it, folded now before me. I extended my arms, and I rested my left upon the scarf and gripped the bottom of my right, which held the heavy Colt, to steady my weapon and give me true aim. My hands felt slick, as if the new blisters already ran their pus and blood. They felt clumsy and thick. But I had no doubt of their ability to grasp the weapon and to shoot it true.

"Is it rescue of the remaining tuns, Billy, or is it revenge?" M's voice was high and hoarse, and I knew that he mourned not only the Negroes discarded, in their barrels, as if they were spoilt goods, but again—and for all of his life—his child, who had gone to sleep and had not wakened.

I called back, "It is nothing that feels right, sir. It is action in the face of the event."

"What a pragmatical man you are, Billy! In your flinty heart, you are a sailor."

I cocked the Colt, and I sighted over the hammer block along the front sight. As the dawn lay out along the nearby shore and on the green, fast water, the river seemed broader, their vessel seemed smaller, and they, upon its deck, in frantic motion, appeared ludicrous to me, like puppets in a children's show who danced to a jig. Yet the cruelty of the morning was in the children themselves, lost at their young age, like Jessie in hers: suffocated, drowned, and thrown away.

By now the vessel was close enough, and the light upon us full enough, for me to read the craft's unobstructed name: She was the *Sweetheart,* out of Cape Sable. Her captain was using his gun. I heard the dry crack of the pistol and I said, "We are under fire."

And Sam, in a tight, familiar voice, said, "It is like old times, Mr. Bartholomew."

I heard the groan as they shipped their oars. We drifted in, and I waited.

Adam said, "All it is, I tell myself, is dying. But I am *not* calmed down."

"A minute more," I said.

I was staring ahead, then I turned to report to them and saw that M had not sat down. "Sir," I said, "you are most vulnerable as a standing target. Will you take cover?"

He opened his mouth wide and seemed about to silently laugh. And then his mouth dropped shut and he, in turn, dropped down to his knees in the stern. "I have mouths to feed," he said in a thin, bitter voice.

I returned my attention to the lighter. I called to Sam and Adam to lie low. Two more shots sounded, and nothing seemed to have hit. As I counted, he had at most three chambers full, though no quantity of cartridges would keep me from him. I saw him kneel beside a half-tun barrel, and I sighted, tried to allow for wind across us from the west, and for the dip of the prow as the current struck us, as the tide surged under us, and I fired two rounds. One or both took him down, and he did not move. I saw a head at the forward hatch, and I put two rounds there. A man began to howl his pain, and I could only think that I had struck him in the jaw or neck, for, surely, if he was not dead, he was very seriously wounded.

I said to them, "Kindly bring us in, gentlemen. Their gun will be silent."

Sam began at once, Adam an instant later, so that we wobbled in our course and then straightened, then made good speed. M stood again in the stern, his gaff hook like a spear in his hand, his shoulders squared, his chin upthrust. No one spoke.

"In the mercy of the Lamb, in the mildness of the Father who is Child," the voice came chanting from the hatch. "Mr. Porter is sorely wounded. I think the bones of his shoulder are shattered." I shook my head in regret for my poor marksmanship. Pistols are unreliable. "Our captain is dead. I alone am left to tell the tale. I throw myself upon your mercy in assurance that it will be as the mercy of the Lamb."

"Come up," I called.

"In the assurance—"

"Up, Mr. North. And you forgot to report on Miss Jessie. Is she safe?"

"Below decks and safe and well, sir."

"Come up, Mr. North."

He appeared as a hat, and then a sweating, round face, and then a good gabardine suit with stains upon its sleeves and matching waistcoat. In his hand was what appeared to be a small, folded handkerchief, stained but once white.

"A flag of surrender, sir. The rules of war. The principles of engagement—I beg all parties to attend. A flag of surrender!"

I put a single .31 round into his belly, at the line of his belt, and I saved the other against emergencies. I wanted the shot in his lower stomach because he would die the more painfully, poisoned by his own bowel. I estimated Porter to be almost bled to death. I lay my head against the warm revolver and the cold, damp scarf. Sam and Adam rowed again, I heard, and we came abutting the lighter, onto which M made us fast. I lay where I was, uncertain for an instant whether we were in a tree in Rebel country or the river off New York. M clambered past me, and I saw the men I had killed and wounded, and I smelled their blood as if it were spilling, all of it, at once, as I lay there, and as if—the scene came through my mind and left, but I remember it—my companions on board the lighter were filling tuns with the blood I had caused to flow. I saw Jessie's face, and I felt her neck and hair, and then I was up, upon my knees, and then standing, and I watched as M and Adam forced the tun and searched inside for someone's missing child.

Soon, for I joined them in the labor, we had opened them all. It was a perversion of Christmas, I thought, unfastening these great casks that were to provide to their inhabitants a gift and to those who shipped them the even greater gift of having given liberty to someone enslaved. Everything was slimy with a mixture of salt and fresh water, the blood from the rowers' hands, and the terrible fluids of the bodies within the tuns. We found only death, and its stink of decomposing bodies in their embarrassing disarray was potent. It made for a liquor I thereafter drank in my dreams. For they were children. They were made of the tender eyelids, the short, thin fingers and soft limbs that we, who were grown in the world, were required by what is proper and right in life to cradle against us, and protect.

M retrieved his gaff, which he had carried aboard the lighter like a spear for great fishes, and he turned from us, by the small cabin among the lengths of rope with which the tuns had been lashed down. They lay beneath his feet like snakes. He stared into the glare above Manhattan that prefigured a lurid dawn. And he only shook his head.

Then, as if possessed of a sudden, he drew himself tall, stepped backward among the serpents, then strode at the side of the lighter and hurled his wooden gaff pole with its iron hook, high and into a darkness that accepted it, as if the morning skies, or what lay behind them, had absorbed his assault.

He stared after his vanished weapon, and then he turned, with a terrible, tortured face, to confront us.

"These babes," he said, "these darksome pips of humanity, abandoned by man and woman and God. How can we? How can *He*?"

Adam sat with his back pressed into the deckhouse, and he stared at the tun. For myself, I committed impracticality, seizing my Navy Colt by its barrel and tossing it, as if with barely a consideration, over the side.

M sought, I saw, to muster a smile for me, but he clearly could not.

And, barely a quarter of an hour later, we fought our way downstream, M at the tiller, steadying our path and correcting, upon occasion, but permitting us to slowly float with a kind of rocking that sickened us as, aided by the sail, we retreated. The day came up, dispersing the golden shimmer under which we had labored at dawn, replacing it with a sullen red light that spoke of dampness and heat.

We were alone on the water for a while in our silence. He swung us out, at Warren Street, and we continued to drift as shipping came up, as a cutter of the river police swung past us—he stood, pulling at his oilskin coat, so that his badge caught the sun—and we began to hear the carts and wagons in the streets, the clash of crates and pallets as they were swung up and set down, the huffing of the switching engines in the yards. Gulls cackled, and the pigeons wheeled above the warehouses, into and out of the soft light.

Adam had begun, on seeing the children, to lament in a deep, hoarse voice that he could not still; I watched him try, for the sake of his dignity, or because he had no wish to share with pale-skinned men the profundity of his feelings. But he had wept, and so had M, who had assaulted the sky. I was emptied, and I sat upon my haunches in the Customs boat and waited. Sam had watched us all. And now we drifted, M steering us, into the Customs wharf, a half an hour before he might go off duty.

"I must make for my office. I cannot speak of what we witnessed and endured. I will not. Adam: You are a man, and a companion, and I offer my salute, my handshake, sir—will you?"

Adam took his hand and promptly released it. His hands, like mine and Sam's, were bloody. His face looked washed clean of energy and will, but I knew better. He would direct his life, and he would never forgive us. He looked at me, then more briefly at Sam, and he climbed from the boat to the dock, and he quickly walked away.

M said, "Billy, you were used, I take it. So was I, by you. But I like you, while I confess to a near womanly love for your Sam. You enlivened me; he will make me live a good while longer, on the pages he will write." Sam's face lit, like the globe of a gas lamp, and his smile stretched wide. "You *will* write them, Sam.

"As to your fishing for the shabby author fish, I know too well the world's waters not to recognize bait, Billy, or lure, or line. But I cannot see it all as insult, and you're a good fellow, and a hero of the republic. I'm a restless man, and I shan't lie down for long. Something further may come of this."

He gathered the skirts of his great, long coat, and he climbed slowly out of the moored boat and turned to us. "The Hudson is a thorough-fare, and crowded with traffic often enough. There are pleasure-seekers, believe it or not, who paddle canoes upon her, and vessels of commerce coming down to us from Albany and Troy, and returning north with passengers and goods. That stubby, terrible craft with her cargo of the dead will be discovered in hours. In a moment, perhaps. What will we need to say to the authorities, if ever asked?"

He took a step, and seemed about to stumble, but he caught himself as, I knew, he had been dragging himself upright for so many years. He shook his head, and of course no one might descry whether it was the elements in the air or the tears from within him that so made his dull eyes, this only time, appear to shine.

"And the black-skinned babies," he said, moving his arms as if to indicate them, "and the girl with the cinnamon skin, murdered by her murderous plotting. No one vouchsafes that she won't soon be found. Nor that those dreadful wooden envelopes containing their shrunk and deathbound seeds will not be opened on the morrow, shipmates and friends. How to account to the world for all this death strewn in and under and through its waters? How to answer to the dreadful shipment that's landed all too soon along our shore? Nothing I know of in a long, dreary life will do. It will not do. It never will do."

He seemed about to speak once more, but his arms lifted and dropped, the heavy skirts of his oilskins flapped and lay still, and his chin was down, an instant, upon his breast as it rose and fell with a futility. He raised his right arm, as if to wave us farewell or to bless us, and he turned toward the steps and moved off in the direction of his office. He would make as if to have been there all the night, and, as he did, he would retrieve a cached bottle of gin, and he would put it to work.

And Sam would soon pack his bag at the Astor and entrain for New England, while I would find myself, days hence, in the office of Lapham Dumont, badgering him for copies of the documents I had required he create—evidence, of course, which I must destroy against the discovery of the lighter, or Jessie's corpse, or those of the other children, buried alive in great casks by the merchants on whose behalf Jessie had duped me, and I had duped M, the merchants for whose calculations she had perished. As Dumont watched me from his straight-backed oaken chair, I swept through his disheveled files and through the drawers and cubbies of his desk.

"You have hidden nothing?"

"I wish nothing to connect me to your . . . business," he replied, "whatever it might be."

"And I to you. I have withheld my participation in the matter and know nothing of its consummation. Do you understand?"

"No, sir. I do not wish to. May I go so far, without prejudicing your goodwill, as to pretend to never having heard of you?"

"If you would. And I, for my part, hereby forgive your debt."

"Forgive?"

"Wholly. I will devise an instrument, I will sign it, and I will cause it to be delivered to these offices. You have wagered and lost on bearskins at my expense. As far as you are concerned, I am as good as dead. If you renege in any manner on our understanding, it is you who will be so good."

He laved his red face with his hands as I have seen a raccoon, at the side of a stream, wash his muzzle. Sighing, he raised his head from the protection of his fingers. "May I say," he ventured, "that I would believe it only from you—the equation of death with the good. Still: forgiven!" His face reflected his disbelief, as if, instead of the William Bartholomew with whom he had conducted business in the past, he thought me somebody else.

CHAPTER 8

THE SECOND DAY, THEN, OF 1868, AND MY PARTIAL investment, the English author, Mr. Charles Dickens, having come to New York to read from his works in December, and having read at the Plymouth Congregational Church in Brooklyn to great acclaim several times, now was about to mount the stage in the Steinway Hall on East Fourteenth Street to offer a program that seemed to me far too long. I sat in a box with Sam, who had come down from Boston; we were far to the rear, and while Sam whispered about the prominent men and women he recognized, I employed my telescope, untouched since the War.

It was, as the newspapers would declare the next day, a gala, and celebrated personages abounded. Mr. and Mrs. Fields, who were book publishing people, Sam said, were in attendance. "Mrs. Fields will remain in her seat, while her husband will shortly walk around backstage to offer his support. I have seen this in Boston. He is Dickens's publisher, Billy, although it is the wife, I have heard, at whom Mr. Dickens enjoys directing his attentions."

I pointed out Mr. and Mrs. John Bigelow, he the diplomat and partial owner of the *New York Post*. Nearby, far down front, were Horace Greeley and William Cullen Bryant. A fellow with a broad, ferocious mustache sat near Mr. Bryant; he was with a woman of remarkable beauty. "Twain!" Sam said. "He is called Mark Twain, he wrote of the life in the gold fields, and he is on the rapid rise." Sam's voice expressed no little envy.

The women wore opulent gowns, and there was much décolletage and jewelry in evidence. The men were dressed, for the most part, in evening suits and boiled shirts, many with diamond studs down the front. I could smell the oily smoke of expensive cigars on their clothing, and the perfume on the warmed skin of the women made a sharp, sweet contrast to the odor of tobacco and—it is inevitable on a cold evening in the city—to the slightly sour smell of the damp wool fabric of their over-coats. They stood, many of them, for as long as they could, so as to see who was present that night and, of course, to also be seen. I sat back in the shadows and looked out with my glass into the rosy light of the hundreds of gas lamps that glowed upon the gold leaf and paint of the ceiling, the molded plaster and carved mahogany of the walls.

It was a happy sound, the hubbub of those voices, and the clothes and jewelry made for a gladsome sight. It had nothing to do with how we lived in the Points, and it was the beginning—I could feel its pulse in the Steinway Hall, and I had sensed it in my accountings of profit and loss: The nation, that New Year's Eve, was commencing to gather itself, and great wealth was in the offing. The result would be named the Gilded Age, and the fellow with the bristling mustache and the angry expression would be said to have chronicled its rise.

The lighting was adjusted, and the audience took their place. Two thousand and five hundred seats were full—he would carry away from New York several hundreds of thousands of dollars—and Mr. Charles Dickens came striding onto the stage. He was smaller than I thought a world-famous writer might be, and I could see the lines of pain about his mouth, as well as the subtle drag of his right foot, as if he bore a wound. His suit was a light gray, with a muted pattern in the weave, and his waistcoat was a bright red silk. As the applause rolled up and the lights came further down, he lifted his head as if to listen to the language in a song. He smiled, and they clapped harder, and several cheered.

He read that night from his *David Copperfield*—"It is the story of a writer," Sam whispered joyfully—which at first seemed persuasive when he spoke of a childhood visit to someplace called Yarmouth Sands, but then a sentimental notion of a sailor or shore-dwelling man spoke in an indecipherable accent and with overmuch servility about a person called Em'ly, whose importance to the story I discerned only with some difficulty. I could not help but compare this sailor to those created by M, who seemed to bear a greater dimension and a more philosophical heft.

A person called Micawber, also part of the Copperfield story, was very entertaining, and Mr. Dickens came into his own as he chirped and twittered and then dropped his voice to moan like a walrus, all the while both telling about this Micawber fellow and, apparently, emulating him. As the audience laughed, Mr. Dickens himself laughed the harder, and went to greater extremes of vocal dexterity, and flashings of the eye, and winks and grimaces, to bind the audience to himself in a mutual affection that I found remarkable.

At times, when the extremes of emotion and humor were unavailable to Mr. Dickens, and he was compelled to read out considerable lengths of narrative, for the sake of the listeners' acquiring certain information, his voice lagged and he even mumbled, and a restiveness went over the spectators. "He ought to quicken the pace," Sam told me with a tone conveying much experience. Embarrassed for the author, and for my friend beside me, and concerned for my investment, I swept my glass along the faces of those in attendance. There I saw Lizzie and, beside her, M, whom I had not seen since our journey up the river and, sorrowing, back down. He did not sit still. He rubbed at his sore eyes, then leaned to whisper at Lizzie, and then sat back, and then, soon enough, he pulled at his collar and straightened the coat of his simple black suit—no evening dress for him—and he made faces when Mr. Dickens did, though M's were effected in neither emulation nor approval. At one point, as Mr. Dickens cried out something about a Poor Pilgrim, M shook his head and slumped, like a middle-aged boy, in his seat.

There was a good deal more of Copperfield, with bodies drifting onto shore from a wreck, and M sat up straighter at that, and so did I. How not to recall the tuns as they spun in the contradictory pull of current and tide? How not to think of those children, and of Jessie? The newspapers called it "Massacre on the Hudson," and it was laid by some at the feet of escaped convicts, and blamed by others on the Irish Rabbits gang from the Bandits' Roost alleys, who were contesting with the remnants of an Africa gang for control of the waterfront. Sam muttered to himself. And then the applause came in as Mr. Dickens, behind his reading table, set down his book, poured water from his carafe—I saw through my telescope that his hands trembled—and he stood in the sounds of his auditors' approval. How fortunate he was, I thought, to be reminded publicly of the esteem in which he was held and, in addition, to receive considerable payment; I knew precisely how much.

Mr. Dickens announced then that in the spirit of the season just concluding, as the year swung round in its infancy, he would read from his *A Christmas Carol.*

Marley, he pronounced in a sepulchral voice, was dead: to begin with. Sam grunted. I watched as M leaned back his head in the shadowed hall and opened his grinning mouth, and gulped the darkness into it, then slowly leaned forward to listen once more as Mr. Dickens told us that every cask in the wine merchant's cellars, downstairs from Scrooge's dwelling, appeared to have a separate peal of echoes of its own. Sam let his breath whistle out from in between his teeth. I saw them roll in the waters of the river, Jessie and Delgado and the little boys, then the casks that were sealed upon the contraband within, spinning, bobbing, drifting, turning in the dark waters upon which we rowed.

I did not know this story of Mr. Scrooge, although Sam had insisted it was justly famous, but Scrooge was clearly indicted by it for his avarice and for the chilly manner in which he treated those who lectured him on charity and love. A ghost, of this Marley who at the beginning was dead, appeared to him in his rooms. I wished to applaud Scrooge's bravery in suggesting to the apparition that it might be merely an undigested bit of beef, a fragment of an underdone potato, but that display of courage went unremarked by the audience, and so I held my peace. I savored, too, the moment when, the phantom unwinding the bandage that he wore around his head, his lower jaw dropped open to lie upon his breast. Once again, my fellow spectators did not celebrate those words. I leaned back, and I watched M as he affected to display the degree of his being unmoved by either the prose of the piece or its performance by the sometimes-grave and sometimes-grinning Mr. Dickens, who spoke his characters as if he brought his children to the front of the stage and introduced them, every one. Sam had spoken of his having to support, even now, all nine of them. I could not begin to imagine how the reception of this material, and the manner of its presentation, must have been galling to M, forgotten by this audience who once, I thought, had read with gratitude the words he wrote. For Sam, I knew, it was all a goad; he wished to emulate—to replace, I suspected—Mr. Dickens with his audience.

At last the small child did not die, the hungry did not starve, the stony heart of Scrooge was said to laugh. A joke was made about spirits and abstinence, and it was always said of him that he knew how to keep Christmas well, if any man alive possessed the knowledge. The audience cheered and cried out *Bravo!* and they clapped and clapped long after M, sitting beside his Lizzie in silence, had clasped his hands in his lap.

Sam gently pounded his fist against the arm of his chair. He slowly shook his head while smiling wistfully. I knew that he yearned to write language so powerful as to cause a crowd of strangers to thank him with their applause for his efforts.

But as for me, I could not believe that such a tattered spirit, even with his author's fervently wishing it, might be so swiftly, so seamlessly repaired.

CHAPTER 9

WE HAD BECOME KNOWN, SEPARATELY BUT ALSO together, in the Five Points. We walked, one early morning in February, on Pearl Street, near Cross. Chun Ho was dressed in a coat I had bought her as a gift. It buttoned snugly at the neck and she could raise the collar to cover her ears. It was long and heavy, and I was content that she could ply her trade in the cold city protected from its winds, which howled down the streets, some days, as if they were canyons of ice. Pages of newspaper blew past us, and the dogs investigating mounds of household garbage steamed at the muzzle, as did the horses' flanks before their heavy wagons in the street. A knife grinder worked the pedal of his wheel and the metal screeched as we passed him, Chun Ho moving her hands in and out of her pockets, enjoying the weight of wool and the luxury of warmth, I supposed, while I worked—it still was far from simple for me—to balance the bamboo pole, and its two heavy baskets filled with clothing and bed sheets, as we made our way.

Two men came abreast of us, laboring fellows, one in an unsavory-looking suit worn over a knitted vest that seemed to afford him little warmth, the other in a coat, dyed green and looking like lichen on a tree, that I recognized as an officer's greatcoat from the War. They stood to the side to permit us to pass, but I suspected that they wished to study us, and I was right. The man in the uniform coat was silent, but the other one sniggered as we went on our way.

I stopped, and Chun Ho did as well. I wondered what they made of what they saw: a tea-colored woman with an oval, impassive face, and a man beside her whose face was a mask of another sort. In silence, these masks, then, which were turned toward them, permitted those who wore them to be regarded in the light of the bystanders' curiosity and, quite probably, their scorn. As they stood and stared, the masks turned simultaneously to move off along the noisy, littered street, and to bob at last out of sight among the ragged and the hungry and forlorn of the Points.

The Night Inspector

FREDERICK BUSCH

A Reader's Guide

A Conversation with Frederick Busch

Q: Of all writers, what drew you to Melville? Was there some particular circumstance that inspired you? And why, writing of Melville, did you use the letter M instead of his name?

FB: What drew me to him? His greatness as a writer—as we know him now—compared to how he was seen by contemporary readers, who scorned his *Moby-Dick* and *Pierre* and *The Confidence Man* and the great stories. They loved his racy, rather plagiarized early novels of adventure, and they detested his great advances in narrative structure and prose. He had the worst luck with his readers! And he mismanaged his career. He is the model of bad luck and mismanagement—and of dedication, of sheer hard work, of brilliance of vision. I wanted to write a novel about this vast man whose domestic problems and financial problems mirrored those of so many of us; he was huge, and as small as we, at once.

    I called Melville "M" because, I think, I was intimidated by him. He is one of the gods in the American writer's heaven—the man who wrote the Great American Novel— and I didn't feel I could approach him more intimately unless I called him something that evoked the actual Melville but that also kept me one decorous pace away from him. As the Hebrews call their God by an approximate name, Yahweh, thus, M.

Q: Where did Bartholomew come from? At what point in your thinking about the novel did he emerge for you as the main character, and why?

FB: I invented Bartholomew because I needed someone in New York City in 1867 to approach Melville on behalf of the reader—he was my vehicle for our getting close to the great writer who, in his present "failure," was difficult and distant. I didn't know who Bartholomew would be, at first; I knew that he would be a Civil War veteran because Melville was so moved and horrified by the war and because it had torn Melville's nation asunder. You cannot write of 1867, two years after the war's end, and not consider the war's ravaging effect. I knew this, and then my wife, Judy, and I went to see a retrospective show of Winslow Homer's paintings at the

Metropolitan Museum in New York. Homer had covered the war for *Harper's Weekly*, and his etchings were as famous as [Matthew] Brady's photographs. The first painting we saw, on entering the show, was a big picture of a Union soldier in a tree, inspecting the landscape through his rifle's sight. *A Marksman on Picket Duty*, it was called. I knew at once that the marksman was my William Bartholomew. In the novel, Bartholomew even boasts of having posed for the painting for Winslow Homer.

I didn't yet know that he was maimed. That came to me from three sources. The first was a reference to a maimed soldier wearing a black silk mask in Hemingway's great short story "In Another Country," and the second was something I read about World War I veterans with their faces shot apart. Then my dentist showed me, as he was preparing a crown, an antique book about post–Civil War dental repairs. The three elements came together, and there was poor William Bartholomew, disfigured and angry and determined to have his revenge on fate by making his fortune.

Q: **As in many of your novels, we see, at the heart of *The Night Inspector*, a fractured family: Melville's. Wrapping this image is the larger picture of the fractured national family of post–Civil War America. Could you comment on this connection, and how you chose to deploy it in the book? I wonder: Does this enlargement of scale represent any kind of culmination for you?**

FB: You're absolutely right about the fractured Melville family and the larger issue of the fractured national family. I have always been drawn to write about domestic issues, especially about the family that is broken in one way or another. But I have always tried to expand my focus so that it would include more and more. Consider, for instance, the campus family in my novel *Girls*, and the scene at the end of that novel where all those men and woman are searching the field. They're searching for the body of one girl, but of course they're also looking for all our missing children. The narrator says, "We were going to move the entire field." That "we" is the human community, toward which I wanted the novel to reach, and on whose behalf I wanted it to speak.

The same is true of *The Night Inspector*. I wanted to deal with the larger national family, as you so well put it. But I must also say that I don't see the enlargement of scale as any kind of culmination. I see it as a continuation, and as a raising of the bar for my own efforts. The next novel, on which I have begun preliminary work, must reach higher, wider, and deeper.

Q: Would you say this is what drives you most as a writer? This "raising of the bar," as you call it?

FB: The raising of the bar, the severity of risk in the dive, the pitch of the mountain—no, that's not what drives me, though it surely does excite me. Actually, I love to write, so I write. I don't feel that I've earned my place on the earth during a day when I have not written. On the other hand, I'm also aware that loyal readers, who know my stuff, expect me to build on what I've done in the past. To one degree or another, each of my novels since 1974 has tried to draw my characters out into the world's concerns, and to draw the reader into the relationship between those two worlds. I want my novels to work in both dimensions, the private and the public. *The Night Inspector*, it seems to me, dives deeper into the darkness of the individual, and deeper into the darkness of the public world, than any of my earlier books. It is an examination—or I wished it to be—of one man's interior being, but also of the American soul.

Q: Building on your remarks about Bartholomew: My own response to him, as a reader, was bound by contradiction. I found myself profoundly horrified by his cold-bloodedness, yet deeply moved by his torment, and fascinated, in an admiring way, by his financial acumen and physical competence. He's a man who gets things done, even if they're awful things—a deeply American character, in other words.

FB: Yes, absolutely! He *is* The American: physically competent in a harsh landscape, a survivor in a dreadful war, a warrior with pleasure, and a man who is also capable of real thought and profound feeling; he is a frontiersman, a merchant, a mournerof-children, a man available to the wonders in women, and, when next you meet him, a cold-blooded fighter. Melville describes Ahab "with a crucifixion in his face," and that's Bartholomew. He suffers *for* the nation and, at the same time, he *is* the nation's cruelty.

Q: **What sort of specific research did you have to do to write this book? How did it pose different challenges from research-ing your other novels?**

FB: I did a fair amount of ambient research, traveling with my wife, Judy, to places Melville had been. It's a matter of sniffing the psychic air, of waiting for the ghosts that the setting gen-erates. Together we visited Melville's Pittsfield farm, and the room—the very desk and chair—in which he wrote *Moby-Dick* while staring out at his beloved Mt. Greylock. We stood in the small piazza, which gives the title—*Piazza Tales*—to his great short story collection. We walked the street in Manhattan—East Twenty-sixth, near Madison Square—where he lived, and followed the route he might have walked on his way to work at the docks. We sat in Madison Square where he might have sat. I read newspapers of the day and studied the works of journalists who wrote about New York City in the late 1860s. I read *Harper's Weekly* to see the ads as well as the news. I looked at hundreds of photos of the New York of 1867, and I read studies of nineteenth-century New York brothels and recollections of New Yorkers. I reread much of Melville's writing, his correspondence, and Jay Leyda's wonderful *Melville Log*. And then I found that I was hiding in the research. Page one had been on paper for eighteen months—the same dialogue, with little changed, with which the novel opens. I flushed myself from cover and forced myself to write page two.

Q: **The Chinese laundress, Chun Ho, who becomes Bartholomew's lover: How did she emerge? She appears at first peripherally—as part of the setting—but eventually she becomes deeply wedded to the story.**

FB: Chun Ho was, indeed, part of the setting. Bartholomew was a warrior and, during the war, as filthy as his environment; it's a novel filled with odors, and he is alive to them. In New York after the war, however, he is somewhat fastidious—he wishes to be clean, enjoys luxuries, and tries to establish a separation between himself and the stench of burning buildings, and killed horses, and men. At first, I simply wanted Chun Ho to rent her tub so he could bathe. She existed to serve that function. But you always owe your characters more than merely a role in the events of your book. Chun Ho, despite my plans, lived, and she wanted more life, and I knew that I owed it to her. How did I know? When Billy Bartholomew, one day, noticed that he had brought over unsullied laundry. She sniffed it and found it clean, and she sensed that he had unbusinesslike motives; and I, knowing that he found his shelter in business, flushed him out of hiding. He was a clumsy and shy lover as he approached her and, finally, Chun Ho—almost in defiance of her nature and her upbringing—took charge. When she asked him to divulge his inner self—to teach her not English, or American ways, but to "teach me . . . you," I have to confess I was close to tears. I loved her way of cutting across traditional American speech and coming up with great ways of saying deep truths. Chun Ho, like Billy, grew from my subconscious and flowered on the page; where they led, I followed.

Q: **I know you to be a native New Yorker. New York City in 1867 is obviously a very different sort of place from the New York of your youth, or the New York City we know now. Or is it?**

FB: I am a New Yorker, born in Brooklyn; a resident with Judy in our early married years of Greenwich Village—Morton Street and Bedford Street. And I have written a good many novels and stories set in the city. The New York I knew as a child, in the forties and fifties, was bucolic. We played stickball on Eighteenth Street in the Midwood section of Brooklyn; when a car turned our corner someone would call out, "Car!" and we would pause. We didn't have to pause that often. I could take the BMT subway—elevated near home, then either descending under the East River or crossing high on the Manhattan Bridge—and ride to the city alone. I could walk back from a Boy Scout meeting on Friday night pretty late, and my mother could take walks through Brooklyn at night when she chose to. Yes, it's a different city. And yet I was able to return to the Manhattan streets that Melville strode and see the same statues and many of the same buildings, the same parks, the same Broadway—looking so different—on which horse-drawn buses might have taken him toward work on the docks downtown.

Q: **You've written about Dickens in the novel *The Mutual Friend,* and now Melville. This has the feeling of a triptych. Who's the third? Is there one?**

FB: I think I might once have wished to write fiction about Kafka, who is in some senses the patron saint of dysfunctional families, paranoia, neurosis, and the general psychic disturbances we think of as modern. But I don't want to live inside that mind. And, anyway, Woody Allen has already done great work along those lines. No, I think I've finished my large historical projects. I think I'll just try to deal with dysfunction, paranoia, neurosis, and general psychic disturbances in a contemporary setting from now on.

Reading Group Questions
and Topics for Discussion

1. Of all American authors, Herman Melville is perhaps most closely associated with the phrase "The Great American Novel." What do you know about Melville and his work? About the book for which he is most celebrated, *Moby-Dick*? How does this knowledge affect your understanding of Busch's novel?

2. On a similar note, what do you know of Busch's work, particularly his most recent novels? What themes and motifs do you see present here that build upon his earlier work? What departures do you detect?

3. The Melville we meet in this novel is a man disgraced and ruined—abandoned by his publishers, forgotten by his readers, consigned to a grim job as an inspector of cargoes in the Port of New York. His career is all but over and ironically, the source of his misery is the commercial failure of *Moby-Dick*—the very novel for which he is now most remembered. Why do you think Busch has chosen this inglorious phase in the author's life as his focus? And what do you make of the use of the letter M in place of Melville's name?

4. The novel's narrator, William Bartholomew, is a Civil War sniper—a trained assassin, skillful at his job. What is your impression of him? Is he a cold-blooded killer? Despite this background, do you find him to be a sympathetic character? Why do you think Busch has chosen him to tell the tale?

5. Bartholomew knows Melville by reputation and early in the novel arranges a chance meeting over dinner. Initially, Bartholomew's intentions in seeking out the novelist are less than noble: "One could turn a powerful profit if the night inspector turned his head at the right moment," he says. "It was chancy, of course, but a businessman must never close his eyes to chance." But their connection soon grows deeper. What is the nature of this affinity? What about Melville seems to be attractive or intriguing to Bartholomew, and vice-versa?

6. Since the war, Bartholomew has remade himself as a financier, "a student of the markets, and therefore a man . . . watchful of human needs." How does this role complement his character and background? In what other ways does his postwar life seem linked to his past? Bartholomew is also a literary man, educated at Yale. What purpose does this serve in the tale?

7. Later in the novel we learn about the first man Bartholomew ever killed—his uncle and stand-in stepfather, whom he drowns in the effluent of an outhouse. Why do you think Busch includes this scene in the novel, with its particularly gruesome form of death and killing?

8. The novel begins with Bartholomew's mask. At other times in the novel, he wears a veil. How do masks and concealment function as a theme in the novel? What other forms of concealment or masquerading do you find? Are there moments when these masks are lifted? Bartholomew's veil could also be understood as a garment of mourning. What is being mourned—by Bartholomew, by Melville, by the novel?

9. The scenes in the novel that describe Bartholomew's experiences in the Civil War paint a grim picture of that conflict. How does Busch's portrayal of life-at-arms differ from your expectations, and from other accounts of the Civil War that you have read or experienced?

10. One of the most poignant and horrifying moments in the novel occurs when Bartholomew and his fellow soldiers come upon a massacre: a shed full of men, women, and children— whole families—cut down in haste by advancing Union soldiers. Why does Busch include this scene, especially the image of the tiny doll's head? How does this scene prepare us for later events in the novel?

11. What do you understand Melville's son Malcolm's role in the novel to be? What do you make of his desire to be a soldier? How does his suicide advance the story and its themes?

12. The weapon that Malcolm uses to kill himself is the Colt revolver provided by Bartholomew at his father's request.

Does this implicate Bartholomew in his suicide? Does it implicate Melville, who arranged for the gun?

13. The children of Chun Ho call Bartholomew *gui*, meaning "ghost." How is this reflective of a larger truth? In what ways is *The Night Inspector* a ghost story? A detective story? A war story? A family story?

14. Throughout the novel, Bartholomew maintains that the Civil War is a purely economic conflict, a practical contest between two competing economic cultures, guided by no overarching moral purpose. He tells his friend Sam Mordecai, "It's about money. . . . Agrarians need slave labor. Industrialists need cheap labor. If we make the slaves free of the Rebels, then the North will use your Negroes in any way they can. We're fighting for the opportunity for men of business, manufacturers, to get their hands on black men, Jews, and broad shouldered girls. It's money, Sam, they're waging the War about." What do you make of his interpretation? Is it cynical, or realistic? What motivates his understanding, and does it seem entirely sincere? How does it square with your own?

15. The main characters of the novel are all outsiders—men and women who in one way or another exist on the margins of society: a forgotten artist, a Creole prostitute, a widowed Chinese laundress, a Negro day-laborer, a Jewish journalist, a faceless war veteran. What do you make of this commonality, and what is your assessment of Busch's intentions in assembling this band?

16. Bartholomew arranges for a tour of New York's Tenderloin District for Mordecai, a "voyage into darkest New York." Melville joins them on this trip, as does the Negro Adam, whom Melville describes as "our dusky Virgil," a reference to Dante's *Divine Comedy*, in which the Roman poet Virgil plays the role of Dante's tour guide to an imagined underworld. What seem to be Bartholomew's intentions in staging this grim outing? Does he want to educate Mordecai, and, if so, what does he want him to see and learn? Is the trip a success?

17. When their outing concludes, Adam refuses payment and professes regret at his role as guide. He tells Bartholomew, "I

showed you a look at bad behavior and sorrow. Like it was minstrels kicking and strumming just for you." What do you make of this moment, and especially of Adam's pain? Do you believe that Bartholomew has taken unfair advantage of Adam's debt to him? In what larger sense does Adam act as a kind of guide—morally, spiritually—for the novel?

18. Many of Busch's novels deal with the subject of endangered or lost children, and certainly this is true of *The Night Inspector*. Driving the story forward is the plan to rescue a shipload of black children, a scheme that brings all the major characters together at the tale's climax. How does this plot crystallize the novel and its concerns? Is it an effective engine for the tale? What does it show about Bartholomew?

19. Thoughout the novel, Busch brings to bear the sense of smell—the stench of war and death, of animal waste and effluent, of the filthy New York streets and the sewers snaking beneath them. What do you think of this strategy? Is it effective? In what other ways has Busch worked to create a sense of the past, and of 1860s New York?

20. From her early appearance as a minor character, the widowed laundress Chun Ho gradually assumes a greater importance to the novel, culminating in the scene in chapter six in which she makes love to the maskless Batholomew in his bath. Did this turn of events surprise you? What do you make of their blossoming affinity for one another? What is Chun Ho asking at the end of the chapter when she says to Bartholomew, "Tell me—teach me—*you*"?

21. The plan to rescue the cargo of black children is ultimately mistaken and thwarted and culminates in a vision of abject horror: a boatload of children drugged and stuffed into barrels to die. How did you react to this scene? Why do you think the writer chose to avoid anything like a "happy ending"?

22. In the chase on the Hudson that follows, Bartholomew is called upon once again to employ his skills as a marksman. Does this occasion differ from those in the past?

23. What do you make of Jessie's role as the Judas figure in the plot? Is her death deserved? After her body is recovered from the river, Bartholomew tells Adam, "At the end . . . I think she must have thought of the children." Why do you think he says this? Does this seem true to you, or is it naive?

24. The novel provides us with a pair of epilogues: A public reading of *A Christmas Carol* by the English novelist Charles Dickens, and a brief glimpse of Bartholomew with Chun Ho, walking together on the New York City streets. What does each scene accomplish? Taken together, do they bring about an effective sense of closure to the tale?

25. Does the meaning of the novel's title evolve for you over the course of reading the book? Who or what is a "night inspector"?

ABOUT THE INTERVIEWER

Justin Cronin is the author of *A Short History of the Long Ball* (Council Oak), which won the 1990 National Novella Award, and *Mary and O'Neil: A Romance*, forthcoming from The Dial Press. His short fiction, novellas, and essays have appeared in many periodicals and received such honors as the *Transatlantic Review* Award, the Baxter Hathaway Prize, and the *Greensboro Review* Award. He has worked widely as a freelance writer and book critic and is currently writer-in-residence and associate professor of English at La Salle University in Philadelphia.

ABOUT THE AUTHOR

Since 1971, award-winning author Frederick Busch has published more than twenty works of fiction and non-fiction, including the novels *The Mutual Friend*, about Charles Dickens, *Rounds*, *Invisible Mending*, *Sometimes I Live in the Country*, *Harry and Catherine*, *Long Way from Home*, and the bestselling *Closing Arguments* and *Girls*. A compilation of his short fiction, *The Children in the Woods: New and Selected Stories*, was a finalist for the PEN/Faulkner Award in 1995. His most recent books are *A Dangerous Profession*, a collection of essays about the writing life, and *Letters to a Fiction Writer*, an anthology for which he served as both editor and contributor. A new short story collection, *Don't Tell Anyone*, will be published early in 2001.

Among the many honors his work has received are the PEN/Malamud Award for achievement in short fiction, an award for fiction from the American Academy of Arts and Letters, and the National Jewish Book Award for his novel *Invisible Mending*. He is the recipient of fellowships from the Guggenheim, Ingram Merrill, and Woodrow Wilson Foundations and the NEA, and his stories have appeared many times in annual editions of *The Best American Short Stories*, the O'Henry Awards, and *The Pushcart Prize*. Mr. Busch has served as acting director of the Writers' Workshop at the University of Iowa and since 1966 has taught at Colgate University in Hamilton, New York, where he is Fairchild Professor of Literature and directs the Living Writers Program. He is also the founder of the Chenango Valley Writers' Conference.

Mr. Busch was born in Brooklyn, New York, and was educated at Muhlenberg College and Columbia University. He and his wife, Judy, a high school librarian, have two grown sons and live in rural upstate New York with their two black labs, Jake and Junior. He writes every day in his studio, located on the second floor of a restored barn on his property.

meditation on those post-bellum, prelapsarian days following the Civil War—days of emancipation but also days of sorrow and confusion in a time when the post-traumatic stress of veterans was as common and uninvestigated as rotting corpses in the Tenderloin of Manhattan, and confidence was a game."

—*Los Angeles Times*

"Out of a rancid stew of vice and misery, Mr. Busch has created a sublimely dark work of almost unbearable beauty. An exploration of evil, hidden identities and the dehumanizing forces of commerce, *The Night Inspector* has a moral heft and stylistic grace not unlike the work of a certain bearded, brooding, ninteenth-century Customs official."

—*The Wall Street Journal*

"The most compelling . . . moments are those describing Bartholomew's experiences as a wartime sniper. This story alone would have made a fine novel and singular character study. But Busch takes Bartholomew, a character finely honed by his horrifying war experiences, and places him in a larger historical and moral context where questions are complex and answers ambiguous."

—*Rocky Mountain News*

"Billy's mask suggests two faces, and indeed he is a man of contradictions. War has made him limitlessly cruel, but he is also generous, a champion of the underprivileged, among whom he chooses to live in the squalid Five Points section of Manhattan. His marvelous Jamesian narrative voice, seasoned by a Yale theology education, is another kind of mask; it's almost as if we can forgive his brutal war crimes, told in explicit, dispassionate detail, because of the measured elegance of the telling."

—*The Washington Post Book World*

"Being a novel . . . about literature, *The Night Inspector* is also a novel of ideas. While grounded firmly in New York's sordid, gritty, industrial realities, it probes some of our broadest and stickiest moral questions, 'the human use of human beings.' How do we use, or employ, people as a means to our own ends? . . .The novel is deep, disturbing, and complex, a meditation on the odds of love and virtue surviving in an untrusting, treacherous world."

—*Denver Post*